THE
SEASON

THE HONEST SEASON

KOTA NEELIMA

RANDOM HOUSE INDIA

Published by Random House India in 2016

1

Copyright © Kota Neelima 2016

Random House Publishers India Pvt Ltd
7th Floor, Infinity Tower C, DLF Cyber City
Gurgaon – 122002
Haryana

Random House Group Limited
20 Vauxhall Bridge Road
London SW1V 2SA
United Kingdom

978 81 8400 585 1

Typeset in Adobe Caslon Pro, Dante MT and Minion Pro by
R. Ajith Kumar

Printed at Thomson Press India Ltd, New Delhi

A PENGUIN RANDOM HOUSE COMPANY

To my father

AUTHOR'S NOTE

Considering the nature of this book, the sources must stay off-the-record in the typical style of political reportage in Delhi. If the words ring true and the incidents trigger a sense of déjà vu, please attribute them to my realistic imagination. I do not write to blame, I write to change. And I hope this is the season for it. It always is.

Two years ago, I had moved away from writing about the way Delhi deals with farmer suicides, the subject of my three previous books, to study procedural and substantive insufficiencies of our democracy. It is at the root of corruption, which exists fearlessly in the name of privilege at high places, behind VIP cordons and guarded gates. We have long waited patiently outside these closed gates of Delhi's power centres. This is the season to run out of patience, and I am grateful for the tall gates of Delhi that inspire to revolt.

The beneficiaries of status quo may defend the inaccessibility of the powerful. But power is not balanced by the corrupt; it is balanced by the honest. It is also unbalanced by them; by bureaucrats and police who wage personal battles against corruption, by journalists who chase truth wherever it may lead them, by teachers who guide youth to hope and not despair, by professionals who chase ethics and not just success, and by businessmen who look at welfare, not just profit. This is the season to unbalance power and I thank the status quo for this desperation.

For those of us who struggle, I have written truthfully about being a woman in India. The rhetoric of empowerment is shattered on our roads, in our homes and in our minds. Exploitation in the name of tradition is a weak man's excuse, and modernity may not have all the answers. One half of everyone is woman, and there is a reason we are all incomplete in our happiness. This is the season for being a woman, and I thank the half that demands to remain incomplete.

This book would not have been possible without the brilliant guidance of Milee Ashwarya at Penguin Random House, who nurtured the book with her wisdom and advice. I am grateful to Gaurav Shrinagesh for his faith in this project, and Caroline Newbury for her support. My sincere thanks to Roshini Dadlani for editorial excellence, and Gavin Morris, Neelima Aryan, Gunjan Ahlawat and Neeraj Nath for the poignant cover of the book. For help with my research, losing my papers and finding them, I thank my assistants Shravan Prajapati and Sudhir Kumar. As always, I am indebted to my family for giving me the space and time to write this book and to believe in it.

December 2015   Kota Neelima
New Delhi

PROLOGUE

New Delhi; July (Six months before the national elections)

It rained in that disinterested Delhi way as if doing a job that would bring neither rewards nor recognition, the same way the government officer in the Free Water department signed an order that afternoon to normalize water supply to areas in south-west Delhi. No one had asked him to expedite the file or delay it by luring him with tickets for the IPL cricket matches or special passes to movie previews. No one even thanked him for making sure that 15,000 households would be pleasantly surprised to find water in taps next morning for the first time in three months. He knew why there had been no supply. The water had been secretly diverted to private businessmen, who had resold it at a profit to the same households. The dry taps were explained to the government by saying that the water supply was affected because of peak demand due to summer heat. No one thought of investigating the matter; the private water lobby ensured that. This informal and hugely profitable arrangement usually came to an end with the arrival of monsoon rains each year, after which there could be no justification for water scarcity. It helped if the rains were delayed, though; people remained thirsty a little longer. This year, however, the rains were on time.

The officer angrily snapped shut the file on his desk and left his room to take a coffee break. The rain that fell listlessly sharpened with sudden focus, and drops found him, choosing their target as he walked to the café across the lane. Settling down at a table with coffee, he pensively lowered his eyes to his cell phone. He had worked in the department for six years now and had made money every summer; all except this one. That was because of the new director, a man famous for his discipline and efficiency. He was specially brought in one year before the elections next January to ensure that water reached the voters abundantly this summer, enough to make them forget the last four very parched seasons. He was so strict that within two weeks of his appointment six months ago, he had launched a full-scale investigation into reports of water pilferage and threatened to take action against any officer found guilty of collusion with the private water business. The findings were submitted in sixty days, collusion was indicated, officers asked to show cause and businessmen issued summons.

Then the summer began. The water supply was once again cut off to households and privately owned tankers reappeared on Delhi roads to sell water at a premium. But there was a difference this year; no one knew what the deal was. The new director was that disciplined, and efficient.

The officer thoughtfully touched the ID card that hung by a cord from his neck. The informal income he earned every summer supported a lifestyle his family was now used to. It paid for the plasma TV and home theatre, holidays in Lakshadweep and Leh, school trips to Nepal and Bhutan, that expensive and unnecessary watch, and that exorbitant but enticing jewelry. He felt poor and deprived today, enough to justify selling the secret details of a multi-crore-government project to the highest bidder. He decided to make the phone call and glanced around once to check. The café was never crowded; there was a couple in the corner who hoped no one recognized them, a young man in the front with headphones peered at a screen, a young woman near the windows was immersed in her notebook and a middle-aged woman and her young son at the counter read the menu aloud, deciding.

The officer made the call.

After the greetings, he had some instructions for the businessman. 'Please make sure no one calls me after this on my official numbers. You told me this cell phone is safe, so I will call if necessary. Don't use your regular numbers to text me either. Do you understand?'

At a distance near the counter, the mother and son chose a latte.

'Of course I'm nervous. And you better be too,' the officer replied on the phone. 'This is an election year. There could be an inquiry into this deal if a different party forms the government after the elections. The companies involved may have to buy immunity from the new government against scrutiny. But if there are loopholes, and if we are not careful today, the contracts may get revoked and officers concerned could be suspended. So, yes, I'm nervous!'

He listened to the other side.

'I know it's all the same to you,' he agreed testily. 'It doesn't matter which party is in power.' He paused to overcome the last tentative tug of his conscience, then said, 'I called to say that I can get what you want; the entire financial profile of the project.'

As he heard the response, he was suddenly upset.

'You did *what*?' he demanded a little loudly, and then glanced around, but no one paid attention. He gathered himself quickly. This was an unforeseen crisis; he could sense from the light-hearted tone that the businessman no longer needed him. 'I don't have a problem if you want to talk to other officers in my department,' he said tersely. 'No one has more information than I do, and that's because of a small detail you seem to have overlooked; I'm the head of the Public Commitments section!'

Apparently, it was too small a detail. His face stiffened in anger at the businessman's reply.

'All right then!' he said, miffed. 'If you believe you want to deal with some other officer, well, that's just fine with me. I would like to see how anyone can get the financial information on this project without my cooperation.'

He was interrupted by an explanation that was too brief to be polite.

'Yes, I know how much this project means to you and I also know you don't want to fail,' he conceded tolerantly. 'But every big company will compete for this project, and I'm just surprised that you want to risk a new source, that's all.'

The officer turned as the young man with the headphones exclaimed at something on his computer screen; probably a catch at the boundary or a missed goal.

'Of course I will help if a colleague asks me to, but the price won't be the same.' The officer retorted in response to a question on the phone. 'Don't get me wrong,' he added nastily, 'I *like* the fact that you are trying out others in the department. Very soon, you will discover exactly how considerate I have been with my demands. I have told you this before; I don't do transactions. This is a relationship of trust between a bureaucrat and a businessman. It has to be nurtured.'

The detailed response infuriated the officer. 'Those were not "gifts" as you call them,' he snapped. 'You gave them to me in return for the information. I earned them.'

The reply was candid and the officer frowned. 'Fine then. I won't compromise on my principles.'

There was a surprised cackle on the phone.

'Yes, you heard that right.' The officer was getting worried by this flippant treatment. 'We'll always be friends, and you can always call me for any information on any project,' he continued with forced composure. 'But you see, I will have to help other companies as well. And that would include exposing the weak points of competitors,' he paused significantly before adding, 'like you.'

There was a sudden silence of realization on the phone and then a swift apology from the businessman.

The officer closed his eyes in relief but said dismissively, 'It's no use. I have made up my mind . . .'

He was once again interrupted by an explanation, this time lengthy and pleading.

'I know,' he smiled to himself, 'you never meant to go to anyone else . . .'

He paused and relished the panic on the other side of the line, then said, 'Sure, you are under a lot of stress.' He had a sip of the coffee.

'All right, calm down now,' the officer chuckled. 'I won't help any other company on one condition. You have to deal only with me, all through and right until the end of the process.'

There was rapid agreement.

'Meet me tomorrow at the usual place, the movie theatre. Leave the payment in the trunk of the car like last time and hand me the keys inside the hall. The evening show is the new Superman–Batman movie, I think.' The officer gently urged, 'Be there.'

He refused a request of the businessman.

'Instalments won't do. I strongly advise you to bring the entire payment tomorrow,' the officer insisted. 'I can't meet you again for some time while the project decisions are being made.'

The woman who had been sitting at the window walked by his table towards the counter. He was distracted momentarily by her slim, tall figure, until he heard the response on the phone.

'No, that's not enough!' he lost his patience. 'We are talking about five officers, one in charge of each step of the contract. Are you sure you can afford this?'

He didn't respond immediately to the reply, and then thoughtfully nodded to himself.

'Fine then. Two instalments, but no more! I'll wait for the confirmation tomorrow morning. Remember; *text me*, don't call. Texts can't be traced.'

'Yes,' he agreed to a suggestion. 'A Blackberry phone would have helped, but I don't have one.'

The alacrity on the other side made him smile again.

'Thank you. That would be nice.' He paused, listening to a question, and then answered, 'Black, please. I like black phones.' After he ended the call, the officer lounged back in the chair, feeling happy with the way he had handled that negotiation. He had not been entirely truthful. He was not the only one who had the financials of the project, this was not the only company he would help and the payment wouldn't be divided among his colleagues; he would keep it all. It was a big project, the last of its kind for Delhi. Pipelines were to be laid for newly developed parts of the west and north-west parts of the city, a vast area with thousands of homes to be served through dozens of government contracts worth hundreds of crores. He had been truthful about one thing though; there *would* be an inquiry after elections into the process of how the companies were selected for the project. This was too large a deal not to interest any new political party in government. It was risky, yes, but just like his new director, even he was efficient when necessary, and disciplined.

After half an hour and a walnut muffin, he sauntered back into his office and settled in his cabin, humming a ringtone of a cell phone he had just overheard in the corridor outside. A smile lingered on his face as he opened a new file marked 'Urgent' and started to estimate the cost to improve water quality in parts of his zone. The air conditioner was set to low. The raindrops on his shirt touched his arms coolly, as if to remind him of his secret deal. His colleague from the next cabin came in to say there had been a phone call for him while he was out. The caller had left a message, and the colleague handed him a slip of paper. The officer read it absently and froze.

'You are wrong,' the message stated. 'Texts can be traced. Keep up Mr Shrivastav.'

He felt his heart slow down, his body turn cold with fear. He glanced up at his colleague warily, but he only seemed confused. No, it couldn't mean anything to anyone but him. His face was drawn as he stared again at the slip; the little white square paper proved that someone knew all about that call he had made in the café to the businessman. His colleague, intrigued by his reaction, inquired if something was wrong. The officer didn't answer; he just stood up abruptly and, in a manner not befitting a man of his rank, ran out of his office.

Outside in the lane opposite the café, Mira Mouli stood under the awning of a shop window and grimly surveyed the shoes on display. These were shoes for mingling, prancing and dancing, not for rush hours and long hours, or for taking the stairs when the elevators didn't work. These were shoes for going places, not going home. One of the salesmen assessed her from inside the shop to check if she was a potential customer. The black heels were stylish, the blue shirt was khadi and the dark eyes were cold as they met his through the glass. He looked away hurriedly. She wasn't interested in the shoes in the shop window; she was interested in the shop window itself because it reflected the café entrance across the street. By now Mr Shrivastav must have read her message and figured out that someone had overheard his phone call in the café. She didn't have to wait long; Mr Shrivastav came running through the rain in his creaseless clothes. He rushed straight into the café but emerged in a few moments, looking lost and bewildered. He didn't appear smug now, Mira thought as she smiled faintly, like the way he had after he struck the deal to sell confidential details of the government contract. The officer shook his head in disbelief and regret, as the rain pounded down on his shoulders in reprimand. The deal would have to be called off, he told himself. He should have been more careful; he shouldn't have been so desperate for the deal. But the season to make money was coming to an end, he thought weakly; the rains were here. Mira studied his reflection among the fancy shoes in the window as he reached for his cell phone and made the call. Though he spoke briefly, it wasn't difficult to guess whom he might have called and what he might have said. The Superman–Batman show would have to wait.

It was good entertainment for her birthday afternoon, Mira concluded as she walked to where her car was parked. It was just a little café on the fringes of a lazy market place where she had stopped for a cup of tea on way to office. But she was intrigued by the officer's angry expression as he had emerged from the government offices across the road and stormed into the café. He had sat two tables away and talked in whispers. But when the negotiation got harder, he couldn't whisper anymore; and that was all she had needed, to hear him speak once. She had already noticed that his shirt was fresh; he didn't sweat through his day. His watch was gold; he had got away with this before. His pen was a ruse and the wedding ring a bait.

Mira had walked by his table to take a better look at his ID. The blue cord round his neck had the initials of his department; the green corner of the card declared the zone and his last name was printed in black. It wasn't difficult to determine his designation either, as he flung it into the conversation. The government directory, accessed on her cell phone, provided his office phone numbers. She left a message just as the head of Public Commitments for the south-west zone exited the café. The officer had been unafraid as he had walked back into his building, as if he knew the public wouldn't bother if he stole from them; they never did. Yes, people would not let him get away if he had touched their homes, their furniture, their vehicles or their parking slots. But their roads, their bridges, their trains? These could be stolen from them anytime. Just like their drinking water.

ONE

Some years ago, Bidur Munshi—the owner of a newspaper in Delhi—decided that enough was enough. There should be a limit to the badgering that the newspaper could take, and this was not any newspaper. It was a political institution, the dream child of those who participated in the greatest endeavour of the nation, its struggle for freedom. It was the voice of unknown Indians, an instrument of change and a mirror of the ideals people aspired for. Today, the newspaper was once again part of a struggle, but unlike the one in 1947, it could lose this one.

Like most symbols of an archaic age, there was respect for the newspaper but no utility. After the round-the-clock reportage on television, there was no news to print for the next morning; nothing that the readers had not already heard, seen, weighed and judged. The line 'At the time of going to press,' was beginning to hurt, and the news didn't seem to care; it just kept breaking. Like, for instance, the minister, whose house was raided, was already arrested by next morning; the actress, who was expecting a child, already had the baby late last night; and the young challenger with the blistering forehand was already the new men's singles champion at Wimbledon.

What was left to report? It was a question Munshi had often grappled with in the last few years, especially while dealing with the plummeting figures of sales of the daily.

He was offered some solutions, which he sincerely tried. There was still scope for political analysis, he was told. Those studied articles that explored new possibilities and tested old theories were so ponderous that nothing but ink and paper could carry their weight. One may love the instant fame of news channels, but, in the end, the printed word was for posterity. And so Munshi got the best thinkers to write for him and launched fresh ideas into the sterile space of what-could-have-been and what-should-have-been.

That improved the minds of the old readers, perhaps, but didn't capture any new ones. Munshi kept discovering, and at a cost, that 800 words of the most thought-provoking newspaper story were equal to roughly a thirty-second 'wrap' on television.

He wanted political reportage, the kind that exposed the ambition and subterfuge of politicians and bureaucracy, the difference between real popularity and voters' lack of choice, the difference between tyranny and parliamentary majority; stories that got under the skin of election promises and government policy. Munshi believed voters would love such news because it empowered them. He was wrong; empowerment now meant being able to recharge the cell phone to watch the live feeds from news channels. The outcome changed the nature of news itself. There was no longer any sanctity of sources, any exclusivity of stories. It was a dull and bleak world of constant updates, which every journalist received at about the exact same time. There was no such thing as selective debriefing anymore, there was only conditional debriefing. And the condition was that the news should be aired at prime time and with a certain spin. Newspapers did not figure in this game; they reached people twelve hours too late.

Munshi went through this churning about four years ago and emerged distraught. He even toyed with the idea of going online, like many immortal brands worldwide that continued life after their death in print. He considered various proposals: 'the first online political news portal', 'the best online political analysis' and 'the only online political newspaper'. It all came down to one thing—an online confession of his failure.

Determined not to buy that last lock for the gates or sign off that final edition of the newspaper, Munshi started to think in earnest. As with anyone at the end of the road, where advice no longer worked, he began listening to his inner voice that spoke to him in an obsolete vocabulary due to disuse and gave him ideas that were extravagant, adventurous and also terminal. There were limited funds left with him and, therefore, limited time to explore all the ideas of his inner voice. But as he had to try at least one of them, he chose the cheapest and least terminal of them all.

Munshi wrote about this idea in one of his page one 'messages from the chairman/editor-in-chief', which were generally famous for kicking in the teeth of deviant newsmakers. This message, however, was a little different. He reflected about the troubles newspapers faced, explained the consequences of decreasing circulation and falling sales. He wrote about his own newspaper and its great history, and referred to daily newspapers as the conscience keepers in a democracy. All this was on the brink of oblivion, he concluded gloomily, but added that life appeared different from the edge.

Munshi claimed that this near-death experience had given him an almost spiritual insight into the truth about political and government reportage. Faced with day-long breaking news, journalists now had to look for other, more unusual sources of information. As the facts were all on air on news channels, newspaper journalists could do the only thing left to do; improvise. This had often led to reading of body language of politicians or putting disparate facts together for a new, although, usually far-fetched result. Journalists in search of an exclusive story now had to cross over into the realm of intuition and special powers of the mind. Things not associated with journalism were becoming common, like *knowing* the future of a bill even before it was made into a law, or *knowing* what decisions were being made in closed-door meetings or *knowing* whose idea it was to arrest the protestors, even though the police said it was the home minister. Different from speculation, this 'knowing' was not factual, it bordered on belief and superstition. And like most belief and superstition, it rapidly took the place of fact.

Munshi suggested a simple solution to end this dilemma. He would set up a department of 'knowers' in his newspaper, which would introduce a new kind of journalism in the country—the reportage of knowing. Not to guess, or speculate, but to know in an authentic, professionally intuitive manner. It was beyond the five essentials of news coverage, and an all-new way of answering the 'why' of every event. He invited men and women from across the country to apply to the newspaper for the new position of a know-journalist. Language would not be a hurdle, qualifications did not matter and age was immaterial. All they required were powers of the mind they were either born with or developed mysteriously, which could range from predicting future to guessing cards. Applicants would be required to do political reportage by knowing events and decisions before they happened. He wrote:

'This could have been an obituary to my newspaper. Instead, it is an invitation. I know this will anger many journalists who may find their careers in jeopardy. I apologize for the inconvenience of an unemployed future this may cause them. But I know they will forgive me because there is no scope for compromise in journalism. In the past, it was the truth we wanted, and we found it every time. We now want faith, and I am sure we will find this too.'

Munshi had always been hated for his words, but his ideas were another matter; he was loved for them. This seemed to be an exception. The subject of knowing was criticized endlessly on television and written about in other newspapers. And as with any free show that promised a possible suicide, the spotlight stayed on Munshi.

He was briefly worried about the general destruction of his relationships that had followed the decision. But he was not the kind to undertake reconstructions of any type without reason, and he wanted to prove that point. As promised, Munshi's advertisement appeared in all newspapers, and it requested applications for the post of a know-journalist. Munshi received only twenty-two applications from all over the country, but the collection was eclectic. From magicians to mind readers, astrologers to arsonists, each candidate had a fascinating power over nature or other human beings. It was difficult to interview them, as they seemed to know the questions the moment they were formed in the interviewer's mind. The suspicion that they knew the answers as well defeated the purpose of the interviews. The selection process now became a test for Munshi and his team instead. Finally, deputy editor, Bhaskar Joshi, developed a template that was based strictly on what was required for reporting about politics and government. After several days of screening, Mira Mouli was chosen for her powers of knowing thoughts just by listening to people talk. That was four years ago.

Then, the previous week, the newspaper had hired a new 'knower' to the department, Salat Vasudev, for his extraordinary powers of discovering patterns and anomalies in complex processes. He belonged to a wealthy and famous business family, a fact Munshi had factored in while recruiting him. That could help in the publicity for his stories and, therefore, the newspaper. Munshi had been right; Salat's debut story last Sunday still made waves, and it was already Thursday. It was an investigation based on a few hundred documents that proved how illegitimate funds were being legalized by ministers for a price with the help of top bureaucrats. Salat had 'known' the irregularity by a mere glance at the records. It had taken the entire editorial team of the newspaper three days to cross check and confirm what he had known in approximately eleven minutes. The response from the government had been decisive, mainly because every word of what Salat wrote had been true. Two top ministers were set to resign, and the officials who colluded with them were suspended from work.

The newspaper now had to make space for Salat, and it encroached on Mira's space. Munshi believed in setting the trend, and he knew that even though Mira had brought credibility to the concept of know-reportage, people were now used to her unusual powers. Her brilliance was becoming commonplace; Salat was the new attraction. Munshi, however, liked Mira for a reason beyond general comprehension; she had proved him right when he had needed it the most. Her sensational gift of knowing had conclusively put all doubts to rest. After the success of Munshi's experiment, other newspapers had employed know-journalists of their own. Know-reportage was the new way of journalism and know-reporters were seen as saviours of the printed news. Even Munshi's friends had returned to him when it became clear he would survive, and his relationships were restored. More importantly, so were the advertisements to his newspaper.

————

The rain had scattered the traffic off the roads, and Mira reached her newspaper office early, much ahead of an interview scheduled at 4 p.m. The lunch hour had segregated the staff into three categories: those who cooked at home, those who did not, and those who didn't care who cooked where. She knew who among the staff belonged to which category not because she lived alone and considered an apple lunch, but because she had no choice. It was more than a habit or a compulsion; it was her nature, the way people made friends or remembered numbers. Her powers worked in a stunningly simple way; it just required she heard people speak, once. It didn't even matter if they didn't speak to her; her mind completed their profile by observing their behaviour, choices or surroundings. For example, the yellow hairband of the chatty receptionist was the brightest thing she had worn in months. She no longer wore her wedding ring, and Mira knew she didn't miss it. Or the clerk who greeted her as he walked by in the corridor; his interest in religion had begun soon after he was overlooked for a recent promotion. People's thoughts seeped through her mind to mix with her observations and rapidly filled up the missing parts of the puzzle. It was as if she moved through a frozen, invisible grid, and if she allowed it to flow, she would know exactly how the day had been for the entire newsroom. But the unwanted detail was a burden, thoughts the weight of water that threatened to drown her if she didn't know how to float. So she learnt to disengage, close her mind to remain unscathed in her office and in her life in general. She survived because of a few uninhabited islands, pockets of relative thoughtlessness that allowed her to come up for air briefly. Her cabin was the usual sanctuary in office, which she entered now, shut the door and took a deep breath of the silence.

Switching on the computer, Mira reached for the apple in her bag. A memory tugged at her heart of another birthday, when she had discovered that it wasn't actually the date she was born. Her fingers froze on the keyboard as her mind returned to that day nineteen years ago in Rishikesh. Professor Raghunath Mouli, who she had thought was her uncle, was merely a stranger who had taken pity on an orphan and paid for her education. She was no one's child and no one wanted her, she had realized on that day.

It was always difficult to douse that memory, as if she had only put out a fire that continued to smoulder under the ashes. Mira forced herself to focus on the waiting messages. The technical team usually disabled readers' comments on her know-reports to protect the newspaper website from crashing with overload. So the readers emailed her instead, and choked the inbox. The messages that day were mainly about the story she had written a few days ago on reallocation of central ministries in the People's Party government. The ruling party was keen to revamp the government ahead of the January national elections, sack the corrupt faces and accommodate electorally useful ones. It had led to the usual game in journalistic circles to predict who would be promoted, demoted, included and dropped from the cabinet, even though everyone knew the list would be finalized only hours before the actual announcement. Promotions had to be closely guarded against sabotage at the last moment; the name of a member of Parliament (MP) could be struck off the list because of controversies, new scandals and new revelations about old scandals. It was, however, easier to track demotions and ousters as such leaders were identified when they vengefully exposed others. The only safety for politicians was in secrecy, and even those who knew they were on the list made every effort to mislead journalists. So, after a week of this game, the media had notionally promoted and demoted every minister, and even sacked a few from the cabinet.

Mira did none of that. She just gave a brief list of politicians who would be promoted, a longer list of the demoted and a very short list of the newly inducted. The cabinet reshuffle was announced that morning, and her list was accurate to the last name. Most emails that afternoon were compliments; readers believed her gift to be a miracle, some even called it a blessing of the gods! Her dark eyes reflected the screen light indifferently as she repeated her polite answer to the mails and thanked the readers. She thought it as no achievement that she had often been right about the decisions of Mahesh Bansi, the president of the People's Party (PP). Four years ago, soon after her recruitment, she was assigned the two main political parties to research and report. She had also been equally accurate about the decisions of Omkar Nuri, the head of the main Opposition National Party (NP).

The reshuffle, she had predicted, would prove that Mahesh Bansi's influence in the party was on the decline, as it would not include his recommendations. The ruling party president's input was important ahead of elections, although as per rule, the PP office-bearers—including the president—didn't contest elections themselves. After a corrupt tenure in office, both the party and the government sought to go to polls with a clean image. Mahesh would consider the reshuffle as the last straw, she explained in her article:

'Mahesh Bansi has thrived in the party organization because he is good with politics, not popularity. He has surrounded himself with people who need him for their political careers. By denying his list of candidates, the government will weaken him and reduce his clout. He will know his opinion won't matter in decision-making during the election process in coming months, especially about who will contest and who won't, a matter that will be of great interest to his followers.

The government's message to the Bansi loyalists will be to rethink their allegiance to him. With restless rivals in the party like Nalan Malik already poaching on his supporters, Mahesh Bansi will see the reshuffle as the final word against his continuation as party president.'

It ruffled feathers, where feathers were left in Delhi. The rest brooded over what could be done about know-reportage of this sort and the menace it posed to political strategy. Every know-report came with a disclaimer that the story was not based on facts but on the special powers of the know-journalist. Earlier, Mahesh Bansi used to call Mira himself to protest about her stories. Those used to be brief conversations that ended with her directing him on how to complain to Munshi instead. But when Mahesh did that, he discovered how Munshi actually enjoyed the complaints and derived pleasure from the finer details of damage the story had done. After several instances of this, Mahesh lost the art of appreciating Munshi's chuckle and stopped calling. Mira often wondered if the politicians who criticized her know-reports realized that the intensity of their protests established the accuracy of her story. Some did, and found consolation in the fact that she was equally accurate and sufficiently brutal about their rivals as well.

The website did not provide the newspaper online but gave a brief description of various departments and their profiles. The most-read section was Mira's background and, as she knew from experience the kind of truth people often preferred, she told them exactly what they expected:

'At the heart of my story, like most mysteries, is destiny. I was born with a unique gift of the mind; the power to think like other people. Given the numerous options and combinations available to us in every moment, it is impossible to know what choices we might make and why we make them. That is how we construct chance and I deconstruct it for you.

I was still a child when it began; at least, they said I was still a child. I could accurately know the choices people had made and might make in the future; know their thoughts, their fears, lies, plans and hopes. Naturally, this made my childhood a busy place. I spent numerous afternoons on school holidays and weekends with family and friends, answering questions important to them. Will the heir take over the business or become the musician he wants to be? Will the daughter leave the city for her career or get married and settle down? Will the troubled couple still be together after three years? I have grown up since those fun- and food-filled afternoons, but going by the emails I receive, the questions seem to have remained the same. As with most things intuitive, I am never really sure exactly what leads to the predictions, and I have never been able to trace my forecasts back to a trigger. Here at the newspaper, I get to write what's behind the decisions and actions of people in politics. In other words, I take the story forward, especially when there are no more facts to be had.'

Since her appointment at the newspaper, Munshi had asked her help several times to assist his friends by studying a situation or an adversary. As a result, she had many acquaintances but no friends. People admired her; she was intelligent, good looking, courteous and engaging. But they were perplexed by her reluctance for relationships especially when, they reasoned, she could read their thoughts. They never understood that it was precisely because she read their thoughts that she didn't want relationships. Her gift protected her from getting hurt emotionally, warned her of intentions and exposed hidden motives. She didn't need people, she wasn't used to them in her submerged world of constant loneliness. But her gift also hurt her sometimes, and when that happened, she wished there was someone who saved her from herself.

Nineteen years ago, she was hurt by her powers of knowing for the first time. The cold river breeze that distant morning on banks of the Ganga touched her face once more now, and made her let go of the waiting fragment of memory. It was her tenth birthday, the last time Raghunath Mouli had visited the hostel at the orphanage. She had then with her a picture of her parents, Sima and Shivnath Mouli. Giving her the photograph a few years ago, Rahgunath had mentioned that his brother and sister-in-law had died following a road accident and left her in his care. She had kept the picture close and tried to rebuild the imaginary life of her parents, working the dream all the way back to their beautiful marriage and a happy home. There had always been something missing about that dream, and Mira had always been worried she would discover what it was. Then on that day, almost instinctively, she had asked Raghunath the date when the photograph was taken. It was a simple question but she knew he had no answer; at least, no answer that was the truth.

'They are not my parents, are they?' Mira couldn't help asking him that morning at the river. 'This is not the photo of my parents.'

Raghunath had tried to stay with the lie. 'How can you say such a thing?' he begged. 'You are the only person in whom I can see a glimpse of my dead brother, Mira. Please don't . . .'

But she could discern his thoughts. 'You took this photo yourself when I demanded proof of my identity. These are your friends, not my parents!'

Raghunath had been shaken by her discovery, she could tell, but he wasn't really surprised. He knew her special powers would reveal the truth one day. It was just a matter of time.

She had fought back the tears. 'I'm right, am I not?'

He had reluctantly accepted. 'Yes.'

Mira didn't know what to do with the truth, it was so hard and so cold that it drained the warmth from everything around her. As the breeze dried the tears on her face that morning, Mira had felt her life was made of temporary matter. She had suspected that her fate lines were drawn in sand. Now she knew they were, in fact, lines drawn in water.

Raghunath had told her the rest of her story, or the little he knew of it. She was found abandoned as an infant at the orphanage on the day that was later registered as her birthday. Raghunath, then a professor at the local college, had often visited the orphanage and offered financial help to as many children as he could afford, given he had a family of his own to support. He had grown fond of the new infant, whom everyone called Mira. He discovered early, like others, that Mira was not an ordinary child and seemed to know things without them being explained to her. She never needed lessons in conduct or discipline, learnt the subjects quickly and excelled at studies. But unlike other children at the orphanage who were reconciled to their reality, Mira constantly tried to know more about her own origin. Her every question led to the eventual assumption that her parents had abandoned her because they didn't want her. She refused to believe that, despite her powers that confirmed it as fact, and continued to ask the same question, hoping for a different answer.

Unable to watch her disappointment, Raghunath built the lie of a family and a home to which she had once belonged. Mira had asked him a myriad questions and wouldn't rest without some tangible proof. His heart was wrung by how desperately she wanted to believe him despite her doubts and so, gave her a photograph of his friends. She was happy at first, but then her mind slowly eroded the façade of Raghunath's lie like a persistent river that triumphed over her belief. This process was so apparent that Raghunath was certain she would soon discover his lie. He just hoped she would understand why he had done it, the same reason why he had given her his name; he truly wished she were his daughter.

At the end, Mira did understand why Raghunath had lied, but at the beginning, she had hated him. The beautiful dream he had built for her had turned an inexplicable misfortune into a deliberate destiny. She could almost hear his gentle voice now, pleading her to never think of herself as being alone. She was well acquainted with those words. She had repeated them to herself a million times until then. But as he spoke them aloud, they created a sudden and permanent gap between her and the rest of the world. She had hated him then for his kind, futile words, for his yet another injustice to her. It took time to realize it was her gift that separated her from the rest, the power to see the invariable truth all the time, without choice, without relief. It robbed her of her mirages, the necessary falsehoods required for happiness. And ironically, none of her special powers could tell her anything about the parents who had abandoned her or the reason for their decision. Her now-famous gift of knowing that could unravel the minds of powerful men and women failed to answer the only question that tormented her: why was she an orphan?

Mira abruptly stood up from her chair, grabbed the apple, and left the office cabin to escape the memories. All cabins of the editorial department opened into the newsroom at the centre, which was a long hall divided into departmental work stations. The glass doors at the end led out to the elevators and stairs, and to the open balcony across the corridor. This was on the second floor of the three-storeyed building that Munshi owned. The ground and first floors were for non-editorial staff, and the third floor was dedicated to offices of Munshi himself, his two deputy editors and the meeting rooms.

Mira paused in the newsroom for the distraction of some random conversation until Lina Kamat, the news editor, joined in. Lina was one of the key people of the editorial department, who brought out the edition every night efficiently and faultlessly. She was also beautiful and single. Lina used to like Mira, until she discovered that Mira didn't need anything from anyone. She didn't need assurances, she also didn't need approval. She didn't care who was promoted, who was reprimanded, the reason for that unfair increment or that well-deserved memo. She wouldn't attend office parties, wouldn't take long coffee breaks and didn't enjoy any gossip based on lies. There was, therefore, not much scope for an office friendship with her. Sensing that Lina hoped for some lunch-hour disagreement, Mira placidly listened to her provocative criticism of her articles and quietly agreed. After avoiding the skirmish, she headed towards the glass doors and, as she passed by the photo section, smiled at the sports photographer who waved at her. He pretended to be a die-hard cricket fan because of his boss when, in fact, he was a die-hard football fan. Then in the city reporting department, she noticed a young reporter diligently typing at his desk to finish a story; she knew he was also considering a job at a rival newspaper.

Crossing the corridor, she stepped out into the balcony where the rain was painting the day silver. The busy main street two floors below was almost deserted as the rain that day was heavy, like a force of nature and not just an urban inconvenience. She leaned against the wall and had the apple. The rain calmed her down in time and she analyzed the inaccuracy of her birthday. She wasn't born on that day; she was merely found alive. She had often wondered if it would be the right day to be found dead as well. Mira considered the edge of the balcony a few feet away and the rain beyond. To reach rain, fall with it, to become rain. To be found again, this time as rain, on her birthday.

TWO

It was almost 4 p.m. Mira was scheduled to meet the young politician of the PP, Kirit Singh, famous for his spectacular rise from college politics to the national stage. He was immensely popular among youth and students, the reason why the PP was considering him for the Middle Delhi seat that included two university campuses. He also had a massive following in the social media network, where he had already begun his election campaign and got enthusiastic support. Then suddenly, earlier that week, Kirit Singh had resigned from the PP and shocked everyone. He said it was a mark of protest against a party that was fast slipping into a dynastic system where the real worth of party men was not being recognized. He revealed he had been denied the Middle Delhi seat as the party president Mahesh Bansi had wanted it for the re-election of his son, Sikander. That was the truth, but as with any truth told without strategy in politics, it was hastily disowned by everyone.

However, it brought to notice a fact that few had engaged with; the future prospects of a little known politician called Sikander Bansi. He had contested for the first time in the last election from a rural constituency and won effortlessly against a sitting MP of whom the voters had tired. And now after four and half years of Sikander's tenure as their MP, the voters were tired of him. It was well-known that his re-election would be difficult. The Opposition candidate had informally begun touring the constituency and was gathering impressive crowds. Analysts agreed that if Mahesh planned a rescue for his son, this was just the right time to change his constituency, and Middle Delhi was just the right place to contest from. Sikander was better suited for Middle Delhi because he was born in the city and had lived there all his life. The city elite had an easy recall of him, although it was mostly about his decadent lifestyle, fast cars, celebrity friends and the frequent cause for embarrassment to his father. Even as an elected MP, he had spent more time in Delhi than in his rural constituency. He never addressed the issues of his constituents and rarely raised questions in Parliament. In contrast, he was a lively participant in Delhi's various social circles, where he could be often seen discussing the cultural scene and international trends. After his election, rivals of his father in the party like Nalan Malik had begun opposing Sikander as well. But they soon discovered that he posed them no threat. He was hardly present in Parliament and never in the party office. And he always, and notoriously, went against his father's wishes. Sikander's conduct constantly violated some rule or tradition; he didn't seem to care for either etiquette or expectations. He never made political statements, demands or suggestions in the press, and was only rarely ever photographed. In a way, it was quite stunning that Sikander Bansi, son of one of the most powerful politicians of the country, almost didn't exist politically.

Kirit Singh's rebellion was bound to have an impact on the party's decision about both Middle Delhi and Sikander's future. That was the importance of the man Mira had invited for an interview at her office that afternoon. Kirit Singh arrived at sharp 4 p.m. and agreed to a cup of tea. He was between thirty and thirty-five years of age, fair and short, with an impatient smile and a manner better designed for confrontation than conciliation. As an introduction, he gave a brief description of how he had grown up in Middle Delhi and that it was more than just his home. Mira listened to him intently, watched his hand gestures, his clothes, words on which he averted his eyes and the issues he was comfortable with. At the end of the first five minutes, she began to get angry with Bhaskar for assigning her such non-stories.

'The Opposition National Party has offered you a candidacy from Middle Delhi,' she noted. 'You have resigned from the People's Party on that issue. What do you plan to do next?'

He shrugged. 'I want to represent the people of Middle Delhi and ensure their problems are solved. It doesn't matter which party gives me this opportunity; people are far more important than any political party.'

'You mean you would join any political party that offers you a ticket to contest the election?' she translated the rhetoric.

He reacted sharply. 'I will go to any party that respects my commitment to the people of Middle Delhi.'

She pursued, 'Are you confident of winning the seat?'

'Absolutely,' he smiled one of his poster smiles. 'That might be the reason why other parties are keen for me to join them.'

'You mean, you can defeat Sikander Bansi if he contests Middle Delhi?'

'I can and I will. He will see a contest of the kinds he has never seen before,' he said derisively. 'He won't find it same as winning an election in a far-flung constituency during a popular wave in favour of the PP. He needs to learn a few things about our democracy, and I plan on teaching him.'

Mira was amused at the thoughts he was prudent enough not to share. 'What do have against Sikander Bansi?' she asked.

'Nothing at all. Never even met the guy! But then, that's true for most of the PP; only a few party men have ever seen him.' He chuckled and added, 'Except for the party president, of course.' Then he turned serious. 'The PP had always been against promoting political dynasties, and that gave hope to common people like me. The PP leadership was dedicated to social service and public welfare, and it made us proud. That was the reason why senior office-bearers of the party never contested elections, because the pursuit of power was not their aim. Unfortunately, the present president is far too ambitious to be good for the party,' he said, sounding disappointed. 'He has run the party with the help of cliques and confidantes, and by rehabilitating former ministers at senior positions. He is enamoured with power and while he himself could never achieve it, Mahesh wants it now for his son. Well,' he observed acidly, 'he might have even succeeded had he not messed with my plans.'

Mira surveyed him. 'What about loyalty? After all, the PP and the same party president gave you many opportunities to progress in politics.'

'I'm grateful for that, of course. But I'm loyal to the people, not to the son of the high command.'

He had just recollected that line from a conversation with Nalan Malik. Mira smiled; she looked good when she smiled, people mistook her to be friendly when she smiled.

'Isn't that one of the secret slogans of the rivals in the party?'

He acted perplexed. 'I don't know what you mean.'

'Your resignation has embarrassed Mahesh Bansi and helped his opponents, like Nalan Malik,' said Mira, as she sipped the tea that had just arrived. 'What do you think of Nalan Malik, Mr Singh?'

'What should I think? He is one of our senior party leaders,' Kirit calmly asserted. However, he was not a politician for nothing, so he added, 'There should be space for every shade of opinion in a democratic political party.'

'Sure. But then, all democracy requires a winner and a loser,' Mira remarked. 'Seems like you are the latter, doesn't it?'

He didn't answer at once. Then warily said, 'The voters will decide who the loser is. I believe in electoral justice.'

'Only if you can afford it,' she pointed out. 'Are you rich enough to believe in electoral justice? Or perhaps someone else is, on your behalf?'

He was uneasy. 'I am not the only one who resents that Sikander is being foisted on the party. But I may be the only one who can do something about it.'

She read his thoughts as if they were printed on paper. 'Surely you discussed this with other party leaders? Like Nalan?'

'I did. They all requested me not to leave the party. Though I refused to change my decision, I was especially touched by Nalan's offer of financial help to my family. He understands these things because he too is a common man. He knows that while I am involved in my politics, I will also need to support my family.'

'That's generous indeed,' she admitted, then said sympathetically, 'You are one of Nalan's loyalists; you think that is why Mahesh Bansi picked your constituency?'

'Exactly. I like Nalan not because of ambition or compulsion, but because he is just like me and thousands of other young men and women from humble backgrounds who seek to join national political parties.'

'Does it mean that Sikander's privileged background will make him a bad politician?'

'Perhaps not,' he granted. 'But I have worked hard and sacrificed enough to be able to contest the Middle Delhi seat. It's my turn now, and Sikander shouldn't be able to just replace me because of his family. This is not why I joined politics, to always be a follower and never a leader. This trend is not good for the party's future.'

'Then your revolt against Sikander is for the greater good of the party?'

'It's a small price to pay.'

'What will Nalan get you in return?'

'I resent your suggestion,' Kirit said cordially. 'Besides, revolts like mine cannot be bought.'

'Really?' She closed her notebook. 'Must be the economy.'

———

Back in her cabin, Mira flipped through her notes of the interview. Kirit Singh's resignation gave the rivals an opportunity to corner Mahesh Bansi, but Nalan Malik could play it both ways. To orchestrate Sikander's defeat in the January elections would be the best way to make Mahesh redundant. And the fear of this possibility would get Nalan leverage with the party leadership. It was precisely such cold and calculating tactics that had ensured his steady rise in the PP. Mira had talked to Nalan only once, when he was promoted a few months ago to be one of the four general secretaries of the party. That promotion required that she researched him as part of her job, and she had called him for an interview. He declined to meet but had politely informed her that he had five minutes, if she wanted to ask him the questions on the phone. His answers were cautious, clear and intelligent. He was neither humble nor proud, but just factual about the promotion, and explained it as part of the party's election preparation.

'Will you contribute to election strategy?' she had asked.

'Everyone will contribute to election strategy, Ms Mouli, before the election.'

The cryptic answers didn't work for her; Mira needed him to speak more. 'Although you do not contest elections as part of your party policy, is your promotion a recognition of your ability to deliver electoral victories?' she asked. 'You have managed to turn around losing battles into winning propositions in the past.'

He had chuckled, 'I wish you were my biographer.'

She focused on his engaging voice. 'How will you help the party in preparing for elections?'

'I shall do the usual, ma'am.' He explained helpfully, 'I shall attend meetings, discuss issues and not reveal a thing to the media.'

She had remained silent.

'I have thirty seconds left,' he said.

'I'm done.'

'You mentioned you were a know-journalist.' He asked, intrigued. 'So, what did you get to "know" about me from this conversation?'

'That you are amused by this promotion.'

She could sense his surprise as he had listened to her in silence.

'But it won't stop you; nothing can,' she continued. 'You want to move forward in the party at any cost, even at the cost of an election defeat, if the blame for it can be pinned on your rival.'

He didn't speak immediately. 'It has been a pleasure talking to you, Ms Mouli,' he had said finally and ended the call.

Nalan had never spoken to her again. She had sought his version on political stories about the PP, but his staff always maintained that he was unavailable for comment. Mira now wondered if she should call his office to get his side of the Kirit Singh story. It felt pointless; Nalan would never speak to a know-journalist about this episode. But she had to try, so she did. And failed.

Nalan's unavailability for comment, Mira had learnt over time, was his general reaction to the free press. He was not available at his office in the party headquarters, at his residence or even in Parliament. He was only partially available on his cell phone and that too, to only those whom he trusted with his number. He had created a moat of silence around himself, which could only be crossed through swing bridges selectively lowered for those he approved of. He seemed to want the rest of the media to remain on the other side of this moat, and survive on the morsels of information he let drop occasionally.

However, in the absence of known facts about an important political person, Delhi usually invented some. Nalan Malik had to be understood from the clothes he wore, the people he met, the places he visited and the secular music festivals he favoured. Then there was that tantalizingly under-reported divorce just a few months ago. He had known his ex-wife, the daughter of a respected judge, for almost a year before they got married. They had been a normal, everyday couple for three years, until she filed for divorce in a Delhi court, stating that he was disloyal and was involved in an extramarital relationship. Nothing was known beyond that, although Nalan had been photographed a few times with Kim Sharma, a businesswoman close to several PP leaders. That didn't count because everyone knew Kim, including the editors of news channels and newspapers that reported the divorce. Nalan moved swiftly and silently, and Kim was never mentioned in the news again.

That was not the only instance when the media was kind to Nalan. Nalan didn't manage the press by engaging with the journalists; he did it by engaging with the businesses that owned the press. All except Bidur Munshi, who hated cultivation of all kinds. That was another reason why Mira wasn't on Nalan's very short list of trustworthy journalists.

While he was usually unavailable on all his numbers, even his secretary was not available to her that day. Amused at the widespread precautions taken to not speak with her, Mira left a message that simply stated that she was writing the Kirit Singh resignation story and that she had a deadline. She was filing the report after an hour when the call came through.

Surprised, she wished Nalan and waited.

'After our last conversation a few months ago,' Nalan explained in his soft, comforting voice, 'I had resolved never to speak to you again.'

'I see.'

'That's because I resent the idea of know-reportage,' he said coolly, 'which is designed to target politicians who are averse to engaging with the media either as part of party discipline or personal principles. I find your style of journalism intrusive and unethical.'

'Exactly like your thoughts, Mr Malik,' she countered, 'which you want to keep from the less intrusive and more ethical journalists.'

'I don't want to debate the point, ma'am,' he said scathingly. 'I returned your call because I had the suspicion that you were once again about to smear my name without any factual evidence.'

'Here is your chance to escape that fate then,' Mira generously suggested. 'Why are you helping Kirit Singh? Or, haven't you heard his name before?'

'Of course I have heard his name!' he snapped back. 'And I have no comment.'

Mira closed her eyes to focus on his thoughts that had always been a little too complex to be known at once.

'Will Sikander Bansi's defeat in elections serve your purpose?'

'What nonsense! His defeat or victory will mean nothing to me.'

She was silent, then said, 'That's a lie, Mr Malik.'

'That, Ms Mouli,' he said cordially, 'is the end of our conversation.'

'Suit yourself.' She didn't hang up.

Neither did he. 'Last time,' he said, in an admirably controlled voice, 'you wrote that I had negotiated a deal with a visiting foreign minister, even though you knew I am not part of the cabinet and merely a general secretary of the PP. I survived that story because I got credit for the rescue of a failing diplomatic relationship. I won't be that lucky every time you write one of your know-reports. And neither will you be.'

'Why not?'

'You're the knower. Figure it out!'

'Is that why you won't meet me for an interview?' she was curious. 'To keep me from figuring you out?'

'The day you have to meet me, Ms Mouli,' his tone was causal, 'you'll wish you hadn't.'

'Can't be that bad, surely,' she mocked. 'You are too hard on yourself.'

There was a few seconds of silence and then he hung up abruptly.

Later, Mira examined his replies; he had not answered the Kirit Singh question, but he didn't have to. He was ambitious, driven and ruthless in his politics. But behind all that, she could also detect an intense vulnerability from his fear of failure and disgust with what it made him do. That's what kept him from meeting her; he knew she would discover his desperation for success, and also, his weakness for it.

———

She had just finished the report when Bhaskar's secretary called Mira about an urgent meeting. One flight of stairs up from the noisy newsroom led to the expensive silence of the third floor and the offices of the editor-in-chief, the two deputy editors and their staff. The rest of the space was used for two meeting rooms, a conference room, the library and an exclusive dining area. Bhaskar's secretary gestured to the door, and Mira walked in.

'Good,' Bhaskar said, his chubby face relieved. 'I was worried you might have been out of office.'

Mira sat down. 'You seem worried for other reasons as well.'

Used to her ways, he admitted. 'Munshi,' he explained. 'He wants to meet you after this briefing; he is waiting with Mahesh Bansi.'

Her dark eyes were intense, as she discerned his thoughts. 'It's about his son.'

Bhaskar nodded. 'Do you know him?'

'Sikander Bansi? No.' She paused. 'Is this regarding the Kirit Singh story?'

'Talked to Sikander on the phone perhaps?' Bhaskar asked again. 'Maybe met him at a party in the city?'

'Never talked to him or met him, Bhaskar.'

'Maybe, you know his friends then?'

'More likely I know his enemies,' she mentioned dryly. 'What's all this about?'

'Sikander is missing.'

'What do you mean missing?' she demanded. 'He is a member of Parliament and son of the People's Party president. He is not exactly a poodle.'

'He can still go missing, can't he?' Bhaskar asked, incensed.

Mira conceded that.

'Now this is crucial,' Bhaskar began, 'under no ...'

'... circumstances must the details of the meeting be revealed without prior permission,' she completed.

He nodded again.

'But what is it to me if Sikander is missing?' she inquired restlessly. 'And why do you or Munshi think I will waste my time speaking about it?'

'No one said you will!' Bhaskar was exasperated. 'Must you take everything amiss? Especially when you know I am only following instructions?'

'I do,' she assured him coldly. 'Just as I knew it was you, and not Munshi, who gave away my Sunday page-one spot to Salat.'

'I thought Salat's story warranted such focus,' he protested. 'And I was right! Look at the impact, and that was just his first story for this newspaper!' He paused and added conciliatorily, 'It's no reflection on you, Mira. But I cannot give you page one if you don't do good stories.'

'I can't do good stories if you give me assignments like Kirit Singh, whom I didn't even have to interview to know him,' Mira said, upset. 'And now you want me to help with a missing person!'

'This can be a big story, Mira,' Bhaskar argued patiently, 'but only if you can focus a little bit here!'

She reluctantly agreed.

Bhaskar forced himself to smile to lighten the atmosphere; it didn't work. 'Mahesh said he won't talk to anyone but you. That's why Munshi and I wanted to check if you were working on any story about Sikander.'

'No, I am not,' she clarified, 'and his father hates my stories too much to ask for my help.'

'You're right,' Bhaskar replied. 'He didn't'.

Mira frowned, as she sensed his thoughts.

'Sikander did,' Bhaskar confirmed.

She stayed silent, puzzled.

'We'll know the rest when you meet Mahesh. Let's go.' He stood up and walked to the door.

Intrigued, Mira followed him out.

THREE

Munshi's room was at the end of the carpeted corridor that was lined with photographs of various famous men and women who had visited the newspaper office over the years. Munshi wasn't in any of the pictures; he did not believe in that kind of endorsement. They found him sitting on the sofa with Mahesh Bansi. Munshi made the introductions, and Mira waited as she registered the three familiar thought processes. Bidur Munshi, fifty-six years old, was not just the editor-in-chief of the newspaper but also one of the most popular journalists of the country, as well as a businessman. He had a flamboyant nature that, along with his unapologetic display of wealth, made him an easy target of attention and criticism. It helped that he was endowed with a keen intellect and sharp analytical skills, evident in his incisive editorials and bold comments. His advice was sought often by politicians and industrialists. It was required for both the construction and destruction of careers. His cooperation, however, was far more valuable, and he never offered it as inexpensively, or as often, as his advice.

Bidur was dressed in his typical style, a pale blue linen suit and white shirt, without a tie. The yellow sapphire cufflinks sparkled as he checked his formal watch. The impatient gesture was not lost on Mahesh, who sat next to him. Mahesh was sixty-seven years old; he had non-committal eyes and a fixed smile, the result of his forty years in politics. He wore clothes in various shades of brown paired with white traditional jackets and a customary miniature flag of PP pinned to them. He had wished Mira when she was introduced. Despite the number of times she had written about him, spoken to him on phone and attended his press conferences for research, they both had never actually met before. It was not required for her know-reports, whose accuracy proved how well she actually knew him. Despite that smile and those courteous eyes, Mahesh detested her, although not as much as he hated Munshi.

Munshi glanced at him and politely said, 'Now that Mira has joined us, why don't you explain the problem, Mahesh?'

Mahesh nodded, his grey hair reflected the concealed lights of Munshi's office.

'My son has decided to go . . . into hiding,' Mahesh told her hesitantly and his smile faded in spite of himself. 'He wants you to find him and . . .'

Then he fell silent abruptly, troubled.

Munshi chuckled, 'Don't be nervous now.'

'What do you expect?' Mahesh demanded. 'I am talking to a bunch of journalists!'

'Perhaps it would help to remember that you asked for this meeting, which I will have to leave in . . .' Munshi checked his watch again, '10 minutes.'

'I don't know where to begin, Bidur. My entire political career, my entire life depends on this . . . this outrageous game!' He closed his eyes desperately. 'Sikander will destroy my political future if I follow his directions. And if I don't, I will lose my son.'

'This sounds promising,' Munshi said cheerfully. 'What does he want you to do?'

Mahesh looked at Munshi with dislike. 'I don't trust you, I don't trust your team. I am here because my son wants me to give you this recording.' He took out a CD from his pocket and threw it on the table in front of them. Everyone watched as the disc in its transparent plastic jacket slid across the glass table and stopped at an idol of meditating Buddha. Munshi followed that journey and then glared at Mahesh; he was beginning to get annoyed.

Before he could speak his mind, Mira intervened. 'You don't like being blackmailed, Maheshji, I get that. The question is,' she wondered, 'why are you scared?'

This was too much for Mahesh. 'Scared! How did . . .?' he stopped with effort. 'Before we go any further, you must answer a question I have been waiting to ask you. Who gives you stories against me? My rivals in the party? Leaders in the Opposition? How do you get to know so much about my decisions? Someone has been helping you, and I demand to know who it is.'

Mira observed him contemplatively. Even in agitation he was calm, as if he had his feelings under steely control. What the world saw was not real; these were just moving pictures on a screen.

'Who are your sources?' Mahesh interrogated her. 'Omkar Nuri of National Party? That mischievous Nalan Malik of my party?'

'Mostly,' Mira answered finally, 'it has just been you. Your words, expressions and gestures are enough for me to know you, although initially I had to hear you speak several times to map your thinking. So I attended your press conferences, political speeches and events, and listened to recordings of your interviews. That let me determine the pattern of your thoughts and helped me know how you make your decisions. And now Majeshji,' she said, meeting his eyes insistently, 'tell me why you are scared.'

Munshi and Bhaskar turned to him, curious.

'Don't you know the answer?' Mahesh challenged her.

'Actually, I do,' she answered. 'The tape reveals information that will anger powerful people whom you had worked hard to keep happy.'

Mahesh was suspicious. 'How do you know what is in the tape?'

'That's what a knower does, Mahesh,' Munshi said testily. 'Now will you please get on with it?'

Mahesh gathered himself. 'As I said,' he addressed Mira, 'my son has disappeared, and I discovered this in the morning today when I received a CD with a clue at the end of the recording addressed to you. There was also a letter for me that explained what to do.' He spoke uncertainly, as if revealing an embarrassing fact. 'Sikander requested me to bring this tape to you; it is the first of several such recordings. The next tape will reach you directly but only if your newspaper publishes this one.'

'The clues will lead to him?' she inquired.

'Yes,' Mahesh said. 'One clue at the end of every tape should help you find him. Tapes will, naturally, cease the moment you find Sikander.'

'How many tapes will there be?'

'He didn't say.' His voice dipped with sadness. 'He won't return home Mira. He will be lost to me forever if you can't solve those clues.'

Mira's eyes sharpened with interest as he spoke in earnest.

'Your son seems indifferent to the risk,' Munshi remarked.

Mahesh agreed weakly. 'This used to be his way to get my attention. He was a child when his mother died. It was about the time my political career had reached its peak. He got into trouble often so that I would rescue him,' he paused absently. 'Then I got too busy with my life, and I guess I stopped rescuing him.'

No one spoke after those candid words.

'Let's call the police,' Bhaskar said, looking for a conclusion.

'Well, Sikander knew that option would come up,' Mahesh clarified. 'The police are bound to get involved in a case like this, but he has forbidden me from going to them.' Mahesh glanced at Munshi, worried. 'Please Bidur, I am here to beg for your help. He is all I've got.'

That plea melted Munshi, and he assured Mahesh all possible assistance.

'Why don't you show us the letter?' Mira suggested. 'I know you have it with you.'

Mahesh regarded her resentfully, then took out a folded paper from his pocket and handed it to Mira.

'It is typed,' she noted and read aloud:

'Dear Father, I can't believe I am saying this but your city of short memories and long ropes has no depth even in its deceit.'

Mira stopped for a second, surprised by the words.

'All it would have taken to deceive me was a little character, a little integrity, and I would have committed my life to politics. Instead, I found effigies running the Parliament, men and women of straw, and I decided they should be properly introduced to their voters. From the time I was elected an MP four and a half years ago, I have had conversations inside Parliament with other MPs, political party leaders, bureaucrats, policemen and businessmen—the separate species of people who are commonly found in corridors of power. These conversations were quite candid because no one imagined I might record them. I was supposed to be in the same boat, equally corrupt and, therefore, safe. I wasn't though, neither corrupt nor safe, as the recordings will prove. I'm sending the first of the series of tapes that will expose exactly what happens inside Parliament. I believe there will be no need for an explanation once you hear the recording. The clue at the end of the tape is for Mira Mouli, the know-journalist. I chose her not because you despise her for her stories against you, although that should have been good enough reason.'

Mira paused, smiling.

'The meaning of the clues will be known only to her; that's why I chose her. Given her extraordinary powers, I'm sure she can find me. In case Mira does, there will be no more tapes, and I shall surrender to your wishes. But until then, you must put up with mine. You see, father, I had to tell the truth; someone had to. But this doesn't exonerate me; I'm a part of you, and I'm equally guilty. In case Mira can't find me, if even a gifted knower can't reach me despite the clues, then there is nothing left of me; I must be truly lost. I shall then have to leave forever. I will never return to Delhi, I will forget home and you can forget about me.'

Stunned, Mira stopped once again, then continued,

'The next tape will reach Mira in her office, but only after I have ascertained the newspaper has published the first one without any deletion or distortion. The following are a few things you've always wanted to hear me say:

You don't have to see my face again.

You don't have to be ashamed of me anymore.

If the tapes are not published or if you try to find me through the police, I promise I won't ever return home.

Only Mira can decipher the clues. So take this tape to her

and explain. But that's only if you want me back. It's a rather simple choice actually. Just throw the disc in trash and return to your important day.

Love, Sb.'

There was an uneasy silence in the room when Mira finished reading. As if to stop the hurting words from resounding in their minds, Bhaskar asked Mahesh, 'How did he manage to make the recordings inside Parliament?'

'I am not sure,' Mahesh was concerned. 'But I once saw him test this new gadget a few years ago. It's part of an advanced surveillance technique that doesn't require wires, receivers and transmitters. This tape here contains the recording made when PP had just won the election and was about to form the government.'

'How did you receive the tape?' Bhaskar asked.

'In the morning post. It was sent from some place within Delhi two days ago; I checked the postmark. The recording, as you will discover, concerns the manner in which the PP had bargained for ministerships and, in particular, the scandalous deal related to the agriculture ministry. It's even mentioned that I may have been aware of this deal,' Mahesh met Munshi's eyes and completed, 'which I was not, naturally.'

'Naturally,' Munshi agreed wryly. 'Who else is mentioned?'

'My colleagues, who else!' Mahesh said, anguished. 'And it's just the first tape. It makes me unwell to think of the impact of more such tapes, especially, if they are made public. When Sikander's subterfuge is discovered, he will be the most hated person in politics. His life will be in danger,' he concluded bitterly, 'and my life will be useless.'

Munshi gestured to the disc on the table. 'And if I don't publish it?'

'I will have to go to the next newspaper or television channel,'

Mahesh explained. 'But as you just learnt from my son's letter, I will still need Mira's help.'

There was a thoughtful silence in the room as the contours of a deal became clear.

Mira studied the unusual letter. 'I will have to hear Sikander speak once, then study the way he makes choices like, for instance, in books, music, hobbies, writing, clothes. You will have to tell me about him, about his career, relationships and share a few photographs. These are some things I would need to know how he thinks and decides.'

Mahesh was dismissive. 'Whatever you want; just find my son!'

'I will,' she told him politely.

No one spoke for a few moments, and she perceived Munshi's decision before he spoke.

'We'll publish the tapes,' Munshi announced.

Bhaskar suggested, 'Let's listen to the recording.'

'Please excuse me then,' Mahesh requested. 'I have a very busy day ahead of preventive damage control with the PP and the government.' Then he added tragically, 'I have even made a copy of this tape to play for my colleagues. You must send me copies of the next ones, Bidur, to help prepare my defense.'

Munshi agreed. Mahesh told Mira to meet him at his residence the next day to talk about Sikander's life and visit his part of the house. When Bhaskar and Mira left the room, Munshi led Mahesh to the elevators.

Mahesh thanked him and stated unhappily. 'It's a fashion among children these days to hate parents and politicians. And I'm both.'

'This is your chance,' Munshi observed quietly, 'to choose one.'

Mahesh ignored that. 'I know the tapes will be good publicity for your newspaper. I also know you Bidur; you might not want

Mira to find Sikander in a hurry so that he sends more tapes and exposes more politicians.'

'The thought had crossed my mind,' Munshi confessed plainly.

'Please be pragmatic,' Mahesh urged him. 'The tapes are only in public interest. They won't help you or me.'

'As the owner of this newspaper, I am at the pragmatic end of journalism. I decide what's in public interest.' He added gravely, 'Your son will make a good story, Mahesh.'

Mahesh waited pensively.

Munshi smiled. 'But there are limits to a good story.'

Mahesh smiled back, relieved.

———

Bhaskar called for an immediate meeting of the editorial team to play the tape, but as some members were not in office, it had to be postponed by half an hour. While Mira waited in his office, Bhaskar played the tape on his computer.

An easy, friendly voice filled the room:

'Today is May 21. The time is 9.30 a.m., and I'm in the Parliament building. I was waiting for Ms Kim Sharma, who has just entered the People's Party office. I am headed there now for a chat.'

There was a long pause and some noises, as if Sikander walked with the recorder through the corridors and into a room.

'Good morning, Kim! What a surprise!'
    'Hi Sikander,' she responded warmly. 'How are you?'
    'Good. Are you here waiting for someone?'
    'Yes, in fact, Nalan is late.'

'Well, it has been an age since I saw you. Let's catch up while you wait.' Sikander paused and added apologetically, 'Can you give me a moment please? I was called to sign some papers here. Will be back in a second.'

'Sure.'

They could hear Sikander enter an office and talk about paperwork for newly elected MPs. He returned after some time to Kim, and they settled down in an adjoining room.

'You're looking good, Sikander. Good and successful.'

He laughed. 'Just a matter of time; I'll be normal again. You look a little anxious though.'

'No, no,' she was uneasy, 'I'm fine.'

'Is everything all right?' Sikander asked gently. 'How is work? Are you still employed with that liaison firm in Mumbai?'

'Yes, I am.' She stopped, hesitant. 'It's just that something important is not working out, you know.'

Sikander waited for her to elaborate.

She laughed nervously. 'Might as well tell you. After all, this cannot be happening without your father's knowledge. You see, your party needs a fall guy for the agriculture ministry, and I thought I might be able to help.'

'Why? What is happening in the agriculture ministry?'

'Something will happen there soon.' Kim paused. 'As you know, I liaison for business houses, especially in political circles.'

'I know.'

'So, before the elections, I mediated a deal with the PP for three cabinet portfolios in which certain business clients were interested. Now, after the elections, I am being told by your party that only two of the three are available.'

Sikander sounded surprised. 'It's unusual for the PP to go back on a promise.'

'It's more than unusual; it is bloody unfair!' Kim was angry. 'I spent money on lunches, dinners, airplane tickets and gifts . . . things I can't even mention as expenses. I won't get paid unless the deal is done.'

'That's sad,' Sikander said sympathetically, 'especially when other business houses get the minister of their choice. Look at Asif; he bagged civil aviation.'

'No, that's different,' she countered. 'I mean, who could have got civil aviation but Asif? He brings with him a contract to buy 200 new aircrafts from a foreign country, government to government, with a hefty commission for the PP leadership. Such deals cannot be ignored; it takes money to contest elections, and you win elections to make more money.'

Sikander asked, 'So, why agriculture?'

'Well, the PP didn't want to offend the business houses, and so Nalan was asked to negotiate with us to accept agriculture as the third ministry in the deal. I think it is a good offer; agriculture is a lucrative ministry.' Kim analysed reasonably. 'A good agriculture minister, also in charge of food and supplies, can control speculation on food production, stocks, imports and exports. By merely calibrating his public statements, he can hike up or drop prices of commodities.'

'Besides, it's useful politically,' Sikander pointed out. 'Food prices can lead to revolutions.'

'Yes, but agriculture is not like ministries of power, defence or even communication, where business houses bid to get a friendly minister,' Kim argued. 'My instructions were if we cannot get portfolio advantage from PP, we must be given policy advantage. The PP government plans to introduce foreign genetically modified seeds for all crops in the country in the coming years. This is being hailed as the new revolution in agriculture that will double the yield and enrich the farmers. Bottom line, the foreign seed company and its local collaborators will enjoy dividends for decades. In other words,' Kim lowered her voice, 'it's a golden egg.'

'I see,' Sikander said. 'So, why isn't there a stampede for the golden egg?'

'Because it will be an illegal golden egg!'

Sikander was puzzled.

'Just picture this,' she requested him. 'Millions of farmers, thousands of seed varieties, hundreds of crops and one international supplier who has already been chosen by the government.' She paused significantly. 'This will be the largest government contract ever, and the agriculture minister will be in charge of it. Losers of bids will complain, expose faults and demand investigation. The minister will be the fall guy, someone who does the job, makes the money and, in return, takes the blame in court cases, audit inquiries, Parliament Committee hearings. When he finally steps aside, a new minister from the PP will continue with business as before.'

'That sounds logical. What do you mean by "fall guy"? Indictment, imprisonment?'

'Both. But the PP guarantees acquittal of the minister one year before the next Parliament elections so that he can contest again.'

Sikander was unconvinced. 'Yes, but there have been doubts raised about the genetically modified seeds before. Won't that make it difficult for you to sell the ministry to your clients?'

'The objections were all non-serious,' she said dismissively. 'I went through some of the studies last evening in my hotel room. The seeds can lead to soil depletion, low yields, high pesticide consumption and extreme dependence on irrigation. Between us, the seeds may not even be suitable for large parts of our country that rely on rain for agriculture. They would also increase the cost of cultivation for the already poor farmers. Hopefully, we will be out of the picture by the time these effects start to show.'

'So what's the problem?'

'We are still searching for an MP acceptable to my clients as the minister,' she added gloomily. 'These days, it's hard to find someone with integrity, someone who is not afraid of a bit of prison time to get ahead in politics.'

'Really? I am surprised; this is such a great opportunity.'

'I know,' she said, dejected. 'Nalan is negotiating on behalf of the PP leadership and the government. We should be able to zero in on a candidate or look for another portfolio, like labour. That would be a disaster though; I mean, who wants to deal with provident funds and wages?' She sighed. 'And I have already refused railways!'

Sikander chuckled.

'Yes, can you believe that?' Kim was exasperated. 'Everyone knows the railway ministry is written off to the coalition party from the east. Who wants to battle it out with him? He built his career with the support of railway contractors, for God's sake!'

'I recall,' Sikander commented, 'that even during electioneering, voters were asked to consider him as the future railway minister if he won the election.'

'Precisely,' she said. 'The regional parties in coalitions win on regional issues, and, at the national level, they are no different from others. You have to wonder how gullible the voter is!'

'That will change.'

'How will it change, Sikander?' she demanded. 'Voters still believe their false gods will one day turn out to be true. In an earlier negotiation, a client wanted environment for an MP who had never cared for it and had never even spoken a word about it. Do you know why? A nuclear power plant was planned for an ecologically fragile region, and his party promised to approve that. But when he returns to his state for the next election, he knows the voters won't question his decisions as a central minister; they will focus only on their state, their lives. He will make suitable local promises and forget them once he becomes a central minister again!'

'Elections are not lost for ignoring the people,' Sikander noted dryly, 'elections are lost for ignoring the business.'

'Well, I wouldn't be required in these negotiations if that were not true.'

'I am feeling a little sad for the next agriculture minister,' he said in a concerned manner. 'He may make money, but his name will be sullied.'

'Perhaps yes,' she accepted. 'But he won't have to spend another rupee on his political career for the rest of his life.'

They heard a door open, followed by mutual greetings.

'Hi Nalan.'

'Hello Sikander,' he answered. 'I'm sorry Kim, to have kept you waiting.'

'That's fine,' she replied. 'Sikander and I got a chance to talk after a long time.'

'You two know each other?'

'Who doesn't know Kim!' Sikander remarked.

'That's true.' Nalan was quiet. 'So, how does it feel

Sikander, being an MP? You seem to have got what you wanted.'

'Not what I wanted,' Sikander corrected. 'Not yet.'

There was an uncomfortable silence.

'I'll take your leave, Kim,' Sikander said politely. 'It was good to meet you.'

'Enjoyed it,' she said. 'Let's do this again soon. Why don't we have lunch? I'm always around Parliament these days.'

'Nice to know that,' Sikander replied. 'I'll call you. Good day, Nalan.'

They heard the recording end. Mira and Bhaskar looked at each other, stunned; this was critical evidence that the PP chose ministers to head its government based on commissions, on willing illegality and to serve business and personal interests. The tape restarted, startling them. It was at a different location; they could tell by the sound of birds in the background. Then Sikander spoke:

'This is the clue for Mira.'

He paused, and then continued softly.

'Choose the knife carefully; none of the fancy types will do. It should be double-edged and long, and made of steel for a warrior. Or decide on the potency after some research. Get the right prescription for the pills; make up stories of insomnia. Or, just take a step forward. Before a train, before a truck, from an edge, from a height. Come die with me any way you want, but not alone.'

The tape ended, and Bhaskar scrutinised her shocked face.

'Didn't you say you never met Sikander?' he asked, perplexed.
She nodded, baffled.

'What does the clue mean?' He frowned. 'Seems like different
ways of committing suicide . . . doesn't make sense.'

Mira was too dazed to speak.

Bhaskar replayed the clue, intrigued. Sikander's first clue was
not about himself or his project; it was about her, Mira realized.
She expected that he must have researched her life and learnt
enough to trust her to be a crucial part of his plans. But the clue
was not about research. He couldn't have known this in a month
or even a year of research. She had spent a lifetime planning her
death. Alone.

Come die with me any way you want, but not alone.

Bhaskar played the tape from the beginning and made notes,
as Mira heard Sikander's easy voice reach deep and hurt her.

FOUR

It rained heavily the next morning. The grey daylight from the windows in Mira's apartment was just enough for her to read the newspapers. Her story looked innocuous enough in print, but every line had blades on both ends. She felt the imminence of the retaliation; the PP would have spokespersons denounce the report from rooftops. It was a day worth waking up to.

The neighbours had left for work after turning the key thrice in their special door lock. They had left fifteen minutes early, probably factoring in traffic delays due to rain. Mira stood at the windows; the driveway of the typical three-storeyed building was now vacant, except for her blue car that looked grey in the rain. The bakery across the road was yet to open; the dogs waited curled up near the door. A boy sullenly reached the bus stop in a yellow raincoat; a failed excuse to skip school hovered about him. Sikander's clue had kept her awake most of the night before. It was unsettling to discover that someone knew her that well. It hurt that the words were genuine and the invitation real. That would be the challenge of Sikander's clue, she understood now; he wasn't going to let her think straight. But how did he manage to do that? How did he *know* her the way she knew people?

The last taxicab swung out of the stand at the street corner and left behind a long and restive queue of umbrellas. No one wanted to walk in rain these days, Mira thought. It was not just the matter of clothes, bags, shoes, styled hair and stuffed pockets getting drenched. Rain was a portable memory now, not an experience anymore. The windows of her third floor flat overlooked the street below and the main road in the distance. Trees obscured houses across the street, but she knew that in one lived a working couple who squabbled over chores, and in another, was a teenage boy who was learning to drink his father's liquor. The foliage did well to blind her from the neighbourhood and turned the house into yet another sanctuary where she could rest her mind. She had rented it four years ago when she had got the job. It was her first real home, unlike the hostels she had lived in until then. The house liked her, she felt. It turned her loneliness into a soft cushion against the world. She loved the absence of another; any movement was only when she moved, any voice was only when she thought. Her address wasn't on the official file at her request, there was no photograph of her ever printed, and readers' interactions with her were restricted to emails. She never invited anyone home; the last visitor had been the cable technician who had fixed the television a month ago. The house was sparingly furnished. The long living room had a desk and two bookcases, the second room a bed and a television, and the last room sundry stuff. The kitchen was adequate for her impatient cooking. Three chairs with wheels clocked mileage across the house.

Besides the landlord who occupied the entire first floor, the second and third floors were rented out as two units each. Her neighbours knew as much about her as the landlord—that she was a newspaper journalist and lived alone. She knew much more about them from their misplaced mail, their lobby chatter and the things left behind in their parked vehicles. During the initial interactions with the landlord and his unexpectedly kind wife, Mira gave Raghunath's name as reference of a family member and said he lived abroad. That seemed to make it easier to get through interviews and applications. In truth, however, she had not met Raghunath Mouli since her tenth birthday. A few months after that day, he had contacted the orphanage staff before he left the country to send her a gift. It was a print of a scene from the Bhagavadgita that now hung in her living room. There had been a brief note with it:

'Be Arjuna the victor, be Arjuna the vanquished; and like him, you too will find your Gita, your song of life.'

There were other children at the orphanage whom Raghunath had helped get through school and college. But she was the only one to whom he still sent money, or someone did on his behalf and made a deposit in her bank account every six months. It was as if the financial assistance was owed to her; it didn't seem to matter that she earned enough to support herself. It also didn't seem to matter that she never used the savings, which had now added up to be a substantial sum and made her a wealthy woman. Mira didn't feel grateful somehow, although she knew she ought to. She was indifferent to his support and to his absence; both had come to her unasked.

Mira checked the clock on the table; it was 8.50 a.m. Time stood still that morning and crawled only once in a while round the clock. The editorial meeting was scheduled for 11 a.m., and it was still far too early to leave home for office. She didn't mind the wait. She didn't fill her solitude with distractions. Those that life brought on its own were scattered in time, and she did not chase them, like others did, to find escapes. She didn't and couldn't see herself in relation to a place, a memory or a person; she was defined by herself. That was the reason why the nonchalance of Delhi had not intimidated her when Mira first came to live in the college hostel twelve years ago. She had just finished school in Rishikesh and had decided to study further in an unknown city or at least a city that didn't know her. After the unavoidable notice that her powers had always attracted, she fell in love with Delhi that couldn't care less. Delhi itself was restless, as if had it not been tethered to the power centre, it would have wandered away along any one of the national highways that crossed it. The tyranny of planning had captured the vagabond in Delhi's character, but not completely, Mira discovered. There was still some moonlight left, some sunrises and some birds that could sing. Mostly though, the unresisting, undifferentiated mass of people was comfortably unconcerned with one more seamless addition.

Inevitably, there were a few friends from school who remained in touch, and invariably, there were a few mistakes in college that were somehow worth the pain. She learnt early that boys fell for her good looks but couldn't stand the scrutiny of her mind. It wasn't easy to take her out on a date; she couldn't be surprised, impressed or in any way misled. And most importantly, she couldn't be deceived. This decimated most of her relationships early. There had been only a few instances when she had felt affection for a man despite his thoughts, like the one in the last year of her master's degree. He had fallen in love with her, deeply and helplessly, and she found herself drawn inexplicably to this form of emotional dependence. It was somehow comforting to know that he couldn't be happy without her, and also, it was the first time that anyone had needed her. Eventually, however, Mira understood why she couldn't sustain such relationships. First, she feared that lack of affection in life could delude her to mistake common kindness to be something special. Secondly, even if it were genuinely something special, she didn't trust love in a world that abandoned newborn babies in orphanages. She had always been angry at her unfair destiny, but her job as a journalist gave her something else to be angry about, the unfair destiny of others. It was her final month at the hostel, her last chance to either find a job or leave Delhi, when she saw Munshi's advertisement for knowers. Waiting among others called for the interview at the newspaper office, Mira had perceived from their thoughts that no one needed the job as desperately as she had. Unlike her, none of them was looking for a reason to live. Or an excuse to die.

The work at the newspaper wasn't easy at first. Munshi's much-publicized experiment drew many skeptics who questioned Mira's powers. These had initially included Munshi himself, which made her job tougher. A few weeks after she joined the newspaper, Munshi had decided to test her powers and asked her to 'know' if he would be chosen by the PP government for one of the nominated seats in Parliament. Mira had told him that he didn't stand a chance, and that Mahesh Bansi didn't trust him enough to back his name. Munshi disbelieved her and countered that he had never given Mahesh any cause to suspect him. As a warning, he advised her to be careful with her predictions. Then the nominations were declared, and his name didn't figure among them. Furious, Munshi investigated who had struck his name off the list. Although he never shared his findings with her, Munshi never again doubted Mira's powers.

Her cell phone rang; it was Mahesh Bansi. The impact of that morning's newspaper report was clear in the strain in his voice. He called to postpone their scheduled meeting; she could sense the story had made him almost hate his son, too much to talk about him that day. Instead, Mahesh suggested that she could visit Sikander's part of the house and do her own research. Mira agreed and said she would reach his residence at 1 p.m. She also answered his unasked question and said she wouldn't stay beyond an hour. Flustered, Mahesh said she could stay as long as she wanted; Mira thanked him wryly and ended the call.

The daily editorial meetings of the newspaper were held at 11 a.m. Munshi met with select members of his staff to outline the agenda for the day. He was often absent but the meetings still took place at the same time, in the same place and for the same purpose. That morning, Mira was the first one to reach the third floor conference room, and by the presence of Munshi's special chair, it was clear that he would attend the meeting that day. The staff arranged the chair at the head of the long table, handling it carefully, as if they could already see Munshi sitting in it.

Salat Vasudev walked in after a few minutes and stopped when he found Mira. He looked around uncertainly, troubled a bit. They had been at other such morning meetings since he joined the newspaper the previous week, but were yet to speak with each other, except that one time when he was introduced by Bhaskar to the entire team. They hadn't been alone before, and this now meant making conversation. When she wished him, he answered her politely and sat across the table. They observed Munshi's staff in silence until they left and the room became still.

Mira glanced at him just as he turned to her. She had already discovered that she couldn't discern his thoughts; knowers were immune to the powers of other knowers.

'I want to clarify something, Mira,' he said in a direct manner. 'You are a legend in know-journalism, and I respect you. I have learnt a great deal about how to handle our special powers from your know-reports.'

She waited, a little surprised.

'One of the reasons I joined this newspaper was because of the opportunity it provided to learn from you.' He hesitated. 'That's why I was concerned when Bhaskar said you were upset and wanted to reassure that I merely aspire to work with you.'

Mira surveyed him. 'Bhaskar told you to speak with me?'

'Yes, in fact, he did.'

She nodded. 'You must wait for Bhaskar to tell you whom to speak with next.'

His face was set. 'I couldn't have stopped him from telling me, could I?'

'Don't play your little games with me, Salat,' she advised him. 'I won't get in your way of promotions and postings. And you please let me mind my own business.'

Salat turned away, offended. Mira reprimanded herself; she knew Bhaskar was always transparent about his decisions so that there could be no scope for office politics. That's why he had informed Salat about their conversation. Munshi's staff returned to the conference room and, having finished with his chair, now started to set the table for him. One man arranged a notebook and pen, another placed an empty glass and a bottle of mineral water, and the third opened a laptop. The chores were, evidently, divided according to departments.

Mira attempted reconciliation. 'Nice first story on Sunday.'

'Routine,' Salat said and continued to observe the staff.

'Couldn't have been easy to get those documents from the ministry,' she tried again.

'A friend copied and scanned the files for me.'

'She has done this before?' Mira inquired.

He glanced at her warily. 'Twice.'

'Why does she do it?'

'Haven't asked.'

'That's a lie,' Mira guessed again.

He smiled. 'How about you?'

'Copy for a man?'

'Or scan?'

'Depends.'

'On what?' He asked sarcastically, 'Wealth, looks, character?'

'No, the usual,' she told him. 'The file he wants.'

They didn't trust each other still, but politely discussed how technology made it easy for journalists to access secret documents. His powers were different from hers, Mira noticed; he dealt with facts and information, rather than thoughts, choice and decision.

The door opened and others came in; the room appeared smaller as they settled around the table and chatted. Curious about another knower, Mira continued to study Salat. He was dressed well, wore an expensive watch and carried a gold pen. His dark hair was combed neatly, his sleeves folded evenly to the elbow. He listened intently to Lina Kamat who sat next to him. He must know Lina liked him, it didn't take any special powers to see that. And Mira could tell he loved Lina's beautiful eyes and dazzling smile. It might take him a few more days to discover another, and a little less endearing, quality about Lina; she never held back her opinion about anything. It was Lina's way of protecting herself from the invariable attention she drew because of her stunning good looks. It was her special threshold. A man had to see beyond her beauty and survive her abrasive manner for her to like him. As she observed Salat nod and smile at Lina, Mira wondered if he was just the man for it.

A few minutes after the chair-and-table ritual was completed, Munshi came in looking perfect in a well-tailored, dull-green linen suit. The emeralds of his cufflinks blinked once as he reached for the paper before him on the table. It was the list of the anticipated top ten stories for the day and the special stories the newspaper worked on that week. Everyone at the table had a copy, and almost every story concerned Sikander's tape. It was the story of the day across the country, mainly because of the way the newspaper had reported it. Dubey's editorial team, under his strict guidance, had excelled in that morning's coverage, tracing down every name, reaching out for every version. Salat had worked out the background of the agriculture ministry scam, something he had written about before at the magazine he used to work for; and Mira had put the main story together. It had also been her responsibility to get Nalan Malik's comments on the story, and his office had informed her that he had none. That morning's list for the day included impressive follow-up stories, new reactions, new revelations and, most importantly, the investigation of the new facts revealed in the tape.

Sikander's tape provided the missing piece in a case that was considered closed. It explained why the then agriculture minister had so blatantly flouted the norms to award contract to a foreign company for seeds. Mira also understood Sikander's smart strategy of choosing to reveal Kim Sharma's tape. He must have known this would revive the rumours about Kim and remind everyone of Nalan's divorce. In the end, the tape did more than expose Nalan's role in the ministry negotiations, it chipped away at his very character.

'What's the progress with finding Sikander Bansi? What do we know about him?' Munshi's question startled Mira out of her thoughts.

'Not much, sir,' she confessed.

'Well, move swiftly on this, Mira,' he instructed. 'We cannot afford to publish too many tapes, and we cannot afford to lose the story. If we fail even once for some reason, Sikander might force his father to go to another newspaper. So find him fast.'

'Yes sir.'

'I've done a bit of research on him,' Salat offered. 'Sikander has spoken only once in Parliament in the last four and a half years and, that too, in support of a government bill. He seemed to have deliberately maintained a very low profile.'

'We know why now,' Bhaskar commented. 'He was a little preoccupied with making the tapes!'

'Businesses, investments, relationships and hobbies?' Dubey asked Salat.

'Nothing newsworthy; he invests along with his father, and they have old partnerships in industry,' Salat answered. 'He has been in two known and serious relationships with women, and several non-serious ones. He has a limited circle of friends, several famous acquaintances and a few expensive hobbies.'

'Is that all?' Munshi was surprised. 'It's as if he doesn't belong among the young politicians of Delhi.'

Dubey shook his head. 'Can't say he does.'

'Are you telling me this, Ashok?' Munshi demanded. 'The man who dug up links between terrorists and bureaucracy?'

'Yes, but this man is neither a terrorist nor a bureaucrat,' Dubey protested. 'There is no money or paper trail to chase.'

'We do have one thing to go by,' Bhaskar pointed out. 'The clue that came with the tape. What does the clue tell you about Sikander, Mira?'

Mira was prepared for the question, as she knew Munshi was keenly interested. 'Sikander likes to challenge himself; normalcy bores him. He can play long strategies, never lose focus of his aim and achieve with precision. He wants more than what destiny has chosen for him. Or at least, he wants to have a say in it.' She stopped, frowning, as the words began to describe her. Unnerved, Mira continued more carefully, 'He is aware of his good fortune and doesn't want to abandon it. But he seeks to be free of it by denying himself its benefits.'

There was a surprised silence in the room after her words, and only Salat smiled faintly at her.

'This sounds a little over the edge, doesn't it?' Lina exclaimed. 'Are we talking about the same guy? The handsome and powerful MP who drives a Porsche and is rumoured to be dating a former beauty queen?'

Bhaskar chuckled. 'Probably not.'

Everyone returned to the discussion, but Mira couldn't

participate anymore. Sikander's friendly voice as he spoke the clue now filled her mind with an unknown fear, as if it was the point of a knife about to break skin. He had proved that she was not alone in her suffering or in her obsession with death. To know why he thought like her, she had to research him and find him. Mira didn't want to know anything more about Sikander, she decided nervously; she didn't feel strong enough for it.

No one noticed that she did not speak again for the rest of the meeting; no one except Salat.

———

Mira was working in her cabin when Munshi's secretary called for a meeting on the third floor. She was sure, as she climbed the stairs again, that it was about Sikander's clue. She wouldn't have spoken about it but for Salat's aggressive display of his research about Sikander. The cool air of the third floor calmed her a little and the deep carpet slowed her down. The secretary asked Mira to wait in one of the smaller meeting rooms. Mira paced it restlessly, around the white table and the four white chairs, and listened to the forced silence of the room. This was an unreal silence extracted with soundproof walls and glass, with muted air-conditioning and soft flooring. Sound seemed to press in on the boundaries of this silence, searching for cracks to creep in and reclaim what belonged to it. Mira observed the silent rain from the windows and wondered what sound she would have attributed to rain if she had never heard it fall before. The door opened and Munshi's secretary held it open for someone. Mira waited, expecting Munshi. Instead, a tall man walked in and thanked the secretary. When the door was shut, he glanced at Mira's stunned face, his brown eyes amused.

'Good afternoon, Ms Mouli,' Nalan Malik said. 'It's nice to finally meet you.'

Mira recovered and returned the greeting, noticing the PP flag that was pinned to the dark jacket he wore over a white shirt.

'I had come to see your editor, Mr Munshi, and requested him for this meeting with you. I hope you don't mind.'

'No, of course not,' she said and gestured towards the chairs. He thanked her but remained standing. He surveyed her in silence, and Mira met his eyes, learning about him. He was a slim man with luminous eyes that brought unexpected character to his good-looking face.

'There is so little information available about you,' he mentioned finally, 'that it had got me curious.'

'That is just to ensure people don't have direct access to me,' she explained. 'It can get difficult for a knower.'

'I see,' he said contemplatively. 'So it's not because you are hiding from the law or have a murky past.'

Mira smiled. 'No. Sorry to disappoint.'

He smiled back. 'I was curious, however, for another reason as well. If nothing is known about you, then how did Sikander Bansi think of that clue?'

'He must have researched me, Mr Malik,' she replied. 'That's the only explanation.'

'I factored that,' he said coolly. 'But the clue is not based on research, ma'am. Instead, it shows a deep understanding of your nature, acquired over a period of time. Clearly, there can be another explanation for that,' he speculated. 'You must know each other very well.'

'I have never met him.'

'That's what Mr Munshi told me. But it's hard to believe,' he commented, 'unless, Sikander was wrong about you in that clue. Now, only you can answer that. Was he wrong?'

Mira was getting uncomfortable. 'He was not.'

'In that case, it's possible that this entire charade has been enacted by both of you. And, therefore,' Nalan paused, 'you know where Sikander Bansi is hiding.'

She could sense his anger, even though he appeared absolutely calm. 'I understand how you might feel, Mr Malik, especially because the tape mentions you. But I'm telling the truth,' she said sincerely. 'I don't know Sikander, and I definitely don't know where he might be hiding.'

He didn't speak; he still stood a few paces from the door.

'According to your editor, the tapes will cease the moment you find Sikander Bansi, and the clues should lead you to his location.' Nalan now slowly walked up. 'Does the first clue give you an idea of where he might be?'

She was frank, 'I haven't been able to work it out yet.'

'Why not?' He stood before her. 'Is that the deal? That you don't find him until all the tapes are published?'

'Of course not!' Mira was offended.

He studied her sardonically. 'Or do you believe in the cause? You think the tapes will cleanse the system of corrupt politicians like me. So you support Sikander in his little project. Is that it?'

Angry, Mira remained silent.

'I'm sorry for the trouble,' he said, smiling stiffly. 'But you see, I have personal interest in finding answers to these questions. It's got to do with my entire political career and everything I have worked for all my life.' His eyes were hard as he added, 'Sikander was smart to disappear; he knows the damage he is doing to me.'

Mira could perceive his thoughts about Sikander; they weren't kind.

'But he has left you right at the centre of this crisis, hasn't he?' Nalan continued. 'Everyone who is in the tapes will look to you for the answers to the questions I just asked. And they could get quite desperate,' he pointed out, 'unlike me.'

Mira lowered her eyes in thought to his white shirt that

reflected the day from the windows behind her, the dark jacket was almost night. The pen was black, the watch was black and the skin fair where there used to be a wedding ring. The much-publicized divorce made sense now, Mira thought, as she recalled the three-year-old marriage that had come to an abrupt end. He wasn't a man who would lie about being in love.

'So, once again,' he said in his compelling voice, 'why have you not worked out the clue yet?'

Mira still remained silent as she read his intricate thoughts and detected the doubts about her. It shouldn't have mattered, but inexplicably, it did. She didn't want him to suspect her motives. He waited in silence and observed how she held the notebook tightly in her hands, her khadi brown shirt the colour of something lost, something deep.

She didn't look up as she said, 'The clue is very real, Mr Malik. It hurts me every time I read it. I cannot look beyond the truth of it and the promise of it.' Mira registered his surprise as she continued, 'That's the challenge of the clue.' She paused and added weakly, 'He knew I won't be able to stand the pain.'

Nalan frowned. 'So you have thought of death in those ways?' Then he apologized quickly. 'I'm sorry, I shouldn't have asked, it's not my business . . .'

'Exactly in those ways.'

He didn't speak at once, then asked, 'Why?'

The shock in his voice left her searching for words to explain. 'Perhaps because I want to change my destiny. It won't let me, and I don't want to escape; I'm not a coward . . .' she hesitated. She had never spoken about this before. It felt unreal as she completed, 'but the only way to outsmart my life is by my death.'

Then she read his unasked question. 'Yes,' she answered, 'I do have everything I want in life, and no, it's not because of failure.

Nothing has ever meant to me more than this final choice,' she spoke quietly, 'and I am grateful that it's so accessible.'

He was silent, distraught somehow. Intrigued, Mira glanced up and met his strangely anguished eyes.

He still frowned. 'Whatever gave you the idea that destiny can be changed?'

'The fact that we constantly hope,' she replied.

'We hope for life, not for death.'

'Death is the best part of life.'

'How can anyone think like this?' he wondered. 'Someone should have changed your mind, Mira.'

'Sikander has,' she said. 'I always thought I was the only one who felt this way. Apparently not.'

'But he hasn't changed your mind about death.'

'No one can.'

That made him smile. 'You shouldn't say such things, makes me . . .'

He fell silent abruptly; Mira was confused as she sensed his unspoken words. His brown eyes stared at her, surprised, and were immediately guarded that she could discern his thoughts. Turning swiftly, he moved to the door.

'As I said,' he paused, 'the people mentioned in the tapes will hunt for Sikander and get to you.' He glanced at her. 'Please take care.'

Taken aback, she thanked him. When he was gone, the words he had restrained himself from speaking aloud, perplexed her.

You shouldn't say such things, makes me want to prove you wrong.

Mira frowned and wondered if she had read Nalan Malik right.

FIVE

Later, as Mira prepared to leave for the Bansi residence, Salat came to see her.

'I wanted to share with you an assessment of Sikander's clue,' he said in his usual candid style.

'Thank you,' she gathered her bag, 'but I think I can manage on my own'.

She was curt and hoped he got the message. He didn't.

'I know you can manage,' he pursued, 'but this is far too important not to tell you.'

She left the cabin. 'I'll be really late.'

He walked with her. 'I believe Sikander is trying to control your mind, Mira, and direct your thoughts.'

Mira didn't respond and crossed the newsroom.

Salat kept pace with her. 'I think the clue is not true. Please don't believe a word of it.' He paused and continued carefully, 'The clue may drive you to kill yourself or to die . . .'

She stopped walking.

'I'm sure you have considered that,' he added hurriedly, 'but the clue has also convinced you that Sikander thinks like you do. You must be relieved to know this, even happy.'

'Probably because,' she said scathingly, 'as you may have realized, that's how I can solve the clue.'

'That's what I'm worried about.'

Mira waited impatiently.

'You have to research this clue, overlooking the way it affects you,' he argued. 'And while you are vulnerable, Sikander can make you think whatever he wants you to.'

Mira stayed silent; she liked his analysis.

'It will not be easy for you to separate the message of the clues from your own life. So I have a solution; I will work the clues with you.'

'Please, no!' she said vehemently. 'I mean, can't you find someone else to haunt?'

'The clues may have many layers, Mira,' he persisted, 'and you can't even get past the mere words. You must let me help you.'

Mira surveyed him, realizing that he was right. But then, she decided, he didn't have to know that.

'That clue about my death got you interested, didn't it?' she challenged him. 'Is that what you will help me with?'

'How heartless, Mira!' He was aghast. 'I just warned you.'

She sounded upset. 'The depths to which you can sink!'

'I can't believe this!'

'The levels to which you can fall!'

'I don't!' he said, harassed.

'You must drive then?'

'I resent that . . .' he paused, confused.

'Let's go to the Bansi residence,' she said, amused, and walked to the doors. 'I'll have my lunch on the way.'

He stared after her for a second, and then quickly followed her out.

———

It still rained heavily, and the roads were invisible under sheets

of water. At the house on Malcha Marg, in the more expensive
part of Delhi, the staff was expecting them. A guard at the gate
handed them blue umbrellas, and an aide guided them around
the premises. They were given a brief history of the seventy-five-
years old residence, and the various renovations that had taken
place over time, including an addition of a separate section for
Sikander. There were two driveways, the one on the left led directly
to a two-storeyed house in the front that functioned as Mahesh
Bansi's home and office. The driveway on the right curved around
this house and vanished into the lawn behind it. The grounds were
beautiful in the rain, and stretched on both sides of the driveway
until the vague line of trees in the distance. A mango tree stood
in the middle, its dripping branches touching the ground, as if
laden with stories waiting to be told. The driveway snaked along
a great Banyan tree, and Sikander's house became visible only
when they walked round it. His residence was smaller than the
main building, although this too was two-storeyed. On one side
were garages, and a door was open to reveal a sleek blue car being
polished by an attendant. As Mira walked up to the threshold
of the house, she noticed its glass windows had no curtains. The
house was at a little height, with a nice view of the lawn and trees
outlined tentatively in the green haze of rain.

The aide pointed out the numbers on the intercom for
assistance or when they were ready to leave. He handed Mira
a large sealed envelope from Mahesh Bansi, and Mira guessed
it must contain Sikander's personal details she had asked for. A
quick silence followed the aide's exit, and they stood amid the
restive bookshelves.

Besides the study and living room, the ground floor also had
the kitchen. Mira switched on the lights and stopped at the
door, surprised at the collection of tea on the shelves. There were
different types, all kept with their labels visible; then there were

many different teapots, all easily accessible. White teacups, true teacups; she too believed that the colour of the cups impacted the taste of tea. He must make his own tea; he chose the leaves by their inclination, brewed them by gentle persuasion and marked their taste as another destination. Just like her. The cutlery was basic, predictable and uncomplicated. Only one plate among the crockery had its label on the reverse worn out from frequent scrubbing, much like the single plate in the set at her home. He preferred to eat in a familiar plate, just like her. Mira stood still, realizing he loved the silences of his loneliness.

Just like her.

Mira touched the shining knives in the holder; the similarities were disconcerting and difficult to believe. But this too could be a façade, like everything else. Mira frowned slightly at the sharp end of the blade. She didn't choose her life, she was born with her demons. How did Sikander acquire his?

The living room and the study on the ground level were upholstered in bright shades of green and red. But as she went up the stairs to the first floor lounge, she was struck by the lack of colour in this more personal space. The subdued greys and browns merged with the cemented floor. There were no carpets like in the study; no marble like in the living room. A simple clock hung alone on the whitewashed walls of the lounge. The view was better from the bedroom next door, but this too was small and bare. His clothes and other personal effects were in an elaborate wardrobe, left entirely behind by their owner, despite the intimidating labels. The lounge was uncluttered, although the shelves were stacked with school and college memorabilia, trophies and plaques. There was no evidence of the celebrity girlfriends; no scarves left behind, no emotional gifts. There was one photograph of a smiling lady and a child; it was clearly Sikander with his late mother.

There were books in the lounge and the bedroom, and it was a more honest collection, unlike the books in the study downstairs. She flipped through a few; he had trouble making his way through the *Inflationary Universe*, the pages had been folded frequently. He had better luck with *The Order of Things*, with only two page folds, and had read through *In Dubious Battle* and *Anandamath*.

Mira glanced up from the books as the rain paused and listened to the birds of the garden. She recognized them from the background of the clue on the tape. Sikander had recorded the clues in that lounge, surrounded by simple walls and personal books. She glanced out of the window at the clearing day; light made a filigree of raindrops over the window ledge. She was reminded of Nalan's words. If the contents of the first tape were anything to go by, powerful people would search for Sikander to stop him and harm him. The clues were the only way to get to him, but he had made sure that the clues meant nothing to anyone except her. Mira realized that Sikander, who was a total stranger to her, had left his life in her hands and wanted her to leave her life in his.

———

Salat was still in the study, making notes about the books, when Mira returned downstairs. She sat at the desk near the window and opened her laptop to study the clue. This was the first time she felt confident enough to listen to those words again, amid the surroundings in which Sikander had chosen them.

'This collection was started by Sikander's grandparents,' Salat said. 'There are roughly 8,000 books here of which almost 6,000 are bound in leather. Others had to be rebound, but not with the same material. Perhaps it was unavailable . . .'

Mira turned and looked at him. This was his special gift, to intuitively find patterns in things.

'There's a water stain on about eighty-two books, which I believe were being transported in cartons. Their edges are bent and some pages have been shaken loose due to the packaging . . .'

She interrupted him. 'What are you saying, Salat?'

'These books have never been read,' he concluded. 'They are just inherited.'

Mira realized. 'Yet another façade.'

Later, when Salat went upstairs to check, Mira replayed the tape. Sikander's voice spread in the study as he introduced the recording. It was mellow and clear, like a parent comforting a child, a voice of someone who knew how to get people's confidence. He did not know Kim Sharma well, but believed she could be charmed into answering his questions. Mira watched as it rained again, but didn't register it. She sensed Sikander believed the world did not deserve the truth; he could be sensitive and rude, he could be humble and irreverent. He could be anything anyone wanted him to be. Just like her.

Sikander may have, at some point of time, had faith in the human heart and mind. Now, he only felt sorry for those who did. The recording ended, and he spoke the clue for her. He could have meant those words, Mira knew. He could have thought of killing himself too. It was so easy to believe him; Mira closed her eyes desperately and buried her face in her arms on the desk. The sound of the rain outside flooded the darkness behind her eyes and heightened the tragedy in Sikander's voice. His light, easy words barely covered his sense of loss that was so overwhelming, it created a destiny of its own. His mask was his brilliant victory against that destiny, and he wore it with disdain.

Just like her.

A memory floated up from the recess where she had buried it, dredged up by Sikander's words, as if it demanded to be understood in the new light of recent excavations.

They said I didn't have parents because I was a girl. They said when people came looking for children to adopt, I didn't stand a chance. If I had been a boy, someone would have adopted me. Someone always needed a son. Who needed a daughter? I had not yet begun to distrust them, those who spoke the 'truth'. So, I believed in that question when I asked it and wanted an answer.

It was a chilly winter evening in Rishikesh, and a Sunday celebration had been organized for something or someone; I don't recall now. We were all gathered in the mess hall for the party and dinner. The students were mostly dressed in informal clothes. I loved the light blue dress of one girl—the daughter of a guest. We all loved that dress. Our own clothes provided by the orphanage were good; they were proper but boring, nothing like the blue chiffon dress with a star.

That evening, everyone had wanted to talk to me, to meet the unusual girl who could read minds. My teachers often spoke of my powers to the townspeople, and the guests were curious. I felt special because of my gift, as it became public for the first time. The guests gathered around me, challenged me with difficult questions and marvelled at my accurate answers. Someone mentioned how unfortunate my parents were to have lost me. Another said anyone would love to have a gifted daughter like me. That's why I asked the question, you see. I could sense that they genuinely felt for me; they truly liked me. So I asked them if they would like to have a daughter like me. A sudden silence fell over the mess hall. I stared, mystified at the people who surrounded me. They had smiled at me and complimented me just a moment ago, but now they were frowning. I asked them again, even though I now knew the answer; 'Who wanted me for a daughter?' They began to step away from me and turned away their faces. One of my teachers was summoned, and she walked up to ask if I had finished my dinner. The warm food and affection were slowly withdrawn, and I realized that the question had displeased people. As my teacher took me to my room, I promised I would never ask that question again. I pleaded that it was all because of that blue dress. I too wanted to be a daughter, I too wanted a star. I had not cried that night, I had not understood that night. I cried every time I remembered that night. I was eight years old.

From the windows of the study, Mira saw the rain lessen. Or at least, it rained less than it did in her mind. The recording had fallen silent a long time ago. Her memories often left her weak, without the will to even breathe. That's why she kept them securely locked, so that they didn't hunt her down like this in the middle of the day. Forcing herself to move, she opened the envelope Mahesh Bansi had sent her. It contained some handwritten notes, newspaper clippings, educational qualifications, shopping lists, restaurant bills, friends' profiles and other stuff that belonged to Sikander. In a separate cover, there was a photograph of an attractive man, 32–35 years of age, with dark hair, large dark eyes and a smile of someone who knew how to appear good for the camera. He seemed to care, but as she looked closer, she found that his eyes ridiculed the camera for trusting the façade. She quickly dropped the photo back in the cover; that's what her eyes would say if she had ever been photographed. Mira decided that no amount of going over his belongings would reveal the truth about Sikander. Everything was a manufactured reality, built exactly the way she expected it to be.

The news that day was all about the first Parliament tape. The Opposition demanded the resignation of the government and a public apology to the people of the nation for misleading them. A memorandum was submitted to the President that sought immediate dismissal of the government on grounds that it had abused people's mandate. The government retaliated by leaking to the media documents that proved the innocence of the PP leadership. The official spokesperson revisited the scandal briefly to remind the nation that action had been taken against the guilty and that the then agriculture minister was now in jail. The Opposition declared that argument futile in view of the tape's revelations. Then the PP's powerful media department swung into action to contain the damage. Munshi's newspaper was blamed for being politically motivated ahead of elections, and old scandals against the Opposition were raked up. There was chaos all around, but not the kind that promised change.

The excitement in the newsroom that evening was electric, and it got further charged as the deadline drew near. Munshi had been down to the second floor twice already to check the assembly line personally. This was the norm with him whenever something big happened, and he couldn't feel its heat in his air-conditioned third floor office. He loved the stress, the tension, the lack of time and the close calls. At 8 o'clock, someone increased the volume of the television on the wall. Mira was in the middle of the newsroom, cutting her story on the computer to fit the space on the page. She turned with the rest to see the news. Kim Sharma was a beautiful woman and as her large eyes flashed in anger, they lit up the screen. The media was camping outside her office in Mumbai and caught up with her that evening. She refused to answer questions, but that didn't stop the journalists from asking them.

'Why were you part of the discussions on government formation?'

'How much does each ministry portfolio pay?'

'Who received the commissions? How much was paid to the PP for . . .'

'No comment!' she turned away indignantly, and the diamonds in her earrings caught the camera lights.

'What is your relationship with Nalan Malik, and did it have something to do . . .'

'I said, no comment,' she glared at the questioner and tried to move through the crowd to her waiting car.

'Which other portfolios did you decide?'

'Let me go!' Kim was losing patience.

She made a good picture, Mira thought. The questions will soon get softer, just to engage Kim and keep her on the screen longer.

'Will you travel to Delhi, ma'am?'

She was perturbed by the polite inquiry. 'I may, yes.'

'Do you travel to Delhi often?'

'No.'

'Is this an attempt to malign your good name?'

That was designed to help Kim Sharma discover the importance of live television. 'Yes,' her voice softened. 'Yes, it is.'

'Which other good names are involved . . .?' There were murmured reprimands from other journalists, and the question was quickly reworked. 'Were you saddened to read the story?'

'Of course . . .,' she stopped speaking, aggrieved, and lowered her eyes; the camera got a high-resolution feed of the perfect lashes, darkened with mascara applied by a habitual hand. 'I have never faced anything like this . . .'

'Is this the first time your deals have been made public?' The question was deliberately tactless.

She glanced around at the cameras, her lovely face emotional. 'I was doing my job, just like anyone of you. Please don't harass me like this.'

Kim was nearing the end of her thirty-second honeymoon with the press. That was the wrong answer.

'Our job is to collect news for television news channels. What was your job ma'am, and who were you doing it for?'

Kim, unwisely, continued with her routine. 'Please, I know nothing.'

'Why were your deals never investigated?'

She desperately searched for her staff, which had been pushed to the fringe by the circle of media people.

'Would you now reveal the details before the nation . . .?'

There was general commotion as her staff jostled with journalists and managed to usher her towards the car. The door of the car shut, and the driver honked a few times to make the crowd move. The cameras caught Kim in the back seat as she reached for her cell phone, her pretty face no longer vulnerable.

There was a brief debate in the newsroom on whether the interview merited mention in the newspaper. Dubey pointed out that some things were best seen on live television and ended the discussion. After an hour, Mira was preparing to leave office when her cell phone rang.

She answered it.

'Good evening. This is Nalan,' the voice said.

Taken aback, she wished him. His voice sounded different on the phone.

'I'm calling about a matter of ethics.'

'So you finally discovered them,' she remarked dryly.

He chuckled. 'They discovered me.'

'How can I help?'

'I want you to tell me your address.'

Mira was perplexed. 'My address? Why?'

'That's not important. I wanted the address from you so that I don't have to find out the wrong way. Like, for instance by following you home tonight, or from your bills, your taxes, your bank details ...'

'All right, I see you can easily find my address.' She frowned, unable to discern his thoughts. 'But I can't give you the address unless you tell me why you want it,' she said decisively.

'I could lie; that I want to send you an important invitation, a subscription to the People's Party magazine, a media pass for a party convention or ...'

'That's enough,' she said impatiently. 'What's the truth?'

'You won't like it,' he warned.

'Try me.'

'I want to make sure you are safe.'

Mira's frown deepened.

'Told you,' he pointed out, 'you won't like it.'

She didn't speak at once. She could feel his worry, he wasn't making that up. Her safety shouldn't have been his concern, but perhaps he also wanted to keep an eye on her to trace Sikander. Yet, he was asking for her address when he could have got it through any means. After some thought, she told him.

He thanked her. 'This is my personal cell phone number,' he said, referring to the number he was calling from. 'You can ring me anytime, and especially when you feel you may be in any danger. Please save the number.'

'I'm grateful for this honour,' she mentioned acidly, 'but I never save numbers on my cell phone.'

He was amused. 'Didn't I tell you before? You shouldn't say such things.'

'I don't,' Mira said, incensed. 'You make me.'

'That's the trouble with ethics,' he said regretfully. 'Drive home safe, Mira. Good night.'

When the call ended, she stared at her cell phone, stumped. That was the first time anyone had asked her to drive anywhere *safe*.

SIX

The second tape from Sikander was in Mira's mail at office next morning on Saturday, proving that Sikander had seen the published story in the newspaper. Gearing up for the Sunday edition, Bhaskar called a meeting to listen to the recording; Munshi was absent that day.

Once again, Sikander's familiar voice announced the time and date:

> 'Today is December 7, Parliament building. The time is 1.25 p.m. I am walking towards Mr Sunil Patel, who is about to leave Parliament. I should catch up with him in less than a minute.'

He moved through the crowded corridor inside Parliament amid conversations, beeping security apparatus and paging announcements for MPs' vehicles at the exit door.

> 'Hi, good afternoon!' Sikander said in a greeting. 'Are you Mr Sunil Patel, the station house officer?'
> 'Yes,' Patel answered.
> 'I am Sikander Bansi, an MP from the People's Party.'

There was a pause. Voices in the background were momentarily louder as a group of people walked past.

'Can we speak alone for a moment?'

'Actually, I was leaving, Mr Bansi. I have to reach somewhere in half an hour.'

'Won't take any time at all,' Sikander invited, then added gently, 'Besides, it may be good for you to be seen with a PP politician. It will build pressure on Nuri to give you whatever you demanded from him.'

There was a long pause. 'What do you want?' Patel asked tersely.

'The real story, of course,' Sikander laughed, 'off the record.'

'And you think, sir, that I go about telling the real story in busy corridors like this?'

'Fair enough,' Sikander said amiably. 'The lounge then.'

After some time, there was a sudden silence as they entered the lounge. They settled down and refused the tea that the attendant offered.

'I will get to the point,' Sikander began. 'Over 200 people were butchered in communal riots exactly one year ago. You were in charge of the area where the clashes started. I would like to know what had really happened.'

'What is the point?' Patel sneered. 'You seem too young to understand, even if I explained.'

'By "young" you mean ignorant. I get that.' Sikander laughed. 'Let me see if I can impress you with my grasp of communal politics. There had been peace for long, and people of the state expected development; they wanted better roads, better power supply and better drinking water. The NP leader who represented the state wasn't interested in development; it would have meant the end of the illegitimate businesses of his funders. And God knows elections require funds,' Sikander sighed. 'The campaigning, the media and the advertising, these cost money. The NP leader knew he would lose the election on the development issue unless he changed the agenda . . .

'No disrespect, but is this how all the young MPs here speak?' Patel inquired.

Sikander did not reply for an instant. 'All right,' he said finally. 'How would you put it?'

'It was always the agenda of the NP to exclude some communities from its plan for growth and development. Far too much money has been spent on the minorities and the underprivileged, and that money would now be spent on the general prosperity of the entire country. That was the promise!' Patel explained. 'The NP had to deliver on this promise. People wanted a better life for themselves and did not care if it came at the expense of someone else's better life.'

'So,' Sikander said, 'you are saying it was a planned riot. And you were part of the plan.'

'I resent that, sir,' he objected. 'I stopped the riot and without me, the toll would have certainly crossed 500.'

'My apologies. As you can see, I am most ill-informed about everything.'

'You are,' Patel confirmed, flatly.

'So why were you suspended if you stopped the riot?'

'I just told you, because I stopped the riot! What's the matter with you?'

'I'm so sorry. So, how did you stop the riot?'

Patel sighed impatiently. 'The houses on a street caught fire, and about thirty families from one community were trapped. They could not escape because the rioters waited outside, and were burnt to death. Everyone was shocked by this gruesome "accident" and that ended the riot. Always remember: in a riot, the cruelest side wins.'

'I will remember that,' Sikandar promised. 'So you saved many lives by sacrificing a few. Did they understand that here at the NP chief's office?'

'What do you mean?' he demanded. 'Are you saying I supervised that riot for my own pleasure? Of course they understood. The entire NP monitored the events that day. They would all have been suspects in the inquiry if I had not signed an affidavit stating there was not enough evidence against them. They know that.'

'Then why did the NP government suspend you?' Sikander was intrigued. 'Is that not bound to upset you and make you expose everyone?'

'I was in charge,' Patel said reasonably. 'They had to take some action.'

'That's what they told you.'

'Yes,' Patel said quietly, 'and I believed them.'

'Why not? You are from the same state as Nuri, and you must be his supporter.'

'Who wasn't?' Patel was earnest. 'That is what I told him today. I worshipped him; he was like a god to me. And I have been waiting, convinced that he will do justice. But I am still on suspension, and there is no hope. I told him this too, that he has lost one of his best devotees.'

They were silent for an instant. Then Sikander asked, 'But what can you do? Who will believe your story?'

'I have proof, Mr Bansi,' Patel said triumphantly. 'That is the reason why I am here today. I played him the tapes of the telephone calls from that night when the riot started. As a rule, I recorded all calls in my police station. There was a call, one of the many made by Nuri, in which he asked me to pull out my men from a locality. Four families were killed hours after we withdrew protection.' He paused and added discreetly, 'I also have log records of the other calls we received that night. My men were all over the area, and did their best to control the angry mobs. Someone complained to the headquarters that the police had succeeded in keeping the peace. So, I got a call from the NP chief's office, from one of his lieutenants who monitored the riots. He was dismayed that I had not grasped the idea and asked me to call back my men immediately. He also stressed that reinforcements were on their way and to await them before taking further action.'

'By NP chief, you mean Nuri's office?'

'Who else? Good god!'

Sikander apologized again.

'Anyway,' Patel continued tolerantly, 'now they know I have the records, but what they don't know is whether I have shared the facts with anyone else. That is the only reason why I am still alive.'

'You mean you may be killed?'

'It's a possibility.'

'I don't understand this,' Sikander said, sounding perplexed. 'Your life is in danger, and your name is tarnished. Why did you do it then?'

'I believed in Nuri's politics,' Patel said repentantly, 'his promise of a golden future for everyone. I too wanted to be a part of that dream. I am not the villain; I am just another supporter of Nuri.'

'But is this all you have? Call logs from a police station?'

'Of course not, sir! You think Nuri would have met me if this was all?'

He fell silent, indecisively, and then said, 'I often carry a hidden recorder, a small thing that we use for undercover operations. I took it with me to an informal meeting with two senior police officials a month before the riots. They guided me about communal tensions and how to "handle" them, and recruited me for the plan.' Patel's voice was forlorn. 'I told them I was ready; this was not my first riot.'

'That's fascinating! Tell me, how does one go about it?'

'Well, it's a delicate thing and has to be thought out well beforehand. I am old school and like to use the traditional trick. Drop a butchered pig outside a mosque and a severed cow's head outside a temple. They race out with weapons, screaming, puppets on strings ready to kill each other. I am actually tired of how easy it can be.'

'Surely, you make it sound easy!'

'Perhaps.' He chuckled briefly. 'Anyway, talking of evidence, I also have a record of the conversation I had with the headquarters, requesting additional forces. They clearly mentioned that it would take two hours for them to reach from a neighbouring district. It took them two days. By that time, 202 people had been killed in communal riots. Job done!'

'You must be proud of such excellent execution . . . of the plan, I mean,' Sikander corrected himself. 'Why are you still suspended from duty, sir?'

'Nuri thinks I wouldn't care. His men take care of my expenses, and I get a monthly payment from the NP. But it's not just about that anymore. It's a matter of my family . . . people call me a butcher. And while cases are pending against me, the real culprits have gone and won Parliament elections'

'Doesn't Nuri realize you might use the information you have?'

'Well, Nuri got to know about it only today,' Patel explained. 'I threatened to go to the People's Party with the information if he does not get my suspension revoked. That is the reason I agreed to speak with you.' Patel added sarcastically, 'I'm sure you didn't know how right you were; it will do me good to be seen with the rival party.'

'You're right, I didn't know,' Sikander admitted coolly. 'So, what's the way out for you then?'

'I return to my state tonight and will soon address the first press conference after my suspension from duty. Activists will ask me questions about the riots, and I will say that I simply followed orders of NP's top leadership.'

'Won't the activists come after you?'

Patel was silent, then said, 'I am guessing here, but have you just returned from abroad, after completing your MBA or whatever you do these days to prove you have administrative experience?'

'How did you know?' Sikander exclaimed.

'Never mind,' Patel dismissed cynically. 'No, the activists won't give me a tough time because they understand and cooperate. Why do you think they have quickly politicized the issue? Why do you think they never ask why I followed my orders without questions? They know everything.'

'Everyone seems to know everything,' Sikander noted, 'except for the people.'

'Don't be so naïve, Mr Bansi. You think people don't know whom they vote for? Communal riots take place because they do not finish a politician's career. Everyone is complicit in this, everyone is guilty.'

Sikander agreed with him. 'Did you tell Nuri about the press conference?'

'Yes, I had to. He told me to be patient and not to tempt fate.'

'That sounds ominous.'

'I don't care.'

'Well, do be careful, and thanks for your time,' Sikander mentioned gratefully. 'It has been educational.'

'I am sure it was,' Patel remarked. 'Please keep it to yourself, sir. You are far too young to get hurt.'

Sikander laughed. 'What do you take me for? A fool?'

'Don't ask.'

The chairs moved back as the two men stood up and took leave of each other. Then there was a break in the recording before it restarted:

'This is the clue for Mira.'

Sikander's voice was somehow pained as he said:

'You asked when you were wounded. What's the difference between blood and rain? One flows over the skin, the other under it. Both are free and can't be captured. You said, fill my veins with rain when my eyes are closed. Let the clouds take possession of my mind and set me free. If I must live, please let me choose the rainbows that are yet to come, over the blood that is yet to be shed in the battlefield.'

————

'Questions?' Bhaskar asked.

No one spoke.

Bhaskar put the pen down and sat back in his chair pensively. 'I find this very predictable,' he observed. 'This is just political rivalry; a PP politician against an NP politician.'

88 Kota Neelima

Dubey disagreed, 'This is much more serious than that, Bhaskar . . .'

Bhaskar interrupted him. 'But is it true?'

'We'll know,' Lina said, 'when we speak to this cop, Sunil Patel.'

'Patel is dead,' Dubey told her. 'He died four years ago.'

'What!' Lina was shocked. Others started at Dubey, stunned.

He explained gravely, 'The news didn't make it to national media, but I remember. It was discovered that he had a weak heart.'

Mira leaned forward keenly. 'When did he die?'

'A few days after his Delhi visit.' Dubey answered, 'On December 11, the day before his press conference about the riots.'

There was silence in the room.

Bhaskar finally spoke. 'We published the last tape because Kim Sharma confirmed that conversation with Sikander. If we can't prove this conversation took place, we won't run it.' He added nervously, 'Munshi will be livid if we can't find the facts to fortify the tape.'

'Perhaps,' Salat pondered, 'Mira can give us some leads.'

Surprised, Mira realized once again that although he couldn't read her thoughts, nothing could be hidden from Salat. He knew she had figured out how to date the tape.

'What are you saying, Salat!' Lina was exasperated. 'We need facts, not fairy tales!'

'Let's talk facts then,' Mira told her and turned to others. 'First of all, I don't see why should Sikander fabricate a tape that can't be substantiated. Why would he give us a recording that can't be cross-checked?' She glanced at Bhaskar. 'Even if it was just political rivalry, as you suggested, it wouldn't be served by unfounded allegations.'

'But that's what they will be,' Bhaskar said, 'if the tape cannot be confirmed.'

'It can be,' she said.

Dubey was puzzled. 'How?'

'Play the tape again,' she suggested. 'Focus on the background noise in the crowded corridor as Sikander meets the cop. For instance, there was a man who recalled how he barely escaped getting caught in the snow storm that shut down most airports in northern Europe. We can date that . . .'

'I didn't hear it,' Lina objected. Dubey and Bhaskar concurred.

Mira turned to Salat asking, and he admitted. 'I heard it. And yes, that can be dated.'

'We can also hear another man speak,' she continued, 'about setting the date for his house-warming before the lunar eclipse in December. We can check the calendar.'

'Snow storm? Eclipse?' Lina chuckled. 'What's next? Someone gave birth in the corridor?'

'There was a woman, probably an actress, who spoke about her movie that was released earlier that year. That can be cross-checked.' Mira glanced again at Salat. 'We could hear vehicle numbers being paged at the nearby exit for the MPs leaving Parliament. With your skills, Salat, you may be able to find an anomaly that can fix a date, such as the end of a term or a change in vehicles.'

He agreed that it could be done.

'If we put together all this data,' she concluded, 'we should be able to confirm the date. That's what Sikander might have expected we would do. We can explain the methodology to the readers and run the tapes in tomorrow's newspaper.'

Everyone stayed silent as they realized it was possible. Then Dubey turned to his notebook and noted down the points. Bhaskar reached for his computer and replayed the tape.

Mira stood up to leave. 'I will be in my room if anyone wants any clarification or assistance.' She paused and considered Lina, 'Or wants to know what happens next in the fairy tale.' Lina uneasily looked away, and Mira walked out.

———

Mira settled at her desk and opened the inbox that was choked once again with messages. Her byline was only on the main story, but readers mailed her questions about all stories related to the tape published in the newspaper. As she answered the mails, alongside, she played the second tape once again to check for further ways of dating it. She heard the conversation, and noticed something enticing about Sikander's voice as he lured the policeman into the discussion. He had displayed, alternately and with perfect timing, fetching ignorance and sharp understanding. It had proved to those who met him that it was easy but also rare to convert him into an admirer. This was a trap few could resist, and Sikander used it to great advantage. Then, as the tape ended with the clue, his words forced Mira to stop her work.

Later, she walked to the balcony; it was windy that day, and the rain paused, as if to let the other elements make their arguments before the world. Leaning against the wall, she stared down at the crowded roads. That accident Sikander referred to in the clue had happened a few months ago. She was walking that morning in the last rain of spring when a van had lost control and crashed into a shop window right next to her. The flying glass had cut her, and she had fallen to the sidewalk. A crowd had gathered, and someone called an ambulance. As she had lain there bleeding, the rain and her blood had mixed on the grey sidewalk and flown along the straight cuts in the cement towards the base of a nearby tree. These were exit routes, she had thought just before she became unconscious. Was death the response to the willing of a lifetime? Was it a desire or a command?

The winds lost the case; it began to rain lightly now, and some of the shower reached into the balcony for Mira. She felt like moving to the metal railing, leaning over and looking up at the rain to meet it halfway to earth. But no; she faintly shook her head, she should want to live, not die. That's what everyone wanted: to live. Another moment, another day. In the hope of what? The rain resounded deep in her mind, like music from behind a closed door, drawing her closer. She moved away from the wall and towards the edge. Her clothes were wet, but she didn't notice, didn't stop. She slipped in the rain, and held the railing to steady herself. Mira froze, as she discovered she stood at the edge, her grip on the railing weak against the rain. She was amused by her fear; it was proof of the end. One more step and she could finally be part of something. Her hand slipped from the wet railing and she gasped. Her feet were inches from the fall, a tantalizingly short distance away but her foot wouldn't move. Mira laughed at herself clinging to a life that had never wanted her.

She could still hear the rain in her mind as she returned to the corridor later; she could still hear it ask her to return. Her legs shook as she rushed towards the newsroom and stopped abruptly at a thought. Perhaps the rain was right, this was the time to return. She had always chosen against it, but it still waited, insistently. Mira willed herself to move and found the newsroom across the corridor too far, tiringly distant. She had to stop again, fatigued with the battle within her, but also elated by it; what could Sikander know about such proximity, such reassurance? He regarded death with suspicion, not longing. That was why he made that mistake in the second clue. She didn't choose between blood and rain. To her, they were both the same.

That afternoon, Mahesh Bansi met Mira, and she introduced Salat to him. They settled in the spacious living room of his residence to speak about his son.

Salat said, 'Could you tell us something about the kind of person Sikander is?'

Mahesh's face was drawn. 'I don't know my son, Mr Vasudev. There is no point in asking me about him.'

Taken aback, Salat didn't know what to say. Mira watched Mahesh seriously; she could feel his sadness in her mind.

'Sikander ensured that I didn't meet him daily,' Mahesh explained. 'He kept different hours and never crossed my path. When I asked for him, he was polite and correct. I don't know who taught him these things, but his conduct was faultless. And every time I met him, I discovered that the distance between us had only increased.'

He paused, his voice heavy. 'My wife and I had decided to have only one child so that we could give him or her all our affection, attention and love. I still want that, but I don't have my child anymore; I don't have my son.' Mahesh was forlorn. 'I know he finds his life complete without me. In time, he may even find people who love him more than I do, but I will never find the child I have lost. And I don't have the time left in my life to search for him.'

Mira stayed silent, overwhelmed by his pain. Salat studied Mahesh sympathetically.

'Despite the respect he showed me unerringly, I knew in my heart that he hated me.' Mahesh paused, disturbed. 'When I asked him to contest in the last elections, he refused and said he didn't want to be part of any plan of mine. I told him it wasn't a plan, it was my dream to see him in Parliament. That's all it took.' Mahesh's voice faltered as he added, 'He changed his mind and his life for me.'

Mira observed him meditatively.

Salat asked, 'Why did he show you so much respect if he hated you?'

'It was his etiquette that made him respect and obey me, not his love,' Mahesh said resignedly. 'He would never degrade his own conduct for me or anyone else. That would be unacceptable to him. Instead, look at what he has done! He has forced me to openly accept that we are estranged. He knew I would have to distance myself from him to survive politically. And he wants me to do it! That's the way he hates, Mr Vasudev, without a chance for reconciliation.'

'And how does he love?'

'I have seen him in love only once,' Mahesh recalled. 'He was really happy then.' He stopped where the memory ended. Then said, 'I have seen him often with women, but I knew he didn't love any one of them. Just one of those intuitive things I can tell about my son.'

'What about his love for the cause?' Mira asked. 'It must have taken calculation and planning to make the tapes. And discipline.'

'He is disciplined and quite brilliant,' Mahesh answered her. 'Always had the best scores throughout his education. He is also very determined. So, if he decided to expose corruption in Parliament, nothing could have prevented him.'

'Does he mean it, as he mentioned in the letter, that he won't return home if I can't find him?'

'Absolutely,' Mahesh said dejectedly. 'I might see him once before I die, because that would be the right and proper thing for him to do, but not before that.'

'What would he do with his life?' She was intrigued. 'Where would he live?'

Mahesh smiled, despairing but also somehow proud. 'He must have got his sense of survival from me, Mira. He can live on nothing; he needs no one. Before he became an MP, he used to vanish for months and live in some corner of the country under an assumed name. I used to try and find him, but it was impossible. He left no trace, no phones and no friends, nothing paid for by cheque or credit card. Then one day, he would return home and join me for breakfast or dinner, as if he had been here all along.'

'But why did he do that?' Salat asked. 'Why did he escape?'

'What can I say?' Mahesh shook his head. 'Perhaps because he didn't want to be my son or he didn't want to belong to my world . . .' He stopped abruptly, too distressed to speak.

'Or,' Mira suggested, 'he gave the world what it expected, so that he could be free of it.'

Mahesh glanced at her, his fatigued eyes, now sharp.

'You are not being honest, Maheshji. You should stop being politically correct.'

There was silence as she paused; Mahesh looked upset.

'I believe,' she continued, 'Sikander didn't want to be trapped in the destiny you chose for him.' Mira met the shrewd eyes evenly. 'He wore that disguise for you to be the son you wanted him to be. You wanted to change him, and yet, *you* couldn't change for him.'

Mahesh didn't speak, but his grey eyes glinted in anger. Mira stayed unfazed by his enraged thoughts about her.

'If you had let him be someone else,' she pointed out serenely, 'you wouldn't have lost him. But you wanted an heir, not a son.'

Salat carefully glanced at Mahesh, who was now furious.

'You wish he hated you,' Mira told Mahesh, 'so that you could blame him for everything. But you know he doesn't hate you, Maheshji, and you don't want to accept that,' she added quietly, 'because then, you would have to blame yourself.'

Salat reached for his notebook; this was clearly the end of the interview.

Mahesh coldly studied her. 'I resent that Mira,' he said vindictively, 'but you're right.'

Salat raised his eyebrows, surprised.

'The evidence is in the tapes, Maheshji,' she said. 'By naming you in his very first tape, he has ensured your innocence throughout his plan. You will appear to be his victim just like everyone else, forced to criticize him, malign him, disown him; it's just what you want to do.'

Offended, Mahesh made to contradict her. Mira followed his thought as it reached a more reasonable conclusion and smiled as he grudgingly agreed with her again.

Later, Salat and Mira walked along the second driveway to Sikander's house. It had just stopped raining, and Mira found the place respond differently to her that day. It was open and accessible, as if she was now verified and approved. Or perhaps, it was her own reservation about trespassing on a stranger's life. Did Sikander feel the same hesitation before dissecting her life? Mira opened a window to let the sound of dripping foliage enter the stillness of the study. It made her feel less lonely somehow, less vulnerable, as she replayed the tape.

Once again, Sikander's words rummaged through her head to pick and choose things that he needed to control her. But she was learning about him as well. It was now not difficult to go beyond the obvious meaning of the second clue that she had wanted to die on that sidewalk after the accident. Mira stared at the garden from the window, her face set. Sikander assumed too much. Yes, she too lived behind masks like him, but there was a fundamental difference. She never had points of reference in life—parents, places and homes like these—which stood witness to her time. Her longest and most loyal companions were the faces she wore, like the ones she put on when she pretended to smile, to trust, to wish and to believe. What could Sikander know of such disguises, façades that ruled her life? He chose his fictions, whereas she was assigned her truths. Mira closed her

eyes and listened again to the rain in her mind that churned up
a memory from the depths.

> That was my first birthday after Raghunath left forever. He had
> made every conceivable arrangement with the school and the
> hostel for my comfort and any eventuality. My teachers told
> me about his kindness and his concern. But none of this really
> filled his absence on the day of my birthday. That was the first
> day when I completely understood I had no one of my own, not
> even as a lie.
>
> Aware of my sentiments, a kind-hearted teacher took me along
> with her to a friend's party. They were all strangers there, but
> they tried talking to me and made me smile. I liked even their
> sympathy, the way they felt sorry for me. It was nice to know that
> someone felt something for me, anything. I was aware of what
> they thought, but I did not say a word. I did not want to change
> anything that evening. They talked about me; spoke when they
> thought I wasn't listening. They said people often killed the girl
> child before her birth; that worked the best. But if the girl was
> unfortunately born, then the child was usually left in hospitals
> and orphanages for the community to take care of. They were
> all very ashamed of this trend and criticized those who resorted
> to such inhuman ways. I was impressed by their words and
> wondered how fortunate their children were. Then I noticed
> that everyone, invariably, had a son. There were two, sometimes
> even three, older sisters for every little brother. No, they didn't
> kill their girls or discard them, but they also didn't think they
> were enough. It was an act of charity, not of affection. There are
> no homes for girls in this country; girls are tenants everywhere.
>
> At the end, I smiled and I thanked them. I lied that I had had
> a memorable time. That's when I acquired my first mask, it was

a great success! Soon I discovered people expected me to wear it
for the rest of my life. I was eleven years old.

Mira sat in the study with her eyes closed. It was the last memory she needed, Mira weakly told herself. She seemed to have abdicated the control over her pain to Sikander. His words shook loose all instances that she made herself forget. Then she realized something else. Deep within her mind, where everything was a different shade of reality, she no longer heard the calling rain. Instead, she heard Sikander's soft voice as his words dismantled her memory of rain, one saved pearl at a time.

SEVEN

Sundays used to be islands of leisure around which one circled the entire week, wading through troubled waters to eventually reach and rest. But this was not one such Sunday. Mira woke up to phone calls and text messages, indicating a day ahead of tension and aggravation. She had to do the laundry at home, get groceries for the week and sweep the floors. Instead, Mira was standing at the gates of her apartment building at 9 a.m., waiting for Salat.

Bhaskar had called her about an hour ago; Nuri was livid about that morning's story of Sikander's conversation with the policeman about the riots. The second Parliament tape once again provided a crucial missing piece of another puzzle. It reopened the unsolved case of the riots and showed who instigated the violence between communities. Predictably, Nuri was shaken and had complained to Munshi that the story revealed a grudge the newspaper held against the NP. Even though Munshi clarified that he never held grudges in secret, Nuri threatened to sue the newspaper for sullying his name unless Munshi could prove he was fair in publication of the tapes. Munshi agreed and promised to send the journalists who had written the story to meet him. As a result, Bhaskar instructed Mira and Salat to reach Nuri's residence to explain the process behind the story to him. Salat called her and offered to drive so that they could discuss on the way. He arrived three minutes late;

they remained silent as he reached the main road and headed towards Nuri's residence in central Delhi.

'What do the clues mean, Mira?' Salat spoke finally, as he slowed at an intersection. 'I can't figure them out.'

'That's not surprising,' she observed, 'because they are addressed to me.'

Mira surveyed the bright sky; the light was linked strands of silver and grey. 'I hope Sikander has factored in Munshi's treachery. What are we to tell Nuri?'

'Bhaskar says that we have to tell Nuri everything.'

'Why?'

'Because Bhaskar wants us to.' Salat glanced at her briefly. 'That's evident, isn't it?'

'What's evident is we write for a newspaper and not for Nuri.'

'Please Mira!' he chuckled impatiently. 'Nuri is the chief of the Opposition National Party. Elections are around the corner, and he could easily be the next prime minister. Don't you see that? How can we displease Nuri?'

'If that's so, then why did we publish the tape?' she inquired. 'What has changed between yesterday and today? Did we reveal the evidence yesterday only to oblige him today?'

'We published the tape because we owed it to the readers,' he replied calmly.

'Then we should write about the phone conversation between Munshi and Nuri in the morning today,' Mira countered. 'We owe that to the readers as well. We must also report our meeting with Nuri, the readers must know that too!'

'Bhaskar specifically told me that everything should be off the record,' Salat cautioned her, 'unless Nuri wants to make a press statement.'

'All right then,' She said reasonably. 'Let's publish tomorrow that we extended this privilege to Nuri to decide what should be off and on the record.'

He turned to her. 'Are you telling me this has never happened before with you? Is this the first time that you have discovered how journalism works or newspaper owners work?'

'No,' she conceded fairly. 'But every time it happens, I am happy that I am still outraged by it.'

'But you do take part in it,' he persisted. 'You couldn't have survived in your job if you had not. Then why do you indulge in this righteous posturing?'

'Because it still hurts my conscience.'

'Even if you are complicit?' he asked.

'Especially because I am!'

'Spare me the classroom idealism, Mira,' he said. 'With every line of news we write in support or opposition, we benefit someone or the other. That's the business of communication. It's communication when we publish a story, and it's business when we sell it. There is no grey area.'

'Then I'll choose either black or white, not both.'

'What's your problem, really?' he asked restlessly. 'Uneasy relationship with parents? Sibling rivalry? Difficult love life? Sorry for being inappropriate, but I want to know.'

'Oh I see!' Mira nodded. 'My morality has to be the result of some insufficiency in my life. Then what's the secret of your immorality?' she demanded. 'The sufficiency of your life?'

'So you know everything about my family,' he noted derisively, 'everyone does. To be brief, we run a few industries, just as the company website says. But I do a job because I want to be someone more than merely the "next boss". It's that simple, really.'

Mira was unconvinced. 'What about the dog?'

'The dog?' he asked, frowning.

'The four-year-old retriever,' she clarified. 'You live alone with your dog, you do a job that you don't need, and you can't sustain relationships. And you talk about problems in my life?'

Salat forgot his annoyance. 'That's really good, Mira! Honestly!' he said, impressed. 'How did you find out? You can't discern my thoughts as another knower, so what gave this away? Clothes, habits, reactions . . .?'

'Facebook.'

He glanced at her amused face. 'All right then,' he said vengefully, 'if you are so smart, why don't you tell me how Sikander knows you this well?'

Mira lost her smile.

'You are not on any social network. In fact, you're barely on our newspaper website.' Salat continued, 'Then how does Sikander come up with his clues that cut you to the bone? It has been hard for you to even *hear* the clues a second time unless you are in Sikander's house, fortified by his life as he demolishes yours.'

Mira stayed silent, unnerved by his perception.

'Don't have an answer, do you?' Salat challenged her.

'No,' she was brief.

He repented at the change in her voice. 'Well, you can always ask my dog,' he recommended lightly. 'Don't read his thoughts though; he too is immoral like me due to the sufficiency of his life.'

Mira glanced at him, surprised, and Salat chuckled, making her smile.

———

Nuri was waiting for them at his residence, and by the number of empty tea cups before him, it was clear that his day had begun early. He gestured for them to sit and continued reading the newspapers. Unlike his counterpart in the PP—Mahesh Bansi, who lived in his own home—Nuri stayed in government-allotted accommodation. Although, as a former cabinet minister and a six-times MP, Nuri was entitled to a large bungalow, he lived in the same small flat where he had begun his political career three decades ago. A simple man with simple needs, that's how he wanted people to think of him. People, however, knew better.

The long living room was crowded with seating arrangements of four different types. The brown sofas at the far end with their plush, rounded corners were like lazy animals resting after a heavy meal. A dozen upholstered skinny chairs were lined up against two walls, as if waiting for the firing squad. Two wooden easy chairs sat uneasily in the middle and divided the room into the plush and the rugged ends. Nuri was perched on a couch, surrounded by different phones and newspapers. They could see he read their newspaper and were forced to wait in a silence that made them appear guilty.

Evidently, he had postponed many things from his morning schedule. He was still in his pyjamas, a rare sight as he had never been seen wearing anything but his traditional starched cotton outfits. Nuri appeared much younger than his sixty years. His hair was without much grey; his face without many lines. The reading glasses accentuated his frown, and as he turned a page of the newspaper, the large pearl ring on his finger triggered a déjà vu. Over the last three decades, that ring had been as much in the public domain as Nuri himself—seen, photographed and televised with him. The hand used to be younger, and the pearl used to be set in silver. Now, the hand was aged, and the pearl was in platinum.

'I was reading your story again,' Nuri said, as he kept the newspaper away, 'because I need to brief my lawyers on the defamation charges. They believe I deserve compensation of up to ₹100 crore from your newspaper for this libel.'

He regarded them accusingly. 'When your office called me yesterday for a version, they never told me it was part of a political game. You should have the basic decency to be honest about who you work for. After all, you are paid salaries as journalists, and people should know who does the paying! And what for!'

As he continued with the tirade, Mira looked out of the window next to her chair. The sun was now out, and there was a slight breeze. She could sense Nuri's thoughts, which were predictably murderous. Her mind sauntered off to Nalan Malik and his unlikely white shirt; she wondered if he had her under surveillance.

'Am I boring you, Miraji?' Nuri demanded.

'Not at all,' Mira turned to him. 'You were talking about the reporter who called you from my office.'

He glared at her. 'The reporter who called me from your office asked me innocent questions! How did I know Patel? Did I meet him on his last visit to Delhi? What did we talk . . .?' Nuri said, working up a rage. 'I answered the questions truthfully. I said we talked about personal issues, which were not meant for the press. Did I say we had differences? No. Did I say it was about the riots? No. Did I say it was about his press conference? No. But that's the story I read today with my statements reported out of context.'

'They were in context and you know why,' Mira noted quietly. 'You were sent the transcripts of the tape.'

'But did it help that I said the tape was baseless?' His dark eyes were furious. 'Does it matter at all that I am innocent, or do I have to be condemned just because I am a politician?'

'I understand your feelings,' Mira tried again, 'and we are here to explain to you . . .'

'No, Miraji, let me explain to *you* instead,' he said harshly. 'I have never protested or questioned your know-reports about me. You exposed my intentions, probably with the help of my rival, Mahesh Bansi. And today, you tried to destroy my career with the help of his son. You must tell me, why are you against me?'

'I am not against you or for you, sir; I am a journalist,' Mira stated. 'I have never needed any help to write know-reports about you, Mr Nuri. If you remember, you gave me an interview once, and that's all I needed to know you, which was to hear you speak once.

And as for our report today, we have evidence to back every word.'

'Every word, is it?' he fumed. 'What evidence do you have of my guilt? How could you insinuate that I was involved in the riots?' Nuri paused, agitated. 'How can you call Sikander's Parliament tapes evidence? It's a random conversation between two biased people against a common enemy.'

'A conversation with a man,' Mira rephrased, 'who was witness to carnage and probably facilitated it. A man who had no idea he was being recorded and had no reason to lie.'

Nuri waved his hand in disgust. 'Please don't talk about lies, not when your byline is on this story. Just say sorry and get lost!'

Stunned and enraged, Mira made to answer when she felt Salat's restraining grip on her arm.

'Your one story has tainted my image, possibly forever,' Nuri alleged. 'My career of many decades of social service is being questioned. It seems now as if I had lied, as if I knew Patel's plans and, perhaps, even got him killed!'

He fell silent, troubled, and his face stiffened with thoughts he didn't share. The breeze made the white curtains of the window flutter and let the sunlight slip into the room.

Nuri took a deep breath. 'Your newspaper published that tape to damage me. And there is nothing you can say today to repair it.'

'Thank you, Mr Nuri, then we won't try any repairs,' Mira said. Contrary to what she felt, she sounded cool and composed. 'However, our editor Mr Munshi thought you should know that we handled the situation with fairness. To give you the general picture, we are publishing Sikander's tapes as a condition for him to return home and on the request of Mr Mahesh Bansi. The tapes constitute important information, which we professionally verify from multiple sources before publication. We side with no individual or party . . .'

'Side with no one?' Nuri thundered. 'Don't play these games

with me, Miraji! You have written the story for Mahesh with the help of evidence his son had concocted against me. You are siding with him and the PP government!'

'The first tape was against Mr Bansi and the PP government, Mr Nuri,' Mira countered calmly. 'I wouldn't call that siding with them.'

Nuri didn't respond.

'The story came to us with a few conditions,' Mira continued. 'First, all tapes must be published by our newspaper. Secondly, every tape will have a clue to find Sikander; and, thirdly, the tapes will cease once Sikander is found.' She paused. 'We have been working on the clues and are reasonably confident that we will get to Sikander soon.'

'Your editor claimed Sikander sent you the clues because you are a gifted knower. So, when will you find him?'

'She can't say when, Mr Nuri,' Salat intervened. 'Sikander had planned this episode very carefully and thoroughly. It won't be easy to find him if he doesn't want to be found.'

'And in the meanwhile, there will be more tapes against me?'

'We do not know what will be in the next tape.'

Nuri asked, mocking, 'You expect me to believe that, Salatji?'

'Yes, although I'm fairly certain that the next tape will once again expose the deals made by parliamentarians.'

'Such as myself?'

Salat shrugged.

Nuri fell silent, thinking. 'Perhaps, I can get the tapes to stop.'

'By suing our newspaper for defamation?' Salat contemplated. 'Unlikely.'

'I meant, by finding Sikander,' Nuri clarified acidly. 'Why didn't Mahesh go to the police to find his son?'

'That was one of the conditions set by Sikander in his personal letter to his father,' Salat revealed. 'No police.'

'Well, I can go to the police, can't I? Let me help everyone by tracking down this meddling son of Mahesh.' Then he regarded them with hostility. 'Tell your editor that I will rethink the legal case against him. And on the way out, please leave your contact numbers with my assistant. He will collect the copy of the tapes from your office.'

'There is nothing left in the recording,' Salat assured him. 'It's all published in today's newspaper.'

'I'm not talking about today's recording, Salatji, I'm talking about the tapes that are yet to come. That was the deal with Munshi.' He noticed their surprise and chuckled, entertained. 'Oh, so he didn't tell you people! Well, perhaps as knowers, you should start by getting to first "know" your own editor!'

After some time, Mira stormed out of Nuri's house, livid. Even Salat was upset. They didn't speak as they reached the car, but had to pause to appreciate the beautiful day. The sun let the freshly painted leaves dry, the sky was an unframed canvas, fine-grained and primed. The light preferred photographs instead, and the breeze dropped raindrops like postcards from the trees. The warmth of the day was dipped in something soft and sweet, as if to change the subject from victory and defeat.

———

The office was deserted when Salat and Mira reached at 11 a.m. The staff on Sunday duty was yet to arrive, and a surprised guard unlocked the door to the editorial department for them. Salat walked off to have a cup of coffee in the canteen, and Mira headed to her cabin. She shut the door and stood thinking. The conversation with Nuri had reminded her of Sikander's letter to his father in which he was confident she could solve the clues and find him. Mira switched on the computer and uneasily read the scripts of the two clues once again. His words were always final and bare, as if to evoke fear of non-existence that entailed she derive her being wholly from his perception of her. She had to admit she was already driven by what he let her think, which made analysis of the clues difficult. The second clue was more tangible than the first because it was based on an actual event. But if Sikander thought like her, why would he refer to the accident and give away his vantage point? She would have never done that unless . . .

Mira stared at the clue, realizing, then grabbed her bag and rushed out of the cabin.

Salat sat alone in the canteen on the ground floor and sipped coffee by the window. He turned, surprised, as she came and sat next to him. He asked for another cup and waited as she glanced out of the window at the parking lot behind the building. Several motorcycles stood there in rows, their rear-view mirrors turned to the skies, like sunflowers in a farmer's field.

'A doctor in the government hospital had treated me after the accident a few months ago,' she said to Salat. 'His name was Gautam something . . . I forget. It is evident that Sikander has met him and, perhaps, wants me to meet him as well. That's why the clue mentions the accident in such detail.'

'Detail?' Salat was mystified.

'Well, Sikander knew I was hurt in the open. He knew it was raining. He knew there was substantial blood loss before the ambulance arrived, and that I was conscious while I lay on the sidewalk.' Mira paused as the coffee arrived. 'These details can't be found in hospital records. He got those personally from the doctor who had treated me.'

Salat nodded. 'You should meet that doctor.'

'You should come along.'

'Need me now, do you?' he asked, amused.

'Need a ride, yes.'

He took a second to recover, then said politely, 'Any time.'

Mira thanked him and had her coffee.

EIGHT

The afternoon sparkled as if it was the first one ever, new and untried, and yet to fail. The hospital reception informed them that Dr R.S. Gautam was not on duty and referred them to his house among the staff residences located behind the building. They parked the car and walked through the empty lanes of the premises amid a lazy Sunday afternoon. The first knock on the door of the doctor's first floor house was met with silence; they waited, sure that he was home and resting. In response to the second knock, the door was impatiently opened by a man in a crumpled shirt and slacks.

He listened sleepily as Salat explained they had a few questions about an accident that took place a few months ago. But the doctor's focus returned rapidly as he recognized Mira.

'You!' he said indignantly and stepped into the corridor. 'I have had enough of your accident for one Sunday! First, it was the policeman an hour ago, who wanted every little detail. And now, you! How dare you, *even you*, come to ask me questions? You know all about it, for god's sake!!'

Salat glanced at Mira; Nuri had meant his words and had already sought police assistance to find Sikander. The second clue must have led them to investigate her accident.

'I am not here to ask about the accident,' Mira clarified. 'I want to know if a man had come asking about it a few weeks ago.'

The doctor's exasperation quickly vanished. 'Eager to know, aren't you?' he asked kindly.

Mira was confused by his thoughts. 'Perhaps yes,' she answered unsurely.

'Well, if you ask me, you still have a chance.'

Mira said, puzzled, 'A chance for what?'

'To get back the man you love.'

'*What?*'

"You don't have to pretend,' the doctor assured her. 'I know everything.'

Mira stared at him, baffled.

Salat cleared his throat gently. 'You see, Doctor Gautam,' he smiled, 'I joined this interesting newspaper only recently. So why don't you tell me what's this is all about?'

'Well, it seems their relationship ended sometime ago,' the doctor confided. 'Sikander was travelling when she had the accident, and when he returned, he was naturally concerned.' The doctor glanced at Mira, who was looking a little dazed. 'Can you believe it? He even said you would come searching for him, just as he had come for you,' he said, getting overwhelmed. 'You two have a true bond.'

Amused, Salat glanced at her astonished face, then turned back to the doctor. 'When did you meet Sikander?'

'About a fortnight ago, I think. You see, I regularly interact with families or friends of patients to help in the recovery process. I pay special attention to accident cases. So, I met with this extraordinary man who sought to know the smallest detail. I mean, if this is not love . . .'

'What,' Mira managed with effort, 'did he ask you?'

'About how you felt during the accident, how you were rescued and how much blood you lost. It was clear how much he still cared for you.'

'Was it?' Mira said, trenchantly.

The doctor assessed her. 'I can see you resent him; you even dislike my praise for him. But let me tell you why I liked him, Mira. I get a lot of questions about accident cases as I work in the emergency ward of this hospital. People ask me about recovery, relapse and rehabilitation—the usual. But Sikander asked me things no one ever had; like how you looked when you were unconscious, what your first words were when you woke up, what your memory was and what your dreams were.'

'Dreams?' Salat repeated, uncertain.

The doctor nodded and addressed her again. 'He wanted to know if I could tell what dreams you had, if you dreamt of finding or losing, of knowing or forgetting. He wanted to know if you smiled in your sleep,' the doctor continued, 'if you cried in your dreams, and if you cried no more.'

As he recalled Sikander's questions, Mira felt the words slip in between her breath like glass to settle deep in her heart, waiting to hurt her later. Then the words ceased and the silence returned her strength. 'I thought he asked about my shoulder injury,' she observed.

The doctor confirmed that. 'Sikander was concerned about your shoulder injury, and I assured him you had a full recovery. I also asked him why your relationship didn't work, I had to,' the doctor justified, 'he was so melancholic.'

'I see.'

'He was unwilling to speak at first, and later, I understood the reason. It's not easy to speak about unhappy love stories. But tell me this, Mira', he asked tragically, 'Was his love not enough? So what if he wasn't rich and successful?'

Mira didn't know what to say and desperately turned to Salat.

'What gave you that feeling, doctor?' Salat asked.

'It was so obvious!' he declared. 'He was poor and struggled to barely survive. His obvious education and perfect conduct couldn't distract me from noticing the torn, borrowed clothes, the grimy face, the dirty beard and the old shoes.'

Salat and Mira exchanged a look; that description was not of the man in Sikander's photograph. It was a disguise.

'And yet, there was something special about Sikander,' the doctor continued movingly, 'something you don't find these days. He had faith.'

'In God?' Salat tried. 'In the government?'

'In Mira, of course!' he informed him. 'Sikander was all about her; every thought about her, every thing about her.'

The familiar fear about Sikander gripped her again as Mira heard the doctor speak about his concern for her. Shutting off the doctor's voice, she turned to survey the day from the doors of the stairwell.

In conclusion, the doctor said to Mira, 'He said you would come here to look for him, and I asked him for his address, just in case you felt remorse and wanted to contact him.'

Mira turned to him sharply.

'He didn't give his address but left you a message. I have it here in the notes on my phone,' he said and reached for his cell phone.

Mira and Salat waited in anticipation.

'Here it is,' the doctor found the note. 'Sikander said to tell you,

'Don't waste time tracing my steps, just go home.'

The doctor smiled. 'Just feel the depth of meaning in those words!'

Salat chuckled and that offended the doctor.

Mira was perplexed. 'Is that the message? "Just go home?"'

'Yes. Try to think about his sacrifice, Mira, his reconciliation with his own fate and loneliness. The . . .'

Salat struggled to control his laughter, and the doctor studied him with disapproval. 'Please look beyond the gold watches and shining shoes of those around you,' he warned her. 'That's what I think, but it's your life.'

'I'm not sure anymore,' Mira said scathingly. 'Did Sikander say he would return?'

The doctor fervently said, 'Men like him don't.'

Mira took hurried leave of the doctor as Salat started laughing again. The sunlight, which was mellow before, now had acquired the edge of sharpened metal. It glinted as they walked to the parking lot and blinded them like the truth they didn't want to face. They had found out absolutely nothing about Sikander, despite knowing so much about him. He seemed to elude them even though he was constantly accessible. He was making them dance.

Somehow, they wished it rained again.

———

Salat drove her home, and they discussed Sikander's message.

'It doesn't fit the pattern,' he reflected. 'It's so direct, unlike his clues.'

'It's not a clue, it's an instruction.'

'So, is he telling you to stop looking for him?'

She shook her head, fatigued. 'It's got to be deeper than that.'

'There can be no limit with Sikander; he can be anyone, the tapes prove that!' Then Salat added appreciatively, 'But you were right that he wanted you to meet the doctor. That's progress!'

Mira leaned against the open window of the car and felt the wind on her face.

'Perhaps,' Salat continued, 'there is another message behind the story he used with the doctor? The story of unrequited love?'

Mira watched the passing trees. 'To know if I smiled in my sleep or cried no more? I wonder that he doesn't know.'

'Know what?' Salat asked.

'That I can't dream.'

Salat glanced at her, astonished.

Mira closed her eyes, the sunlight fell on her face from in between tall buildings, and she answered Sikander as he waited in her mind.

'Happy dreams; what are they made of? Complete circles and happy endings? A body that's not a cage; a soul that's not a guest? But I like this arrangement, this hurtling down the slope towards the abyss. I like the transience of happiness. I like finding it somewhere between two desires and a lack.'

The car halted suddenly, and Mira opened her eyes. They were at the corner of her street, and she saw two police vehicles in the distance; they were parked in front of the gate of her apartment building.

Salat's voice was urgent. 'What do you want to do?'

Mira wearily said, 'Kill Sikander when I find him,' then added, 'All right. Let's go and see what they want.'

The car didn't move. Salat smiled kindly and said, 'Need my help again, is it?'

'If you mean, do I need you to drive again,' she said tersely, 'then yes.'

His face was set as he restarted the car. 'You know, it's hard to say this about a girl, but you have absolutely no regard for other people's feelings.'

'Nonsense, Salat,' she said reasonably. 'You can always say that about a girl.'

The car drove round the corner and headed towards the waiting police vehicles.

———

Additional station house officer, Sita Patnaik, stepped out of the van and met them as they reached the gate. She was an attractive, unsmiling young woman with small, keen eyes. She introduced herself to Mira and explained that Omkar Nuri's office had informed the police of a disappearance. She scrutinised Salat. 'This investigation has to be carried out discreetly; those are the special orders. Who are you?'

Salat answered that he was working with Mira on the case. Sita asked if they could sit and talk somewhere, and Mira led them to her third-floor flat. On the way, but too late, she recalled the messy state of the living room. They discovered plates on the desk, newspapers on the floor, unwashed cups in the corners, half-read books in the middle and laundry in chairs. Salat was especially intrigued by an apple kernel that sat outside on a window ledge.

When they were finally settled in the chairs, Sita recorded Mira's name, address and age in her register. Sita spoke slowly and deliberately, as if she not just wrote, but memorized each fact. They answered her questions and explained the disappearance of Sikander Bansi.

'What do you mean you have special powers?' Sita demanded, her sharp eyes on them. 'Who authorised them?'

'No one . . . I mean,' Salat attempted, 'these are special abilities. We are both know-journalists and we . . .'

'Oh, that!' Sita said, relieved. 'I know what you mean, and I have been curious for some time now. You do sensational stories, Miraji, and it's hard to believe that it is all derived from your mind. Honestly now, who are your sources?'

'That's the point,' Mira said briefly. '*We* are the sources.'

'I see. So what do your powers tell you?' Sita asked indulgently. 'Where is Sikander Bansi?'

'I don't know yet.'

'The controversial tapes are getting you and your newspaper huge publicity. That's good enough motive for Sikander's disappearance.'

'Motive for *what!*'

Salat intervened, a little dazed. 'You think we have kidnapped him, Ms Patnaik?'

'Have you?' Sita inquired calmly.

'Of course not!' Mira was outraged.

'Then why are the clues addressed only to you?'

'And that makes me a suspect?' Mira asked incredulously.

Salat explained, 'This was entirely Sikander's idea. You can ask his father, Mahesh Bansi.'

'My colleagues will speak with Mahesh Bansi and also Nuri. But the real question is how to find Sikander, and the real problem,' she pointed her pen at Mira, 'is you.'

Mira sat quietly enraged.

Sita studied her closely. 'When did you last meet Sikander?'

'I have never met him.'

'Talked to him on the phone?'

'No.' Mira was distracted as she began to sense Sita's thoughts.

'How do you know the tapes are from him?'

'His father showed me Sikander's letter and provided his handwriting and voice samples,' Mira replied, keenly following Sita's thinking process.

'Is it not possible that Sikander's father had fabricated these tapes, forged a letter from Sikander and got you to publish the tapes?'

Mira knew Sita was about to ask that. 'It's possible, but why would he do that? The newspaper would have published such explosive recording anyway, irrespective of who got them to us or why.'

'As the tapes were made by Sikander,' Sita deduced smoothly, 'Mahesh Bansi must have known he was bound to get involved. But by claiming that his eccentric son *forced* him to publish the tapes, Mahesh has become an innocent victim.'

Mira disagreed. 'I know Mahesh Bansi, and he is far too shrewd to come out into the open like this. If he had planned the tapes, he would have stayed behind the scenes, not in the spotlight.'

'Ah! The special powers again!' Sita remarked gravely. 'Convenient, is it not, to attribute all crucial facts to just "knowing" them?'

Mira did not answer that, offended.

'Have you used your gift to figure out the clues yet?' Sita asked. 'What have you found?'

'The two clues represent the same agenda . . .' Mira fell silent as she read Sita's thoughts ridicule her and then continued patiently, 'He has established familiarity with my life and thoughts, as a counter to my own powers to read him. The first clue described my wish to die, and the second was about when I thought I was dying.'

'That's vague!' Sita commented, dryly. 'How do you plan to find him?'

'By surviving his clues, which I know he thinks will be difficult for me, I can know his mind . . .'

'That does it!' Sita put down the pen decisively on the page. 'I have had enough of this "knowing" business! Exactly what does it mean, when you say you will know his mind?'

'Exactly that, Sitaji,' Mira informed her.

'I am not convinced,' Sita pursued. 'As I see it, you don't want to expose your elaborate plan behind this show. Fine, but at least lie creatively. Know his mind? What rubbish!'

'Rubbish?' Mira repeated the word, infuriated.

'You can make all the allegations you want, Ms Patnaik,' Salat intervened, 'but we are not lying about our powers to know.'

'If that's true, sir,' Sita suggested, 'then you must "know" where Sikander Bansi is.'

'We will know, but we don't yet,' he said. 'Please believe us.'

'Fine then. Make me believe you,' she challenged. 'Let's see what you can "know" about me.'

Salat raised a hand. 'I don't think that's a good idea.'

'No, I didn't think you would,' Sita sighed. 'I want both of you to accompany me to the police station, where you will be detained until you "know" how to get out.'

Mira considered her, curious. 'If that's how you will believe us then . . .'

'No, Mira, please,' Salat stopped her hurriedly.

'She asked for it,' Mira pointed out.

Then she turned to Sita. 'Let's see.' She smiled in her deceptively friendly manner. 'Well, I "know" that you are unhappy in your job and wonder if you were right to join the police force. The last two years . . . no, three years in the service have revealed the truth . . .'

Sita interrupted derisively. 'That would be true of almost any idealist who takes up any job in the system.'

Mira admitted that and then said, 'You don't want to investigate Nuri's complaint; you rather that the Parliament tapes are published. But your disinterest is in contrast to how diligently you write down facts and how passionately you interrogate . . .'

'Is this all you got? Really?' Sita demanded, taunting. 'I myself told you I like your stories, and everyone in my police station knows I love police work. Perhaps, you knew I was assigned to this case and checked up on me before this meeting.'

'Fair point,' Mira chuckled, enjoying herself now. 'All right then. Let's try something *outside* your police station,' she said, her dark eyes intense. 'You are not sure about your fiancé anymore, you don't know if you want to marry him. But you don't have the courage to break the relationship, not because it will hurt him, but because you are afraid of being alone.'

Salat winced. Sita was enraged but also a little confused. She asked suspiciously, 'Who have you been talking to?'

'You,' Mira said.

Sita frowned.

'You keep tugging at that ring,' Mira gestured to her hand, 'as if it was not yet part of your life. You have said yes to the marriage, but you don't mean it anymore.'

Sita checked the ring, concerned.

'You don't take it off. The sheen is gone from the gold, and that's not because you like the ring,' Mira explained methodically. 'He should have noticed how you mistreat the ring. You hope he does.'

Mira paused, serious now, as she detected the real cause for Sita's doubts.

'He doesn't want you to be a cop,' Mira concluded uneasily. 'He objects to it because you are a woman, and that's unacceptable to you.'

Sita didn't speak, hurt. Mira glanced at Salat, apologetic, and he shook his head in a reprimand.

Then Salat gently analysed, 'Your fiancé wants you to choose between the marriage and the police force. And, although you may hate him today for making you choose, you'll thank him for it some day.'

There was absolute silence in the room for a while. Then Sita said with effort, 'This is remarkable.'

They remained silent in remorse.

'I have to report this, so I will leave now.' Then Sita hesitatingly asked, 'What do you think I should do?'

'Go ahead and file your report,' Salat assured her. 'Don't worry about us.'

Sita listened to him uncertainly, Mira knew that's not what Sita had asked.

'Do exactly what you had decided,' Mira told her. 'Get posted away from Delhi and let the distance take care of the relationship.'

There was respect in Sita's sharp eyes. 'This is incredible! My colleagues will never believe it when I tell them.'

Salat settled back in his chair. 'Which ones?'

NINE

There was no sunrise the next morning, and the clouds descended many levels of existence to rain away insidious plans. The story about Nuri continued to make headlines as news organizations across the country did their own research and connected the dots. The NP suffered damage due to the second clue, as much as the PP had done due to the first one. The NP's response was exactly the same as the PP. The NP spokespersons repeated what the PP spokespersons had said, that the tapes were politically motivated and aimed at ruining the leadership's image ahead of the national elections in January. Sikander's disappearance was now an open fact, and his personal letter to his father was widely circulated. The newspaper was criticized by both the PP and the NP, which ensured that everyone else supported it. Know-reportage went through the usual dose of skepticism, especially on the assumption that Mira's special powers would help find Sikander. But not everyone seemed to share that doubt, as Mira found herself under surveillance through the day and even at night. From her living room windows, she spotted a non-descript jeep with two watchers parked at the street corner.

The first meeting on Monday morning was a tedious discussion with the legal team about the special investigation initiated by the government into the new allegations made in the tapes. All documents, transcripts and notes made by the reporters were explained to the lawyers and copies submitted. Every phone conversation and interview was replayed, and every word spoken on record was cross-checked. Then they discussed the police investigation following Nuri's complaint, and Mira informed them of her meeting with Sita and also about the surveillance on her. Munshi instructed that there should be complete transparency and full cooperation. 'We are not the ones who have anything to hide,' he maintained. Observing his easy conscience, Mira recalled his deals with Bansi and Nuri, and wondered whether being unscrupulous could be a virtue in the fight for truth.

The third tape reached her by the afternoon post under considerable limelight. A number of copies were made immediately and sent to Bansi, Nuri, the police and other investigative authorities. Though the tape was not yet released to the television channels, there were far too many copies circulating in Delhi for them not to reach journalists. The atmosphere in the conference room where the editorial department had gathered was sombre, even without the presence of Munshi. Every decision they took would be watched and weighed, every value measured, every opinion dissected. This noticeably reduced the chatter, and the room quickly settled down to listen to the new tape. In contrast to their subdued agitation, Sikander's voice was strikingly calm.

'Today is 5 April . The time is 12.30 p.m. I have just entered the Parliament building and turned left in the main corridor in pursuit of Ajay Sarkar and Bharat Kumar, as they walk ahead of me. They are headed to the lounges, and I'm following them in the hope of eavesdropping on their conversation from a seat close by.'

This was followed by sounds of the corridor and a medley of voices. Then there was silence, as if Sikander followed his targets into a room, and only a single conversation was now audible.

'I don't owe you an explanation, Ajay,' a man emphasized coldly. 'You can't threaten me with meetings like these. You are free to leave the party if you don't like my style of functioning, or,' he added helpfully, 'I could expel you.'

'I just need an answer to a question, Bharat,' Ajay noted flatly.

'And I need you to be loyal to your leader,' Bharat snapped back.

There was a moment's silence. Then Ajay said, 'You're the leader of my party, but we are also friends. We founded this party together to work for the people, to cleanse the system, to make politics answerable. Our movement was about being different, being better than other political parties and politicians,' Ajay's voice was pained. 'But what have things come to, Bharat? A poor farmer committed suicide at your public meeting, and you didn't even blink!'

'Don't get dramatic now,' Bharat said derisively. 'You get passionate about little things like honesty and accountability. But what about power? How can I maintain power if I go about telling people the truth all the time? Have you ever thought of that?'

'Our vision,' Ajay pointed out tolerantly, 'was that we wouldn't have to lie to the people.'

'Truth in politics is overrated,' Bharat dismissed. 'I won't survive a day in government if I told the truth.'

'That's what I thought,' Ajay was forlorn. 'Answer my question and then you can leave, if you want. It's about the

farmer suicide. You knew the farmer was there to commit
suicide; he had announced he would hang himself when
he climbed the tree inside the meeting ground. Everyone
could see him but your meeting continued in a cold-blooded
disregard to this man's life. Even after the man killed himself,'
Ajay accused him, 'you continued with your speech; you
insisted, ironically, that your party stands firmly with the
farmers . . .'

'I know all this, Ajay, I was there,' Bharat interrupted him
impatiently. 'What's your question?'

'Why didn't you save the man?'

'You mean, personally?'

'Yes. Why didn't you stop your speech, suspend your
meeting and save his life?'

'I don't know,' Bharat replied bluntly. 'I didn't think of it.'

'Was it because you were sure he wouldn't go that far?'

'I suppose so.' Bharat's voice turned cautious.

'There was a suicide note found at the site that was not
written by the farmer. Who wrote it?'

'I can't say.'

'The police said that the farmer was called to the public
meeting by your party colleagues. The police investigation
will expose how the farmer was incited to commit suicide.'

'I have already dismissed the police investigation as
politically motivated,' Bharat countered. 'That's the best way
to deal with such crises.'

'But you are in charge, Bharat. You must work with the
police, not against it.'

'What nonsense! If I work with the police, who will I
blame for the rising crime in the city, for the dismal protection
for women, for the general feeling of insecurity?'

'Convenient, isn't it?' Ajay was sarcastic. 'The central

government should take care of living standards in the city, and the police should ensure security. What about you? What are you responsible for?'

'I talk about curbing corruption all the time.'

'You talk!' Ajay's voice was restrained. 'You're right Bharat, you were elected for your rhetoric, not for your work.'

'I don't have time for your sermons, Ajay. What's that you wanted to ask me?' Bharat said, tersely.

Ajay was direct. 'Did you know this farmer would be at the public meeting?'

Bharat didn't speak.

'Did you or any of your colleagues arrange this to get the attention of the media? Was it an accident, was he never supposed to die? Answer me.'

Bharat continued to be silent for a few seconds. Then said, 'And you say you're my friend! How can you even ask me this?'

'Because I know you,' Ajay explained. 'I remember you from the days when you were not a politician. A few years ago we were all part of the movement to demand for transparency in government. Ratanbau, your mentor, was on a hunger-strike for many days to protest the government's apathy. You and I negotiated with the government for consensus on our demands, but you stalled for time to stay in the limelight. You delayed resolution even at the risk of Ratanbau's life. I know what you are capable of!'

'And I know what you are capable of, Ajay,' Bharat said, scornfully. 'You want to be in my shoes and you are envious of my political rise. But you forget one important thing, my friend; none of you can be me. This party is not about Ratanbau or anyone of you. It's about me! Understand?'

'The party is about lakhs of people who donated funds for you,' Ajay said sternly, 'supported you and worked for you, because you promised clean politics, transparent governance and subsidies. You must deliver on what you promised.'

'Which politician delivered on his promises in this country?' Bharat demanded. 'Clean politics and transparency are good slogans, but doors of a government must be kept closed for the public. Secrecy is power, transparency is for the powerless. Free water and cheap electricity won the election, but I can't subsidize these for long. So I am already thinking of other impossible promises, just as a diversion.'

'You ought to be ashamed!'

Bharat chuckled. 'It got me elected!'

'And how will you explain to the voters why you failed?'

'I'll blame the central government for stalling my work; blame the local agencies for not cooperating with my policies; and, blame the private sector companies involved in public works.'

Ajay asked sardonically, 'Then you must have someone to blame for the suicide as well?'

'Of course. I blame the police, the media, the Opposition parties,' Bharat paused. 'They were all there but didn't help the poor man.'

'You were there too.'

'You want me to climb trees to rescue people?'

'You would have climbed that tree if it was required to win the election.'

'Are we done?' Bharat said angrily. 'I have a busy schedule today.'

'Aren't you worried what people may think, Bharat?' Ajay wondered. 'They had watched as you continued with your cold-blooded speech live on television news even as the man committed suicide.'

'I know, the visuals were brutal,' Bharat said pensively.

'Perhaps, I will apologize. That seems to work always.'

'What do you mean?'

'Politicians have never apologized for anything in this country, Ajay,' Bharat explained. 'People feel good to have an influential man apologize to them; it seems like an empowerment, as if I serve them and they are my masters. It's theatrical, costs me nothing and the people don't have to know if I mean the apology or not. It just makes them feel in charge.'

Ajay sounded distraught. 'Don't cheat the people Bharat, that's not the right way to power.'

'The right way to power is neither through the minds of the voters, nor through their hearts. It's through their pockets.' Then Bharat added, 'They will forgive me anything.'

Ajay didn't speak.

'I hope that answers you question. Now, let me leave . . .'

'I see no difference, Bharat,' Ajay told him tragically. 'No difference between you and any other politician in this country. I was wrong to think you loved the nation, you just love yourself.'

Bharat was patient. 'Next time, let's do this on phone. I'm tired of your disappointment with my success.'

'That's fine, Bharat,' Ajay commented sadly. 'Just don't let people seek the satisfaction of your failure.'

They listened as the men left and the tape ended. It began again a little while later with birds chirping in the background.

'This is the clue for Mira,' Sikander said in an optimistic voice.

'Why do you despair if you are a river? Others try a lifetime and die as ponds and puddles. Look up and choose the sky for

today, that's your destiny. Draw from the river at any point,
that's your origin. You will find me when you find yourself,
in that place you go to recover your faith.'

———

Dubey was upset with the tape. 'I don't believe this conversation
took place,' he shook his head. 'Absolutely not!'

'But Ashok . . .,' Bhaskar tried to reason.

'Don't try to convince me! I know Bharat and I simply cannot
believe he is capable of such heartlessness.'

That was expected. Dubey was a staunch supporter of Bharat
Party and an emotional follower of Bharat Kumar. It usually
coloured his judgment, which was why no one took him seriously
now.

Bhaskar was firm. 'If the story is confirmed, we will carry it.'

'Can't you see this is a conspiracy?' Dubey protested. 'The
traditional political parties, like PP and NP, are trying to discredit
Bharat Kumar and his revolution.'

'We will run it only after verification . . .'

'If we run this story, we would help all those with vested
interests against clean politics.'

'You heard the tape, Ashok. Is this clean politics?' Bhaskar
inquired.

Dubey couldn't answer.

Bhaskar glanced around the table for any further objections,
but there were none.

The discussion began about people's versions required for tape
verification and further questions that required answers. The new
recording was set to start another controversy, and after the last
two tapes, Bhaskar wanted to be prepared.

'The earlier tapes were posted on our website on the day of

publication,' Bhaskar mentioned. 'But this time, the tape will reach the channels much before we publish it. So, we need a media strategy.'

'Someone should represent us on television and articulate our coverage process,' Lina suggested. 'For instance, someone like Salat.'

Salat disagreed with her and said it had to be Mira. Everyone countered that Mira never allowed any publicity, a reason why even her photograph was not on the newspaper website unlike other assistant editors. Mira clarified that she had no objection if Salat spoke about the tapes on television. After a brief discussion, Salat was nominated for the job.

Lina then turned to Mira. 'I noticed there is something personal about every clue, Mira,' she remarked, intrigued. 'Does Sikander really want you to kill yourself?'

Mira cordially asked, 'Don't you?'

'Not always,' Lina said evenly, then repeated with great forbearance. 'Why are the clues so personal?'

Mira decided to answer this time. 'Sikander Bansi believes his clues will overwhelm me and make it impossible for me to find him.' She paused. 'He is right; I do get hurt by every clue. But with every clue, he gives himself away too. It's almost worth the pain.'

Everyone was quiet, astonished.

'Well, if you were to ask me, Lina,' Salat intervened to end the uncomfortable silence, 'about why Sikander sends such personal clues, I would say that the man is struggling to impress Mira with his poetry. And seems to know it won't be easy.'

There were chuckles around the table, and even Mira smiled. Putting aside his reservations, Dubey plunged into the preparations for the day. 'Let me call the reporters who covered Ratanbau's hunger strike to revisit their experiences. We should get the background stories from Patna.' Bhaskar approved the idea and they discussed the general deployment of reporters to cover all angles of the story.

Mira glanced out at the grey rain from the windows. Like the rest of the clues, the third clue of Sikander was designed to damage and kill her slowly from inside out. But he also made mistakes, and in the third one, the mistake he made was very special. In the first clue, he misconstrued her wish for death as an escape; she wished it as a destiny. In the second, he mistook that rain set her free from herself; rain returned her to herself. But the third clue proved that Sikander believed there was nothing left for him to know about her. Origin and destination—Sikander was convinced that the two things that defined her life would decide her death as well.

'Look up and choose the sky for today.'

It was not that easy, however. How does one find the perpetual source of meaning to everyday existence? Is there a physical junction where everything mundane intersected with something greater?

You will find me when you find yourself.

It was not that simple either. In his attempt to know her, Sikander had taken her apart and expected she would come together again on her own. But she had never been whole; there was no place, no thing and no one from where she could recover the parts that were lost. She had always been much less than the sum of her parts.

———

In a way, Delhi was where all the residual powers of fate were stored, preserved in the delicate layers of chance, folded along seams of time and perfumed with ancient dawns of autumn. Delhi never dissolved in blood or ink; didn't vapourise or disperse. Naturally, there would always be attempts to disprove any claims of such tangible immortality in this world, even though they may only strengthen it at the end. One such attempt was scheduled for that evening, as the television channels aired the third Parliament tape and announced the demise of the political class of Delhi. No political party—the ruling PP, the Opposition NP or even the revolutionary new BP—was fit to rule the nation. Delhi had failed, perhaps for the last time.

The noisy day crashed into the static evening like glass against concrete. Salat began his rounds of television studios, and the editorial department followed him on different news channels from the newsroom. The discussions were packed with experts who served aces at each other, and the anchors turned into umpires, counting points. It did not take long for everyone to discover the main problem with the tapes; the recordings did not pick sides and told the truth the way it was. The facts could not be manipulated to produce the truth of one's choice. No one liked this kind of truth, the kind that made no one happy.

This led to a frantic search for weaknesses in the news reports instead, and Salat defended it based on the extensive verification process that preceded it. Then the scrutiny reached the bylines and the question arose why know-reporters wrote stories that were based on hard evidence. Salat explained that Mira was the best political know-journalist in the country, and she was the reason why the tapes had come to the newspaper. She was also the only one who could trace down Sikander, as his clues were addressed to her. The question then was whether there was collusion between the newspaper and Sikander Bansi.

'Based on the tapes,' Salat answered, 'the PP government's business deals are being investigated, the NP government's role in riots is being inquired into and the BP's personal ethics are being questioned. Collusion should have benefitted someone, I can only see damage all around.'

Mira watched the discussion from the back of the newsroom; she knew Salat was not finished.

Responding to another question, Salat added, 'There will be more tapes, and there will be more allegations. We could blame the media for being partisan and forget about the charges, or we could find out if there is any truth in them. What we decide to do with the tapes will decide the kind of society we are.'

Lina exclaimed that it was a good answer. Almost everyone was there, Mira noticed—the newsdesk, the city reporters, the national correspondents, the sports desk, the photographers and Bhaskar. And everyone was falling in love with Salat, Lina was not the only one. Salat appeared good on television and adopted a strategic demeanour while defending the tapes. He was humble, ordinary, conciliatory and polite. He was judgmental but understanding, hurt but considerate, and helpless but resilient. He was like any average television audience, and as the anchors realized that, they stopped criticizing him and started to seek his opinion.

'I was shocked,' Salat said, when asked about his personal reaction to the tapes. 'Was this how the men and women who swear by our Constitution chosen? For how long has this been going on?'

The television anchor heard him sympathetically.

'Does nothing matter more than wealth?' Salat asked. 'Why do honour, truth and integrity matter more to me than to my nation's leaders? And why do we get hurt by what they have done?'

On another channel, he agreed that there may be different points of view about know-journalism, but that shouldn't minimize the importance of the tapes. 'We are not here to debate the tapes because we think they are false,' he said. 'We are here because we fear they may be true.'

'Now, let's be honest, Mr Vasudev,' the anchor said frankly. 'Did your newspaper doctor the tapes to make the stories sensational? You have to admit, surely, that this episode has made you famous.'

Salat nodded. 'Valid doubt, but we didn't have to tamper with the tapes. They were already sensational.'

'You are not answering my question,' the anchor pursued. 'Media houses are routinely blamed for pandering to popularity. Is this charge true in case of your newspaper?'

'Let's not underestimate the people,' Salat advised cordially. 'The average reader of a newspaper or viewer of your television channel knows why a story is getting played up or down. And can figure out who is telling the truth. That's what we did at our newspaper. We told the truth, and I'm glad we are now popular for that.'

The next channel got into the morality question. 'It's just a tape, Salat, obtained without the permission of the speakers. Is it ethical?'

'It's not just a tape,' Salat explained. 'It is evidence. The events mentioned in the tapes have been thoroughly investigated by every journalist in Delhi and outside. If there is an ethical question, it is this: shouldn't Sikander Bansi be praised for bringing all this out into the open?'

'Sikander Bansi could have gone missing anytime in the last four years and given your newspaper these tapes,' the journalist objected. 'Why now, at the very end of the government tenure and just ahead of the elections?'

'I can only speculate, and I see two reasons—political and personal,' Salat reflected. 'First, Sikander wants these facts to be made public just before the elections for the benefit of the voters. Secondly, well, it takes time and courage to destroy the career of one's father,' he paused, as if confused. 'Not sure which reason is personal and which political, though.'

The newsroom broke out in laughter. Leaning against the wall at the back, Mira smiled. Salat seemed to be that rare thing in journalism, a print journalist who was good on live television. The newsroom soon returned to work, every word written was backed by evidence and on-the-record statements. That evening, additionally, the legal team vetted their news reports in the upstairs conference room, and Munshi walked in and out at a feverish pace. As the deadline grew closer, there was silence of caution among the reporters who fine-tuned their stories before submission and once the deadline passed, the room was abuzz with conversations. Driving through the misty night, Mira reached home late and found Nalan waiting across the road from her gate. He leaned against a black car and read something on his cell phone. Puzzled, she stopped her car, and he glanced up. Mira stepped out as he crossed the road and greeted her.

'Sorry for this unscheduled meeting,' he said. 'I had something to ask you.'

'Which you couldn't on the phone?'

'Never.'

She frowned faintly.

'Bet you can't find it in my thoughts,' he challenged.

'No,' she admitted. 'They are too murky.'

He chuckled. 'What did you expect after a day spent doing politics?'

Mira smiled warily. This wasn't the first time he had successfully hidden his deeper thoughts from her. They were alone on the road, and the streetlights made his brilliant eyes sparkle. Even the night waited to know more.

'So, tell me,' he said, interested, 'why do you wear khadi all the time?'

Mira stared at him. 'That's what you wanted to know?'

'Yes.'

'At 11 p.m. on the road outside my house?'

He shrugged and waited.

'I guess,' she said tentatively, 'I like handspun cotton.'

'I see. Have you always worn khadi?'

'Since college.'

'Right,' he noted meditatively. 'Don't you want to follow the latest fashion?'

'I'm happy to set my own trend,' she answered. Mira was mystified that she still couldn't discern his thoughts. He improvised on so many levels that it was impossible for her to know what he would think next.

'Don't you wish for change?' He surveyed the road, as he asked, 'Try to wear something different?'

Mira decided to help him focus. 'I like predictability in some things.'

He glanced at her, curious. 'What things?'

'Like the white shirts,' she gestured to his shirt, 'every time we meet.'

Nalan regarded her in silence and Mira, amused, found his mind concentrate on her.

'I'm glad to know that,' he said finally, his brown eyes still unsure of her.

'This is what you couldn't talk about on the phone?' she repeated her earlier question now. 'Why I wear khadi?'

He smiled meaningfully. 'Doesn't seem a very safe conversation now, does it?'

Mira raised her eyebrows and he apologized smoothly.

'As you have probably noticed,' he explained, 'you are under constant surveillance by the people affected by the tapes. They wanted to confront you tonight and interrogate you about Sikander's whereabouts.' He spoke quietly. 'I got to know of their plans and offered to ask you myself on their behalf.'

'So you're asking me?' she inquired.

He met her eyes. 'No.'

'They're watching us?'

'Yes.'

'That's why you wouldn't call,' she inferred. 'My phone is being monitored.'

He nodded. 'Besides, on phone I couldn't have expressed adequately my feelings about the way you have interpreted my request to be careful, by driving home alone at midnight.'

'It's not midnight yet.' She couldn't help smiling. 'But what *are* your feelings about it?'

'Utter and complete dismay,' he said seriously. 'You have no sense of precaution.'

'I shall acquire some.'

'Please do.' He pointed to her car. 'Need help parking that . . . thing?'

'No, thanks.' She returned to her car. 'And I'm still paying instalments on this "thing". So be respectful.'

He held the door for her. 'Find Sikander fast, Mira, for your own good.'

Nalan wished her a good night, shut the door and crossed the road to his car. Mira watched him drive away, impressed with his strategy. He had managed to convey to her the dangers she faced without producing any evidence and without making it sound like a threat. Then as Nalan's car turned the corner, the headlights momentarily lit up the surveillance jeep parked in the darkness. Troubled, Mira recognized it to be the same vehicle that had followed her through the day and wondered whether she had, perhaps, read Nalan wrong.

TEN

On Tuesday, Mira requested Mahesh Bansi to let her visit Sikander's house once more. Salat had been exact with his intuitive conclusion; that was the only place she wasn't afraid of the clues. Fear stalled her mind if she studied them anywhere else as they plunged her deep within herself and choked her. His words were like devices of destiny, mechanical and not given to common mercies, unwinding her past with precision. The words did the same with his life when she heard them in his home.

The surveillance jeep halted at a discreet distance as Mira entered the Bansi residence at 10 o'clock that morning. As before, the aide kept the house keys on the table near the intercom, and left. She stood alone in the questioning silence and felt the house once again surround her. Then she smiled; Sikander shouldn't have sent that third clue. But how could he stop? He was enjoying himself too much.

As she replayed the clue on the laptop, Mira could sense his thoughts far more clearly than she had before. Things that couldn't be changed, he justified them for her, like her destiny. And yet he challenged her merely for fun, Mira noticed as she paced the study. There was laughter behind the voice in the recording, a little mocking laughter. He seemed to be entertained by her nature. . . no, that was not all. She stopped and listened keenly. There was compassion as well, and even affection, but there was also derision. He found her weaknesses pointless yet inevitable; thus, the solutions about origin and destination. And at the very back of the words, where they were still attached to thoughts? There was sympathy towards her need for answers.

The place you go to recover your faith.

That should have been Rishikesh, she thought. That was an easy place to find faith, as she had discovered many years ago.

It was difficult not to believe in God in Rishikesh. There was tangible evidence everywhere. Temples, ashrams, prayer halls and religious organizations. Then there was the river, flowing with conviction and belief. Rishikesh was not the place for doubt; it was where one discerned the grand design of God. I knew I should be grateful for the grace of God, for the way every need of my life was taken care of by the benevolence of a charitable man and for finding home in a sheltering institution like the orphanage. Gratitude, however, was no answer to curiosity. I believed in God, but I also questioned his creation. I loved God but I also hated his design. I knew we should emulate God, but also knew we never would.

The moments of great hope in my life were when new children were brought into the orphanage. I knew, like we all did, that these children had been saved from the misery of streets and possible death. Most new infants were girls, but there were some boys as well. They all looked the same, they all looked like us. I felt like believing in God's design at that point. Everything was made equal. Everyone had an equal chance of survival. Until one morning when the boys among the infants would be taken away, adopted by people eager for an heir. Perhaps these

desperate couples were poor and could not afford to raise a girl
along with a boy. Perhaps these helpless parents had a daughter
or two already, and wanted a son. Perhaps these realistic men
and women thought daughters were a liability, while a son would
be an asset. Perhaps these sensitive citizens knew they couldn't
protect a daughter in a nation that didn't want them and found
new ways of killing them. No, God had not created this world
equal, at least not for women. As I mentioned, it was difficult
not to believe in God in Rishikesh. But I have never been grateful
again, or curious. I was fourteen years old.

Mira closed her eyes, tired. This was yet another memory that
she had kept tightly sealed under the dark waters of her mind. The
clue handicapped her, blinded her, just as the other two clues had
done before. But there was a difference this time. Even Sikander
seemed blinded by her pain.

The place you go to recover your faith.

He should have known faith was just another one of her masks.
This mask was most worn out and frequently damaged. So the tools
of its repair had to be handy. The truth couldn't repair her faith, so
it had to be a lie—the only lie she allowed in her life. She opened
her eyes suddenly as she discovered that she was wrong. Sikander
wasn't blinded, he could see the lie she needed to keep her faith
alive. Dazzled by the solution, Mira held her breath as pieces
clicked into place in her head to complete the puzzle. Everything
made sense now, including that impatient instruction Sikander
had left for her with the doctor:

Don't waste time tracing my steps, just go home.

The day was cold as calculation, but the sky was the colour of wood smoke and promises. When the aide returned after half an hour to check, he couldn't find her. She was already gone.

———

The new Parliament tape had revealed yet another secret, this time about the ruthless politics of Bharat Kumar. His party's reaction to the publication of the third tape that morning had brought the city to a standstill. Even the first tape had led to protests; the PP spokespersons had defended their government, and the Opposition NP had demanded resignation of the ministers involved. The second tape too had generated heated reactions; the NP spokespersons had defended their president, and the PP leaders demanded his resignation. This was normal for Delhi, and life remained undisturbed on the streets. Normalcy, however, was not something that the Bharat Party believed in. And even though the third tape was actually a confession of his disregard towards the farmer suicide that took place at his public meeting, Bharat Kumar charged that it was sabotage of his revolution. Like most BP street protests, this too started at morning peak hour when Bharat Kumar's supporters blocked arterial roads and drained the city of life. Forced to take control of the situation by detaining the BP cadres, the police restored the traffic flow of office-goers.

After battling with the police live on television for a couple of hours, the supporters conceded to contain their protest to the road in front of Munshi's newspaper. The building gates withstood the charge of the protesters who demanded to meet Munshi. Then a BP spokesperson made an emotional media statement that the outrage was legitimate because Munshi's newspaper had published lies against their beloved leader. He said this 'river of rage' would only stop if Munshi personally apologized, failing which, that day's

newspaper wouldn't be allowed to publish. In response, Bhaskar
sent out a message that Munshi was not in office, and was in
Andhra Pradesh for a business meeting. The protesters called
Munshi a coward, who ran scared from the popular backlash.

'Come out Munshi and say "sorry"!' Their slogans could be
heard inside the building. 'Liar! Liar!'

Bharat Kumar expressed helplessness at the chaos unleashed
by his men in the city and stated it just showed how much people
loved him. As the protests continued, the staff of the newspaper
was forced to use side entrances to the building. In contrast to
the noise outside, the office was unruffled and peaceful, although
the morning meeting was held in the afternoon, presided over by
Bhaskar. Mira had called him early to say she would be away for
half a day. That had not affected anything; she was not required
for the follow-up stories about the tapes. Bhaskar treated BP
protests as he would any other news; one reporter covered the
BP demonstration at the building gates and another verified
the allegations made against Munshi. At 2 p.m., Bharat Kumar
held a press conference and, in a stunning statement, blamed
the police for the traffic crisis in the capital. He also advised the
media on how his news should be reported so that his supporters
were not upset.

'The media should exercise restraint and think before writing
against honest and upright politicians like me,' he suggested. 'We
are here to rid politics of corruption; that is the reason why the
entire corrupt establishment is targeting us. The newspaper report
is one such attempt.'

The newsroom television screens were tuned to the live coverage
of the press conference. The room was busy as usual. Those in
charge of foreign news, business news and sports were in a meeting
with Bhaskar. Lina's team compiled stories from other cities and
Dubey tracked developing stories with his reporters. Salat and

Lina returned from lunch and stopped before a television screen to watch. A questioner at the press conference asked Bharat Kumar, 'You had no problem when the same daily newspaper published other Parliament tapes against the PP and the NP. You had even hailed Munshi for his fearless journalism. And yet, you denounce his newspaper today for writing against you. Why such double standards?'

'The two situations don't compare!' Bharat declared. 'The earlier tapes against my opponents were true. This tape against me is not!'

The questioner pursued, 'But when the NP and the BP said the earlier tapes were a lie, you refused to believe them. Why should we believe you now?'

'I blame the media for being biased and not believing me,' he charged.

'According to the tape,' another journalist said, 'you confessed that you have fooled people in past and plan to do it again.'

'It's a conspiracy against me and my honest politics.'

'Why didn't you stop the farmer from committing suicide at your public meeting?'

'That wasn't my job; I blame the police.'

'Your colleague in the party, Ajay Sarkar, confirms the facts he had stated in the tape about Ratanbau's hunger strike.'

'Doesn't matter now.' Bharat Kumar added with satisfaction, 'I have expelled Ajay from the party this morning.'

A senior journalist stood up. 'This is cold-blooded ambition, Bharat, this is neither clean politics nor real revolution.'

Bharat was furious. 'Not real revolution?' he repeated scornfully. 'Revolutions require martyrs and heroes, and the leader decides who among his men will become what. The tape only reveals the price of opposing my clean politics.'

The next questions naturally were about why the BP cadres protested when the story wasn't wrong. Cornered, Bharat Kumar re-enacted theatrics based on popular themes of police brutality, political corruption, media apathy and corporate interference. Then he stormed out of the press conference.

'They should have asked him about his false promises,' Salat said to Lina, as the cameras chased Bharat into his office.

'You'll get your chance tonight on the news channels.'

'Can't wait,' he replied.

'I see that you enjoy this!' she smiled. 'Mira never cared for the publicity. She never cared for anything, except the know-reports and their subjects.'

He scanned other news on the television screens. 'You speak as if she is part of the past.'

'She may soon be,' Lina speculated, 'if she fails to solve Sikander's clues.'

'They are not easy clues to solve,' he defended. 'It's difficult for her to handle them. They affect her personally.'

'That's impossible!' Lina said, laughing briefly. 'It's nice of you to make excuses for another knower, Salat, but you are wrong. Nothing can affect Mira, she has no feelings.' Lina paused. 'Well, I won't miss her if she leaves; I have never really liked the way she plays around with one's thoughts.'

'What did she do?' Salat asked, as he surveyed the bustling newsroom around them. 'Read your next move?'

'Much worse. She read my boyfriend's next move.'

Salat glanced at her, interested. 'Don't tell me that didn't help.'

'It did. I escaped from that relationship in time.' Then she turned to him. 'Now I wish Mira had told me something else.'

'What's that?'

'Your next move.'

He smiled. 'I could tell you that.'

Lina nodded. 'You should.'

He watched as she walked away to her section of the newsroom, then turned to check Mira's cabin. It was dark, and the door was still shut. He knew she was away for half a day but she should have returned by then. Salat checked his watch, it was almost 3 p.m.

———

About the same time across the city, the landlord of an unauthorized building in the dark end of Sangam Vihar read the visiting card Mira had handed him. She explained that she represented a charitable educational trust that set up schools in the poorer parts of the city. As the dark end was one such part, the landlord had no reason to doubt her story, and especially when she said she would pay cash. She was interested in the room on the first floor of his house, and he was interested in skipping the paperwork. The room was built by illegally extending the unauthorized house in violation of various municipal rules, and the landlord didn't want to sign on anything that identified him as the owner of such a structure. She heard him in silence as he explained the additional charges, and he listened to her with patience as she said she required the room only for a month or two. When they entered the dusty room, the landlord apologized for his old furniture that was packed into it and promised to sort it out. Thus, with the formalities out of the way, and with half of one month's rent paid, Mira got the key to the room and exclusive access to the staircase. After the landlord left, Mira untangled a chair from the pile of furniture and dragged it to the covered balcony—the main reason why she had rented the room. She could covertly observe the entire street from there, and especially the ground floor house across the lane of the address 1221/11/OC.

Mira sat back in the chair and observed how the lane was still flooded from the brief rain that morning. She had the apple she carried in her bag, and traced back her steps that day to check for mistakes. She had been in Sikander's study when she had discovered what he had meant by the 'place' in the third clue. He knew exactly what it was; the place she visited to recover her faith was not a town or a location, but an object. Using that as a template, Mira searched for words in other clues that supported this conclusion. She could find none at first, and so eliminated words that did not fit in. The words 'ponds', and even the 'place' made another set that was just a diversion. She had to listen to the tapes several times to further distill his thoughts from his words. Finally, Mira isolated 'warrior' from the first clue and 'battlefield' from the second. There was only one way to ascertain if she was right, and she rushed out of his house and headed home. The surveillance jeep had kept up with her through the traffic. She smiled now, taking another bite of the apple. It had been one of the longest drives of her life. At home, in her living room, Mira had paused for an instant. To recover faith? She had thought he meant that deep place in the heart where the other self waited and used faith to complete circles that life left unfinished. But no.

He had meant something frustratingly tangible, something real and available. A picture on her wall! The warrior Arjuna in the battlefield, dispirited and disillusioned, struggling to recover his faith in his destiny as he understood the Bhagavadgita. Sikander must have stood before the picture in her living room, she realized. What did he want her to think? He wanted her to be disappointed, as she was, that the answer was right before her eyes. He must have known she didn't need faith, it was too fragile for her life. That picture was a gift from the only person she had ever trusted—her uncle who turned out to be a stranger. And yet, she had kept the picture because it reminded her of what faith had felt like. It helped to repair her masks.

It was easy to think like Sikander, he thought like her. She discovered the address taped to the back of the picture, it belonged to the house across that flooded lane. Mira had studied the clean tape and the small piece of paper, and wondered when Sikander might have had access to her home. She recalled the landlord saying he had let a cable technician into the house while she was away. She hadn't cared to ask what was repaired; the television worked fine. That was almost a month ago. Mira looked around her house; what else had Sikander touched? What else had he changed? Everything seemed different for a moment. What did he make of her home? The absence of furniture, the absence of food, the space and the silence?

Before she could visit the address, Mira had to get rid of the watchers who followed her. Thinking of a way, she drove to a crowded bazaar in South Delhi and left her car in the parking. Walking through the maze of shops, she finally managed to slip away from a different exit to reach the nearest metro station. She had arrived in the lane around noon and found the door of the ground floor house locked, as it was now. She had to keep a watch on that house, and a quick search revealed the room available for rent across the lane. Mira left the lane again to withdraw money from a distant ATM. On the way back, she got a few visiting cards made at a printer and hoped the landlord didn't call the phone number given on the card. It didn't exist.

Her cell phone buzzed and startled her. It was one more message from Salat, asking if she was safe. Ignoring it, she leaned forward in her chair pensively, and wondered what was that ground floor house about. The landlord was in his office when she went to meet him again and asked about the general profile of the residents of the lane. To her surprise, she found he owned several houses in that area, including the one across the lane. He said that a farmer named Gopi had rented that single room house many months ago. He had come to the city looking for work, but found the going tough. He was unable to keep jobs and was already on his third one. But as he could read and write, and was ready to work for low wages, Gopi was presently employed at the storage facility of the shopping mall on the main street. The landlord, however, didn't seem to give him more than another week at this new job and explained the man had a habit of vanishing for days, a reason why he was sacked from the earlier jobs. Mira nodded indifferently and moved on to ask about other neighbours.

The rainwater receded from the lane that evening just before people returned home from work. As the doors and windows were opened on neighbouring floors, Mira found her secret vantage point suddenly compromised. She shifted indoor and sat next to a window in another chair retrieved from the furniture pile disturbing its thick layer of dust, which rose up in protest. From the twilight of the room, Mira looked out at the homes that came alive as the day ended. A mother called for her children as she returned from work, and a father carried fruits for his family. There were smiles, laughter and plans for dinner. Mira leaned to the window and heard the sound of television, many channels playing at the same time. Younger children came out to play some more and found the failing light inadequate. They sat together on steps of houses and discovered stories to tell in the deepening shadows around them. The kitchens were all busy, there was something different about the smell of food cooked for one's own. It didn't smell fancy, it didn't even smell familiar; it just smelt good. A girl ran to the corner bookshop to buy something for school the next day. A boy darted to the grocer and returned with onions that his mother needed in the kitchen. Every house was lit by 7 p.m., except the one she was waiting for. Mira decided to call off her vigil.

Locking the room, she walked through the damp lane towards the main street to take the metro at Saket. She paused at the tea stall at the lane's entrance and decided to have a cup, which turned out to be a glass. It was dark and damp inside the shack, and she settled on a bench near the back to watch the traffic of the main street. It started to rain a slow, monsoon rain. The wet, dark road reflected the streetlights, and people were silhouettes as they rushed for cover. It was almost 8 p.m. The tea stall offered a sketchy dinner, but the tea never stopped. Those who returned from work mingled with those going out on night shifts to stop and chat over tea. She sipped her second glass, and wondered about her next step. It was a mystery why that address should be locked, or even belong to a farmer. Gopi might know something about Sikander, but if Gopi had vanished, as the landlord said he did periodically, then there may be no way left to find Sikander. Perhaps, it would take another day's watch to know for sure, she felt. The rain thrashed on the tin shed above as Mira prepared to leave. She paid the bill at the counter at the entrance and opened her umbrella in the porch light. From the darkness beyond, a man ran up to the tea stall and paused at the counter.

'I see that the roof has stopped leaking,' he said to the owner, laughing. 'No fun having tea here anymore.'

Mira froze. She could recognize that voice anywhere.

'And I thought you came here because you liked me, Gopi,' the owner chided.

'Liked you better with a leaking roof, my friend,' Sikander remarked and walked in. 'Tea please.'

Mira held the umbrella tightly to stop her hands from trembling and restrained herself from looking. She had found Sikander, she told herself, thrilled. He stood just a few feet away! She desperately wanted to register the expression on his face if he saw her there; it would be worth remembering for a lifetime. But not yet, she resolved. She had to know how he did it. Sikander appeared to be so much like her that it almost felt like a lie; no one could understand her life so precisely. But if he did, it would prove to her for the first time that this world was worth living in, after all. She smiled at the thought and left the porch without glancing back into the restaurant.

Much later when she was on the metro, she realized that Sikander might have known she wouldn't make his whereabouts public, even if she discovered him. He might have known she would be compelled to learn about him and forced to share his secret. Mira was disconcerted; what gave her thoughts away? She was under pressure to find him, and even under surveillance. No one wanted more tapes to be published, and everyone wanted to settle a score with him. So, how could he be sure she wouldn't betray him? Was it because she was an orphan, too lonely to lose someone who pretended to care for her? Or as he had stood in her living room, there amid her empty house, he had discovered death was equal because she didn't live at all? When did Sikander know that she *couldn't* betray him?

Still lost in her thoughts, Mira recovered her car from the bazaar parking and drove home. She could see the surveillance jeep now with three watchers instead of two. Whatever his plans to manipulate her, she couldn't deny Sikander gave her the address also as a last resort to give him up if she was in danger. This was more than anyone had ever thought for her, she realized, overwhelmed. He was right, she decided as the headlights of traffic reflected in the faint tears of her eyes. This *was* the place to recover faith.

ELEVEN

The next morning was covered under a bright blanket of clouds that held back rain, as if expecting sunlight for ransom. Munshi was back in town and began the editorial meeting on a menacing note.

'I get the feeling that I am addressing a bunch of newcomers to this newspaper,' Munshi announced acidly, as he settled in his carefully arranged chair. 'I was away for one day and look what happened!'

Everyone knew what he referred to. The Bharat Party members had stayed outside the office the day before and made various threats, ranging from hunger strike to storming the building, to extract an apology from Munshi. It made the headlines, along with other news about the tapes. Being absent from the scene, Munshi seemed like a fugitive. And that was a first for him.

'This tells me that I should not leave Delhi,' Munshi concluded, tragically. 'I should probably not even leave this office. I should stay somewhere in this building. Perhaps, live in the basement to keep an eye on the printing process.' He remembered, 'Where on earth is Mira?'

There was nothing unusual that he searched for Mira, almost everyone did. There was an intense but new-found interest in know-reportage after the damage caused by the third tape. The threat of more tapes on their way helped everyone develop a sudden admiration for Mira's powers and curiosity about how she was tracing down Sikander. However, she was nowhere to be found that day, she did not answer her cell phone and no one in the office knew if she was on leave or would report to work. So, when Bhaskar said the newspaper had no comments in response to inquiries about Mira, he was not being coy. It was the truth.

He now tried to answer Munshi's question. 'Mira may be late for this meeting.'

'She told you that?'

'No,' Bhaskar spoke with an attitude of someone lighting a cigarette at a petrol pump. 'But she has never gone missing like this before, so I assume she will be here shortly.'

'If she is, Bhaskar,' Munshi said dangerously, 'then make sure she is never out of sight again!'

'Yes sir.'

'What do you mean "Yes sir"? If you can't keep track of your own journalists, then forget about tracking news!'

Bhaskar stayed silent.

Munshi glanced at others with his small black eyes shining in anger. 'I was at a meeting yesterday where no one carried cell phones and no one answered calls. They could afford that kind of peace and focus, because their deputies were efficient and could handle any crisis. But not me!' he thundered. 'It's clear that I did not belong in that meeting!'

No one breathed around that table.

Munshi collected himself with effort. 'Why were the BP members allowed to gather before the gate?'

Bhaskar cleared his throat. 'There was no notice. We were not prepared.'

'Not prepared?' Munshi repeated. 'They were gathering there, right in front of your eyes!'

'Yes sir,' Bhaskar said uneasily, 'That's why we shut the gates and used the side entrances . . .'

'I know,' Munshi said and added bitterly, 'and now the whole world knows what you did. That's what I am asking you, why did you do it?'

Bhaskar said, confused, 'It was the only thing we could do.'

'It was not!' Munshi exploded. 'You should have let them come in, dammit! You should have kept the bloody gates open!'

There was a stunned silence.

Salat recovered first. 'Kept them open?'

'Yes!' Munshi slammed the table. 'They would have damaged property and hopefully even burnt a few copies of the newspaper. They might have even refused to leave the building until one of us apologised. Think of the drama it could have been. Think of the free publicity this newspaper has lost!'

Bhaskar was still unsure, and his face showed it.

Salat asked Munshi, 'But what if they had prevented us from printing the newspaper last night?'

Munshi dismissed the argument. 'I can get this newspaper printed from half a dozen places in Delhi. You are missing the bigger picture.'

'No, I get it,' Salat said. 'The vandalism would have threatened the freedom of press, and we would have looked like the champions of it.'

'Exactly! Thank God we hired you,' Munshi said fervently. Then he glanced at Bhaskar again. 'Instead of using a good opportunity, you thought to save us from the mob. You are turning into a scared rabbit, Bhaskar!'

Bhaskar seemed ambivalent about that.

'Last evening for me was hell,' Munshi was pained. 'I emerged from my meeting just before dinner and discovered the news channels were full of BP's protest against our newspaper. We appeared guilty,' he lamented, 'and we could not even produce Mira as a face-saver.'

'We can make a statement today,' Bhaskar suggested. 'We can include a line or two from Mira to explain how she worked the case.'

'This is a good time to showcase know-reportage and how we pioneered it,' Dubey pointed out. 'We should have a story based on her past cases and the way she made this new branch of journalism credible.'

'It's just an aberration Ashok!' Lina objected.

'All that matters,' Bhaskar asserted, 'is that it has provided pathbreaking news to the readers.'

There was a knock on the conference room door and Mira entered. She apologised to Munshi for being late and settled in an empty chair at the table. When she finally glanced up, she found everyone looking at her and was intrigued particularly by Munshi's expression. He was livid.

'Where were you yesterday?'

'I was on leave,' she said.

Munshi searched for a way to hold that against her. Then he admitted, 'Well, at least I cannot blame you for what happened here yesterday. How about today?'

'I was busy working the clues,' she explained. 'As I have mentioned before, I am being watched, and it's sometimes difficult to keep to a regular schedule.' She paused. 'I may also need more days away from work.'

'What for?'

'I'd rather not say.'

'Then don't,' Munshi snapped. 'I don't want to know about things I don't have to deal with. Instead, tell us what have you discovered about the clues. How close are we to finding this mad man?'

'I can't be sure, sir,' Mira replied frankly. 'Sikander has been quite comprehensive about this disappearance. His cell phones are at his residence, and his email ID has not been accessed since the day he went missing.'

'Are you saying you can't find him?' Munshi asked impatiently.

'On the contrary, sir. I am saying no one else can find him, not even the police. The clues are the only way and they are addressed to me.'

'So?' he demanded. Mira could detect the question he didn't ask.

She answered it. 'Yes, we can afford to take our time and publish more tapes in the meanwhile.'

Munshi nodded. 'I am being asked rather frequently these days if I don't like living in Delhi. I think it's a threat, but we'll see. You take your time.'

Mira thanked him.

'There is another thing I am asked quite often,' he said. 'What is Sikander Bansi's motive behind making the tapes?'

Mira remembered Sikander's one-room house in the swampy lane and felt she was more certain about him now. 'To tell the world what takes place inside Parliament,' she answered Munshi.

'What about political motive?' Munshi asked intently. 'He doesn't want to fix his opponents? Smooth his way to power?'

'Perhaps he does,' Mira conceded. 'But I believe he is also teaching his father a lesson.'

'I know! That's another good reason to continue publishing the tapes. Never have I been able to do so much damage to someone by helping them,' he chuckled finally. 'I love it!'

Making quick use of the improved weather conditions in the room, Bhaskar steered the discussion to the fallout of the Bharat Party exposé. Dubey informed them that Ratanbau was ready to reveal the facts to the newspaper's Patna correspondent. And there was to be a special feature on Mira and why only a know-journalist could find Sikander Bansi.

———

Salat followed her downstairs to her cabin after the meeting.

'I called you eighteen times yesterday and left eleven text messages,' he said, incensed. 'Where were you, Mira?'

She noticed his anger and was brief. 'On leave.'

'Couldn't you call back or text?'

'Didn't have to.' She went to her desk and added 'There was no danger.'

'Really?' He raised his eyebrows. 'Here is a man who has researched your life with the penchant of a psychopath, you are under the surveillance of people who have been exposed by your stories and you tell me there was no danger?'

'You didn't have to worry.' She was curt. 'It was unnecessary.'

He frowned. 'Why?'

She shrugged. 'No one has to worry about me. Or call.'

'There *is* no one to worry about you,' he snapped back. 'Or call.'

Mira glanced at him, astonished. They were silent for an instant, and then upset with what he said, Salat stormed out of her room.

Later Mira walked into his cabin and found him sitting at his desk, looking guilty.

It was her first visit to his room, and she surveyed the papers everywhere—graphs, tables, and charts—even on the floor. Mira leaned against a wall and met his eyes questioningly.

'How I never refer to my family?' she asked. 'Is that what gave it away? How I don't talk of my home?'

He was uncomfortable. 'Sikander's clues.'

'Could've been misleading.'

'They were systematic,' he explained quietly. 'He targeted your weaknesses.'

'That was enough to tell you I was an orphan?'

'Not entirely,' Salat said, hesitant. 'There were some patterns about you as well; for instance, you constantly disbelieve and test people.'

'You do the same, even with your family,' she pointed out.

He thought about that. Then tentatively said, 'You also disregard relationships.'

'You make short-term mistakes just to escape loneliness,' she told him.

He was pensive. 'You think emotions weaken you,' he said cautiously.

'You listen to sad songs when you are drunk,' she remarked.

'Is this about you or me?' he demanded, hassled.

Mira waited in silence.

'Sikander chose you for your vulnerability, not just for your strengths,' Salat regarded her critically. 'You like him, Mira. Can't blame you if you do. He is a smart, good-looking man who has turned your life inside out.'

Mira didn't speak at once, then said, 'Wish it were that simple.'

He nodded in grim understanding.

'Hopefully,' Mira said, 'Sikander doesn't know that.'

'He doesn't?'

They were both silent, sure of the answer.

She finally said, 'That's not why I came here. I wanted to . . .'

'It's all right,' Salat interrupted. 'If it's about what happened before, I didn't mind it. Really.'

Mira patiently tried again. 'I need to . . .'

'No need to apologize,' he assured her. 'You were upset and said some things. That's fine.'

'Actually, I didn't . . .'

'Didn't mean what you said?' Salat nodded approvingly. 'Good to see you care for the feelings of others, Mira."

'I do,' she agreed dryly. 'Especially about Munshi's feelings for Bharat Kumar.'

He was puzzled.

'Munshi and Bharat Kumar have reached some understanding,' Mira told him. 'We are to explain to Bharat Kumar, much like we did in the case of Nuri, how we work this story.' Then added calmly, 'That's what I came to tell you!'

'Was it?' he asked, unperturbed. 'Well, then why didn't you say so?'

Mira tried to answer, then shook her head helplessly and left his room.

———

Unlike on the drive to Nuri's residence, they didn't discuss Munshi's tactics on the way to the BP office in Sarojini Nagar. There was no point; it was clear that Munshi made deals with people mentioned on the tapes after and not before the tapes were published. The baseline of ethics was getting obscured with all this cross-court play, but it was not altogether lost.

The afternoon was the same grey as the morning, without sunlight or rain. No anticipatory breeze opened a window in the blue; the sky was just a canopy of mirrors over a concrete city. Mira wondered, as Salat discussed corporate funding of political campaigns, that she had rarely talked with someone who knew the truth about her but was unaffected by it. Salat dealt with it routinely, as if it was something that had happened a long time ago to someone he barely knew. That, in a way, was right.

The BP office was situated in a government house originally

allotted to a BP supporter. It was prohibited to use such residences as offices, but this was Bharat Kumar's way of showing that he made the rules in his government. He was a middle-aged man with a look of enforced anger about him.

'Don't you want to end corruption in this country?' he interrogated them when they were seated. 'How could you write against me, the only man struggling to improve the system?'

'We believe,' Salat answered sincerely, 'that our stories strengthen that struggle.'

'What?' Bharat Kumar said, his face childish in rage. 'Who do you think you are speaking with?'

Prudently, they didn't answer that.

'I know exactly what you tried to do and you better make sure this never happens again,' he said in mock fury. 'You underestimate the power of my voice and my image. I ended the agitation against your newspaper as a favour to you guys. But if I demand that the newspaper never be published again,' he paused significantly, 'it won't be.'

'Nice to know that, Bharatji,' Mira commented. 'However, we are here to explain to you the manner in which we investigate the tapes before each publication . . .'

'No ma'am,' he interrupted, amused. 'You are here because I demanded an explanation from your editor.'

'Fine, then.' Mira refused to get provoked, as she continued, 'The tapes came to our newspaper because Sikander Bansi's clues can be deciphered only by a know-journalist like me. We did not ask for the tapes, and we don't know what the next tape may contain. The readers get to know as much as we do about the tapes in the very next edition of the newspaper. We don't alter the tapes in any way, and we don't report anything more than what is in the tapes . . .'

'I don't care what you did with other tapes,' he said, cutting her short. 'Just make sure you don't publish anything against me again.'

'Why not?' she asked fascinated. 'What's so special about you?'

'If I have to tell you,' he seethed, 'then you haven't learnt the lesson yet.'

She considered that. 'I get the same feeling about you, Bharatji.'

That made him lose his temper. 'The people will rise in revolt on my one gesture, ma'am,' he shouted, reaching the edge of the chair. 'You take a great risk by angering me. I am a leader of the common people. I am a saviour of the voiceless . . .'

'Let me,' Mira suggested helpfully, 'continue with the explanation. The way it works is that we get the tapes in the mail, which we then send to our newspaper offices in the relevant cities across the country. In this case, we sent the tape to Patna, where it was taken to Ratanbau for confirmation . . .'

'This is a conspiracy!' he declared darkly. 'You want me to fail because you are corrupt!'

'The verification process is all on record,' she proceeded, unfazed, 'and has been published along with each story and with every transcript of the tapes.'

'You want me to fail because you serve corporate interests!'

'I would recommend,' she spoke calmly, 'that you take a look at our process and suggest improvements to make it more effective and fair.'

'You want me to fail because you are against the revolution!' he charged, ominously.

'And now, if all your doubts are at rest,' Mira concluded amiably, 'we would like to thank you for your time and take your leave.'

'You are on the payrolls of my political opponents!'

They stood up. 'It was good talking to you.'

'No, wait!' He came to his feet quickly. 'You must promise that you won't publish anything against me again.'

Salat unhappily said, 'We can't publish anything against you.'

'That's good.' Bharat smiled, relieved. 'Then I promise we won't vandalize your office.'

'I meant,' Salat clarified, 'we can't publish anything against you because we don't have the next tape yet. If it turns out to be against you, we will publish it.' He added cheerfully, 'This I can promise.'

Bharat Kumar's small face once again stiffened in fury.

'However, as Mira mentioned,' Salat was conciliatory, 'we will know the contents of the next tape only when we get it, as will our readers, which includes you.'

'Make sure you send me a copy,' he instructed sternly. 'Your editor agreed to that.'

Salat and Mira were stumped. They had both forgotten that the deal had already been struck between Munshi and Bharat Kumar, just like it was before with Omkar Nuri and Mahesh Bansi.

They coldly wished him a good day and marched out.

———

Salat pointed out as he drove back to the office that they were being followed and Mira recognized the surveillance jeep. Salat felt that with every new tape, her delay in finding Sikander would worry more and more people. Mira knew that; it would also get further difficult for her to visit Sikander's lane. She pondered about how to go to that lane in the evening without being followed. She couldn't confide in Salat because he mistrusted Sikander and might expose him to protect her.

Deciding not to take her car out of the parking, where it had been the entire day, Mira left her office from one of the side exits at around 6 p.m. She took a bus to the nearest metro station and after changing lines, finally headed to Sangam Vihar. It was crowded, and the aisle was full, but there was not much chatter. The evening rush hour was quieter than other times. People were too exhausted at the end of the day. Their faces were clear and strong, as if they didn't want to give away their fatigue to strangers. But their shoes, they told another story; the day was etched on their shoes. Some had the thick dust of busy sidewalks, others had the fine dust of carpeted offices. Some were cheap and comfortable, others were expensive and difficult. Some were honest about failures and others were dishonest about success.

As the metro took the elevated path, Mira saw the crowded eight-lane roads below, four lanes for going home, four for leaving it. If she had a home, she would never leave it, never waste time on escapes. She would throw away her travelling shoes and just belong . . . be home.

Mira closed her eyes, and remembered the shoes she had once got as a gift.

How well must you know a person to gift them shoes? The size, the colour, the style, the heel, and finally, the look. Perhaps nothing packed so many clues about a person's character as shoes did. I got these beautiful shoes once, wine red brocade embellished with tiny beads. My room-mate in the college hostel had brought them for me from Punjab. They were beautiful, but a size small, so I managed to get my feet into them, but couldn't walk without wincing. Others couldn't see me suffer and suggested that I should give them away. But how could I? They were bought specially for me, unlike the random stuff we usually got from donations at the orphanage. I enjoyed this difference, the knowledge that someone had thought about me long enough, imagined how I would look when I wore them, imagined that I would be happy. So, I didn't give away the shoes and pretended that they had finally fit me. I wore them a few more times, even if they cut my feet. Finally, however, the physical pain overpowered the pain of their loss. With a heavy heart, I offered the shoes to the girl who stayed a few doors away in the hostel corridor. They fit her feet perfectly. They made her so happy that it almost felt like I wore the shoes myself, and this time, without the pain. It was almost my dream that had been fulfilled. That was a breakthrough for someone like me who didn't dream, because I couldn't think of myself in any place or any life, not even my own. I couldn't own things, I realized, because I knew nothing ever belonged to anyone. I couldn't desire things, like those shoes; I didn't see myself wearing them in the first place. I didn't dream for a better life, a better place; I had no idea what that would be like.

What the girl felt was not my kind of happiness, but it was close. It wasn't my kind of dream, but it was close. Since then, I began collecting things I could give away to be that close again, my halfway to happiness. I was seventeen years old.

The lane was settling in for the day when Mira reached it. All the houses across the street were alive except Sikander's room, which was still dark. As promised, the landlord had got her room cleaned and tastefully arranged his discarded furniture. The sinking couch, the shaky chairs and the stoic dining table stood questioningly when she walked in. Mira touched their clean surfaces, as if apologizing for the trouble, and switched off the single light blub. Once again, she sat in the darkness and watched the street merge with the main road in the distance. She followed people as they returned home, but no one reached Sikander's room. Then, around 8 p.m., a tall figure walked into the lane and, as he passed under a lamp post, the light fell on Sikander's face. Mira quickly moved to the balcony to observe him better. He walked slowly, unhurriedly. He wore a loose shirt and trousers, and carried a paper bag in his hand. He had his eyes lowered in thought and glanced up only when a motorcycle drove by. She couldn't see much of his face from that distance, except that his eyes reflected the lights before he lowered them again.

She pressed back into the shadows as Sikander opened the door of his room. From across the narrow lane, she could even hear the turn of the lock and the rustle of his rough shoes on the uneven floor. He switched on a light and opened the single window through which Mira could see the peeling paint on the walls and a wooden table with an empty plate, a glass and a water bottle. The packet he carried had dinner, which he put on the plate. He then pushed a chair to the table, washed his hands, and sat down to eat. From her post in the balcony, she could see him only partially. He wore no rings, his wristwatch was cheap, and his shirt was folded till the elbows. There was nothing noteworthy about him, except the way he evenly placed the napkin, and neatly finished his food using plastic cutlery. His behavior wasn't just habit, which changed when he was alone and there was no one to see. It was discipline. And pride.

After washing, he placed the cutlery and plates in the same spot on the table as before. Then he set his room in order, and as he moved around, she caught the first clear glimpse of his face. Sikander looked just as the doctor had described him; his dark hair was long, his cheeks gaunt, his beard days old, his eyes fatigued. He didn't merely wear the disguise, she realized, surprised. He brought it to life.

She couldn't leave, couldn't look away from the square, lighted window in the night. And after two more hours, around 11 p.m., the light went out and the window remained open. It took a while for Mira to move. Her body was frozen where she had been sitting for hours on the balcony floor. Returning to her room, she settled in the dark on the sinking couch and thought about the life he lead with such punishing accuracy. Sikander did not pretend to be Gopi. He was Gopi—one of the millions who came to Delhi to be rescued from the poverty of their villages. He didn't allow himself anything that Gopi wouldn't have got. He too didn't have any money, any place to go and any job that lasted. He didn't just borrow the suffering; he immersed himself in it and lived it, one day at a time. She couldn't help admiring his strength, his decision and his silence. No one knew he was there in that lane—no cameras, no media and no opinion makers. No one was ever in that dark room to see how men like Gopi lived in Delhi. And no one was there for Sikander either.

TWELVE

That Thursday morning Salat was surprised when he entered the conference room at 11 a.m. for the editorial meeting. Everyone was already there, everyone except Munshi. Bhaskar fixed the volume on his computer and played the fourth tape that was received in the morning post. This recording too began with Sikander stating the date, time and place, but his voice was unusually low.

'Today is 13 July, and the time is 4 p.m. I am in the Parliament canteen to have tea. At the next table are three men: Anand Mohan, president of the All Rights Party, and its MP, Dwakaranath—alias Don—and Fernandes, a senior official of the People's Crime Bureau or PCB.'

There were sounds as the equipment was suitably arranged to record the voices from across the other table.

A relaxed voice said: This is the last place we should be seen talking.

A much-ruffled voice replied: Yes, Anand bhai, but I am afraid I may be arrested. At least here in Parliament, there are permissions to be obtained, and I'll get time to escape.

Anand Mohan: Good to see you quoting rules, Dwaraka, but you will have to go home sometime.

Dwarakanath: Perhaps, I will leave when it's dark.

Anand Mohan: (chuckling) Tell him, Fernandes, that it's not such a crisis.

Fernandes: It is not, sir. We are yet to issue arrest warrants in your name.

Dwarakanath: But you will one day, won't you?

Fernandes: Yes, I am afraid so.

Dwarakanath: (desperate) This is all because PP made that stupid statement that criminals have no place in Parliament. What a cruel stand to take, especially when we are one of the allies in government! It stalled the ordinance that allowed people with criminal backgrounds to contest elections. Someone in the party even said the PP was ready to sacrifice power, but wouldn't issue that ordinance.

Anand Mohan: So what's bothering you? The PP did not say it would sacrifice the criminal. You are safe.

Dwarakanath: I hate that word! Don't tell me I am safe. Are you?

Anand Mohan: (quelling) Calm down now. The case against you is rape and murder. And yet, you are a third-term MP because of me. Try gratitude sometime.

Dwarakanath: I am grateful, Anand bhai. Don't get me wrong. But I was drunk that night. It was a mistake . . . Is it fair to hold it against me after ten years?

Anand Mohan: Yes, because you were not punished for it.

Dwarakanath: If you're going to talk about the law, then I'll have no option but to call Omkar Nuri. No, bhai . . . listen to me. Remember the witness I had kidnapped for you, the one who got killed? Or when you were caught at the airport with excess cash? Anyone else would value a commitment like mine. If I told Nuri all your secrets and asked for his help in return, I'm sure he would lend me an ear.

Anand Mohan: (amused) This is getting a little funny now!

Dwarakanath: (warning) Please don't provoke me, bhai. I am rattled enough by PP's stand, which has upturned all my plans. People have invested in me. They believed I will make them huge profits, and will be very upset if I get arrested. I cannot even return the investments. I don't even have the money here; it was way too much to be kept in this country.

Anand Mohan: (sighing) You have been in Delhi for fifteen years now, but have not learnt a thing about staying in power in the city. There is a solution to everything in Delhi, and everyone. Isn't that true, Fernandes?

Fernandes: Very true, sir. If I may, your friend here has been convicted, and will have to begin serving his life sentence shortly. If you remember sir, eight years ago when you had asked me to file the charge sheet against him, I had informed you that if he gets convicted, he would be finished. You had asked me to go ahead.

Dwarakanath: Bhai! You did *what*?

Anand Mohan: (quietly) Must have been necessary.

Fernandes: It was, sir. At that time, he refused to support the PP coalition and had threatened to join the Nuri coalition instead. I had asked if you would prefer a case of disproportionate assets, irregularity in an election or one of his old cases. You had said he should not be able to change camps easily and chose the murder and rape case.

Dwarakanath: (heartbroken) I always suspected it. Bhai, how could you . . .

Anand Mohan: Shut up, Dwaraka. Now, Fernandes, can it be undone?

Fernandes: Of course, sir. There were two witnesses to his crime, who were his close associates. I had to lodge false cases against the witnesses. That was how they deposed against him, even at the risk to their own lives. I could promise to withdraw the cases, it could make them change their statements.

Dwarakanath chuckled in relief.

Anand Mohan: (impressed) Remind me, Fernandes. What was it that you wanted?

Fernandes: To investigate the case of black money, sir, stashed abroad in Swiss banks.'

Anand Mohan: Done. And is the Reddy charge sheet ready?

Fernandes: Almost. We are charging him with criminal intimidation, fraud, forgery, etc. Unfortunately, he is an educated professional, not a criminal. So we had to look really hard for something against him.

Anand Mohan: Make it nonbailable please, I want him behind bars immediately. Now, about the ordinance, can you think of an argument in support of it? That criminals should be allowed to contest elections?

Fernandes: (contemplative) One could say that it was a Constitutional right, sir. Convicts could contest from behind bars and add a new vantage point to the mainstream discourse of the nation . . .

Anand Mohan: What! Have you been reading Parliament speeches?

Fernandes: (defensive) Yes sir, I was asked by the minister to prepare an answer for the debate on the difference between being a caged parrot and the lapdog of a government.

Anand Mohan: (after a pause) I don't see any difference.

However, can you please send me the points in favour of the ordinance? I plan to push it through. Don't email please.

Fernandes: Don't worry sir. Your mail is not being hacked by the Chinese anymore.

Anand Mohan: That's a relief! But . . . what have the Chinese got to do with my mail?

Fernandes: That is what we are trying to find out, sir, by hacking your mail.

Anand Mohan: (ironically) I see. I somehow prefer the Chinese.

They could hear people leave the tables and walk away. The tape ended there and restarted after some time. Birds in the background chirped busily as Sikander's easy voice said:

'This is the clue for Mira: Sleeping with the lights on at night won't help with the inner darkness. You can't see because it's too large, that of which you are a part. You are too close. Don't think of running away, instead, think of letting go. Be a cause that does not expect an effect. Pause the wheel of life, switch off the lights and close your eyes. I'll be waiting there for you.'

——————

Dubey was pensive. 'Sikander must be speaking metaphorically.'

'Of course he is speaking bloody metaphorically!' Bhaskar was unusually ruffled. He glanced at Mira, who was absorbed in the clue copied in her notebook.

'What does he mean, Mira, by "pause the wheel of life"? Why does he talk of death all the time?' he asked.

She shrugged. 'Because I think of death all the time.'

No one spoke for a moment.

Then Bhaskar declared, 'I'm beginning to see what he is doing. After defaming political parties, he is now demolishing the institutions of this country.' Then he reluctantly accepted, 'The PCB might have been misused for political purposes by ruling governments. But we have written about it and criticized it often. We have done enough; there is no need to publish this tape.'

'No need?' Dubey was intrigued.

'I am not comfortable with this tape,' Bhaskar announced. 'It attacks our institutions, and I don't like it. Investigating agencies like the PCB shouldn't be dragged into this controversy.'

'Not even when we have evidence?' Dubey was still perplexed. 'We published against politicians because we had similar evidence. Should we employ different yardsticks now?'

'I am not saying that,' Bhaskar argued. 'But these are senior policemen, Ashok. My father was a policeman and I have great respect for the force.'

'So do I. Does that mean we ignore evidence of corruption among the police?' Dubey inquired.

'Of course not! We can reveal the matter privately to the PCB and bring it to their notice,' Bhaskar suggested. 'We don't have to publish it and tarnish their image!'

'Then why didn't we just call the political parties and privately disclose what their party men were doing?' Dubey countered. 'Why did we publish the tapes against the politicians and tarnish *their* image?'

'That was about corrupt politicians. They deserve it.'

'Only politicians deserve it?'

There was sudden silence in the room.

Bhaskar was grave as he admitted, 'You're right.'

The dust settled quickly after that.

'As you all know,' Bhaskar addressed them, 'copies of the tapes have been already sent to the police and other agencies, along with Mahesh Bansi, Omkar Nuri and now, Bharat Kumar. By noon, I expect the first stories to start appearing on television.' He glanced at Salat and asked, 'Can you handle the news channels again today?'

Salat said he could.

The discussion moved forward to the various points on which versions from the PCB, the All Rights Party and the PP would be required for running the story in the morning edition. Mira heard them without comment. So many colleagues working on the story simplified her job, she could continue her own investigation and visit Sikander's place of work that day. She wanted to listen to him actually speak, not on tape, not on recordings, but in person. That's all she would need to really know him, and she couldn't wait.

———

Later, Mira walked out of the building to the parking lot, a little preoccupied with the new clue. Like the ones before, even this clue referred to the picture in her living room—Lord Krishna's advice to the warrior Arjuna, to believe and to let go. And like with every other clue, this one was also personal. It wasn't difficult to discover she left the lights on at night, a causal glance at her apartment windows could have revealed that. Mira wondered, instead, about what Sikander meant by the line:

I'll be waiting there for you.

Did he mean he waited for her to find the address? Or that he knew she had already found it?

'Slow down, for God's sake,' Salat called out and she turned around, startled. 'Where were you lost?' he asked. 'I have been calling your name!'

Mira apologized, and they stood talking. It was a bright day, the sunlight reflected off vehicles in the parking lot like white gold.

'The new clue must have upset you,' Salat said, 'but let me come along.'

Mira said worriedly, 'Come along where?'

Salat shielded his eyes from the light. 'Aren't you going to the Bansi residence? To work out this clue?'

'Not right now, no,' she replied hurriedly. 'I'm meeting someone . . . a friend.'

'Oh, I'm sorry. I didn't realize.'

She hesitated, it felt rotten lying to him. 'It came up suddenly. This friend. . .he is in town and called me.'

'Sure,' he said politely. 'We'll talk in the evening then, after I return from the studios.'

Mira thanked him and walked to the car, troubled deeply that Salat might detect her lie. But as soon as she started to drive, she forgot all about Salat. It had slipped her mind that the surveillance jeep now had three watchers. They could monitor her far more efficiently and pursue her through crowded buildings or market places. It meant she had to go to a place with limited access and strict security. It had to be a government office, she decided. Thinking up a few good questions, she used her cell phone to call a media spokesperson in one of the ministry offices and sought to see her immediately for a news story. She drove there sedately to give the surveillance jeep every chance to locate her in the traffic. As she had expected, none of the watchers followed her into the ministry building. The spokesperson for Tourism was helpful and Mira diligently wrote down the government data, which she had no intention of reporting. After the meeting, she left from another exit of the expansive building and took a bus to the nearest metro station.

In about half an hour, she was in Sangam Vihar and at the mall where Sikander worked. It had three levels, and, as she walked in through the main entrance, Mira immediately felt the risk of being seen. She needed a disguise, she realized. At a nearby clothes shop, she bought a discounted yellow dress that came with a long scarf and changed in one of the rest rooms. Wrapping the scarf round her head, Mira checked her reflection in the mirrors. She appeared different and fashionable, and as she checked the shops, merged easily with the lunch-hour shoppers and movie goers. Gentle music played in the background; some movie had just ended, and the audience lounged about. Sunlight poured in from the glass skylight and reflected in the pool on the ground floor. An-hour-long search revealed two things about the popular mall; every second shop sold clothes or cosmetics, and there was no sign of Sikander. Disappointed, Mira took a break and entered the single bookshop. Browsing through new arrivals, she resolved to follow Sikander the next day to know exactly where he worked. A door at the rear of the shop opened, and Mira glanced up at the sound. Sikander carried a ledger, and the man next to him wore a tag named 'Manager'. Startled, Mira turned away quickly and tugged the yellow scarf into place.

They walked past her, and she heard Sikander explain about the stocks to the manager. When they moved to the next aisle Mira glanced up cautiously. Sikander wore the shop uniform, black shirt and trousers. He noted down the manager's instructions, answered questions and explained about stocks in other locations of the bookshop in Delhi. As they walked away, she moved to the section on Astrology to get a better look. Sikander's disguise was complete and convincing. His large, dark eyes were intense and calm. He smiled politely at the manager's words as they walked through Business Management. She slipped into Philosophy aisle to listen to their conversation; Sikander was saying he made no excuse, but the senior man wasn't buying it. Sikander heard the reprimand respectfully, neither defensive nor angry. They moved away again, and she slipped into Self-Help and grabbed a book.

'I am aware of that, sir,' she heard Sikander say, his voice sincere and self-assured.

'I am not so sure, Gopi,' said the manager, perceptively. 'Start doing the shift at the counter. Deal with customers and sell books! I can't waste you as Storage in-charge.'

'But I like being Storage in-charge.'

'What's wrong with you?' The manager sounded impatient. 'Why would you turn down a promotion?'

Sikander didn't answer.

The Manager continued, 'You work ten hours in the heat and dust of the warehouse sheds, handle the labour and manage the deliveries. Instead, I want you to work in the front of the shop.' The manger was a little baffled. 'Just the air conditioning is worth saying a Yes, damn it!'

Sikander gently pointed out, 'I applied for the job of Storage in-charge, sir. If that job in unavailable, I will resign.'

There was a moment's silence.

'What is it, really?' There was a change in the manager's tone. 'I can see you are hiding something.'

'I'm not, sir.'

'We are yet to get your certificates, and we don't even have a valid ID from you.' The manager was stern. 'You do realize you will have to provide these documents before the end of the month.'

'I do.'

'Is that why you can't work at the front?' The manager was suspicious. 'Are you hiding something?'

Worried, Mira stole a glance at Sikander but he was as serene as before.

'I insist on an answer, Gopi.'

'The truth is, sir,' Sikander convincingly rueful, 'I'm not one of those impressively smart ones who can sell anything to anyone. That's just not me,' he said apologetically. 'I like to work in the background, amid people who make it all happen for those who enjoy the airconditioning.'

The manager frowned. 'What's that, an ideological stand?'

'Ideology is for the elite, sir.' Sikander's dark eyes were serious. 'What difference has it ever made to the poor?'

The manager surveyed him at length. 'Are you feeling all right today?'

'Just answering the question on why I don't want to work at the front of the shop, sir,' Sikander answered simply. Then added, 'I'm not hiding anything. I went through an identity check at the time of appointment, but if you want, you can run a recheck.'

'Won't be necessary,' the manger responded shortly. 'We had confirmed your address and that you don't have a police record. But we still need the other documents, Gopi. We have to be careful. We run a respectable book shop and crimes here are committed only between pages of a book.'

'Or by authors who can't write,' Sikander said quietly.

The manager laughed. They walked away chatting and left through the back door of the shop.

As she walked out, Mira realized why Gopi could not keep any job for long. Sooner or later he had to provide paperwork to prove his credentials, and he couldn't do that. So, the only way for him was to quit and find a new job. Besides, there was a compelling reason why Sikander didn't want to work at the front of the bookshop. The television news was full of stories about the missing MP. Although his photographs and footage were limited, and his disguise convincing, Sikander wasn't going to risk being recognized.

The mall's storage facilities were located in a lane behind the building. Several doors connected them to the mall, but none led outside the premises. The entire mall was secured by a single heavy gate that was always guarded. With a few hours left to return to the ministry building before the offices shut, Mira settled in at the café across the street to watch that gate. Around 3 p.m., Sikander emerged carrying a backpack. He was once again wearing his faded blue shirt and dark trousers, and was headed up the main street. The sun kept the skies clear, as if it expected skirmishes with rain clouds any second. It was so bright that she could follow Sikander at a safe distance and saw him enter an internet kiosk. That was where he must make the CDs of the recordings, she concluded, as he didn't carry any electronic gadgets of his own. As she waited for him, Mira decided she too must leave her cell phone in her car whenever she visited the lane in future. Sikander left the kiosk after half an hour and headed to the metro station. He changed lines twice, walked through the crowded lanes of Old Delhi and found an unassuming post office to mail a familiar brown envelope. She recognized that envelope in which she usually received the CDs.

When she was convinced he was headed back to Sangam Vihar, Mira left him and travelled towards the ministry building to recover her car from its parking. As the metro wound its way to the heart of Delhi, Mira heard Sikander's voice in her head again, formulating itself into a character. It wasn't just one of his many facades; Sikander could send her those personal clues because he *was* like her. That was the real reason why he chose her, the knower he knew as well as himself. No one could trace him down the conventional way. The only way to catch him was to think like him. Or her.

———

Back at the office that evening, Mira attended a meeting with Dubey to discuss an old copy of Dwarakanath's confession of his crime that a reporter had unearthed. Her cell phone rang, and she silenced it without checking. The meeting continued, and Mira agreed with the general assessment that the document could be published. They then discussed the contours of the reportage, and Mira suggested she could refer to the document in her main story for page one. There was a knock on the door and one of the assistants came in with an urgent message for Mira that was left at the reception. Everyone waited in silence, expecting him to deliver the message. The young man uncertainly surveyed the four faces as if weighing whether he should reveal the message, then shrugged and read out from a note:

'Tired of waiting for a reason to meet you. Please run into me by chance. Nalan.'

Mira stared at the assistant, stunned, and managed to thank him. Then she turned to her perplexed colleagues and assured them that the matter could wait till after the meeting. When the discussion finished after ten minutes, Mira angrily walked out to the reception on the ground floor. Nalan wasn't there at the busy entrance of the building, and she recalled his message *Run into me by chance*. Sensing his thoughts behind those words, Mira stormed out of the office towards the shopping area across the street. The clouds gathered above, and grumbled about the delay in the rain. Then a few drops fell on her shoulders, as if to test her reaction. It was difficult to miss Nalan even in a crowd, she thought infuriated, as she spotted him turning the pages of a magazine at a news kiosk. And it was not because of his usual good looks, the usual white shirt and dark jacket, or the usual silver pen that reflected the light usually. He would look special anywhere with those knowing brown eyes that smiled in a greeting.

'Fancy seeing you here!' he said, breezily. 'Don't you work somewhere nearby?'

'I do,' she said, and added witheringly, 'when I'm not dragged out of office by impertinent messages communicated publicly.'

He winced. 'You should've known better.'

'And you shouldn't have given your name!' She was indignant.

'I thought there might be others,' he explained.

Mira refused to understand. 'There were, a room full of other journalists.'

'Not what I meant,' he clarified, amused.

She demanded, 'Is this about another threat, like last time, in the guise of a warning?'

He didn't speak. Then turned a page of the magazine. 'Isn't this about protecting a man who you know is manipulating you?'

Her dark eyes were instantly guarded.

Nalan scanned the magazine. 'Or perhaps you slept at your desk yesterday, considering your car was in your office parking lot the entire night.'

She stared at him; she had forgotten all about that and was astonished he knew. It began to rain and enclosed them under the awning of the kiosk.

'Someone gave me a ride,' she replied evenly. 'I didn't need my car.'

'That's what I said,' he assured her. 'But I don't think they believed me. You are risking your life for a man who has put your life in danger, Mira. A man who didn't have the courage to fight this himself and is in hiding.'

'He had no choice, did he?' She reproached him. 'If men like you had known what he was up to, you would have ensured the tapes were never published. You would have forced him to surrender the truth.'

Nalan nodded sympathetically, and turned another page. 'But

then,' he noted indifferently, 'it's men like me who warn you, even when you think it's a threat. Because it's important for me that you are aware of the danger, and that you are prepared.'

He glanced at her. 'Still, I have to admit. There is an allure about the rebel that cannot be denied. But just for your information, there are no rebels in politics. There are only politicians.'

'That's not true,' she insisted, speaking above the sound of the rain around them. 'Sikander is not playing politics.'

He chuckled and kept the magazine back on the shelf. 'So, who do you think the tapes will help in the end? Me? Or the others named in the tapes? Or Sikander, the man being hailed as the new hope in Indian politics?'

Mira stayed silent uneasily. His words made sense.

Nalan's smile slowly faded as he met her indecisive eyes and his own turned earnest. 'I won't forgive Sikander for many things,' he told her, 'but most of all, I won't forgive him ever for leaving you in the middle of this storm.'

He regarded her, worried. 'You have to be careful, Mira,' he said intensely, 'promise me!'

Unsettled a little, Mira did and thanked him for his concern. She knew he had meant those words.

———

There was absolute silence in the newsroom that evening. Every eye was turned to the television screens mounted on the walls. Mira leaned to her cabin door to watch the news; the PCB had just released a statement that if the latest tape was authentic, action would be taken against the erring officer and also the All Rights Party chief Anand Mohan for manipulating evidence. This breaking news filled the screens and Mira returned to her desk to finish her report.

Almost an hour later, Salat came back from the studios and after briefing Bhaskar, met her. Mira surveyed him as he dropped weakly in the chair across her desk.

She observed, 'I see the limelight is making you sweat!'

'So is Dwarakanath,' he remarked, fatigued. 'For instance, he asked if we checked whether the conversation was meant just as a joke. I noted that only he could joke about a crime. Then he asked if Sikander played fair, why didn't he confront him with the tape that was recorded secretly? I said Sikander would have if everyone else played fair.'

'Good answers.'

'I am tired!' He rubbed his eyes. 'You know, our newspaper seems heroic doing the right thing, but we walk a fine line here. We absolve ourselves every time because the tapes don't spare anyone. The day we hold back a tape from publication, the day *we* spare someone, will be the last day of our glory.'

Mira nodded, she had realized that.

'The problem is, I will be left holding the bag.' Salat smiled cynically. 'I will have to defend our fall on television, and I will fail. Not Munshi.'

'That's the price of the ride you enjoy today.'

He agreed. Then said, 'Bhaskar says you filed a very good story today.'

'Just getting used to the tapes.'

'Or, Sikander.'

Mira was silent, taken aback.

'Oh, I forgot,' Salat corrected himself. 'You must have been too busy today to work the clues.'

'I was,' She recovered quickly. 'My friend was in Delhi only for a few hours.'

Salat assessed her. 'Someone special?'

She remained silent, unwilling to lie any further.

'What about Sikander then?'

Startled, Mira asked, 'What about him?'

'Surely you see that Sikander has written you four beautifully crafted love letters and announced them to the world.'

'*What!*' Mira was flustered.

'He asked you to die with him, hasn't he?' Salat raised his eyebrows. 'That's love; modern, urban, side-effect-to-anti-depressant kind of love.'

She smiled tensely.

'If you ask me, it's a little too upfront,' he said, thinking. 'I mean, you can't just ask a girl to die with you. You need to get to know each other first.'

Mira managed to laugh and dismiss him.

'No, Mira,' he argued, 'you have to like the fact that he spent time working out the details. Seems like a caring man!' He analysed. 'It's also nice that he didn't decide for you. How many men really leave it to the woman to choose how to die? That's very progressive, you must agree.'

Then he leaned forward keenly. 'But seriously, Mira. Here is a man who watched you and waited outside your house to know when you switch off the lights at night. Just the language of the clues shows how much he thinks about you.' He stopped smiling. 'He seems more real than that friend of yours today!'

Mira grimly met his eyes.

He nodded, as if he understood her silence, then abruptly stood up and angrily walked out of the room.

THIRTEEN

Mira had a sleepless night and came to office early on Friday. The empty newsroom seemed to still vibrate with last night's edition, like strings after a symphony. She stood at the windows and recalled the thought that had kept her awake—that Nalan might be right about Sikander's motives. It had rained all night as the monsoon reached its peak in Delhi. She watched the cement of the building indifferently receive the rain and channel it to the waiting drains. Whatever be his motive for the tapes, she could feel the truth of Sikander's thoughts for her. And yet, the fact that he knew she was an orphan changed everything. There was reason for her mistrust. She had known deception to lurk, waiting, in the cool shades of affection.

I had not noticed him before that day, before he told me at the college canteen that he really liked me. At first, it had meant nothing. My every effort was focused towards education and deciding on a career to support myself. If there was time left, as a habit I spent it learning about the thoughts and lives of strangers. So, I had no idea what to expect when we started seeing each other. It was simple at first and we met with friends on the campus. Then we went out alone to watch movies, to theatre, or to just have a cup of tea. I was drawn to his kindness, the nice words he had for me. I got addicted to his attention, his concern. This looked like the place I had been waiting for; I thought I could rest my soul a while in his gentle arms. And so, I told him about myself. He seemed pained by my fate and was sympathetic; he even talked of a rescue that I had never imagined I deserved. There was still a degree of disbelief in me, I had seen a bit of the world by then, and people like him didn't exist. I knew as an orphan I had no past and probably no future. But he said it was enough for him, and he meant it, I could tell. He said exactly what I always told myself, that I should be what I choose to be, destiny had no say in it. I understood, tentatively and vaguely, the meaning of love. I didn't have to search for proof, I found it in his eyes every time I looked. Until he invited me to his hostel room one evening and suggested that it was time we got to know each other better. I consented, I thought I was prepared. But I stopped despite myself and said I wanted to wait. He was hurt, but I told him it wasn't about him. He asked if I didn't trust him or his love for me. I said I could refuse even if he loved me, and even if I loved him. It had to be my choice too. He laughed at that word 'choice' and said it didn't suit me at all. He asked me what choice did I have in life? He reasoned that I had to accept whatever came my way. So, how could I refuse this?

Well, I did refuse and it was the end of that relationship. Although I was upset at my wrong assessment of the man, I was also grateful for the practical insights it gave me about the places I shouldn't rest my soul. It taught me the truth about love. I was twenty years old.

Overcome by the memory, Mira sat alone in the empty newsroom. The silence in the long hall was unnatural and eerie. Words could be weapons, even if they were cloaked in kindness. The lessons were hard earned and couldn't be forgotten; she couldn't trust the affection of anyone who knew she was an orphan. That's why she kept it a secret in the first place.

The phones started to ring at around 10 a.m. Callers gave information about press conferences, press statements and timings for photo-ops. The earliest calls to newspaper offices came from government departments, hospitals and the police, the first people to get to work in Delhi. Later came the calls from businesses, public relation firms and informal lobbyists, those who came in to work after a late night's work or play.

The staff brought rain up to the office door, dripping from umbrellas, raincoats, shoes and bags. The peace of a newsroom was always uncertain, as if it was due to some malfunction of a device that should have already exploded. The nature of silence had changed from that restless recalibration before to a suspended detonation now. Mira shut the door of her cabin and reached for the envelope in which Mahesh Bansi had provided samples of his son's bills and addresses. Vantage points, she thought, were important for her special powers to work. Like a street with a signpost in the corner that waited for birds and bystanders, or the shop window that changed the observers into the observed, or the traffic signal that kept the red longer than the green. Like the conversation she had overheard at Sikander's work place in the mall or his habits she recorded from her secret balcony. His bills showed Sikander preferred repetition in certain things and risk in others. They were mostly from a handful of shops, restaurants, theatres and spas. The bookshops didn't change and neither did the music shops. He drove jeeps and motorcycles, but owned three cars. He watched different movies with friends in theatres, different ones alone at home, he liked to party in clubs but preferred to drink alone at bars. His facades were his shields; he used them as a protection from the more abrasive materials of life. That's how he learnt to break through her masks.

Sikander's political career had been like a furnished apartment. He moved in immediately and could leave anytime without baggage. There were rites of passage he was exempted from and circles of trust he was born into. It was a given that he should shift to a visible, more urban constituency like Middle Delhi from the rural seat that he presently represented. Visibility was one of the burdens of his legacy; secrecy was another. And the Parliament tapes proved how much he wanted to rewrite that legacy, which predestined his life. This may have been an ingenious way to get the tapes out to the press and yet remain untouched by the impact, but that was not all. Nalan was right; the tapes would be the making of Sikander Bansi.

The newsroom was buzzing by now, every chair was busy and every computer alive. Even though she couldn't hear the noise in her closed cabin, looking through the glass, she perceived the constant ringing of the phones, the attempt to keep conversations low, the patience and forgiveness of mornings and the anticipation of a news day yet to be reported. It was almost as if she had imagined the peace before.

———

The PCB headquarters at Connaught Place was built of red brick and metal on some futuristic lines. Mira and Salat were escorted to a small conference room so clean it appeared guilty of hiding microphones and cameras. Even the green plant in the corner appeared dubious, and Salat walked up to examine it closely.

The fourth Parliament tape managed to provide evidence of something that had been speculated for a long time—that the PCB investigations were politically motivated and served whichever political party was in power. Soon after that morning's editorial meeting, Bhaskar had directed them to meet PCB Officer

Fernandes to dispel any notion of partisanship on the part of the newspaper and establish its innocence, if possible. Munshi had also reached an agreement with the PCB on how to deal with the fallout from the tape and wanted Mira and Salat to give the officer an opportunity to accept a face-saver.

Fernandes didn't look like he had any use for face-savers. He walked in for the meeting exactly on time, and after introducing himself, wished them curtly. He was neatly dressed, and from his close-cropped hair to the shining shoes, he was sharp and angry.

Salat briefly explained the reason behind the meeting and Munshi's instructions. He spoke about the newspaper's process of investigated the tapes and their verification. Even though it appeared like he already knew everything Salat told him, Fernandes politely thanked him at the end.

Then he glanced at Mira.

'As you might be aware, ma'am,' he said formally, 'I could be under suspension from the PCB pending inquiry following the recent Parliament tape. Even if I am found innocent at the end of the inquiry, it will remain part of my record to be mentioned every time I am considered for any position or promotion.'

Mira remained silent and hastened to perceive his thoughts. 'There is one thing, however, that could prevent the inquiry, and that is, if I can prove the newspaper had concocted the tapes with the help of Sikander Bansi,' he said steadily. 'All it would take is a confession from you.'

Mira wasn't surprised.

'I know,' Fernandes added kindly, 'you must be thinking why would you ever make such a confession as it would discredit the newspaper and destroy your career.'

She wasn't thinking that. He was. Mira waited.

'You must be aware,' his voice was toneless, 'that you are under surveillance of the government, political parties and also private agencies. A lot of people are interested to know the whereabouts of Sikander Bansi. Every moment of your day is being recorded and reported to higher authorities. I have studied your life, and I admire you, Ms Mouli.' He paused, his face devoid of expression. 'You are from a humble background, but have never done anything wrong to reach where you are today. You have only an uncle for a relative and have lived alone all your life. You take pride in your independence and never used the funds regularly sent by your uncle. Despite the obvious lack of guidance and affection, you haven't made many mistakes. You have an extraordinary gift, which could have made you famous, but you opted to remain unknown. Fame and wealth don't inspire you. You are driven by purpose. You seek larger meaning in life, a goal beyond your personal motives.'

Mira was speechless, impressed not only by his analysis but also by what he was about to say next.

'That, Ms Mouli,' Fernandes concluded, 'is the reason why we think you will never find Sikander Bansi, even if you could. You believe in his ideas and support his fight to expose corruption at the highest levels of our government. You have found your purpose, and you won't let it go easily.'

Salat glanced at Mira to check whether he should answer that.

She gathered herself. 'That's very good, Mr Fernandes. If the rest of the PCB is anything like you, the intelligence apparatus of our nation is in safe hands.'

Fernandes allowed himself to smile faintly.

'However,' she continued, 'I am committed to finding Sikander, as I assured his father. Now about the confession, unfortunately, I am not intimidated by the surveillance. In fact,' she pondered, 'I think the only man who needs to make a confession here is you!'

'How interesting!' Fernandes regarded her coldly. 'That's exactly what your editor, Mr Munshi, said to me this morning. To that, I answered that we have had him on our radar for almost a year now, and that the findings are hardly pretty. But just then,' he added absently, 'we recalled that some things should never be discussed on the phone. Instead, we will meet for dinner this weekend at the Gymkhana Club.'

Mira didn't know what to say.

'So you see, a confession from you will be appropriate,' Fernandes negotiated. 'As you are the one entrusted with finding Sikander, it won't be difficult to believe that you colluded with him. Such a confession is the only way to ensure that the case is closed.'

Salat objected. 'But it would be a false confession.'

'Please don't confuse confession with the truth, Mr Vasudev.'

'And what if she doesn't cooperate with your scheme?' Salat challenged him.

'Then the PCB will be forced to summon her for questioning as part of the inquiry into the allegations made in the tapes. But one never knows about such interrogations,' he noted menacingly. 'People have walked into this office thinking it would take an hour and left after serving fifteen years in jail.'

'That explains, Mr Fernandes,' Salat was contemptuous, 'why you are so effective with stitching up coalitions for political parties.'

But Fernandes was unfazed. 'Yes, I have been fortunate to have had many opportunities to try my skills.' Then he glanced at her. 'So what will be your choice? Confession or interrogation?'

Mira considered him evenly. 'You tell me. You are the expert about my life.'

He conclusively nodded. 'I was afraid of that, Ms Mouli. Unless you can find Sikander, you will have a tough time at the questioning.'

'You don't have to worry, Mr Fernandes.' She smiled. 'I won't refer to this conversation at the inquiry.'

Fernandes met her eyes steadily, then took their leave and left the meeting.

———

Salat didn't speak as Mira drove back to the office. It was 3 p.m., but the rain had continued at an even pace, as if making a point. She stopped the car at a signal, and watched as the surveillance jeep halted right behind them.

'That's new,' she remarked. 'Now they no longer want to be inconspicuous. They are right behind us.'

'Who are?' Salat asked absently.

'The watchers,' she answered, and Salat turned to look.

'There are now four of them instead of three. One for each tape, I guess.'

Salat abruptly opened the car door and stepped out into the rain. Surprised, Mira checked in the rear view mirror as he walked up to the jeep and tapped on the driver's window. They had a brief conversation as the other three men watched them with various degrees of incredulity. Salat was almost drenched when he returned and apologized for dripping rain on the seat. Mira waited in silence.

'I've had enough, Mira,' he spoke angrily. 'We are only doing our job and shouldn't be harassed like this. They think we can't do anything about it . . . I just wanted to show them that we could.'

Mira knew he resented Fernandes' threats at the interview. 'Come on, Salat. You put it perfectly when you asked me before,' she paused. 'This isn't your first time, is it?'

Salat smiled and recalled his words about negotiations with Nuri after the second tape.

'But I'm curious.' Mira chuckled. 'What did you say to the driver?'

'I invited him and his friends to ride with us,' Salat replied. 'I said it was the most logical thing to do as we were all headed to the same places. And they would be less anxious if they were in the same vehicle with us.'

'What did he say?' she asked, wondering.

Salat now laughed. 'The driver mentioned that his surveillance manual specifically prohibited sharing transportation with the subject. I pointed out that the PCB informed us that men working for different patrons were in that vehicle and that my invitation extended to them as well. They have promised to examine my offer,' he added hopefully, 'So let's wait and see.'

Mira looked away in disbelief and drove again as the signal changed.

They were silent for a second, then Salat said, 'Fernandes was right, wasn't he? You don't want to find Sikander, do you?'

She didn't respond, unsettled by his question.

'I know you, Mira,' he reminded her. 'Fernandes might have bought your answer that you are committed to find Sikander, but I didn't.'

Mira quietly said, 'That's the truth.'

'Then why are you not working on the clues anymore?' he inquired. 'Why have you not visited Bansi's residence again?'

She remained uneasily silent.

'There is just one answer to this,' he reminded her severely.

'You should not read too much into my way of working, Salat. It's neither precise nor predictable.'

Salat studied her. 'Where is Sikander Bansi?'

'For one thing,' she said testily, 'he is not at his residence!'

'Answer my question.'

Mira shook her head helplessly.

'You weren't bothered about the fourth clue, I could see,' he pursued, inexorably. 'You didn't meet any "friend" yesterday, I know. So where were you?'

This was inevitable, Mira thought as she drove the car in silence. She knew Salat would discover her lie.

When she didn't answer, Salat said, 'The tapes are worth the trouble, Mira. I see what you are doing. You can keep Sikander from being discovered so that the tapes continue to be published.'

He paused, worried. 'But just remember who you are dealing with. Sikander knows how you think and can lead you to do what he wants.'

Mira didn't tell him she already did what Sikander wanted.

———

They had to brief the legal team and Bhaskar about the meeting with Fernandes. Then they waited for the legal team to get back to them with advice. After that, following Salat's request, there was a special meeting about the surveillance on Mira, which ended with the conclusion that nothing could be done without evidence. Salat argued that the 'evidence' was sitting in the parking lot outside the building and they could submit a photograph as proof. Then that was debated. Mira sat through all and barely spoke a word. It occurred to her, as one meeting led to another, that she couldn't visit the lane that evening. She was free finally at 8 p.m., but she didn't feel like going home. She didn't feel like being alone amid the gathering doubts about Sikander. As Mira walked to her car, she decided to try the only escape there had ever been from her thoughts, the thoughts of others.

The café at Hauz Khas Village was crowded with people coming in from the inauguration of an art show at a nearby gallery. The scene was most creatively deceptive. Men and women were dressed in their best clothes, brandishing their best conduct. The surface was so dense that it almost appeared to be real. Also, Mira noticed from her corner table, there were no cracks in the veneer.

It was a well-rehearsed scene that had run successful seasons at other such theatres.

The painter was a young man with long hair and slow beer, who answered questions in a way that they led to more inquiries. There was a special table in the centre for special guests at the show. There sat a grey-haired patron/investor, a well-dressed gallery owner/businessman and a silent girl/girlfriend next to the artist's empty chair. She was still on her first glass of white wine and observed everything with her lovely eyes. The artist frequently came back to the table from his rounds of the room and always spoke to her before leaving again. And every time he left, she checked whether he went to the table at the back. A woman sat there sipping a lemonade, her blue dress the colour of sapphires in moonlight. She was gorgeous even when she didn't move, but when she raised her eyes to see where the artist was, she was devastatingly beautiful. Mira gave it five more minutes. That was fine; she would be finished with her tea by then. She also noticed, as she glanced around, that the four watchers who followed her were waiting outside the café. This wasn't normal, Mira was mystified.

The artist now moved in a less systematic way and returned to tables already visited. He was establishing an erratic flight path, which could later explain how he ended up at the woman's table at the back. But before that, he returned to the girl/girlfriend once more and shared a joke that made her smile. This was going according to her schedule, Mira thought, and once again checked the men in the lane. They watched her from outside; one of them smoked a cigarette. They were never together out of the surveillance vehicle at the same time, she recalled. They always left one man with the vehicle, as if she might make a run for it.

The artist drifted around a bit and finally reached the woman's table. Mira paid the bill and waited for just a moment longer. The future of that scene, and probably of the artist, depended on one decision of a person in that room in that instant. The most obvious person with that kind of power seemed to be the dazzling woman in blue or the wealthy grey-haired patron/investor, or the evidently successful gallery owner/businessman. But it was the girl/girlfriend, who kept down her glass of white wine, made polite excuses to the guests at her table and decisively walked out of the café.

It had taken ten minutes instead of five, Mira analysed, mainly because of the ineffective circumspection of the artist. It was of no use; the girl/girlfriend knew exactly where he was headed the entire time. Perhaps, there was a knower in everyone; it was just that not everyone was ready for the truth.

Mira left the café; it was a pleasant night with light rain and gentle breeze. The four men walked up to her, and one of them stepped forward.

'Ms Mouli,' he said swiftly, as if in a hurry, 'we need to talk.'

'At this hour?' she inquired. 'You know my schedule. Talk to me tomorrow at my office.'

Mira turned and walked towards the parking lot at the end of the lane. She could make out her car amid the drizzle. Most of the shops were shut for the day, and the lane was well lit but deserted, except for the watching mannequins in the shop windows. Music came in from an occasional open doorway of a restaurant. The first watcher followed her briskly, brushed past and blocked her way. She turned quickly to return to the café but was prevented by the others. There was silence as the situation became clear to her, and she finally faced the man. He wore an informal shirt and jeans, and seemed fond of silver rings; one was on his finger, one in his ear and another on his keys. He had to speak to her once more for her to sense his thoughts, so she said, 'I just told you that I don't want to talk now.'

'We need to ask you a few questions. That's all.' He was restive.

He had to finish this job and get somewhere in time. 'No need to be nervous,' he advised habitually.

Mira was alarmed as his thoughts flooded her mind. They wanted to give her a little demonstration of the dangers of further delay in finding Sikander.

'You know,' he stepped closer, 'you were supposed to look for someone.'

Mira stepped back and saw the other three men draw closer.

'I'm working on it.' She moved back further and stopped at the wall of a shop.

'How long will you take?' His silver shone in the light from the shop window beside her. The rain slowly drenched their clothes.

'I don't know.' She knew her answer didn't matter.

'You don't know?' he repeated, as if marvelling at her audacity.

He moved again, and she quickly said, 'You do realize that I'm the only one who can find Sikander?'

He didn't know that. He stopped, irked.

'I won't find him if I feel intimidated in any way,' she informed him calmly. 'I'll give up the case, I swear.'

The man impatiently glanced at his colleagues for advice. They shrugged. Irritated, he reached for Mira and viciously pushed her back. She crashed into the wall and fell down on the wet ground. Her shoulder was hurt, and she winced in pain.

'You won't give up the case and you will find this guy,' he said nastily. 'Don't play games with us!'

Mira glanced up, acting unfazed. 'Now I'm really upset and I'm not sure I want to find Sikander. Tell that to whoever sent you!'

That stopped him again, but he was also getting restless. He had expected this to be over by now. Mira held her breath as he reached for her again.

'There you are!' A familiar voice called from the road. 'Didn't you say dinner? What are you doing here? And who *are* these people?'

The man veered round, startled. Equally surprised, Mira stared as Nalan stepped out of his car into the falling rain. The man glanced at his colleagues asking, but they just turned and quietly walked back into the lane. The man moved away from Mira, but didn't leave the scene like his colleagues. Mira could detected he had further instructions to follow.

'Go ahead,' she said encouragingly, 'tell me what you were asked to convey.'

He stared at her, astonished, then glanced furtively at Nalan who stood nearby, waiting inquiringly.

Finally, the man said, 'Remember these questions. Someone will come to get your answers if you don't find Sikander soon. I'm warning you . . .'

'Try warning me!' Nalan invited him and briskly walked up.

The man rushed away into the lane and shouted back to her. 'You won't be lucky next time.'

'Why don't you come back, you little . . .' Nalan restrained himself.

Then he turned to her as she struggled to her feet and helped her lean against the wall. 'Are you hurt? Do you need to go to a hospital?'

'I'm fine. Just a few scratches,' she whispered and pushed his hand away. 'What are you doing here?'

'I was in the parking lot . . .'

'A little overplayed, wasn't it?' she was sarcastic. 'Saving me from thugs?'

He stared at her, shocked, his anxious face illuminated by the shop window.

Mira held her arm that hurt. 'I said too much yesterday, I knew. I shouldn't have told you I didn't trust you.'

Nalan was quietly outraged.

'Guess what,' she said defiantly, 'I still don't trust you. So try something different next time. Make me bleed a little, perhaps. That could help, but I don't promise . . .'

'And you read this in my thoughts?' he demanded harshly.

She didn't, of course; she could only read concern for her in his thoughts.

'Why don't you tell me what you really want to?' Nalan challenged her. 'That I had *sent* these men to hurt you.'

'You could have,' Mira accused him angrily. 'I know you can do anything to serve your ambition.'

He was stunned. His eyes were on fire as they met hers through the rain. 'Anything?' he repeated, furious. 'You are right, I can do anything! But do you know why?'

'Oh, let me guess!' she said scathingly. 'You were a poor kid who wanted the world, the common man who dreamt of making it big. It doesn't matter how you get there, does it?' Her incisive dark eyes reached deep into him. 'It only matters that you do.'

'Don't talk about things you don't know, Mira,' he warned her, tersely. 'What can you know about being a nobody? To be someone so small that you are almost invisible. That was until I made the first cut.' He paused with satisfaction. 'Then when it hurt them, they registered that I too existed in this world. That's how I learnt my politics, on the streets and by winning prize fights!'

Mira heard him in silence, his words were beginning to hurt her now and, somehow, so were his wounds.

'I struggle because I hate being owned, unlike other politicians! And I succeed because I'm unscrupulous!' He surveyed her with conceit. 'If that's not good enough for you, it's fine by me!'

Nalan picked up her bag from where it had fallen and strode back to his car. Furious, Mira stayed in the rain as his words echoed in her mind. Then her own words returned to question her. Wasn't she against Nalan only because he was ranged against Sikander?

Mira was undecided for a moment and observed the car that waited impatiently. Then she walked to it.

He drove them out of the lane in silence, his thoughts still simmering.

Mira glanced at him. 'So once again, why were you here?'

'To save you from the thugs I hired!' he told her bitterly.

Mira waited and his anger melted as he thought of her.

'I came round to your office earlier to meet you after work,' he explained finally. 'But you were about to drive away. So I followed and thought I'll catch up when you got home. Instead, you drove up here.'

'Then why didn't you join me in the café?' she wondered.

'I thought you might have come to meet someone,' he hesitated, 'like a date or something. I didn't want to get in the way. I was about to leave but had a few calls to return. That's what I was doing in my car in the parking when I saw those men attack you.'

He didn't ask but she still told him. 'I wanted to be around people tonight,' she confessed. 'Didn't want to go home yet, didn't want to be alone.'

Nalan spoke after a moment. 'Those are the worst mistakes, the ones we make to escape from ourselves.'

Mira was intrigued. She could detect his doubt and disbelief about his own feelings for her. But that didn't explain his vehement restraint not to let her know his thoughts; his determination was almost as strong as her caution. He didn't speak again throughout the drive and neither did she. When they reached her home, Nalan took her car keys and said his driver would bring it from the lane in the morning. Then he bid her a brief good night, forcing her to do the same, and drove away.

FOURTEEN

There was something about that Saturday morning that reminded Mira of Sikander. It was almost as if she missed the experience of watching him. The encounter the night before proved that she would have to make a choice very soon. She would have to either give him up or face the consequences for herself and her life. But before that, she had one last thing to do in that lane, she had to find the rest of the tapes. She had to ascertain if Sikander had the tapes with himself or he had a collaborator in this game. If he had the tapes, Sikander wouldn't risk keeping them on his person, and so she had to search his room. Mira finished the apple for breakfast and anxiously observed the jeep on the street from her living room window. Fernandes had claimed that the PCB recorded her every move. There were just two watchers that day, and they were new men, as if to ensure that she couldn't identify them from the attack last night. One of them went away to get a coffee, and the other man in a crisp blue shirt stayed behind the wheel. It was just 7.30 a.m. and far too early to go to office, but she had no choice. The jeep followed her closely all the way, she could even see the dark, cold eyes of the driver. At the office, the unprepared guard unlocked the newsroom and remarked worriedly that she had arrived one hour earlier than the day before. Mira explained that she would work in her cabin and requested that the cleaning crew not disturb her.

198

When he was gone, Mira took the stairs to the basement and left the building through a side exit that opened into a narrow lane. The air was still thick with the residue of rain and a ten-minute walk got her to the nearest metro station.

Sikander seemed to have already left for work by the time she reached the lane, and the single window of his room was shut. From her balcony, Mira scrutinised the door; it looked so much like her room door that she wondered if it had the same kind of lock. It wouldn't be surprising, considering the same landlord owned both the buildings and might have used the same locks. She waited for the courage to check and then, finally at 11 a.m., walked across the lane to Sikander's house. It felt the entire world watched her in silence, and at any moment, would point to her and start screaming *thief!* The sky was gloomy, the light was subdued, and she hoped she merged well in her grey khadi shirt and black trousers. It might all end up as a joke, she told herself just to stop her hands from trembling as she took out her room key and fixed it in the lock. The key might not even fit, she chuckled nervously. This was a stupid idea and she would be back in her balcony in no time. There was a click as she turned the key, and Mira held her breath, shocked. The door to Sikander's room was open.

Glancing hurriedly around the lane, she quickly stepped into the incomplete darkness and shut the door. Recalling Sikander reach for the light on the right side, she found the switch for a bulb hanging in the middle of the room. It was like any low-rent room with a single electrical point and no water. The walls were mouldy, the floor was cracked, the wood rotted and the taps were unused; there was a bucket of stored water in the corner. And yet, the room was neat; a few clothes were folded on a broken shelf, the table was set, and the bed was made.

Mira couldn't help recall Sikander's other home, the one where birds sang for him. It had also been neat, as if he was far too arrogant for such insignificant indiscipline. A travel bag in the corner was empty, and the backpack in the chair held just a pen, a notepad and a dozen brown envelopes for posting the tapes to her. But where did he keep the recordings? She desperately looked around. Even though she was sure Sikander would return only in the evening, she felt being chased and out of time.

Driven by panic, Mira once again rapidly assessed the room for chinks in its correctness, but found nothing. She took a moment to think; everyone needed things that reminded them who they really were. Not expensive acquisitions or prestigious trophies, but ordinary things that were available easily and possessed the power to orient life. Like, for instance, a brand of toothpaste, a kind of pen or a type of shirt—things that are portable identity of a person. And unlike the grand landmarks of life, these didn't have to be chased, protected or sacrificed for. Sikander had found such a thing in her home—the picture on her wall. It was nothing special, just one of the many common prints. Perhaps even her uncle hadn't thought much of it when he gifted it to her. But it was now her Bhagavadgita.

Mira calmed her mind to be able to focus, and after a moment, returned to the backpack. It was old, and its green canvas was faded to almost grey. The buckles were dull and the zippers were overworked. Mira smiled; she had found Sikander's portable identity. He would buy another one if this failed him, but there would always be a backpack in his life. She carefully went through it once again. It was empty except for the pen that was attached to the notepad, and the brown envelopes. She knew he wouldn't carry the tapes on his person; that would be too risky. Besides, he would leave the tapes for her to find, just as he had left the address. That was his contingency plan. Mira thoughtfully turned the empty pages of the notepad and examined the pen again. It was just an ordinary white pen made of plastic with a cap. She unscrewed the cap and discovered it was a normal ball point that wrote blue. Disappointed, she reached for the cap to cover the pen again, and then froze. Hidden inside the cap was a slim memory chip, lodged perfectly at the very back. It shone dully in the light of the bulb, and could be shaken lose with a few taps. Mira was still, as she held the cap in the palm of her hand. These were the rest of the tapes, she told herself, invaluable evidence of wrongdoings behind the closed doors of Parliament that had already plunged the political world into turmoil. Who knew what these new tapes contained? Or how it would all end? The fate of political leaders, the government and even the coming elections depended on these tapes.

Mira felt a surge of determination run through her, as she considered walking out of that dingy room with the tapes. She closed her fist over the cap; she could control the tapes herself, and write about them. She could prove wrong the allegations of collusion against her. Her fist tightened over the cap; these tapes would be free of Sikander's political motives. They would just be the truth, just a good story. Mira paused and tensely weighed the consequences. If it were known she had the tapes, her life would be in danger. She recalled the thoughts of the assailant from the night before; they would stop at nothing to get the tapes. As for writing about the tapes, she couldn't even be sure that Munshi would publish them. She opened her fist worried and helplessly studied the cap. She wouldn't be able to part with the tapes, protect them or publish them. It explained why Sikander lived in that seedy room in disguise and distanced himself even from his father. The cap felt heavy in her palm, heavy and hot, like a bullet. Making a decision, she returned the cap to the pen and clipped it to the notebook exactly as before. Then she replaced it in the same pocket of the backpack and kept it on the chair precisely as it was. Her sweaty fingers slipped as she locked the door and hurried back to her balcony. There she waited for Sikander to return and to see if he would find out that someone had been in his room.

Sikander was home at his usual time and Mira watched tensely as he entered the house. What would he do if he discovered that someone had gone through his things? After some time, he opened the window as he always did and had his dinner alone at the table. Then he settled for the night, switched off the lights and merged his room with the rest of the dark lane. Relieved, Mira slumped back on the floor of the balcony, exhausted. She would never ever do that again, Mira resolved, she simply didn't have the nerve to break into people's homes.

———

Not wanting to take further chances with her luck that evening, Mira headed directly home from office. The watchers, who had waited the entire day in the parking lot with her car, restively followed her now. To her surprise, the vigilance was scaled down the next day, a Sunday. There was just one watcher, a new man, and even he sauntered away often. She wasn't even followed as she went shopping for groceries and collected the dry cleaning. They seemed to be losing interest in her; she seemed to have tired them out. It made her wonder if she could see Sikander once more, observe him in yet one more situation. Then it got too tempting to resist when she found the watcher sound asleep early the following morning. Taking the precaution to leave her cell phone at home, she slipped out of her house unnoticed in the pre-dawn darkness.

Mira reached the lane just as the sun rose above the sleepy outline of houses in the lane. It was a shining, outdoor kind of day; the rain clouds were in their corner, as if waiting for the umpire's whistle. Sikander followed his Monday morning routine; he went to the corner shack for a cup of tea and read the newspapers sitting outside on the wooden benches next to the road. Then he returned to his room and got ready for the day. He appeared different in the mornings, she noticed; he had a resolved, rested look about him. Mira edged forward from her post at the back of the balcony and watched him as he locked the house. He walked to the mall in his typical, unhurried way, observing every little detail of what happened around him. He seemed interested in everything — the road, the people - as if he had a great big space within him, which he wanted to fill with new experiences. Mira wondered as she watched him from across the road if that's what helped him merge into the background. One couldn't describe him, except to say that he was ordinary. The sidewalk was filled with ordinary people, young men from distant places, who were slowly losing themselves to the city. They all walked to their places of work from neighbouring settlements to do jobs that didn't pay them enough, that didn't demand training, talent, mind, heart, soul, and that just required them to be alive. He would have never been found if she had not looked for him, Mira realized as he entered the guarded gates of the mall. Sikander didn't have to go far to disappear, he just had to merge in the dust under the feet of Delhi.

That evening, Mira was already at the tea stall for dinner when Sikander walked in. She had chosen her table carefully. It was at the front, and she sat with her back to the rest of the room. Her face, now covered with a dull brown scarf, was in the shadows. The only vacant table was in the corner, which she expected Sikander to take. But people at the next table invited him, and he joined them. They were his colleagues from the mall and seemed to have known Sikander from before.

'Nice to see you settling down, Gopi. Do you like this job better than the last one?' one of them asked, his voice was soft and barely audible.

'Yes,' Sikander chuckled. 'But it lacks the excitement of counting rotten cabbages at the day's end in a grocery store.'

'If you ask me, you were a fool to have left that job,' said the other man, his voice heavy. 'You got free groceries, man! What else do you need in life if the food is free?'

'Food is never free,' Sikander remarked. 'You always pay for it, one way or the other.'

The soft voice agreed. 'It's well known that the grocer leaves only spoilt supplies for his workers. You probably can't even eat the cabbages.'

'Well, you definitely can't eat the books,' the heavy voice countered.

'I am glad you think so, Ramesh,' Sikander sounded relieved. 'Now I can let you into the bookshop.'

'That's why you are alone, Gopi, you fool!' Ramesh retaliated. 'Forget the books and find yourself a woman.'

The soft voice was intrigued. 'Never asked you before, but are you married, Gopi? Do you have a family somewhere?'

'No Manoj,' Sikander was patient. 'I am not married. And how exactly did the conversation go from rotten cabbages to my life?'

'But there must be someone you care for,' Manoj pursued delicately. 'There always is, even if she doesn't know and even if she will never belong to you.'

'No, no, there is really no one.'

'Ah! You are lying,' Ramesh smacked the table loudly. 'I know that look, my friend. You are in love.'

'What nonsense!' Sikander dismissed him. 'I don't have time for love.'

'Why not?' Ramesh was offended. 'You are young. You might even look good, but I can't tell unless you clean up. You have a job, but for how long one doesn't know. You have a house, for which the rent is due for only a month. I mean, you are practically irresistible!' Ramesh declared. 'But if you want to lie to us because we are not important enough,' he paused theatrically, 'that's a different matter!'

'This is extortion,' Sikander laughed. 'I will have to imagine a woman for you now, is it?'

'Go ahead,' Ramesh urged. 'Imagination is the better part of love.'

'That's actually good, you moron.'

'I know things you don't, brother. I have been married twice.'

'Tell us, Gopi,' Manoj prompted politely. 'Tell us about someone you admire. It will take our minds off our lives and its difficulties.'

'And this chicken curry!'

'All right,' Sikander sighed. 'I guess I'll have to make up a little story to help you plod through dinner. I have never done this before, so you are both the first to know of my dream.'

'Start talking,' Ramesh instructed.

Sikander took a minute to organize his thoughts. 'Everything about the girl of my dreams would be not just perfect, but also interesting,' Sikander began. 'She will be intelligent, attractive and passionate about some profession or the other, I don't really care.' Then his voice softened. 'But there will be something special about her. She will have this unique gift, the gift to know people's thoughts by just listening to them speak.'

Someone at the next table choked while eating and they turned to check, but the woman had her back turned to them.

They waited for her to stop coughing. Then Ramesh said to Sikander, 'Now, who in his right mind would imagine something like that?' He protested. 'God forbid women were to know my thoughts!'

'That's not all,' Sikander told him. 'She will also be able to predict what you will do next.'

'Come on. That's hardly a gift! What, for instance, will any man do after dinner? Pick up a quarrel with the neighbour he doesn't like over something he doesn't want.'

'You are an animal, Ramesh,' Sikander informed him. 'Anyway, just try and imagine a woman who can feel your thoughts. Someone who will never misunderstand you and always trust you, because she knows you.'

'You are right,' Ramesh concluded gravely. 'This woman can only exist in your imagination.'

'And so,' Sikander continued, 'it would be natural that such a woman would be desired by other men. They would want her to be part of their life and their story. And she should have the choice, I would never take it away from her.'

'Forget about choice!' Ramesh was restless. 'Say some sweet things to her, gift her a few trinkets and get married, my boy, before someone else does.'

'No Ramesh,' Sikander reasoned soberly. 'A woman like that would be difficult to win over. That's part of her charm. Other men would have tried before, and she knows how to say no.'

'She sounds too stuffy, man!' Ramesh was troubled. 'Is there no one else, someone easy?'

'In my imagination,' Sikander clarified, 'it's just her.'

'Then damn your imagination!' Ramesh recommended. 'Can't you imagine someone simpler?'

'Haven't tried.'

'I feel,' Manoj reflected, 'such a woman is sure to like you, Gopi.'

'Not necessarily. There is no reason why she should like me.'

'You're being modest now,' Manoj told him kindly. 'You are honest, hard working and humble. Women like such things.'

'They also like food on the table!' Ramesh pointed out.

'She wouldn't care about such mundane things,' Sikander mentioned.

'Women never do in our dreams.'

Sikander agreed sadly.

'If it's not too impertinent,' Manoj hesitated, 'what would you say to her, if you met such a woman?'

'Well,' Sikander pondered, 'I can't think of anything to say to her. But perhaps I'll just ask if I could kiss her.'

A spoon clattered to the floor at the next table, and the attendant rushed to replace it.

'Now you're talking!' Ramesh approved. 'Tell me, how does it go in your imagination?'

'Not very well.' Sikander was melancholic. 'I get slapped.'

Ramesh said sportively, 'That wouldn't stop a man like you!'

'It does. You see, in my imagination, she loves me too.'

Manoj was happy, but Ramesh was earnest. 'You know you're lost, Gopi, don't you? I mean, you have no idea what's happening out there in the world. Girls like that don't exist!'

'They don't for idiots like you!' Sikander told him cordially.

'Really? So why don't we find out who is right?' Ramesh challenged. 'Take a day's leave from work and find such a girl tomorrow. Then I'll believe you.'

'Yes, but you see,' Sikander said, 'such a precious girl would be under constant vigil. She would get into trouble if I met her.'

'You're all talk, man.' Ramesh was disappointed. 'You'll never find a girl like that.'

'She might find me.'

'That's going too far!' Ramesh objected. 'Look at this dump we live in. You think a girl like that will come for a guy like you? It's crazy, just Bollywood crazy!'

'Some dreams do come true,' Sikander said hopefully. 'She will come to me, and perhaps, we will sit at the next table here and have dinner.'

A glass of water spilled at the next table, and the attendant hurried with a mop.

'Hate to break it to you brother,' Ramesh said with regret, 'but even if she did find you, you can't afford her dinner today.'

Sikander was repentant. 'Should have stuck to cabbages.'

'Told you.'

'That's a beautiful dream, Gopi,' Manoj complimented him. 'I hope it will come true some day for you.'

'It never will, Manoj,' Sikander chuckled. 'As Ramesh put it so eloquently, damn my imagination!'

They all laughed, and then it was others' turn to tell their stories. They didn't look up as the clumsy woman at the next table finished her dinner and left. They also didn't notice that her hands shook when she gathered her bag or when she held out the payment at the counter. Mira walked out in a daze and somehow made it to the nearest bus stop. That's where she discovered she was drenched; she never noticed that it had begun to rain.

It rained darkness that night, and everything seemed to be at various stages of invisibility. As Mira walked home, she wondered if the watchers in the jeep at the corner of the road could actually see her. Her mind was still preoccupied by Sikander's words, spoken in his liquid voice, thinking of her. She could sense the depth of his feelings for her, but she had no courage to go that deep yet. Unlocking the front door, she left the dripping umbrella in the corridor and entered her house. She was glad she had dinner, she thought, there was not a thing to eat in the kitchen. Then she saw the light in the living room and wondered if she had left it on. She walked in and froze; there were four strangers in her living room. Three men sat in the chairs, and the one standing was the driver of the surveillance jeep; she recognized those cold dark eyes. She had never seen the others before. One of them vacated a chair pointedly; there were no escape options. She sat down.

The bald man at her desk said, 'Apologies for this, Mira, I don't like surprises either.'

'Who are you?' She felt the question superfluous, but still asked it for the sake of balance.

'We can't give you names, but let me just say that each one here represents a different client hurt by the publication of the Parliament tapes,' he explained slowly. 'Four tapes, four men. Get it?'

Mira had already got that part. 'You are from the PCB?'

'No. But I will file my report for them. They are very keen to clean up their image after what you have done. Questioning you officially wouldn't have helped.' He added pleasantly, 'So, I am here to do it unofficially.'

Mira glanced at the bottle of water near the sink, an open shelf in the kitchen and the book next to one of the chairs. They had been waiting for some time. She had to listen to each of them speak before she could decide how to get out of this situation.

She began, 'How did you enter my house?'

'That's insulting,' the PCB man noted. 'Anyway, you should be more bothered about why we are here.'

'All right,' she conceded. 'Why are you here?'

'Because we know you have found Sikander Bansi.'

Mira couldn't help her expression of dismay.

'It's traditional to deny,' he reminded helpfully. 'But let's skip all that and move to the part where we get down to the business of threatening you with consequences if you don't tell us.'

Mira tested an idea. 'I could complain to the police.'

'And say what, my dear?' The PCB man said, 'We don't exist.'

'But you are wrong,' she tried. 'I don't know where Sikander is.'

The PCB man considered her patiently. 'Are you sure you want to go with that answer? We won't give up until we find him.'

Those were their instructions, she could discern his thoughts now. 'I can't help you,' she was apologetic. 'I am still working on the clues, and I don't know . . .'

'You think this is a joke?' The fat man in the other chair interrupted her. 'You think what you did to Bharat Kumar was a joke?'

He stood up suddenly and reached her. Mira gasped and made to get up from the chair, but he rudely pushed her down again.

'Listen to me carefully, woman,' he said maliciously. 'We know you have been missing for several days from your office and home. Where do you go? What do you do?'

'But . . . that may be none of your business,' she said, experimentally.

That was too much for Bharat's man. He grabbed her shoulders and pulled her out of the chair. 'We will beat you up and leave you for dead here. No one,' he promised darkly, 'absolutely no one will know how you got killed, and no one will be interested to find out. Every important person in the city is hunting for Sikander Bansi, Mira. They won't mind the methods we use to find him,' he said, and shook her shoulders hard as a sample.

Mira winced in pain. His fingers dug into her arm that was hurt from the other night. One of the two standing men intervened and politely restrained the fat man.

When she was seated again, the rescuer spoke to her. 'We know because you left your cell phone behind, Mira. Smart thing to do, but a bit too smart,' he told her regretfully. 'Just like when you published that tape against Nuri. We also know from your call records that you didn't answer calls, or make any, for long intervals in the last few days of this week. In other words,' Nuri's man paused, 'you have left your cell phone behind often to go somewhere. Where did you go?'

Mira was now shaken a little, both by their findings and their thoughts. She glanced up at Nuri's man, he had a friendly face. 'Is it a crime not to use my cell phone?'

'No. But then we are not the best people to define what strictly constitutes crime.'

'Oh.'

'Now please tell me,' he smiled. 'Where were you tonight?'

She smiled back. 'I was out for a walk.'

'In this weather?' he asked tolerantly.

'I like walking in the rain,' she revealed.

'For two hours?'

'I didn't notice the time. I was working the clues in my head.'

The man thoughtfully glanced at the PCB man. She could detect that he believed her, but Bharat's man didn't.

'How would you like your head smashed against that wall?' he inquired. 'Will that help you with the clues?'

Mira was fairly certain. 'I don't think so.'

The driver, who watched in silence, now said decisively, 'I think I will give it a try.'

He strode to her, and Mira pressed back in the chair, perceiving the violence of his thoughts. The driver regarded her scornfully. 'You thought I didn't see you in the morning today?'

Mira stared at him, as she understood that the slackening of the surveillance had been just a trick.

'You thought I was asleep, you little fool!' he sneered. 'We were giving you a long rope. We knew you would do something stupid if you thought we were not looking.'

'I didn't do anything stupid,' Mira protested, as she calmly registered his thoughts. She continued desperately, 'I don't know why you even watch me. I am not hiding anything.'

'We watch you because you made the fatal mistake of writing against Kim Sharma.' The driver reached out deliberately and held her hair. Mira gasped in surprise and pain. He said, 'I have wanted to do this for a very long time now. You, in your silly car, driving all over the city with your arrogant colleague.'

Others objected to this form of revenge for her driving preferences.

He pulled back her head roughly. 'Tell me what I want to know. Now!'

Mira winced in agony but something in what he had said earlier caught her attention. Her mind rapidly assessed if others would buy the story she fabricated. The man's grip on her hair tightened, and her eyes filled up in anguish.

'Please let me go,' she begged. 'I will tell you everything.'

'Good girl,' the man left her and glanced triumphantly at his colleagues. 'I was sure that would work. You have to know what kind of person responds to what type of force.' He was smug as he told them, 'It's almost a science.'

Mira felt her head ache fiercely. 'The truth is,' she said in a feeble voice, 'I have been seeing Salat for some time now.' She paused, discerning the immediate doubts in the minds of the four men. She resolved each as she explained, 'His family is against me. They even monitor our cell phones to ensure we are not in touch. So, we meet during office hours on some pretext.'

'Your colleague?' The PCB man repeated, a little incredulously. 'Salat Vasudev?'

Mira nodded, and then said tragically, 'But Salat's parents don't want their daughter-in-law to be a poor nobody from nowhere.'

Kim's man chuckled. 'They've got that right!'

Mira stayed silent, apparently hurt by the words.

Nuri's man glanced at him in reprimand. 'Don't have to talk to her like that. What if someone said that about your sister?'

'Why do you mention my sister here?'

'Calm down,' the PCB man said. 'You don't have a sister.'

'No reason why she can't be mentioned.'

'Refrain from referring to families,' Bharat's man said, vexed. 'Now where were we?'

After a moment's search, they returned to the point. 'So you were with Salat?' The PCB man asked, 'Anyone who can vouch for that?'

'Of course not!' Mira alarmed. 'The idea was that no one should be able to.'

'I'm telling you she is lying!' Bharat's man was on his feet again. 'Let me just crack open her skull and look for the right answers ...'

'Wait!' Nuri's man stopped him and turned to Mira. 'I agree that if you and Salat were escaping attention, it is unlikely that you would have any witnesses. But how about Salat? Can he corroborate your story?'

Mira knew they all wanted that. She had hoped that they would not call Salat from fear of exposure, but they didn't seem to care.

'Of course he can,' she said, confident. 'Call him if you want.'

Kim's man reached into his pocket for a notebook, which seemed to contain Salat's cell phone number. He dialed it from his phone and waited.

After a moment, he glanced at Mira accusingly. 'There is no answer.'

Mira shrugged. 'I can't help it. I mean, what can I do if ...'

'Call him from her number,' the PCB man suggested calmly.

Mira waited, worried. Salat wouldn't ignore a call from her. Kim's man took her cell phone from the desk and dialed Salat's number. He answered it immediately.

'Mr Vasudev?' Kim's man put the phone on the speaker.

'Who ... where is Mira? Who is this?'

'She's here. We have a question . . .'

'Is she safe?' Salat's concerned voice filled that silent room. 'Let me talk to her.'

'No, Mr Vasudev. You talk to me.'

'All right. I will,' he retorted, and Mira knew he understood there was something wrong. 'But what's with that gangster tone?' He chuckled, startling everyone. 'Is this a joke? Are we on reality television or something?'

'Just answer the question.' Kim's man struggled to stay focused. 'Were you with Mira today?'

Mira held her breath for the answer. She hoped Salat remembered his own words to her—she had no one who would worry. Or *call*.

'Of course I was with her today,' Salat said. 'Who is this? What kind of dumb question is that?'

Mira lowered her eyes in relief.

'You were with her, fine,' Kim's man spoke ominously. 'But at what time of the day?'

Mira wasn't bothered. She knew Salat would immediately know which answer would best fit the pattern.

'Just left her a short while ago,' Salat said easily. 'Hasn't she reached home? Are you from the police? Has something happened to her . . .?'

'Yes, she is home. No, I'm not from the police. Nothing has happened to . . . wait a minute, I will ask the questions.' Kim's man remembered, annoyed. 'Why were you with her today?'

'What do you mean?' Salat demanded.

'It's a simple question. Why were you with her and not with anyone else today? There must be girls your parents approve of.'

'But I don't approve of them.' Salat paused, suspicious. 'Why are you asking me all this? Have you been sent by my parents to spy on me?'

'Of course not!' Kim's man was offended, and the others smiled discreetly.

'Then get out of the way!' Salat was blunt. 'Let me talk to Mira!'

'Only after you answer one last question,' Kim's man said and added nastily, 'You get this wrong, and you will never speak to Mira again.'

'All right, but you must reconsider your style of talking,' Salat said, and added disapprovingly, 'Really doesn't suit your voice, you know. You have the potential for an urbane and sophisticated . . .'

'Will you please,' Kim's man said with immense patience, 'tell me about her cell phone?'

Mira still sat with her eyes lowered to her hands. She knew the others watched her but couldn't help stiffening at that question.

'You mean why she doesn't use it much? Doesn't answer calls or texts?' Salat asked.

'Yes. I find it strange.'

'You wouldn't, if you knew my parents! I mean, if they can't appreciate my emotions,' Salat said upset, 'I have no reason to respect their feelings either.'

'I know what you mean.' Kim's man was distracted for a moment. 'Didn't you try to explain to them?'

'Explain?' Salat was agitated. 'What can you explain to parents who keep track of our cell phones to see if we are in touch?'

That confirmed Mira's story, and the others in the room exchanged glances.

'I see what you mean.' Kim's man frowned. 'But you can't abandon your parents just because they are crazy. It's a given.'

'I know. But I also can't leave a girl who never answers her cell phone, just because it's a call from me. She is an angel!'

Mira uneasily glanced around to see if anyone got the sarcasm; no one did.

'Can I talk to her now?' Salat asked. 'Please.'

Kim's man gravely handed her the cell phone and sauntered away, lost in thought.

'Salat ...,' she put the phone off the speaker. 'These guys think I have found Sikander. They are in my home ...'

'I'm on my way,' Salat told her. 'So will be the police. Don't worry.'

The call ended, and Mira regarded the men as they prepared to leave. Kim's man shook his head at some thought, Nuri's man consulted about logistics with the PCB's man, and Bharat's man sat alone, despondent.

Mira wondered if she could prevent them from leaving her house for just another ten or twenty minutes more, until the police arrived. Then she reproached herself for her simple thinking; the police would never arrive while the men were still there. They wouldn't be that suicidal.

FIFTEEN

It was a little after 9 o'clock when Mira finally woke up on Tuesday morning. She sighed with relief. There was no headache, but she was still groggy from the pain medication. Mira closed her eyes again as memories of last night came to her like forms through winter fog. The four men had left soon after the phone conversation with Salat, and, as she expected, the police had arrived a little later. When she was done explaining, Sita Patnaik had checked her notes clinically.

'Let me get this straight. You were being watched by one of these four men for some days now.'

'Yes.'

'But you have no names.'

'No.'

'They told you they work for the People's Party, the National Party, the Bharat Party, the People's Crime Bureau and the individual known as Kim Sharma.'

'Yes.'

'But you have no evidence.'

'No.'

'They asked you about Sikander.'

'Yes.'

'Whom you haven't found.'

217

'No.'

'There is no evidence of a break in.'

'No.'

'No proof that they used force, like bruises or cuts.'

'No.'

'So,' Sita summarized, 'four unknown men working for unverifiable employers threatened you tonight by using unseen violence that left you unscathed. Correct?'

'Undoubtedly,' Mira confirmed.

'But not undeniably,' Sita countered.

Mira had been searching for ways, and words, to convince Sita when Salat had arrived. After that, things settled down rather quickly. He searched the house and found a medicine for her headache, corroborated the police complaint and sent Sita away. Then, having discovered milk in the refrigerator, he made Mira have a glass before she went to bed. She also remembered he had vaguely mentioned about not leaving her alone ever. . .

Mira slowly opened her eyes again, and this time, they were clear of all sleep. The house sounded empty, but she wasn't sure. There had been more people there during the last twelve hours than there had been in the last twelve months. She moved around, assuring herself, then stood in the living room reliving the cold fear she had felt last night. If it hadn't been for Salat, she wasn't sure how she could have escaped unhurt. Then she tentatively glanced out of the windows. The surveillance jeep was parked exactly where it used to be with the same watchers from last night and the same driver behind the wheel, the man who reported to Kim Sharma. It was as if they knew she could do nothing about them, nothing she could prove.

Mira stepped away from the window, intimidated, and got ready for the day. As she recalled the thoughts of the four men from last night, Mira was glad Sikander was in hiding. They were employed to stop him at any cost, and use of violence was a small price to pay to prevent Sikander from doing further damage. She picked up her bag to leave and hunted around for the front door keys. She was still searching when she heard the key turn in the lock. She froze in fear and then quickly reached for her cell phone to call Salat. The door opened, and Salat walked in to find Mira in the living room; her panic turned into surprise.

'Good. You are alive . . . awake, I mean awake,' he corrected hastily. 'Thought I would take a chance, so got you some breakfast. Sandwiches?'

Too relieved to speak, Mira nodded, and he went into the kitchen.

She hesitated. 'Thank you for helping me with that phone call, Salat. I don't remember if I thanked you last night.'

He checked the microwave. 'You did,' he remarked, 'about fifty times.'

'It was really good thinking!'

'Not really, it was just instinct. No one else in your life to worry or call, remember?' He smiled at her. 'Besides, as a journalist, I could spot leading questions, especially regarding my parents. It was easy.'

She smiled with him. 'You know it wasn't.'

He shrugged. 'Anyway, I just emailed Sita the picture of the surveillance jeep that's parked outside. I hope now the police will take our word seriously.'

Mira disagreed. 'That police complaint will never be lodged, whatever evidence we may have.'

'I'm not bothered about the complaint, Mira,' he said and placed the sandwiches in the microwave. 'I want the police to keep a watch; that may deter others from planning another assault like last night.'

'And you think the police will interfere with the business of PCB or any of the political parties?' Mira inquired. 'Sita Patnaik herself was investigating on behalf of Nuri. Remember?'

'Yes, I remember,' Salat said, upset. 'Look, I know it may be useless, but I have to do something to help you be safe. I can't forget that man on the phone last night or your voice . . . or that long drive here from my home.'

Mira was still, her dark eyes suddenly cautious.

Salat chuckled, apologetically. 'Clearly, I have had very little sleep. Do you have coffee here, by any chance?' He rifled through the cabinets. 'Or rather, do you know, by any chance, that you have coffee here?'

'Yes,' Mira said absently. 'There's Assam, Darjeeling, Green, Jasmine . . .'

'Thank you,' he said, amused. 'I spotted them last night, quite a collection of tea. Reminded me of Sikander's kitchen.'

He turned away to make tea, and Mira stood in silent desperation. He was just a friend helping her out in trouble. Why couldn't she let him be? Because he knew the truth about her, he knew she was an orphan! She didn't need his help, his concern. It would all turn out to be a lie, and she couldn't be disloyal to the lessons of her life.

'I see that you like to keep your kitchen neat and clear of any kind of food,' he was saying. 'But what do you generally eat? Anything that's visible and tangible?'

She interrupted him. 'Will you lock up the house when you leave?'

'Lock up the house?' Salat turned around. 'I thought we were having breakfast.'

Mira collected her bag from the living room and walked past him to the door.

'Why are you leaving?' he asked, worried. 'What happened?'

'I'll see you at the editorial meeting in office.' She opened the door, then paused. 'I had to ask for your help last night because I was unprepared,' she said, her dark eyes cold. 'Won't happen again.'

Salat was silent, his handsome face grim.

Mira waited until he understood.

Then said, 'Sorry about the sandwiches,' and left the house.

———

By 11 a.m. at the newspaper office that day, the next tape had reached Mira in her post. She handed over the recording to Bhaskar as always and walked to the conference room on the third floor for the morning meeting. She was ten minutes early and settled in a corner to think through what had happened the night before. The four watchers had been candid; they couldn't give up until they found Sikander. She feared what they might do if they found Sikander in that lane, unprotected and unknown to the rest of the world. Mira closed her eyes and tensely felt her forehead. She just hoped she was strong enough to protect Sikander. That's why she had to resolve the familiar fear she had felt last night after a very long time. It wasn't the fear of pain or death; it was a cold, unresponsive chill of knowing that she was absolutely and irrefutably alone. This wasn't the first time she had faced it, she told herself. Won't be the last, either.

> I never had to tell anyone every morning before leaving home what time I would return. I never had to call if I got delayed at work. I don't have people who visit me or call me to check if I was all right. It is an easy thing to notice, if you are looking for the signs. There are those who do, and they always find me. They don't go by the lie I have in my record that states I have an uncle. They don't go by records. They know I am all alone, not just in this world, but also deep in my heart.
>
> That was my last year at the university. The exam results

*were out, and students were moving out of hostels. I had to
find a job quickly, and I also had to look for a place to stay.
That night, I was walking back to the university, delayed from
my efforts, when I sensed I was being followed on the deserted
road. The gate of the university was still some distance away
when I felt them rushing towards me. Who were they? What
did they want from me? I didn't turn to find out, and ran to
the gate, shouting for the guard to help. Alerted, he came out
of his post as I reached the gate. We turned back to look at the
road. I was now concerned about the guard, he wasn't safe from
them either. They couldn't be defeated, those shadows, not by
other people anyway. The guard said he didn't see anyone, and
perhaps, that was just as well. I knew how strong they were,
I had grown up with them. They came every time I believed I
was truly alone. I have battled against them long and often.
But they don't surrender. That wasn't in their nature, because
it wasn't in mine.*

*I carry fear in me, fear of being alone, like people carry hope.
I preserve it on a high, inaccessible shelf, so that mere men can't
reach for it. Not unless they promise something better, like my
death. I realized I didn't care for anything less. I was twenty-
two years old.*

The door opened and startled her. Salat entered the conference
room and came up to sit in a nearby chair.

'I'm sorry, Mira,' he said, frankly. 'You're right.'

She blinked, surprised, 'About what?'

'I should've explained the reason I was back at your house in the
morning,' he said. 'After the story we made up yesterday, it would
have seemed very strange if I had not come to check on you. The
four men might have disbelieved us and returned to question you.'

Mira felt that was possible.

'I thought you would get it,' he said. 'That's why I didn't think it necessary to explain.'

'It wasn't important.'

'Wasn't it?' he asked quietly. 'I thought that's why you ran away.'

'I didn't run away!' Mira countered sharply. 'As I told you before, I just don't like anyone to be concerned for me.'

'Or was it because you would have had to explain where you were yesterday?' he was persistent.

'I don't have to tell you where I was,' she said, flustered. 'It's personal.'

'Like that friend you didn't meet the other day,' he reminded her. 'That kind of personal?'

Mira helplessly fell silent. Salat was offended because he could detect she kept the truth from him. She knew that very soon his mind would work out what it was. The staff came in to begin the chair ritual, indicating that Munshi would attend the meeting that day. He joined them a few minutes after 11 a.m. and nodded to Bhaskar, who played the fifth Parliament tape. Sikander's voice was the same, but Mira now felt anxious thinking of him in that narrow, dark corner of Delhi. He sounded very far from it indeed as he introduced the location of the recording:

It is 9 March and the time is 10.32 a.m. I am at the People's Party office in Parliament, where the meeting of the party's members of Parliament has just finished. I am walking up to the room of one of the deputy spokespersons, Lochan Reddy, an MP from a southern state. The corporate friend I will refer to in the following conversation doesn't exist and has been introduced just as an excuse (my apologies to Lochan).

There was silence for a few minutes.

'Hello, Sikander bhai!' A male voice called out. 'Coming to see me?'

'Yes Lochan.' Sikander chuckled. 'You look hassled, my friend.'

'What did you expect? Come in and sit down, and shut the door . . . thanks.' There was a pause. 'I mean . . .for God's sake, inform the MPs before deciding to divide their state. People are burning my effigies back in my constituency.'

'I thought the division was taking place on popular demand and had the backing of the people of the state,' Sikander countered. 'After all, over a million people attended that public rally recently in support of the division.'

'And another million attended the public rally that sought that the state should remain unified,' Lochan argued. 'This decision was not based on merit, Sikander. This was something else.'

'What do you mean?'

'It's a long story,' Lochan sighed, 'And I feel hopeless every time I think about it. Anyway, you tell me, how is your father? Do give him my regards.'

'I will, thank you.'

'What did you want to see me about? Is there anything I can do?'

'Well, yes,' Sikander hesitated, 'But don't mention this to my father. He doesn't understand the new fund-raising methods. He still believes in the old-style politics that if you work and deliver on your promises, people will elect you. He doesn't realize that it takes money, and not work, to make people *believe* that you have delivered on promises.'

'Or not delivered on them, yes,' Lochan agreed. 'The Opposition will convince voters about the inefficiency of our government and will win the coming elections. The new government will be equally inefficient, but no one will complain because no one would have spent on the campaign against the new government. Until the next elections!' He paused, helplessly. 'People will never get to know these deals.'

'Was the division of this state also a deal?'

'Everything is a deal in the running of this government,' Lochan reflected, cynically. 'The question is who has bid the highest.'

'That is what I wanted to see you about,' Sikander said. 'I have a friend, a corporate businessman, who has been a supporter and has contributed to my election. He seeks to invest in the state and wants the real picture from inside the party.'

'A businessman would know more about my party than the party men, Sikander,' Lochan felt. 'But here is what I know. The division of the state would have never happened if the PP had not refused privatization of natural resources and had not cracked down on militancy in the north of the state.'

'I don't understand.'

'Neither did I at first,' Lochan said sadly. 'Local PP leaders opposed major industrialists who wished to privatize natural resources in the state. Fearing an impact on lives of common people, politicians of my state including myself, opposed it.'

Sikander heard him in silence.

'The PP had curbed militant groups in parts of the state, and their movement was affected,' Lochan continued. 'Then, when resource privatization was stalled by PP, the demand for separate state was raised in the same parts, and was backed by industrialists. At first it was just as a warning to the local PP leaders to back-off, but when they didn't cooperate, it became a full-fledged war between the industrialists and the PP government. No democratic government can survive for long

against the unlimited funds of business interests. Then about
a year ago, our colleague in the PP, Nalan Malik, proposed
that the PP should support division of the state. Naturally,
this idea was immediately backed by the industrialists and the
process for the division began.' Lochan added dryly, 'This has
ensured that no local leader of the two states will ever have
the stature to oppose big business houses again.'

'That's unfair.'

'Yes, but who asks the real questions these days,
Sikander?' Lochan reflected, 'Did anyone ask who funded the
demonstrations in the state capital? Who paid for the travel
and food for thousands of people who were transported to
the cities to disrupt normal life? Who brought people to Delhi
to meet leaders and address the press here? Who started new
news channels to propagate the idea?'

Sikander heard him in silence.

Lochan was dejected. 'Nalan didn't have to do much.
The system was already in place. But he was exquisite with
his control of the events, the slow turning of the press,
the damning reports of think tanks and the tragic hunger
strikes.'

'All the democratic tools of legitimizing undemocratic
practices.'

'Well, they work. We don't want violent coups anymore,
we will settle for opinion polls instead.'

'What did Nalan get out of it?'

'He is the most trusted politician in the country for
businessmen today. His plan had ensured no industry suffered
a loss in the state's division, manoeuvred party politics and
government policy to suit the funders, and where required,
facilitated the exodus of investment, business, employment
to better destinations.' Lochan's voice was forlorn. 'My advice

to your friend, Sikander, is to forget about my state. It has been set back by a hundred years.'

'Won't history judge?'

'I doubt it,' Lochan sounded resigned. 'When people organize on the streets for personal gain, we have arrived at the end of history, my friend. What follows is various stages of the epilogue.'

'But you are the people's representative,' Sikander urged. 'Surely you can speak against what's happening?'

'There is a party whip that prevents politicians of the state from opposing the party decision. Besides,' Lochan asked, anguished, 'where will I be heard? Didn't you see how they passed the bill in Parliament for the division? Elected MPs of the state, who believed they owed their loyalty not to the party but the people, protested against the bill. The doors were sealed to them and others when the bill was passed.'

He paused. 'We forget to question the system at our own peril, Sikander.'

The ringing of the quorum bell interrupted them.

'I guess we should go in,' Sikander said.

Lochan refused. 'This is not the Parliament I want to be part of. I cannot occupy the same benches as people whose silence or support is up for sale. It weighs on my conscience that I couldn't even make my arguments before this House. I can no longer attend such a gathering.'

'Then let's leave,' Sikander suggested. 'This country is more than its Parliament.'

There was the sound of a door opening as they stepped into the corridor.

'You listen well for a politician, you know,' Lochan complimented. 'Listening to people is a habit that governments lose when they gain power and find when they lose power.'

'Then I hope I always have the power to listen,' Sikander replied.

Their voices merged with the crowd, and the recording ended. When it restarted, Sikander said:

'This is the clue for Mira: Layers of different lives obscure what you truly know. You know that you don't have to find me. You are never without me, and I, never without you. The masks we wear must be discarded because they are just masks. Let's not hide anymore, let the sunlight shine on that indestructible soul, which neither fire nor water can touch.'

———

'This is the second time Sikander Bansi has targetted Nalan Malik through the tapes,' Munshi observed and glanced around the table. 'Can this be seen as political vendetta?'

Bhaskar considered that. 'It can be, yes. But if the tape can be verified, then it won't matter.'

Munshi agreed. 'Get the confirmation from Lochan Reddy, and give Nalan Malik the opportunity to respond to each allegation made in the tape.'

'He doesn't talk to the press usually,' Dubey said, 'But I will try myself.'

Munshi was particular in his instructions. 'Let's be fair in our reporting of this story to both Sikander and Nalan. We can't let a story go because the source may have hidden motives. Truth has no motive; people do.'

'I suspect Lochan's motives,' Lina declared. 'He could have staged this with Sikander.'

Bhaskar objected. 'Until now, all of Sikander's tapes have proven to be genuine. The tapes have also been authenticated technically', he pointed out. 'No one can deny their existence.'

'All except the policeman in the Nuri tape,' Dubey mentioned with his usual diligence. 'He's dead.'

'That shouldn't have stopped you from getting his confirmation, Ashok,' Munshi remarked, amused, and then turned to Lina. 'You were saying?'

'What if Lochan and Sikander had a deal to tarnish the corporate businesses in the state?' Lina contended. 'We all know the amount of money that could have been spent on publicity of this kind.'

Munshi studied her shrewdly. 'That point can be made about every story we do,' he paused, 'and is usually made.'

'But I have personal knowledge that this tape is biased and untrue,' Lina insisted. 'The businessmen referred to in the tape have been friends of my family. They have always stood up for fair and just business practices. I don't believe this tape!'

There was a surprised silence in the room.

Salat hesitated, 'My apologies, Lina,' he said, 'but as you know, my family too is in business, and I have known such things to happen.'

'Perhaps, they do,' she accepted, pragmatically. 'But this tape could be an attempt to expose selective facts by rival companies.'

'That's how we get our stories, isn't it?' Bhaskar pointed out. 'Most of our sources are selectively against someone or something.'

Lina had to concede that. The discussion turned to the reportage of the tape and Mira agreed to the parts that she had to work on. She continued to write the main story. Her byline now attracted huge attention, especially because of the mystery that surrounded

Sikander's disappearance. The clues also gave tantalizing insights into her life, about which the readers had always been curious. All this, along with the controversial tapes, was doing wonders to the newspaper's circulation. Mira hoped Munshi never found out she had already discovered Sikander's whereabouts and didn't tell him. He could kill her with his bare hands!

'Now, about these clues, Mira,' Munshi said at the end. 'Very philosophical, but what do they mean?'

Mira was prepared. 'He refers to the Bhagavadgita.'

'The Gita!' he mused. 'I thought ordinary young men these days were not interested in the Gita.'

'He is not ordinary.'

'That's true,' Munshi agreed and added appreciatively, 'He has turned this city inside out, and that takes some doing. Everyone is looking over their shoulders, and there is a general fear of exposure. Everyone wants Sikander, Mira. You have to find him first and get his first interview,' Munshi stressed. 'That decisive moment must belong to this newspaper.'

'It will, sir,' Mira promised in a hollow voice.

Later, back in her cabin, Mira weakly slumped down in her chair. Munshi had been right; there was an equal chance that someone else might find Sikander. Delhi was a dangerously restive city, and it usually got what it wanted. Sikander's clues were now all in public domain and anyone could work out what they meant. All it took was a little research about her sketchy life, and one visit to her living room to connect the words to that picture on her wall. She just hoped that the four men last night had other things on their minds then to appreciate art inspired by Indian philosophy.

SIXTEEN

By that afternoon, two things became very clear. It was not going to rain that day, and Nalan Malik was not going to speak to Dubey. He stormed into Mira's cabin, looking upset, and slumped in a chair.

She was sympathetic. 'I sense that you have been dealing with Nalan's staff.'

Dubey nodded. 'That's a nasty bunch. First, they gave various excuses why Nalan was unavailable. Then, they diverted me to the party spokespersons for the official reaction to the tape. And when I persisted, they told me that Nalan will speak about the tape, but not to me!'

Mira waited, she knew what he meant.

'Nalan wants to speak with you!' Dubey said, exasperated. 'He could have revealed this three hours ago and spared me an ulcer!'

Mira was uneasy about meeting Nalan and tried to think of a way to refuse. She couldn't, however. She had to get Nalan's version for the newspaper, and she was sure Nalan must have known that when he asked for her. She didn't want to meet him. She felt guilty for her words on that night when he had rescued her. It should have helped that Salat would come along, but even he was unhappy with her. Dubey briefed them about the interview and the supporting statements that had already been recorded by reporters from Lochan and others.

They arrived ten minutes ahead of the appointment, and, as the waiting room next to Nalan's office was crowded, stood in the corridor outside. The PP headquarters on Sansad Marg was a sprawling building with pillared corridors that overlooked patches of a well-manicured lawn. The bright sun brought alive the insect world of the grass, and much like the lawn outside, the corridor was also a busy place. It was full of action, and crawled with visitors and party men who made the most of the election year. Door signs announced offices of a former commerce minister now in charge of coordination, a former Speaker in charge of publications and an ex-bureaucrat in charge of campaigns. They were appointed by Mahesh Bansi himself to rehabilitate them when they were either sacked from government or lost an election. The ex-commerce minister, wearing a saree the colour of a praying mantis, emerged from her office briefly to see off a visitor. The office assistants in their brown uniforms were everywhere like ants and made everything possible. The former bureaucrat had just arrived and walked briskly to his office, like a busy beetle headed for a lucrative crevice.

Then a visitor entered the corridor, and the food chain paused to assess him. He moved heavily like a caterpillar, the sunlight reflecting off the rings and the Rolex. The former Speaker, anxious as an aphid, received him quickly and hurried him away protectively. The canteen boy gathered the empty tea cups with the apparent disinterest of a fly on the wall and watched victors replacing the vanquished, who would be victors again; fiction replacing fact that would be fiction again. History was a mayfly moment that lived short and died young to be born again. And again.

When they entered his office, Nalan Malik came around the desk to greet them. He wore his usual white shirt and dark jacket with the party flag, and his brilliant eyes smiled at her, as if the past was forgotten.

'I asked to see you alone,' he said, then added without glancing at Salat, 'No offence meant, Mr Vasudev.'

'Salat and I work on the story together,' she explained. 'He is also a knower.'

Nalan now regarded Salat briefly before he turned to her again. 'Then promise me a few minutes to speak with you alone and off the record.'

She agreed uncomfortably, aware of Salat's surprise. Nalan invited them to sit in the sofas in the corner and went to his desk where an aide waited with some papers. It was a wood and steel desk on which files were neatly stacked on one side, a computer was on the other and a laptop was open in the middle. His chair was simple, and, unlike most offices, exactly the same as the chairs for the visitors. The walls had the required photographs of the present and past presidents of the party, important moments in history and the government. Nalan sent away the aide and returned to them.

'Let's begin.' He sat back and crossed his legs. 'I have made sure we have more time.'

Salat handed him a transcript of the tape and waited as he glanced through it. Then he switched on a tape recorder and briefly recounted what the new Parliament tape contained. Finally, he asked for Nalan's response.

Nalan pondered. 'It has been my endeavor to ensure that every decision I support benefits the common people of our nation. To those who don't like my decisions, I have only this to say: please think of those on whose behalf you stand in Parliament.'

The stock answer didn't surprise them, and Salat asked the

next question from his notebook. 'Was there corporate interest involved in the division of this state?'

'The PP has always had one and only one interest at heart—the public interest. Our history provides evidence of this, and I am certain that with Mr Mahesh Bansi as the president, the PP's values have only become stronger and more transparent.'

It was a routine answer again, and Salat made his questions more specific. 'Your party MP, Lochan Reddy, has alleged that you had helped organize support for the division of the state. What do you have to say?'

'I don't know why my friend Lochan said what he did, but I recommend that none of us underestimate the power of the people,' Nalan mentioned politely. 'No one can *organize* millions of people to support or oppose an idea. It is the idea that draws people to the streets, and I, for one, do not question people's judgment.'

Getting impatient with these evasive manoeuvres, Mira requested Salat if she could ask the next question. Nalan turned to her, his brown eyes formal.

'How much money was made in the division of the state, Mr Malik?'

He studied her evenly, then said, 'I believe that money will be spent by the government, and not made, in the division of the state. For instance, a whole lot of expenditure is envisaged for building infrastructure.'

'What are your views on the manner in which Sikander Bansi has recorded the tapes that expose what happens inside the corridors of power?'

'Reminds me of something I learnt in school,' Nalan told her. 'You may be a star, but you still have to do your homework.'

Mira inquired, 'That's your message for Sikander Bansi?'

'That's my message to every child going to school.'

He wasn't smiling, but his eyes were amused as they met hers.

Giving up on her attempt to get a personal comment from him, she asked Salat to continue. Mira sat back in her sofa, impressed by Nalan as he answered the questions. His composure was remarkable, even when Salat repeated the allegations made in the tape against him of collusion with industrialists. So was his focus. Every word Nalan used was carefully planned and placed. And every word did exactly what he wanted it to do.

The interview came to an end without Salat finding any conclusive answers. Nalan stood up to thank him and shake his hand. Just before leaving, Salat told her that he would be waiting right outside in the corridor.

When the door was shut, Nalan said, puzzled, 'I wonder what he meant by that.'

Mira closed her notebook. 'He is just being protective towards me.'

'Is he right?' Nalan sat down again. 'Do you need protection?'

'What do you think?'

'I think you do,' he said coolly, 'and I found out about the four men who visited your home yesterday.'

She wasn't surprised anymore that he kept track.

'This is the time to give up Sikander, Mira,' he said directly. 'I know he must have told you where he is; he cares for you too much not to.'

Mira didn't answer him.

'This is the second tape against me that Sikander has offered you,' Nalan mentioned placidly. 'You may still want to believe in him. You may still think he has no political motives, but I just wanted to inform you that if this story is published, it will be the last Parliament tape that your newspaper will ever print,' he said, and added softly, 'I shall see to it.'

Mira heard him silently. His thoughts were serene, as if he was meditating.

'Unfortunately,' he continued, 'that's the only way to keep you safe and also stop the damage being done by Sikander. We'll find him eventually, and hopefully, with your help.'

'Splendid!' she said sarcastically. 'You seem to either warn me or threaten me every time we meet.' She stood up to leave and he didn't stop her.

'That's strange,' he said, as he accompanied her to the door. 'All I ever want to do when we meet is make you smile.'

Mira glanced at him, surprised; she hadn't detected that line in his thoughts.

'See that as a threat or warning, Ms Mouli?' he asked seriously. She admitted, 'I'll have to wait and watch, sir.'

'In that case,' he held the door handle, 'let's meet off the record again tomorrow to find out for sure.'

Mira waited for him to open the door. 'I think I have had enough of meeting you briefly on roads.'

He laughed. 'Lunch then,' he invited her, 'at any place you like.'

'That's not what I meant.'

'Where do you generally eat?'

'You may not be able to afford it.'

He nodded. 'I usually can't.'

She glanced at the door that he held, as he waited for her answer.

'Fine then,' she said. 'Tomorrow, 1 p.m. My office canteen.'

'Now that,' he said, troubled, 'I really can't afford, Mira.'

'Thought so.'

'But I'll be there,' he said valiantly.

He opened the door for her and they were met with the waiting crowd of party men outside. As she walked away, Mira heard the aide call the next appointment and the door shut.

———

There was unusual activity around the fifth Parliament tape back at the office. The story developed fast with stunned reactions coming in from other political parties. The tape had already reached the television channels, which headlined it in the afternoon news. Mira briefed Bhaskar about the off-the-record meeting with Nalan and his threat that this would be the last tape they publish. Then, Munshi came down to the newsroom and declared that he would personally monitor every word written that day in the newspaper about the tape.

'This is the best tape so far. I have never had so many threatening phone calls about any story before,' he announced cheerfully. 'Let's ensure we don't provide a reason for the threats to come true. Check every word and every fact. And when you are done,' he directed, 'check once again!'

He was right. The story about the division of the state reached the top headlines and stayed there. Every political party joined the game and played to their own audience. The PP took the heat in a sporting manner, and blamed the media for concocting stories that were designed to hurt the party's chances in the elections. Salat, therefore, had his hands full that evening when he represented the newspaper in television studio discussions. Despite the evidence, no one found Nalan guilty or seemed to want to. Salat's defence of the newspaper was spirited and imaginative, but he was repeatedly attacked on the question why Sikander had not been found yet.

'There have been five clues, five tapes until now,' said an anchor, unusually upset. 'Why has Sikander not been found?'

'This is not scrabble, ma'am,' Salat retorted. 'These things take time.'

'And meanwhile, the tapes will continue to be published?' asked the PP spokesperson on the discussion panel.

'More reputations would be destroyed based on evidence given by a man who is himself absconding?' the anchor asked, almost taking it personally.

Salat calmly heard them out. 'It may sound crazy, but we journalists keep our promises both to our readers and our sources. The tapes are for readers, and Sikander is our source.'

His words were drowned in charges of collusion and political partisanship by the newspaper. The entire newsroom watched in enraged silence as the panelists alleged that the story against Nalan Malik was being published as part of a deal with his rivals. Lost in all the noise was Salat's explanation that the newspaper was neither singling out nor sparing any political leader, bureaucrat or corporate house.

'The tapes provide a glimpse into what happens behind closed doors of our Parliament where common people are not allowed,' Salat argued. 'The question that you, the viewers, should ask yourselves today is who keeps the doors closed, to exclude you from the crucial decisions about your lives, your nation? Are these the same people who want to prevent publication of these tapes by attacking me, a journalist from the newspaper that has exposed them? The answer is yes!'

Salat returned to the office at night and requested Mira for time to speak. She gestured to a chair, and he shut the door of the cabin. He wore a dark suit that day and a formal blue tie. He looked angry and good.

Mira smiled faintly. 'It was rough today, wasn't it?'

'It was,' he said shortly. 'I have wanted to speak to you about an issue for sometime now, and it can't wait any longer.' His sharp eyes examined her. 'Why do Sikander's clues refer to the Gita? Has it something to do with the picture in your house?'

Astonished, Mira couldn't speak.

He sternly inquired, 'When did you find out?'

Mira hesitated, saying, 'After the third clue.'

'Have you met him?'

'No. I watched him.' She told him about the lane.

'What is he like?'

'Complicated.'

'Like his clues?'

'The clues were easy. He wanted me to find him.' She added defensively, 'And give him up if I were in danger.'

Salat was still angry. 'So he has left it to you to decide until when the tapes can be published?'

'Yes.'

Salat frowned. 'You don't trust people who know the truth about you. Sikander does, so why do you trust him?'

Mira uneasily turned away. 'I don't . . .'

'No, please.' Salat dismissed her. 'Don't answer that. You can't!'

Mira responded sharply. 'What do you mean?'

'You would only lie, the way you have been lying to me,' he accused her. 'You like this game that Sikander plays, you want him to succeed, despite you!'

She stared at him, infuriated at his accuracy. 'Yes, I do!' she said severely. 'I suspect the charade of Sikander's perceptive clues, his uncanny understanding of the way I think. But I also want someone to know me that way, know me to my bones. Including all the parts that are vicious and vulnerable, all the parts that want to hurt and also bleed when I am hurt.'

She paused anguished and then said, 'He knew I would love this game and that's why I wouldn't betray him, because no one has ever come this close to me. Even as a lie!'

Salat heard her in silence, overwhelmed.

'That's why I didn't tell you that I found him,' she explained, 'I wanted Sikander for myself, just for a few days or a week, before I gave him up.' Mira stopped speaking as her voice faltered. She stood up and walked away from her desk. 'I wanted to know him the way he knows me, wanted to learn how to become another human being, as he had become me. I didn't want facts, knowing is not facts, it's truth.' She said forlorn, 'Facts have always hurt me, truth has rescued me. I was sure the truth would rescue me from Sikander.'

'But there was still time for that, I thought,' she leaned against the wall helplessly. 'I fit his plan perfectly—a lonely, single woman, suspicious of all affection. He chose pieces of my life when he put me together for himself. It wasn't the complete me, but I hoped he grew fond of his idea of me.' She glanced at Salat. 'This is too good to be true, isn't it? Tell me I'm deluded. Tell me there can be no such thing for me in this world!'

'I can't tell you that,' Salat said quietly. 'It would neither be truth nor fact.'

Mira remained silent, waiting.

'I'll keep this a secret,' he said, finally, 'but I hope you realize you have now chosen a side in this battle, Mira.' He cautioned her, 'It will hurt.'

She smiled. 'It'll be worth it.'

———

That night, Mira lay in bed listening to the rain trickle down the window panes like a relationship that had run its course. Not all endings were literal, just as not all beginnings were tangible. There was something personal about Sikander, something close that could only be detached with pain. There was something inevitable about Nalan, something necessary that had to be returned to her despite the pain. She wondered if she had become incapable of anything else but ending things. It was so difficult to seek anything more after a lifetime of practice.

Over the years in Delhi, I kept in touch with the orphanage
in Rishikesh and made an annual contribution of whatever
I managed to save from my own scholarships and tuitions.
I wanted it to be money that I had earned, I never touched
Raghunath's 'charity fund' in my bank if I could help it. Most of
my teachers were by now retired, but it didn't matter. I talked
to whoever was in charge. A few years ago, I made the usual
phone call to inform them about the cheque I had written for
the orphanage. The person at the other end thanked me, then
asked why I made the contribution. I said it was my way of
helping other children like me. The person concluded by the size
of the contribution, which was meagre, that I couldn't afford it.
A little offended, I pointed out that it should be more valuable
then. Besides, I said I would get a job soon and the contributions
would improve. The person explained that I didn't owe them
for their kindness. It was unconditional. How could that be? I
pondered later. I had to be grateful for everything I got, because I
didn't deserve even to be born. And then, as a girl, I must belong
to family, to society, to relationships, to parents, to brothers, to
husband, to children and to everyone, but myself. Instead, I was
still free. That seemed like a random kindness of destiny. But it
wasn't unconditional, I realized. There was only one condition—
that I stayed free. It took me a while to delink myself, and finally
I discontinued my annual calls to the orphanage. I was finally
free. I was twenty-four years old.

SEVENTEEN

Mira thought that the next morning on Wednesday might have easily ranked as one of the worst in Nalan Malik's life. In fact, he would have wished he didn't wake up at all that morning. The story, which had been aired on news channels the evening before, was now splashed across the newspapers. As the tapes were available to multiple sources, they were already posted on the internet and were doing damage online as well. Whatever Nalan's plan was for containment, it became clear by afternoon that nothing could have stopped such an avalanche of coverage. It might have slowed it down a bit, as was evident from the tone of the television discussions that were severely critical of Sikander's methods.

Mira wondered what Sikander thought about that day's news. The fifth Parliament tape provided evidence for something that had been suppressed as untruth. Whenever people had expressed such doubts about the state's division, their reputations had been tarnished and their voices stifled.

Nalan Malik's career as a politician appeared to be finished. Even the PP spokespersons couldn't defend him. Mira watched the television in the newsroom after the morning meeting, as she waited for it to be 1 p.m. She wished she were back in that narrow lane where Sikander lived; she hadn't been there in two days. She missed watching that open window, the silent night, the working day; she missed him. Just then, the news channels recapped the Parliament tapes and Sikander's photograph flashed on the screen. There was mention of the Parliament tapes and how they had reached her. There was no photograph of her. As part of the segment on Sikander's personal life, there were some more pictures, mostly taken accidentally, and one with a girl at a polo match where he smiled a non-smile for the cameras. The feature ended with an earlier recording of Mahesh Bansi, as he answered a question for the cameras and Sikander stood behind him, looking away as if bored. It was one of the masks he had recommended they should discard in the latest clue.

The masks we wear must be discarded because they are just masks.

Mira smiled at the file footage on the screen, familiar with that expression on his face; it was the same mask she wore. It covered the fatigue with the millionth replay of mundane moments that must be considered precious because that's all one would get instead of the one special moment that could change it all.

'Handsome man, isn't he?' a voice teased her.

Startled, Mira turned. It was Nalan, who looked cool as if the day's top headlines had nothing to do with him.

'Your type?' Mira inquired politely. The lunch hour newsroom was sparsely populated, but even then every eye was on them and every ear tuned to their conversation.

He smiled like he meant it. 'Yours, I believe.'

Mira could feel the room fall silent around them.

'Because we published the tape against you?' she questioned him.

'Because I saw you smile at his picture,' he disclosed.

Mira uneasily said, 'I thought I recognized a look of

indifference to hide a certain helplessness—a quiet and constant desperation.'

'That's understandable,' Nalan noted generously. 'Not everyone can have lunch with you.'

There were chuckles in the aisles behind them, and Mira ushered Nalan out of the newsroom. His aides waited in the corridor with a phone and a few messages; Nalan asked them to hold his calls for an hour. The functional steel and white canteen had a short menu. Nalan glanced through it as he said that he came from a meeting with the chief of the party disciplinary committee who gave him a scolding for the tape. Mira listened to him as they both chose the vegetarian options and carried their steel trays to the seating area. By then he had managed to silence the noisy lunch hour with his presence. Most journalists there recognized Nalan Malik, the influential PP general secretary. And the few who didn't were now familiar with him because of last night's news and that morning's papers. They were astonished that he should eat at their notoriously disastrous canteen with their notoriously silent colleague on an already punishing day.

They sat facing the open windows that overlooked the parking lot behind the building.

Nalan scrutinised the dark brown-green sticky material in his plate. 'Seems like something from the Yamuna river bed, but I might be wrong,' he said considerately and turned to her. 'Do you cook? I do. Very well, I'm told.'

Mira began to eat. 'Whom do you cook for?'

'Used to be for my wife, now I cook for myself.' He paused, the spoon suspended in his fingers. His voice was distant, as he added, 'It's not the same.'

'Why not?' she spoke lightly. 'Don't tell me it was love!'

Mira stopped, realizing what she had just said and glanced at him, hurriedly.

He smiled. 'I won't.'

'I'm so sorry!' she said, flustered.

His face was drawn as he responded, 'It may not have been love, but it was a marriage. And its end has left a gap that I don't know how to fill. Like a fractured bone with a piece missing; it can't heal, it won't.'

Mira knew what he meant. 'You would be lost without the pain,' she reasoned. 'Loneliness makes sense of the incomplete, so that we can endure again.'

He frowned as if he disagreed, but didn't speak. She could once again feel the distance at which his thoughts stopped, as if he was afraid she would hurt him.

Then he sought to verify if his fear was valid. 'That was a smart lie about Salat, which you told those men at your house the other day.'

Yes, the fear was valid, she wanted to tell him. 'Was it a lie?'

His eyes reflected the light from the windows. 'Wasn't it?'

'Question is: How do you know what I told the four guys?'

'I told you, I keep track.'

'How?'

'Everyone affected by the tapes is aligned against Sikander. And you.' His soft voice distracted Mira for an instant, as he observed, 'I can survive the damage in the media, I always have. But there are those who won't. So it's either your survival or theirs. The stakes are very high.'

Mira continued with her lunch. 'So, which side are you on?'

His fingers gently moved the spoon around, as if to test the indeterminate curry for life. 'You don't seem to need my help. It was a good lie about Salat. They believed it.'

Mira glanced up and he met her eyes again, waiting. She couldn't escape this time, she couldn't lie like before.

He looked away at the windows, and she breathed again.

'Sikander has hurt me viciously,' he remarked. 'I have to retaliate; it is expected of me. I wouldn't be much of a politician if I let him get away with it.'

Nalan then reached for his cell phone, opened an email and handed it to her. Intrigued, Mira saw the image of a letter on the screen, written on Sikander's Parliament stationery with his signature at the end.

'Two years ago,' Nalan explained, 'Sikander wrote this letter to the government requesting that an infrastructure company may be considered for an airport contract in his constituency, as it fulfilled the project criteria. This is routine, all members of Parliament write such letters, most of which are never taken seriously. And neither was Sikander's letter,' he paused gravely and then continued, 'but it assumes importance now because the company he recommended was recently blacklisted by the government for anti-national activities.'

'He may have been unaware of it when he signed that letter,' Mira argued.

'How can you be sure?' Nalan inquired.

'You mentioned it was routine. He must have written many such letters.'

'He must have,' he granted. 'But I have the one in which he supports a company suspected of subversive activities.'

'It could be an honest mistake, Nalan. Perhaps his staff didn't check the antecedents of the company.'

'And perhaps you have been helping a criminal,' he mentioned gently, 'just because he made you believe in his words!'

Mira turned away, concerned, as her doubts about Sikander resurfaced.

'Is it really that easy, Mira?' he asked her, his luminous eyes hurt somehow. 'All it takes is a smart man who says what you want to hear? If someone could aggregate every loss in my life and promise to set it right, I would be her slave.' He continued, his voice distant, 'But I would also know these are mere words. They will stay much after that person is gone and much after the words have been proved wrong. Like a shrapnel in the mind,' he whispered, 'that hurts every time I think of it and leaves every reality incomplete.'

Mira heard him, distraught. He once again seemed to speak about her life, not just about his.

'But I can't blame you for searching among words.' He lowered his eyes, disturbed. 'Words are the missing pieces of bone, missing pieces of heart—every missing piece. You never know what you might find in the debris of our language.'

He collected himself, then said, 'I came today to show you the letter that is scheduled to reach every newspaper and television channel tomorrow. When that's published, it will be for the people to judge what kind of a man Sikander is and the motive behind his tapes.' Nalan added clinically, 'We can also show that he has links with a particularly unpatriotic group that has international support.'

Mira could sense the smouldering anger in his thoughts against Sikander.

'The tapes, then, would appear to be part of an elaborate strategy to destabilize the country by attacking the most visible and efficient symbol of our democracy, our Parliament.' Nalan glanced at her, saying, 'It's treason, and it will destroy Sikander.'

Mira noted bleakly, 'I knew you wouldn't stop short of that.'

'Neither did Sikander.'

'It is not the same. The tapes don't single out anyone, Nalan,' Mira objected. 'They expose our failure as a nation and a people, so that we can change and grow stronger.'

He disagreed with her. 'The tapes are about breaking down a structure that has been our dream,' he said. 'We chose democracy because we thought it will best serve our people. It has fulfilled many of our aspirations, sometimes beyond our expectations. Yes, it might have also fallen short of our goals. But the democratic system hasn't failed, we can correct it because we built it.'

'But *who* will correct it?' she mocked his words. 'You? Why would you change a system whose problems benefit you? Sikander's tapes prove how good you are at manipulating the system; why would you ever reform it?'

'The tapes also prove that I didn't draw any benefit by creating problems. I might have, by finding solutions.' He pointed out, 'Unlike Sikander.'

'But unlike Sikander,' she countered, 'your hands are dirty!'

'That's because I am part of the system,' he contended. 'Sikander trashes the system without offering options for a new one; I don't. His hands are clean because he doesn't want to mend it. I do.'

'And yet, he is the one being hunted,' she pointed out, ironically. 'He is the one who has to hide from the system and people like you.'

'Don't be naïve, Mira,' he chided her. 'Sikander is hiding because he has a past too, just like me or anyone else on the tapes. And it is equally indefensible.' He reached for the cell phone. 'If I mail this letter in the morning tomorrow, Sikander won't stand a chance.'

Mira perceived he seriously weighed that option.

'What if people still believe him?' she challenged him.

'Then they will change their minds,' he promised her. 'After all these decades of democracy, we should know by now how to construct a good scandal.'

'If you must distrust him just because he is a rival, then I have to ask you what you asked me before.' She regarded him severely. 'Is it really that easy?'

Nalan surveyed her for an instant. 'You mean, all it would take is a smart woman who says what I want to hear?' He smiled. 'Want to try?'

She stared at him patiently.

He chuckled. 'Yes, it's easy, because it's Sikander,' he answered her question. 'All it will really take is to address one common email from my cell phone to every newspaper and television channel in the country and abroad. And just press "Send".'

Mira shook her head, as if to clear it. 'Can we please have lunch now?'

He apologized for his negligence and considered the flotsam in his plate. Picking up his spoon again, he tentatively tasted it.

'Beans!' he discovered, relieved, 'and not dead fish in an oil spill. The chef deserves to be complimented. What an excellent disguise!'

———

The response to the fifth Parliament tape that day was widespread and sharp. Members of every political party, including some PP leaders loyal to Mahesh Bansi, condemned Nalan for siding with business interests. Action against Nalan appeared imminent as PP looked for damage-control and he made a brief statement in the press to say the tape was one-sided and unfair.

Mira was preoccupied as she sat through various meetings in office for the rest of the day and offered little or no input. Then she went to the office balcony to be alone for a while and to think. It rained again in that sad, dripping way. Perhaps she was wrong, she thought, maybe there was something common between Nalan and Sikander. Perhaps both had secrets to hide, which if exposed, could threaten their political careers. And as Nalan mentioned, perhaps, that was the reason why Sikander was in hiding. Because he knew that for every allegation he made against others, there could be one made against him. Mira glanced up at the monsoon sky. She had felt Sikander's detachment, just as she now felt Nalan's restraint. It was hard not to like Nalan. He was both a strong and a weak man, who hated and cherished his ability to get hurt. But it was harder not to like Sikander who cared for the pain of others, the fate of others, even if it was for his own political gain.

Reaching a decision, she went back into the newsroom and walked to Salat's cabin. He was typing his story and without turning away from the computer screen, asked her to sit down.

'Thanks for offering to write the main story today,' Mira said. 'I am a little distracted.'

'No problem.'

'I had agreed Nalan's lunch would be off the record,' she clarified. 'So we don't have to mention that.'

'That's a pity,' Salat continued to type. 'Everyone is talking about the mighty Nalan Malik in our humble canteen.'

She didn't answer.

'What did he have to say?'

'Told me about a letter Sikander had written in support of a company with anti-national links.'

'Wow!' Salat glanced at her for a second before he returned to the screen. 'Did he show you the letter? Are we getting a copy?'

'We will tomorrow,' Mira said, 'along with the rest of the world.'

Salat nodded. 'This was expected. It's Nalan Malik.'

Mira hesitated, then said, 'I need to warn Sikander about the letter.'

Salat laughed briefly. 'You can't mean that.'

'I do, Salat. I have to tell him,' Mira said seriously. 'This will ruin all his work, and the Parliament tapes.'

'He would have seen this coming.'

'Yes, by counting on me to warn him.'

Salat shrugged. 'You will lead the surveillance team directly to him if you visit that lane again.'

'That's why I need your help. Besides,' she said uncertainly, 'I owe you sandwiches.'

Salat stopped typing now, his sharp eyes, surprised.

'Let's try your place this time,' she offered tentatively. 'We could leave office together . . . then I might sneak out of your house in the night and return early in the morning. It'll just take a couple of hours.'

Salat pondered. 'That could work. Sure.'

Mira relieved, smiled. 'Do you ever say no?'

'Not to good-looking women who want to go home with me.' He paused in doubt. 'Or, perhaps, it's the sandwiches.'

She laughed, and he smiled with her.

———

Salat's house turned out to be a sprawling place with several exits to choose from. She opted for the garden door obscured by the foliage of an enthusiastic creeper. Salat warned her that every door would be visible from outside during daytime, and she promised to return before sunrise. It was 8.30 p.m. when Mira finally reached the main road at Sangam Vihar, it had taken much longer during the extended peak hour traffic. As she turned into the lane, she stopped in her tracks, astonished. The lane was transformed. The dark, damp end was shining with light and echoing with music. Flowers decorated facades of residences, and a sign glittered over the entrance of the lane to announce the wedding of a resident's daughter. Amazed by the number of people milling around, Mira slowly made her way to Sikander's room. But it was impossible not to get involved in the festivities all around her. Someone rushed along with flowers and handed her a garland, a few boys danced around to a melody and a lady handed her a glass of almond milk. It was difficult to tell whose daughter was getting married as every house celebrated, and every threshold was filled with colour.

Mira reached Sikander's room and was perplexed to find it locked. He was usually home by that time and usually never went anywhere else. Except for the tea stall, she recalled. To check, Mira headed back to the entrance and prepared herself to brave the wave of celebrations again. On the way, she managed to turn down the sweets someone offered but was intercepted by two girls, who wanted to decorate her palms with henna. They were disappointed when Mira refused, and unable to see their beautiful smiles fade, Mira agreed and selected a pattern each for her palms. They settled on a step of a nearby house. The chubby strong girl in a green dress made the designs on the right palm, and the slim delicate girl in red on the left one.

The girl in green smiled at Mira. 'You are married, aren't you?'

'No,' Mira answered, taken aback.

'Really?' She was disconcerted. 'I have never been wrong before.'

The girl in red was intrigued. 'How can you tell?'

The green girl confided, 'It's simple, really. Married women look at peace.'

Her friend was unconvinced. 'That's not true. Look at Rima, I have never seen her smile. And have you forgotten Nina? She is so unhappy.'

'Of course she is. I didn't say married women look happy,' the green girl said impatiently. 'I said they are at peace, because they don't have to listen to the daily rants of their parents to get married. They are finally free of the guilt of spending one more day unmarried in their parent's home.'

'Oh yes!' The red girl agreed. 'Last month, when I turned nineteen, my mother found an eligible boy for me on a marriage website. I told her I wanted to graduate, but she said I couldn't afford to study any further.' She stopped, suddenly conscious of Mira's presence. 'My parents are saving money for my brother's education.'

Mira nodded politely.

'But didn't your brother fail in the last school exam?' the green girl asked.

'So what?' The red girl was sad. 'It's his money, his house.'

'I don't understand really,' said the girl in green. 'Why do our parents tell us that we are merely guests in their home? They don't even consider me in their plans for the future because they are sure I will be married by then.' She paused, distressed. 'It's as if I will be dead or something; just a closed chapter.'

Mira frowned at her words, but didn't glance up from the henna.

The red girl's face turned tragic. 'My parents wouldn't care who married me, as long as the dowry is cheap.' She paused. 'I don't get it. They had an option. It's illegal, but people do it, right? They could have just killed me ...' She hurriedly glanced again at Mira. 'I mean, that would have saved everyone a lot of trouble, right?'

Mira couldn't look up at her.

The green girl disagreed. 'I'm glad to be alive. I just wish my parents had left me at one of those orphanages, you know. That would have made my life!'

Mira's hands shook, and the girls glanced at her questioningly. She apologized and made an effort to hold still.

'If I have children, I hope I never have a girl child,' the red girl continued. 'I cook, clean and take care of the house and also study, while my brother plays cricket and fails at school. I wake up three hours before him every morning and sleep two hours after he sleeps at night. When he is married, his wife will do these chores. I don't see why I should produce one more slave to this society. I will never have a girl child.'

As before, the green girl was more optimistic. 'That's why I want to be an orphan, someone who will live for herself and not for everyone else. She would just be a human being, just like the boys.'

Overwhelmed, Mira turned away to observe the lane.

'What a stupid thing to say!' The red girl exclaimed. 'You think boys are human beings? I'm so disappointed in you!'

They argued the point, and that made Mira finally smile. But as she considered their pretty faces and sad eyes, she knew she too could have been one of them. She too could have been a so-called cherished daughter in a so-called loving family; an almost orphan in an almost home.

———

The feasts of the marriage were organized at different places, and one of them was the tea stall. It was packed with people celebrating, drinking and eating, and Mira tried to locate Sikander from a distance. As the crowd moved a little, she saw him in the middle, laughing at something someone had said. She couldn't see him as people closed in, but she still heard his laughter. Glasses clinked, and people began to sing, drunk. Standing in the darkness outside, Mira was incensed by his freedom, for the way she felt responsible for him while he let go of everything as if he knew she would stop his fall. She glanced up at the starless sky and wondered. Nalan plotted Sikander's downfall with inspired planning, and she understood that. There was passion in that hatred, but there was only surrender in Sikander's love. It was difficult, it asked for too much because it asked for nothing at all.

Mira looked around helplessly, thinking. She was glad he wasn't home; she now had a choice. If she went up to him to speak, it would change everything. Not because she would tell him about Nalan's plans, but because it would prove her affection for him. And he would be forced to respond, Mira knew. She didn't want anything from him, she couldn't afford it because he knew everything about her. She saw him once more in the distance. He replied to someone, and there was laughter again. Mira studied his grimy face, dirty beard and old clothes, the way he drank liquor from the same glasses in which he had tea. This wasn't equal, she told herself, this wasn't fair to him. He still had something to lose; he still had everything. She never had anything to lose. And she still had nothing.

Determined, Mira turned and walked back into the lane. Careful with the henna in her palms, she used her key to open Sikander's room and reached for the backpack in the chair. The notepad with the pen were still in it, and she wrote down a message for him.

> 'Nalan has your letter in support of an anti-national company for an airport contract in your constituency. He will make it public tomorrow. Wanted to get your version, but didn't feel like spoiling your evening—Mira.'

She stared at her words seriously. This would prove to Sikander that she had solved the clues but had not yet given him up. Wasn't that what he had expected? That she would do anything for him? Well, he was right, Mira thought weakly. She dropped the notepad back in the backpack and left the house. On the way out of the lane, she paused at the tea stall and saw Sikander still surrounded by his friends. Mira watched him for a moment, letting him go. He smiled at something, and somewhere in the darkness outside the stall, Mira smiled back.

EIGHTEEN

The rain beat down her bedroom window, but Mira suspected that she heard it in her memory. Not possible, she told herself, as she also heard the doorbell. Mira's eyes snapped open, and she sat up in her bed to listen. It couldn't be Salat, she was sure, he had just brought her home earlier in the morning. After that, she had taken a bath and fallen on the bed, tired, and slept deeply. Mira heard the doorbell again and rushed to the main door. Nalan was speaking on his cell phone when she opened the door and frowned at him in sleepy confusion. He regarded her coldly and continued with the phone call. Mira didn't move for an undecided instant, and as he waited, his brown eyes registered her hesitation. Then she stepped aside reluctantly, and he walked in. He stood in the living room looking around and replied to the caller, explaining a voting process. She wondered why he was there. Then she checked her crumpled shirt and open hair. Mira moved towards her bedroom to change and reached the door when she heard him end the call. She turned, and Nalan glanced at her. The silence in the room seemed to be made of inflammable material that came with fire hazard warnings. He surveyed her for a long moment, his eyes hard with disbelief.

'I got this email in the morning, online from a random address,' he said and took out two folded papers from his jacket pocket. Mira could discern from his thoughts that it was Sikander's response.

'Let me read it to you,' he continued levelly, 'it's just two lines:

"You have a letter I had written two years ago. Please find enclosed the list of sixteen senior leaders from all political parties who had recommended the same company before I had."

Nalan turned the papers. 'Needless to say, the list has every important name on it. So I can't use the letter against Sikander.'

He glanced up at her, and she looked away hastily.

'How did Sikander get to know about the letter, Mira?' Nalan's voice was calm, but the anger in his thoughts made her take a step back from the doorway.

'How did he find out something that only you and I knew?' he asked again.

Mira didn't answer, didn't look at him.

'You warned Sikander, you told him of my plans. And now I can't use the letter.'

She was silent, guilty.

'But,' he said trenchantly, 'I never planned to use it.'

Mira frowned.

'It was just a trap, Mira,' he confirmed her conclusion, 'and you walked right into it. I never meant to use that letter; it was just to make you go to him.' Nalan threw the papers on her desk, infuriated. 'And you did. Thank you!'

Mira was stunned by her oversight; Nalan had done this before. She shouldn't have trusted him. But her concern for Sikander had been much more than her suspicions about Nalan. However, there was no need for guilt, she told herself. Even Nalan had hid his deeper thoughts and misled her with distractions. Just like her.

And even Nalan manipulated her mind, or thought he did. Just like Sikander.

'I know you sensed that I would use the letter.' His voice was soothing, despite the damage it did. 'But you see, this was the only painless way left to make you reveal where Sikander is.'

Mira struggled with his thoughts, then finally spoke. 'You are lying. You don't know where Sikander is,' she managed. 'You're just trying to fluster me.'

'Am I?' he wondered. 'Let's find out if I have succeeded.'

He quickly walked towards her and, alarmed, she stepped further back. Nalan's eyes were friendly until he noticed the colour of henna on her palms.

'This wasn't there yesterday when I met you,' he said curtly, as he examined her palms. 'Salat seems to be an artistic man,' he mocked.

Mira faltered a little. She had forgotten about the henna.

'I know you are not in a relationship with Salat.' He moved closer, his black shoes touched her bare feet. 'I also know you left his house in the night and returned in the morning. Question is,' he asked gently, 'where did you go?'

'There were men watching the house. Why don't you ask them?' she suggested steadily. 'I was with Salat the entire time.'

'I don't have to be a knower, Mira,' he said severely, 'I can tell just by your touch that you're lying.'

Mira tried to free her hands, and he let them go. She could detect the familiar controlled intensity of his mind as he shut her out. However, from past experience, Mira knew how to open those closed doors.

'You want a knife?' she asked encouragingly.

'What!' Nalan took a second to recover. 'Of course not!'

'You might.'

'Sadly, I like you too much for that,' he informed her. 'Now, where is Sikander, Mira? For God's sake!'

Annoyed, Mira forgot strategy for a second. 'Why is it so hard to believe that I spent the night at Salat's house?'

He smiled forgivingly, and then glanced at her open hair.

'I mean,' she argued, 'is it not possible that we had dinner together and ...'

She stopped suddenly as he reached out to feel her hair.

'And?' he said helpfully.

Mira saw his fingers run through the strands. 'And we didn't sleep at once, although ...'

He touched her neck faintly and traced it to the collar of the shirt.

'Although?'

Mira tried to focus. 'Although we saw the sunrise between ...'

He pushed away a strand of hair from her forehead.

'Between?'

She closed her eyes. 'Between the clouds and had breakfast before ...'

He vaguely felt her face, as if he recalled her from a lost time. 'Before?'

She heard the change in his voice as she continued, 'Before he brought me home.'

Nalan waited.

Gathering her courage, Mira opened her eyes. 'I slept until you...' she couldn't complete as she met his serious eyes that were also, somehow, sad.

'Where did you go,' he asked absently, 'from Salat's house last night?'

Mira didn't answer, the question didn't matter anymore. His mind now opened to her, unfettered, and let her reach as deep as she wanted. It was then that she discovered his restraint was not to spare himself the pain she may cause; it was to spare her. Nalan's intense eyes were honest and apologetic as he touched her face once more. Unsettled by his thoughts, she moved away to escape him, and even he stepped back, as if to escape himself.

He stopped at a distance and said, 'This is no longer about the Parliament tapes, Mira. This is about retribution, and I don't want you to get hurt.' He paused, then added affectionately, 'Not with that henna on your palms.'

Troubled, Mira turned to him. He smiled reassuringly and was gone.

She heard the door close and shakily reached a chair to sit, realizing she should never meet Nalan again. Ever.

———

The next tape was on Mira's desk the same morning when she reached office about an hour later. Following instructions, Bhaskar made quick copies and took it to Munshi first, even before the editorial meeting. This was unusual, and everyone waited inquisitively in the conference room.

Munshi walked in after some time. 'Let me inform you all that I have already heard the new tape.' Then he smiled, making everyone reach for their shields and armours. 'Excellent work on the Nalan tape,' he said instead. 'If we do not have a court case against us today, that's because of your unexpected efficiency.'

They thanked him cautiously.

'This is the longest-running campaign in the history of the newspaper,' he told them and added acidly, 'thanks mainly to Mira, who could not find Sikander despite almost half a dozen clues.'

Mira glanced up from her notebook.

'But we have opened the doors to Parliament,' Munshi continued harmlessly, 'which have remained unfairly closed to the people to whom it belongs.' He paused. 'It is not every day that we get to know a man like Sikander Bansi, who seemingly sacrificed his own interests to expose what goes on in the corridors of power. I would have liked nothing better than to help him in his endeavor, but to be honest, I am not sure of his motives, and neither is Mira.'

Mira could sense where Munshi was headed with this talk, and she prepared herself quickly.

'Sikander had faith that a knower would understand his reasons and his clues. Of course, he was wrong on both counts,' Munshi said sarcastically. 'Mira has spent the last two weeks making up exciting new excuses about how she had been unable to solve the clues or to figure out the motives of Sikander.'

The silence in the room subtly changed to incredulity at Munshi's criticism of his most famous staffer, his protégé.

'As a result of her behaviour, I have been accused of making a deal with Sikander and even hiding his whereabouts.' Munshi took a deep breath, as if to control himself. It didn't help. 'Usually, I enjoy this sort of thing, but it is getting to be too much. I don't care where Sikander is! I don't care if we never find him! I want Sikander off the front page and out of my life! Is that clear?'

It was urgently clear to everyone.

'Now, I have had enough with the clues, Mira.' He turned to her, and his voice softened a fraction. 'I understand that your gift is not precise, but I also happen to know how powerful it is. And I'm not the only one. Most of this city has been at the receiving end of your accurate analyses for years. So, it's a little unusual and difficult to believe that your powers have suddenly failed you.'

Mira silently heard him.

'I have no doubt about your loyalty to his newspaper,' Munshi said sincerely. 'That's something I have always liked about you, and is also the reason why this city admires you. Even though you could have, you have never used your powers to derive benefit for yourself or against anyone. You have always employed them for this newspaper and its reportage.'

'You are a true knower,' he concluded and added apologetically, 'and I'm sure you already know my decision.'

Mira nodded. 'You want me off the story.'

Everyone stared at Mira, astonished, then glanced at Munshi questioningly.

'Wonderful!' He smiled sadly. 'So, given your powers, it appears that the only reason we have not been able to find Sikander is because we don't want to. It appears that we have been lying to the readers. We need to hold someone responsible for this lapse to appear neutral again. We need to be able to say that once you are gone, we shall deal with the tapes, and Sikander, in a more professional way.'

Salat glanced at her, worried, but Mira just listened to Munshi.

'I am a great believer in thin lines, Mira. You should too, and I'll tell you why.' He explained paternally, 'They appear exactly at a time you are about to take a difficult and important decision. Today, the thin line is between you and the newspaper. That's why you need to go.'

Mira agreed quietly, but everyone could see Munshi was unhappy with the decision.

'You see, Mira,' he spoke again, his small eyes earnest, 'the readers have to believe in us like an audience believes in a magician. Journalists isolate truth from the thin air of a newsroom with the help of a few facts; we need to show the people that our hands are clean. The strings should never be seen in a good newspaper, like in a good puppet show.'

'I understand, sir,' she assured him.

Munshi thanked her, then glanced at Bhaskar inquiringly. 'What time is your wake up alarm?'

Startled, Bhaskar said he would play the tape and reached for his computer.

Mira sat back in her chair and lowered her eyes to her notebook. She wasn't surprised by Munshi's decision. There would be no need to trace Sikander if no further tapes were published. That's what she expected Munshi to announce next, that he was dropping the story. Considering her non-cooperation, this was the only other way the tapes could have been blocked — by getting Munshi's cooperation instead. Nalan's warning in the morning made sense. This was not about the tapes anymore because there would be no more tapes. Mira had intended to seek Munshi's intervention to get police help formally to prevent further attacks against her. That wasn't possible anymore. She ceased to worry about it when Sikander's friendly voice filled the room.

> It is 15 January and the time is 2 p.m. I am in the chambers assigned to me when I was recently made a deputy parliamentary secretary for PP. In a few moments, I have an appointment with a weapons dealer known only as the General and his local counterpart, Pran Gupta. I will refer to a deal that was behind the government decision to use drones against rebels in parts of the country.

There were noises of a chair being adjusted and papers shuffled, as Sikander arranged the recording equipment in his office. Then the phone rang.

> Sikander answered, 'Yes Suresh?' There were faint words heard on the phone line. 'Please send them in,' he said.
> There was silence again until the door opened.
> 'Good afternoon, Mr Bansi,' said someone with a foreign accent. 'So kind of you to see us at such short notice.'

Sikander wished them and invited them to sit. He offered them coffee, then they chatted a bit about Delhi winter.

'I always tell my friends,' the General remarked, 'you can't prepare for India. It's a land of infinite surprises, like its weather. I am happy to find Delhi freezing. I find this very pleasant.'

'I'm glad you do, General,' Sikander said formally.

Pran explained, 'The General loves this nation, and this nation loves him back. Do you remember the case of the night vision goggles for the Army, Mr Bansi?'

'I do,' Sikander replied. 'The Army discovered that the night vision equipment didn't work at night. So, they were just regular goggles that cost the country a fortune.'

'Then why did the Army place a new contract for more of the same goggles?' Pran asked significantly.

'The goggles started working?' Sikander guessed.

'No, that's the point!' Pran said. 'They don't have to work, when the General is involved in a deal.'

'Nice to know that,' Sikander said, sounding impressed. 'Then, perhaps, you can help me with the problem I wanted to discuss with you. This is a well-publicized case, and I'm sure you have heard of it. The government is stuck in a matter and, well, I want to work out a solution that is beneficial to everyone.'

They assured him their support.

Sikander thanked them and continued, 'As you must be aware, the country faces violence and terrorism in over 150 districts. Millions of lives are affected, and development is hampered. The state wanted to take action, smoke out the rebels from these areas. This plan was called Operation Green Horn and had included the use of drones, which we would have procured and loaded with other equipment.

It was worth billions in contracts. Then the politics began,' he sighed helplessly. 'Should we attack our own citizens? Won't the drone strikes kill the good along with the bad? And similar such rubbish! So, the plan was shelved.'

'Yes, I know this story. It's a pity really!' The General said, 'So you want to revive the operation?'

'The rebel influence is spreading,' Sikander said gravely, 'and if nothing is done to stop them, the movement will threaten the nation at large. I see no option but to revive Green Horn.'

'Oh. I understand now,' the General said appreciatively. 'You want to do this in national interest.'

'Naturally.'

The General chuckled. 'There would be no weapons industry without the concept of national interest.'

Sikander hesitated. 'Also, my re-election is due in a year, and I've got to procure the funds soon.'

'Of course,' said the General, understanding. 'Can you tell us who were opposing the deal?'

'The usual, predictable people! The pro-rebel activists and a bunch of politicians from the Opposition who wanted incentives to keep quiet. That was a bit unfair, considering we in the PP government have already paid our allies in the ruling coalition.'

'Yes, but this is a democracy, not a dictatorship. You have to bribe everyone.'

'I realize that now.'

'So you want us to smooth the way for the deal in Parliament and also find a way of selling it to the people.'

'Exactly.'

'Fine,' he agreed. 'Give me a week, I will do my research here and get back to you with a proposal.'

'Thank you,' said Sikander, as if relieved. 'I have heard you are very good at this sort of thing.'

'Well, I won't promise you anything yet,' the General was candid. 'But by the time I'm done the drones will appear to be the only way to deal with the rebels.' He chuckled. 'There may even be a public demand asking for their expedient deployment to contain the problem!'

There was laughter.

'I wish it were not a moral problem,' Sikander said with regret. 'How can we defend drone attacks by the government against its own citizens? It's unpatriotic, unethical and inhuman.'

'So is all force, my friend,' the General reasoned. 'The difference is who has the right to use force. The state has the legitimacy, and the voters elected the government to take difficult decisions on their behalf. Use of force is one such decision.'

'That may be true in theory, but in practice, it's about killing people of my own country.' Sikander maintained, 'It's treason.'

'Agreed, but no nation wants to be cowed down by violence unleashed by rebels. There wouldn't be many nations left if that were to happen.'

'Perhaps, there shouldn't be.'

'We are experimenting with that notion in other parts of the world,' the General revealed. 'We discovered that it makes no difference to us whether it's one nation or three states. Every state will have its rebels, and both sides will buy weapons from us.'

'I see. When you say "we", you mean your company?'

The General and Pran were surprised.

'I had no idea you were doing this for the first time, Mr

Bansi,' Pran said kindly. 'It's not a company or even a group of companies. These are weapons lobbies that cut across nations and ideologies of all kinds. If you want to kill for reasons of justice or protest, religion or nation, vision or politics, we can get you the bullet.'

Sikander inquired in disbelief, 'Is there never any opposition to your methods?'

'Of course there is. And there is a price list to deal with the degrees of opposition,' Pran said. 'But there has never been any real challenge to the weapons industry.'

'Except for one,' the General pointed out. 'Democracy.'

Pran conceded that. 'If you can't sell the idea to the people, it cannot be done. And that's where we come in.'

The General seemed experienced with these aspects of public scrutiny. 'The beauty of defence purchases, my friend, is that no one can be found guilty.'

'Please don't talk about guilt, General,' Sikander pleaded. 'We are all very nervous about defence deals in this country.'

'And for good reason,' he agreed, sympathetic.

'We address our anxiety by appointing the most honest and usually inefficient men as defence ministers; men who won't buy even a garden tool without a global tender.'

'I noticed,' the General said, then added, 'But hopefully, not everyone will be that honest.'

'Hopefully, General,' Sikander said politely, 'they will be.'

'That remains to be seen,' he answered. 'Meanwhile, it helps us to talk about corruption in India, the many hands that need to be greased all the way to the top. That makes it easy for us back home to negotiate for larger margins of profit.'

'How do you manage to sell us anything?'

'By lowering the quality, of course!' The General explained, 'We don't mind because you are the only guys who still want our obsolete weapons. We want to earn whatever we can for them and recover our investments.'

'So that's why the goggles don't work.'

'They do,' the General corrected him. 'They just don't work at night.'

Sikander chuckled. 'Well, I hope the drones will fly!'

'Yes, let's hope so. Then again, to the people on the ground it would make no difference if the drones fly or crash,' the General observed. 'They will be dead anyway.'

They scheduled the next meeting in a week's time and, after noting down private phone numbers not listed on visiting cards, they stood up to leave. The door was opened, farewells were exchanged and the door shut. The tape ended in a few seconds.

There was silence for a while as everyone waited for the clue at the end of the tape. Then Sikander's voice once again lightly filled the conference room:

'This is the clue for Mira: You are wrong, you have options. Surrender to desire is acquisition, to power is fleeting, to religion is escape, to knowledge is incomplete. Surrender to truth because there can be no one truth. Surrender to faith, because it can be unfounded. Be a fugitive from fate forever and surrender to that which sets you free.'

———

No one spoke immediately. Everyone was aware that Munshi had already heard the tape and that meant he already had an opinion.

'It's a good tape,' Munshi said, 'but there is a problem. Can anyone tell me what it is?'

Mira once again glanced up from her notebook. 'Nalan Malik. He vowed not to let us publish any more tapes.'

That was the truth, but it was also too much truth.

'Apart from that,' Munshi patiently asked, 'is there any other problem?'

There was silence.

'I thought you should have seen it right away, Ashok,' Munshi was surprised. 'This tape cannot be confirmed.'

'Why not, sir?' Dubey was confused. 'We can try and get the two weapon dealers on record and also get their associates. They seem to have operated in Delhi, so it can't be very difficult to contact them.'

'That's not enough.' Munshi turned to Bhaskar. 'What do you think?'

Bhaskar said, 'The time, date and location of every tape are given and, as Mira once demonstrated, Sikander left clues in the recordings that could be cross-checked. For instance, in the present tape, this meeting of Sikander Bansi must be still in the books of the PP office where it took place. We will get a copy of the page, and, if possible, a comment from Sikander's secretary who showed the men into the office.'

'I see,' Munshi said thoughtfully. 'I just felt that we may not be able to defend ourselves on a tricky issue like this. What do you feel, Salat? You are the one, after all, defending us on live television.'

'It's well known, sir,' Salat answered, 'that the government is looking to revive its strategy to deal with the rebels in the troubled districts of the country. This conversation is the missing link and reveals the real motives of the government. I think it is invaluable information. We have gathered much appreciation for the tapes published until now. We have shown courage and character.'

'Courage,' Munshi repeated meditatively, 'and character. People usually use those words to describe someone posthumously.'

'I didn't mean that . . .' Salat hurriedly clarified.

'I know you didn't,' Munshi reassured him. 'You meant it as a compliment. The truth is that the tapes have made us proud,' he glanced around the table. 'But do we have *the right* to feel proud? Not really. These tapes were not recorded by us. They didn't even come to us because of our "courage" or "character".' He paused, then said decisively, 'Let us do something that makes us proud, friends. Let us find our own stories and report our own investigations. Let us no longer publish these tapes.'

Everyone stared at him, stunned.

Munshi glanced at Mira. 'You knew I was about to say that, Mira, but it's not due to pressure from Nalan Malik. I wouldn't have published that tape against him if I could be pressured.'

She knew that wasn't true, that was not how he thought. Munshi had published the tape against Nalan because he liked to defy, and he wouldn't publish any more tapes because he had to survive.

'What if we find a way to publish this tape?' she asked him.

'What way?' he inquired. 'This is evidence. You can't tamper with it.'

Everyone turned to Mira.

'What if we exclude the names mentioned on the tapes?'

Dubey glanced at Bhaskar. They both knew about Munshi's close links with the weapons industry, which had funded his bid for a nominated seat in Parliament four years ago.

Munshi answered her carefully. 'Naturally, I have no problem with the names, Mira. I'm just against this entire idea.'

'Or, we could even exclude specific defence deals and publish the rest of the transcript,' Mira suggested, persistent. 'It would still remain a very important story.'

Lina leaned forward keenly to hear Munshi's response. She

remembered the newspaper had repeatedly favoured purchase of various defence equipment.

Munshi smiled tolerantly. 'That's not necessary. I have no problem with the defence deals either.'

'Or, perhaps, we should edit the transcript,' Mira pointed out, 'and cut out the parts that criticize drone strikes.'

Salat glanced at her appreciatively. The newspaper was known for its support of action against rebels.

Munshi's smile was turning cold. 'No problem with that either.'

Mira stayed silent. There was nothing left to say. She didn't want to remind him that he had asked her to assess his chances for the Parliament nomination. She knew who had backed him at that time.

There was now a questioning silence in the room.

Mira glanced around. 'We have all had reservations about the tapes at some point. With all due respect, it shouldn't be different because it's you, sir.'

Everyone turned to Munshi, waiting.

Munshi's small eyes were glinting angrily. 'But it is different, isn't it?'

Dubey cleared his throat. 'The tape is already with news channels. And it may go to some other newspaper if we don't publish it.'

'Yes, but first it will go into my dustbin!' Munshi informed him.

Lina protested. 'We will be blamed for not publishing the tape because it goes against the weapons industry.'

'Then that will give you a chance to deny it,' he said, generously.

Salat frowned and said, 'The readers will question the newspaper's decision.'

'Well, at least there will be a newspaper to question,' sighed Munshi.

Bhaskar contemplated. 'I'm against drone strikes, sir, but I have never objected to our stories supporting them.'

'That's because you don't own this newspaper,' Munshi explained. 'I do!'

There was little to discuss after that. The list of other news stories for the day was summarily accepted, and the meeting ended. Dubey, Salat and even Lina came to Mira's cabin later to condole the end of Parliament tapes, and she thanked them. Later, Bhaskar sent her an email to officially grant her indefinite leave from work, starting the next day. In view of Munshi's decision, Mira thought it was fair to inform Sikander not to send any more tapes as the newspaper would no longer publish them. She wondered how she could visit the lane and discounted asking Salat for help. He was occupied with his stories for the day. Besides, as Nalan had conclusively established that morning, no one seemed to believe her lie about Salat. Mira was sure it would take only a few hours, she didn't need a very elaborate cover. Deciding to try an old trick, she called a media spokesperson in the health ministry this time and made an appointment for a briefing about a story. After the meeting, she planned to leave the ministry building from a different exit without the car and return before the offices shut to collect it from the parking lot. Like last time at the tourism ministry, the watchers wouldn't follow her into the health ministry building and believe she was still inside.

It was 1 p.m. when she drove to the health ministry, and the skies were brooding over Delhi.

NINETEEN

It was raining heavily by the time Mira reached Sangam Vihar around 3 p.m. The waters swirled around her ankles when she entered the lane. As she had expected, Sikander's room was locked and she opened it with her key. Mira was glad she didn't have to meet him. She wouldn't have known how to face him with the news or what to say to him. Mira reached for Sikander's backpack kept in its usual place in the chair and opened the notepad to write the new message. She turned the leaves absently and then froze. She stared at the page on which she had left the message about the letter Nalan had threatened to make public. Under that was now a new message in a few handwritten lines:

'How do you find it? Is it comfortable? Is there light? Is it pleasant? It might be a little crowded with the incomplete and the unfulfilled. Is there enough room in my heart for everything you brought with you? My universe.'

The lines were even, the writing habitual, the ink blue and the paper cheap — the kind that left an imprint on the subsequent pages. Mira touched the words in disbelief to check if she was imagining them and if they would just vanish in a mist of blue ink. She couldn't see them clearly any more, as her eyes filled up. But she didn't have to, she already remembered them forever.

Mira averted her face and controlled the tears. This could be a game too, she warned herself just to get over the pain in her heart. It didn't take a genius to guess that she would have never known such words before. He toyed with her emotions for some end she couldn't see yet. She nodded, getting convinced. Besides, she asked herself, who wrote such words these days? She glanced at them again, now more clinically. Also, how did he even know she would see them? It was a shot in the dark. He had nothing to lose . . .

But Mira closed her eyes, anguished. There was no escape from the point, she had been wrong not to trust him. It was her caution as always, but her tears were the proof, her heart, her mind, everything told her she was wrong. This once, this man was different. Feeling weak, she wanted to fall to the floor and stay there. Or walk to the book shop in the mall and tell Sikander she had been a fool. Instead, she turned the page of the notebook, unable to write anything below those beautiful words. The pen felt heavy in her hand as she wrote:

'Munshi won't publish the last tape. It's over. I'm sorry.'

A little later, she emerged from the house and stopped abruptly on the threshold. She stared at the flooded lane in disbelief. The rainwater already lapped at the steps of the house and threatened to enter it. People were trapped in their homes, and no one came in or left the lane. Mira, worried, observed the rapidly rising water levels and the pouring rain. The four watchers, who had followed her to the health ministry building earlier, were waiting in the parking lot where she had left her car. If she didn't return before the ministry offices shut in a few hours, they would know she had escaped from the building. They would suspect, and correctly, that she had come to meet Sikander. Troubled, she realized that there was little chance for her leaving the flooded lane. Deciding to wait, Mira waded through the water and reached her room, breathless from the effort. Tired, she slumped next to the window in the room and surveyed the flooded area with concern. A cool breeze touched her face gently, and her eyes were heavy with sleep and fatigue. She hadn't slept well in two days. But this was no time to fall asleep, she told herself. She had to leave the instant the rain stopped; yes, but that didn't look imminent, she argued back. Perhaps, there was no harm in resting for ten minutes, Mira concluded. Just *ten minutes*, that's all.

It was dark when she woke up, and the streetlight outside the window sent a column of illumination across the room. She sat up, shocked, and checked her watch. It was 8 p.m. Mira frantically glanced out of the window. It was still raining hard, and the lane was completely inundated. Sikander's room was still locked, and the water was now a few inches away from the window, it had long crossed the threshold. Mira anxiously watched the dark waters below. The rain didn't want her to leave, as if it owned her now to do as it pleased. But why would the rain want the watchers to discover her lie? She noticed the streetlight sharpen the raindrops into glass before they fell to earth. She feared the morning, knowing it would change her life. Mira would have to decide whether to return home or not. Should she return to the only life she had, because she would be lost without it? Or should she escape, as she had always wanted? There was still time for the decision, this was just the night. Mira settled down on the floor again and fell asleep.

The rain ceased just after dawn, as if a job was done. In about an hour, the water drained out of the lane, and people ventured out of homes to assess damage. Mira felt refreshed, she had slept the entire night. From her balcony, she watched the misty sunrise over the unauthorized colony. Everything seemed possible at that moment. Everything was a choice, and every choice was inevitable.

Mira knew she didn't have to return to that parking lot outside the ministry building. The watchers must be waiting for her with a final plan to make her reveal Sikander's whereabouts, and they could hurt her or even kill her. They must know the tapes wouldn't be published anymore. They no longer needed Sikander to stop the tapes, they needed him for revenge and, they must either find him or force him to surrender. The mist refused to lift despite the sun and clung to the local addresses on earth instead of returning to heaven. Mira had always found two promises renewed every day: the promise of life and the promise of death. It was reassuring that if one failed, there was always the other to count on. She realized, as she watched the sunrise, that this was the first time in her life when both promises appeared equally possible. She could stay for Sikander, she wanted to. She could discover the truth of his words, the face behind his masks, and tell him the truth of his clues, the faces behind her masks. But if she left, she could escape the inevitable failings, his human errors, his mortal greed, his natural malice and his unfinished circles. She could escape knowing if he meant his words to her or had just tied up loose ends.

My universe.

Perhaps, if there was ever an escape required, it was from finding the truth about love. She took the decision to leave and, there was a moment as she walked by his door, when Mira wondered if she would ever see Sikander again. He didn't have to, he didn't need her any more. And neither should she.

A bus took her to the metro station, and she reached the ministry building around 7 a.m. There were two more vehicles in the parking lot beside her car, the usual surveillance jeep and a van she did not recognise. She waited near her car and regarded the watchers, who seemed prepared but still stunned that she returned. She felt nervous, frightened of the end, but she was also eager, and even thrilled. A man she had never seen before stepped out of the van and came to her. He requested her to drive home and Mira agreed. Taken aback a little, he waited to see if Mira had any questions. She had none. As she got into her car, she found her cell phone dead. Mira didn't care, she wasn't going to call for help. The two vehicles followed her home, and the van driver accompanied her to the apartment and shut the door. Mira stood in the living room in a silence hand-picked for that morning.

'My employers have set two conditions,' the man said without preamble. Mira studied him in silence, learning his thoughts as he spoke in a flat voice. He appeared disciplined and efficient in a beige shirt and dark trousers. From a shopping bag that he carried with him, he took out a waterproof jacket and wore it, zipping it up carefully. Then he put on disposable covers over his shoes, and finally, he wore plastic gloves. It was obvious that he was not a watcher like the other men who waited outside on the road. This man meant business.

'The first condition is that no one else but I deal with you. You'll find that I'm a professional. And secondly, I don't touch you except to hurt you,' the man informed her. 'My employers desired me to explain that these two conditions are based in respect and concern for you.'

She liked the irony of the message. His employers would feel neither respect nor concern for her, considering they figured on the Parliament tapes she had reported about. But Mira thanked him nevertheless. 'You are fortunate to be working for such kind people.'

'I don't work for anyone, ma'am,' he clarified. 'I freelance. I specialize in women targets.'

'It's a specialization?' Mira was surprised. 'I thought women died the same way as men.'

'They do,' he confirmed, 'but many people in my line of work don't like hurting women.'

'Not you, though.'

'No, it doesn't bother me. My childhood cured me of that, I grew up watching my father hit my mother.'

Mira noticed there was no bitterness. 'May I ask why I am to be hurt?'

'A message has to be sent,' he said. 'That's all I know.'

She nodded. That was expected.

'Now, if you please,' he requested, 'my time has been cut down significantly due to a sudden development. I have been given just twenty minutes to do this job. So, I have to get on with it.'

She asked apprehensively, 'It takes that long?'

'No ma'am.' He smiled faintly. 'The actual job takes just 5–10 seconds. The rest of the time is for setting up the place before the event and to sanitize the premises after it, if required. This will be a crime scene for the police very soon.'

Mira stayed silent. His thoughts were organizing themselves into a sequence.

Once again from the shopping bag, he took out an object covered in a black cloth. He put it on her desk and unwrapped it. Mira surveyed the knife from the distance as it shone coldly, its eager edges darker where they had just been sharpened. She couldn't help her panic and turned away to the windows. The mist hung by the trees and pressed against the glass, obscuring them. Then, as if it waited for her to look, it began to rain. Mira smiled.

She still clutched her bag nervously. He took it away and kept it in a corner. Then he pushed back the chairs to the walls and calculated her fall.

His thoughts were meticulous, but unsure of the end. 'While you visualize the scene,' she said, 'can you tell me if you see me dead or merely hurt?'

He considered her, a bit mystified that she should know his exact thoughts. Then said, 'Well, it gets a little messy if you try to escape. But I have been assured that you may not.'

'Your employers know me well,' she noted dryly.

'They believe there may be others who know this about you as well. They could try hurting you,' he said and reached again for his shopping bag. 'That's why I need to ensure that it doesn't seem like a suicide.'

He took out plastic strips from the bag and secured her hands behind her. She winced as the tight grips cut into her wrists. He apologized but didn't loosen them and went on with his work. Finally, he made a call from his cell phone and reported that he was ready. There were a few instructions to which he agreed, and ended the call. Mira frowned suddenly, astonished, as she detected the name of the employer whom he had called. She stared at the man in shocked disbelief. The person had identified himself, and the assailant now repeated the name in his mind. Her legs shook, and she thought she would fall, shattered, as she discovered who wanted her dead. All the doubts she had fought against had been true all along. But she always knew she couldn't trust affection in this world. Mira pleaded with her fate, she didn't need this lesson!

'I have been instructed to ask you,' her assailant said. 'Would you like to have something? Something to eat? A glass of water, a cigarette, a drink?'

Mira couldn't answer at once, still shaken, then said, 'A last wish!' She whispered, ironically, 'I wish that you make sure I don't survive this.'

'I have my instructions, ma'am. You are to bleed to death, so it's really as much up to you as me,' the man reasoned practically. 'Also, I have been asked to find out if you have any last thoughts?'

'Last thoughts?' Mira pondered. 'That's going to be easy, there is just one.'

Mira glanced at the rain that had delivered her to this moment of truth. 'Do you think there was a time without rain?'

'Pardon me?'

'Was there summer before this?'

The man was perplexed.

'But I don't remember the spring,' she wondered. 'Do you?'

He cleared his throat. 'No.'

'Or the winter?'

'No.'

'That's what I thought,' she concluded, distantly. 'Don't you think it is the rain that makes us forget?'

'It's possible.'

'Or perhaps, there are no other seasons,' she said. 'Just the honesty of rain and the absence of it.'

He listened to her in silence, then turned and went to the desk.

'Perhaps,' he suggested, 'you would like to close your eyes and pray or something.'

'I would rather see the rain for one last time.'

He examined the knife. 'Why do you love rain?'

'Because I was born of it.' She glanced at him. 'And I shall return to it when I'm dead.'

He regarded her seriously, as if to tell her it was time. Then he quickly walked up to her, and Mira noticed the instinctive fear that made her step back from him. He restrained her and held her shoulder. She didn't see his other hand move, but the fierce pain in her stomach made her gasp. He supported her as she leaned to him in agony, then he stabbed her once more. She heard him exhale, and she could sense he was relieved that she didn't fight him.

Then he let go of her shoulder, and she fell, the floor cool on her face, her insides on fire. She thought she screamed in trauma, she thought she fainted, but she did neither. She could see her blood

on his covered shoes as he went back to the desk and wiped the
knife clean with the black cloth. Placing it back in the shopping
bag, he moved around arranging the room. The puddle of blood
on the floor spread slowly, and Mira felt her heart heavy as it beat
with effort. He stood nearby and watched as life drained out of
her, emptying her. Then he knelt and checked her pulse, as if to
assess the time it would take for it to stop. Mira felt cold. Even
the pain in her stomach was getting dull, as if it was someone else
who was hurt, someone close. She sensed her mind slip away from
her too, like her body, and she felt sadder for this loss.

As she paused on the brink, Mira heard the man make another
phone call and report that it was done. His thoughts floated to
her, and she expected it to be the same employer as in the first call.
But as the assailant repeated this name in his mind, Mira held
her breath suddenly, agonized. She must have read him wrong,
she fought with herself desperately; after all, her mind was half
dead. But there was no doubt as the assailant answered a series of
questions about the attack, describing it. How much blood, how
much pain, how long has she got? Mira stared numbly at her blood
on the floor as every word sliced through her mind and hurt much
more than the knife had. The assailant paused again for a question,
and then replied that he was about to leave. Then he ended the
call and walked out. Mira heard the door shut and closed her eyes,
ready, and the tears fell to the floor a short distance from her blood.
It was the rain and Mira in that silence, until her heart faltered
and her breath slowed down. Then everything was just the rain.

———

That day had the texture of a thick quilt, as if it took many days to
make it and would take many days to live. The copies of the last
Parliament tape reached other newspapers and television channels.

Nothing was as big as this and, for the first time, the tape received response from across the borders. As with most defence deals, there was a doubt of treason attached, and that made it dramatic fodder for the Opposition. The story was devastating, easy to understand and vaguely familiar. It was, therefore, the complete entertainment package, and the journalists couldn't type as fast as the news poured in.

That is, all except the journalists at the newspaper's editorial meeting, which Munshi presided over moodily. They felt like a collective blind spot in Delhi, that was somehow missing all the excitement. But as it was one of those occasions when Munshi couldn't blame anyone but himself, the atmosphere at the meeting was relaxed. Like the diligent journalist he was, Dubey read out the top ten stories that made news that day. All of them, however, were about the tape that they hadn't published.

'The top story today is the Opposition's reaction,' Dubey began methodically as always. 'The NP wants the resignation of the prime minister, the home minister, the finance minister, the law minister, and, of course, the defence minister, blaming them for their support to drone strikes against citizens and for using it as an excuse for defence procurement.' He paused, then said, 'The second important story is the government's response. We have statements from the PMO saying that it was not involved, from the home ministry that it gave no recommendation, from the finance ministry that it only checked the budget, from the law ministry that it was never asked and from the defence ministry that it will look into the matter.'

Everyone glanced at Munshi. He played with a pen, distracted.

'Among other stories making headlines is the statement of the defence minister, that it was an attempt to tarnish the community to which he belongs,' Dubey said. 'He is on a visit to his constituency and is expected back in Delhi for this evening's emergency meeting at the PMO over this issue. Should I send a reporter to the airport to get a quote from the minister when he arrives?'

'No.' Munshi didn't even glance at him.

Dubey fell silent, helplessly. It was clear that Munshi wouldn't care what the top news stories were if they were about the sixth Parliament tape and the arms deal. So, Dubey read out the list of stories that had nothing to do with the tape. Munshi finally approved the coverage of a bilateral pact scheduled to be signed that afternoon and a follow-up of the staff strike at the local municipal corporation. They had no good story for the first page of the newspaper, and everyone wondered how to break it to Munshi.

After much thought, Lina mentioned it with her usual tact. 'We have no good story for page one.'

Munshi turned to her. 'No?' he asked indulgently. 'That's where I come in. You don't worry. Just send a photographer and a make-up artist to my room in about half an hour.'

Everyone waited, curious.

'We'll have a full page spread, my friends,' Munshi said vengefully, 'of the photograph of my face! I assure you, it will be an exclusive!'

They all looked away, disappointed.

'That won't work sir,' Bhaskar remarked, as if after due consideration of the idea.

'Then we will have your photo as well!'

'No, I mean, it won't work to keep silent. We need to make a statement about this issue,' Bhaskar said. 'Every media organization has contacted me since morning to ask for our version.'

People quietly marvelled at his courage.

Munshi, however, looked murderous. 'They want me to explain how I run my newspaper? What I choose to or not to publish?'

'No sir,' Bhaskar replied. 'They want us to clarify why we have asked Mira to go on leave.'

Munshi frowned slightly.

'As you remind us often, we are keepers of our own conscience in journalism,' Bhaskar continued valiantly. 'There can be no secrets in the media. We have to be transparent ourselves before we can point fingers at others.' Bhaskar paused and then confessed, 'I told a few friends last night that we have sent away Mira on leave indefinitely.'

Munshi's small dark eyes were wide in surprise. Amazed at Bhaskar, Salat leaned forward to hear him better.

'By taking action against her,' Bhaskar said, 'we have accepted the possibility that the rumours of collusion between her and Sikander were true.'

Munshi heard him in angry silence.

'But I knew for a fact the rumours were wrong,' he continued in the same samurai fashion. 'I had briefed her about the story, and I knew she had never even met Sikander. And I believe her.'

'So do I,' Dubey said. Lina agreed.

Salat mentioned, 'I too believe her, but that's not enough. We need to speak about this to the press. I agree with Bhaskar,' he said to Munshi. 'We need to make a statement.'

'You mean,' Munshi said sternly, 'I do.'

Salat hesitated. 'Yes sir.'

Munshi surveyed his team with misgivings. Then he shook his head. 'And to think I hired every one of you! Makes me shudder at my sense of judgment.'

There was absolute silence in the room.

'It also makes me proud of it,' Munshi declared, and then glanced appreciatively at Bhaskar. 'Fine! Put out a statement. I'll draft it in an hour. Now, can we get on with this damned meeting? I can't stand so much conscience so early in the morning!'

There were smiles all around, and Dubey continued with the rest of the list, pausing significantly at the inauguration of a convention of footwear manufacturers in the city. The meeting ended soon after that.

In an hour, Munshi made one of his typically scathing statements on behalf of the newspaper that was immediately telecast by news channels. Salat read a copy of it sitting in Bhaskar's room. Munshi started his statement by emphasising that as the editor and owner of the newspaper, he had every freedom to publish or not to publish any news. Aware of the scope of free advertisement, Munshi then recapped how the newspaper had published five tapes and the impact of those stories. He also cleverly underlined, for the benefit of the uninitiated, the kinds of pressure he had faced while he printed stories against politicians, bureaucrats, investigative agencies and businessmen.

Then he got down to the point. 'This is not the first time that our newspaper has done something explosive and detrimental to the subterfuge of the people in power. This is also not the first time that I have been ascribed motives for choosing to publish such stories. Some of those making the accusations are my best friends. Some of the people against whom we have done stories are my best friends. But that's the nature of journalism. No one is greater than the story that has to be told. And no one dictates how to tell the story. But I don't mind the accusations, I understand that everyone has to survive. If my reputation were not tarnished enough, then every word I published in the newspaper would have to be the truth. That would be a nasty inconvenience! So, I need to be devalued by such allegations, even if they are never proved. That's how Delhi works, and it has worked for me. But not when one of my best journalists is involved.

'That's where I drew the line, and I sent Ms Mira Mouli on leave in the wake of the allegations that she and Sikander Bansi, someone she never even met, had colluded to bring out the tapes. You might argue, some of you anyway, that an agreement must have been made for the tapes to be published by us. We explained to our readers what that arrangement was and how we got the tapes. We informed the people we were writing about, notably Mr Omkar Nuri, Mr Nalan Malik, Mr Bharat Kumar, Mr L. Fernandes and others, on how we worked on the tapes before publishing them. I can tell you what they had to say to us, but I shall keep it for my next statement on this issue, if I am ever forced to make one. I wanted it to be clear that we have always considered ourselves very fortunate to have the country's first know-journalist working with our newspaper. Nothing has changed, we continue to be very fortunate—Bidur Munshi.'

Impressed, Salat asked Bhaskar, 'That's the truth?'

'Let's just say, it's not a lie,' Bhaskar remarked.

'Then why did he send Mira on leave?'

'Because he was under pressure,' Bhaskar explained.

Salat was surprised. 'So why did he make this statement then?'

'Because he doesn't stay under pressure for long,' Bhaskar smiled.

Salat nodded, realizing.

Bhaskar casually observed, 'I knew she worked out the clues that Sikander sent. Everyone in the office knew it; everyone except Munshi.'

Salat was astonished, but didn't tell him that he knew it too.

'She was too smart for the clues,' Bhaskar shrugged. 'And she was too smart to tell Munshi if she found Sikander. We published these stories, which were potentially impossible to publish, because of her,' Bhaskar admitted, appreciatively. 'She knows Munshi.'

'Mira would be happy to see his statement,' Salat commented.

Bhaskar agreed. 'Are you meeting her today?'

'Yes, I plan to go round to her place later,' Salat replied. 'I called her in the morning but couldn't reach her. In any case, she never answers my calls, and says I don't have to worry.'

'Anyone would worry, with those vicious clues from Sikander and veiled threats from Nalan.'

'And watchers round the clock.' Salat shook his head. 'But she acts so cool, as if she knows the end right at the beginning.'

Bhaskar inquired, 'What end is that?'

Salat's cell phone rang. 'This is rare. Mira is returning my call!' He chuckled and answered the phone. 'Hi Mira. What? Already missing the morning meetings . . .?'

'This is not Ms Mouli,' a woman's voice interrupted him. 'I'm Sita Patnaik from the police, Mr Vasudev.'

Salat was puzzled. 'Why are you calling from her number?'

'I was looking for someone to inform,' she said tonelessly. 'Her phone was dead, and we just recharged it. The phone book was empty except for one number. Yours was the last call on her cell phone.'

'Where is she?' Salat asked anxiously. 'Is she in some trouble?'

Bhaskar frowned, listening.

'I have identified her, but I would like a quick confirmation from you. You can do it later formally,' she said. 'Can you describe Ms Mouli?'

'She . . .' Salat faltered, too worried to speak. 'She is about twenty-nine years old . . . about five feet, six or seven inches tall, dark hair, dark eyes . . .' Salat couldn't go on. 'Please, tell me. What has happened to her?'

'She is in the South Hospital. It's a case of attempted murder, she was stabbed.'

'Attempted murder!' he repeated, dazed. 'Who stabbed her?'

'I'm investigating that.' She hesitated, 'Look, I know you are just a colleague, but can you please come to the hospital now or to the police station later? We just need a statement, it won't take any time.'

Salat got up from the chair. 'I'll meet you at the hospital,' he told Sita.

Then he saw Bhaskar stand as well. He gave his secretary a few instructions and left the office with Salat.

————

It was windy that afternoon. Drops of rains were swept away from their destination, destitute forever. As they rushed from the parking lot of the South Hospital towards the main entrance, Salat recognized the surveillance jeep that had been following Mira. Furious, he walked up to it but found it empty. When they entered the hospital, he found the four watchers standing with Sita Patnaik.

'These men, Ms Patnaik,' he pointed to them, 'are your culprits. These are the men Mira complained about, and you wouldn't believe. I can identify them because they have been following her. They had assaulted her before,' he said, agitated, 'and I am sure they have now tried to kill her!'

The watchers uneasily turned away from him.

Salat spoke to Sita again. 'I want to lodge a police complaint against them now. Please, help me do that.'

Sita observed him, unaffected. 'I tried to lodge a complaint the last time you tried to frame these men, Mr Vasudev. I failed because there was no evidence. These men say they were protecting her, and I tend to believe that.'

Salat was aghast. 'Protecting her? Against whom?' He gestured to them. 'These were the four men who broke into her house and threatened her. Don't you see they are lying?'

'I do see, Mr Vasudev,' Sita smiled patiently. 'Two of these four men report to the top investigating agencies of the country, and they vouch for the other two. It is the job of such men to protect citizens, not try to kill them.' She paused. 'So I suggest you revise your opinion about these men. That way, we can focus on the real culprits.'

Salat stared at her helplessly.

Bhaskar said, 'Where is Mira?'

Sita pointed to the door marked surgery at the end of the corridor. 'They wheeled her in about an hour ago. Her condition wasn't good when she was brought to the hospital.'

Bhaskar asked, 'Is there anything that needs to be done? Anything we can help with?'

Sita didn't think so. 'The paperwork required signatures, but that's been taken care of.'

'Thank you,' Bhaskar smiled. 'That was kind of you.'

'No, I didn't sign,' Sita clarified. 'The man who brought her to the hospital did.'

'Who was that?'

'Sikander Bansi.'

Amazed, they turned as she gestured to the waiting area in the distance.

TWENTY

Sikander sat in the last row of chairs along the wall; it would have been difficult to recognize him if the policeman had not guided them. They were astounded to find that he looked nothing like his handsome photograph on political posters. He was much thinner, his face gaunt, his clothes dusty and his shoes worn, but in his grimy hands was an expensive cell phone, and his two aides waited at a distance. Sikander was lost in thought as he studied the phone, as if he was weighing a decision. Then as they reached him, they saw the blood on Sikander's shirt. Distressed, Salat knew it was Mira's and lost control of his anger.

'You little coward,' Salat said sharply. 'Now you turn up? Now, when she is dying?'

Sikander slowly glanced at him, his large, dark eyes neither hurt nor angry but just curious as they surveyed Salat. One of the aides stepped closer, alerted by Salat's tone.

'I have been waiting to say this to your face, Sikander!' Salat was furious. 'Don't think for one moment that you can get away with everything because she has no one. Yes, you might have needed her help as a journalist and as a knower, but you had absolutely no right to play those personal games and hurt her.'

Sikander stood up now. 'Then who does?'

Salat frowned. 'Is that what this is about? Who can hurt her?'

'Not entirely,' Sikander remarked and extended his hand. 'Salat, I presume?'

Salat didn't take the hand. 'You presume bloody correctly!'

Bhaskar stepped forward to shake his hand and introduced himself. 'Forgive us, Mr Bansi, if we can't think of anything else but the danger Mira faces right now.'

'I thank you both for that.' Sikander then glanced at Salat, and met his enraged eyes calmly. 'But I don't owe you an explanation.'

'Oh, I already have one!' Salat snapped back. 'You are an arrogant, bored son of a big shot, who developed a conscience one fine morning. So you wanted to expose the system, get people's attention and be hailed as a rebel.'

Bhaskar uneasily glanced at Sikander who listened to Salat in respectful silence.

'And while recruiting for this project,' Salat continued harshly, 'you wanted someone who could be manipulated, someone weary of this world and ready to even die to change her destiny.' Salat stopped, choked. 'She was the perfect choice, wasn't she?'

Sikander's face was drawn by those words, but he remained silent.

'What part of your game is this?' Salat demanded. 'How did you get her to the hospital?'

Sikander hesitated. 'I guess you know that she discovered me through the clues. I'm not sure she told anyone, even at the newspaper.'

'She told me,' Salat assured him, avoiding Bhaskar's surprised eyes. 'Go on.'

'Well, yesterday Mira came to the lane where I live to leave me a message that the sixth tape would not be published by your newspaper. Clearly, she must have taken a series of precautions to visit the lane without being followed there. She cared for my safety too much not to.' He paused, forlorn. 'But even then, she couldn't go missing for long stretches of time. She had to return soon not to arouse suspicion among those who watched her.'

Sikander's eyes turned hard, as he said, 'You see,' he explained, 'they would have discovered she knew my whereabouts if she had not returned from the lane yesterday. But she couldn't leave because the lane was flooded in rain.' Sikander stopped speaking again, tormented every time he spoke of her. His voice was low as he continued, 'She must have known those waters that rose at her feet and the rain that fell mercilessly forced her to take the only decision left. Never to return, not just today but ever. She must have known she couldn't survive if she returned home. Not without me.' Sikander affectionately touched the blood on his shirt. 'And yet, she left.'

'That's nonsense!' Salat said bluntly. 'Every clue you sent her proved you understood her life was just a constant search for death. If the choice was between you and the possibility of death, you should have known she would choose the latter.'

Unable to respond, Sikander turned away. The afternoon light from the windows reflected in his emotional eyes, and the loss on his face made Salat feel better.

'I'm a knower too, you see,' Salat informed him with satisfaction. 'So what happened this morning?'

Sikander collected himself. 'When the waters receded, I went back to my room and found her message. That's how I realized that she must have been trapped in the lane due to the rain. I rushed to check the room she had rented across the lane, which I had discovered earlier.' His voice was filled with desperation. 'I was shocked that she wasn't there. I couldn't believe she chose to leave instead of . . .' He stopped again, defeated. 'I immediately called my aides and came to her house. But I was too late, she was already unconscious.'

'Then how did you enter her house?'

'I have a duplicate key. I had once got a fix on the lock posing as a cable technician,' Sikander said absently. 'That's how I had accessed the picture in her living room to leave my address there.'

Salat heard him in silence and didn't have the courage to ask Sikander how hurt she was when he found Mira, and even Sikander fell silent, reluctant to revisit that scene.

But Bhaskar asked, 'Did you find her badly hurt?'

Sikander spoke with effort, 'She was barely alive . . . lying in a pool of blood.'

'Who could have done this?' Bhaskar asked. 'Who attacked Mira?'

Sikander considered the blood stains. 'I can't answer that.'

Bhaskar frowned, and Salat was speechless.

Bhaskar tried again, 'So you know who it was?'

Sikander's head was still lowered. 'I'm sorry.'

'You know, any leads would be most helpful to find the assailant, Mr Bansi.'

Sikander didn't answer. Salat took an angry step towards him, but Bhaskar restrained him.

He asked a third time. 'Who attacked her, Mr Bansi? Why won't you tell us?'

Sikander just said, 'Because it's my score to settle.'

'That's rubbish! You are shielding someone,' Salat accused him. 'It's someone you know, someone more important to you than Mira!'

Sikander looked up at those words, offended deeply, his dark eyes enraged. Salat frowned at the challenge and moved closer. The waiting aide rushed to intervene, but Sikander gestured him not to. Bhaskar could see Sikander was taller than Salat, but Salat was stronger. They were all still for a moment, the confrontation pending. Then surprising everyone, Sikander stepped back from Salat and lowered his eyes again. Salat glared at him and spoke mockingly. 'This is the man Mira was ready to even die for. I wish she never finds out.'

Bhaskar noticed Sikander's control as he turned away from Salat. That made Salat hold his shirt and make him turn back.

'Who tried to kill her, Sikander?' Salat demanded, outraged. 'I don't care what it takes, but you will tell me!'

Sikander met his eyes indifferently, and then glanced at Salat's hands on his shirt. That's when Salat suddenly saw he touched Mira's blood stains and hurriedly pulled away. He stared at his hands distraught and glanced at Sikander who regarded him steadily.

'It speaks, doesn't it, her blood?' Sikander inquired. Salat stepped back from him, unnerved.

'It tells me things I don't want to know,' Sikander spoke, his voice low with agony. 'It makes me think the way I don't want to think. I could even kill to make these stains disappear . . .' He paused, too anguished to speak. Then said, 'Because I shed her blood, and she won't stop thanking me for it.'

———

Soon, Salat and Bhaskar started receiving calls asking about the attack on Mira. A few photographers, who wanted to get a picture of Sikander, were intercepted by the hospital security and politely herded out to the front porch. There they were allowed to set up their cameras and wait for Sikander to emerge. Visitors to the emergency area were screened, and anyone with a press card was disallowed. As measures such as these inevitably made journalists more curious, they managed to sneak in through other entrances and on other pretexts. They found Sikander in the waiting area and jostled with his aides to ask him questions.

'Why did you make the tapes?'

'How did you select your targets?'

'What recording equipment did you use?'

'Why did you choose Mira Mouli?'

'Who do you think hurt her?'

'What will you do next?'

Sikander sat in silence, lost in thought. Salat observed him from a distance without rescuing him. He was still angry with him, but he also noticed something special about the peace on his face, as if he knew he deserved the punishment. Salat leaned forward in his chair, his knower's mind working out patterns of what he knew about Sikander. Intrigued, his eyes narrowed as he saw Sikander sit absolutely still amid the open notebooks and poised pens.

After about an hour, the doctors came out to speak with friends or family, and led the three of them into the briefing room. They informed that Mira had survived the surgery, but until she regained consciousness, there was still a serious threat to her life. Sikander asked when was she likely to wake up and they said if not within the next six hours, then probably never. That made others hold their questions.

The doctors were almost finished when Nalan walked in. He anxiously questioned the doctors and seemed to breathe again only after he learnt she was still alive. He heard their report mention the risk factor and wanted to know what it was.

'Since she was brought to the hospital,' the head of the team said, 'we have struggled hard to keep her from giving up. Her blood pressure, her heart function and, almost every important parameter has slipped despite our best efforts. We have been unable to find any physical cause and believe it to be psychological. We usually see this in suicide cases, wherein the patient doesn't have a will to live. But this was an attempted murder, so that doesn't apply.' The doctor finally admitted, 'Honestly, we are mystified.'

No one responded to that.

When the doctors were gone, Nalan glanced at Sikander, his brown eyes on fire. They were seated across the briefing room, which appeared to shrink somehow. Even the small, featureless table between them now looked like a weapon. Bhaskar turned to Salat, apprehensively, as if to suggest they should leave.

'This is not fair to her,' Nalan said, his fury barely under control. 'She could die.'

'She would,' Sikander agreed coolly, 'if she could.'

'You knew this could happen when you started this game.'

'And you didn't?'

Nalan face stiffened with rage. 'She doesn't deserve to die.'

'No, but she wants to,' Sikander pointed out. 'You heard the doctors.'

Nalan surveyed him with hatred. 'Thank you for making the call. On your request, the PP leadership has put me in charge of deciding your future in the party.'

Sikander chuckled. 'Just thought it will give you something to do.'

'You're right,' Nalan remarked sternly. 'I will enjoy making you squirm.'

'Then I must warn you,' Sikander's smile was intact, 'I don't squirm very well.'

'I am a patient teacher,' Nalan assured him. 'You'll learn.'

He stood up and walked to where Salat sat in the room. 'Please do give Mira my regards if . . . I'm sorry . . . when she wakes up.'

Salat thanked him. Sikander, who also stood up, smiled at him in farewell before leaving with Nalan. Salat and Bhaskar followed, and saw them emerge through the main exit and reach the journalists who waited on the porch.

'Why did Sikander ask for Nalan of all people?' Bhaskar pondered. 'They hate each other. It doesn't make sense.'

Salat watched them face the press, and their aides cleared the way to their cars. 'No Bhaskar, it makes perfect sense. When you lose a battle, you surrender to your enemy who has been waiting to kill you.'

Nalan advised Sikander not to answer the questions. Then he addressed the journalists. 'I won't speak personally, as a mark of respect for a dear friend who is battling against death in this very hospital. But I'm also here on behalf of my party, which has taken a decision that I would like to convey. I shall read the statement here. You can collect the copies at the PP headquarters.'

He glanced around, his expression melancholic, his face drawn. Then he read the statement from the paper:

'The People's Party has been most concerned about the cases of corruption in the highest corridors of power that a party leader and member of Parliament Sikander Bansi has boldly exposed. Unlike other political parties, the PP has a commitment to provide a clean government. The PP is always eager to take action against those who are guilty of any degree of misconduct in public life. To this end, the PP will question Sikander Bansi about the evidence he had produced and assess whether it qualifies for action.' Nalan paused, then resumed evenly. 'This investigation will commence immediately and under the supervision of party general secretary Nalan Malik. The PP leadership expects a report on the matter within twenty-four hours, based on which necessary directions will be given to the party and the government for taking appropriate action.'

That statement made the top headlines of the day. Stories circulated in Delhi like quinine in blood, killing any hope of Sikander's political future. Politicians, bureaucrats and businessmen, whose carefully built facades had been demolished by Sikander, got to work against him. It was rare for the shadows of Delhi to join actual battles, but it was not unknown. Sikander Bansi was no longer a promising politician by the end of that day.

He was just a bad idea that had slipped through while no one was looking.

Somewhere on the margins of prime time news and corners of the first pages of newspapers next day, there were brief stories about Mira. These reports talked about the attack against her, the state of her health and Munshi's statement that the newspaper stood by her. It didn't seem to matter anymore who helped Sikander in his endeavour or why. There was no time to waste remembering, when the whole idea was to forget. And like an honourable person with a clear conscience, Delhi was very good at forgetting.

———

Salat was not surprised when Mira didn't wake up that night or even the next morning. She was tenacious about death, and as Sikander had discovered, she didn't care for one man's love or another man's respect. She was from that end of the spectrum where all these emotions merged into nothingness. It would take more than that to get her to return, more than mere refracted light.

He was still wondering about it when, at a formal meeting at the PP headquarters, Nalan Malik submitted his inquiry report to the party president Mahesh Bansi. That would have made a good photograph, but it was done inside Mahesh's office and beyond the reach of cameras. The report, according to the news channels, had three sections. The first one was an exhaustive list of people mentioned in the tapes and the allegations against them, which showed how dangerous Sikander could be. The second section was an interview with Sikander, which proved how dangerous he really was. The third part contained the findings of the investigation, which suggested how to deal with such danger to the party.

As with all internal reports of political parties not open to the press, it was on the news within one hour of its submission. In two hours, the full copy was with senior journalists in newspapers, including Dubey. Shortly afterwards, Munshi called a quick meeting at 4 p.m. to discuss the implications of the report and the impact on the newspaper's stories about the tapes. This was the second meeting of the day, and everyone had kept tabs on Mira's condition in the hospital. There was a moment's silence as they all sat round the table, aware of the possibility that she might never attend another meeting with them again. Dubey shook his head, as if dismissing a nasty thought. Lina's lovely face was flushed with emotion, and Bhaskar frowned broodingly. Munshi sat with his eyes lowered, grim. Then he looked up at Salat.

'Salat, can you please ensure that the hospital agrees to a special request?'

'Sure.'

He glanced around the table impatiently. 'If Mira can't come for the meeting, let's take the meeting to her.'

There was a wary silence.

'Call your contacts and please arrange visitors' passes for all of us and deal with whatever hospitals do to keep away loved ones from patients. We will be there immediately.' He paused, and then threatened, 'And we will stay there for as long as it takes!'

Salat stared at him, astonished, and then rushed out of the room to make the calls. Munshi glanced at the stunned faces in a warning. 'Now, don't think this sets a precedent. You have to be on the death bed for me to do this, all right?'

Everyone nodded, then smiled at his warning. Eventually, even Munshi smiled back at them.

The hospital allowed them only half an hour and with only two extra chairs in the room. They had to lose their shoes, wear surgical masks and wash their hands. Munshi commented that if Mira did wake up now, she would never stop laughing at them. He occupied one of the chairs, and the other was given to Lina.

The rest leaned against the walls, with notebooks open in their hands. Mira lay still, a blanket pulled to her shoulders, her hair still covered. An oxygen cannula reached her nose, and wires connected her to monitors on the wall. They sat in frozen silence, the fear of losing her was more real now.

As always, it was Dubey who remembered his duties. He referred to the summary of the inquiry report. 'I have here the gist of the report submitted by Nalan Malik to the PP leadership today. He was given one day to complete his investigation and question Sikander. It's believed that Sikander asked his father to put Nalan in charge of this investigation, a choice that other leaders had no problem with supporting. This happened yesterday and surprised everyone that Sikander should prefer Nalan, a man who expressly worked against him. Today we find an answer in this report . . .'

'You know Ashok,' Munshi said, his voice muffled from behind the mask, 'if you don't get to the point soon, I might end up in the next room of this hospital.'

Dubey hurriedly nodded. 'In brief, the report had found various faults with the manner in which Sikander recorded the incidents. Nalan has questioned the ethics of hidden recordings and contended that it is human nature to be inaccurate about events when making informal remarks. And yet, he has left it to the courts to consider the evidence. He has also strongly recommended action against members of government and party who have been mentioned in the tapes. That includes himself.'

'Brilliant as usual!' Munshi noted. 'Nalan Malik knows he must not be seen as shielding the corrupt. He knows people have already judged the tapes through the media. And that Sikander is a hero.' He paused, 'There will be no action against anyone. I talked to Mahesh Bansi on phone in the morning today. This is just an exercise for public perception. The Parliament tapes will be given a decent and quick burial, and Sikander an equally decent and quick promotion.'

'But how can the PP brush aside conversations inside Parliament that revealed sordid deals?' Lina asked.

'Who will demand action?' Bhaskar countered. 'The Opposition National Party? Omkar Nuri? There is a tape against every one of them, but they cannot denounce Sikander's work either.'

Munshi glanced at Dubey. 'You were saying something about how this report explains why Sikander chose Nalan to investigate him?'

'Yes.' Dubey pointed to the CD of the report on the table next to him. 'The politics of the investigation should have been to reprimand Sikander for his methods and later build a case for his expulsion from the party. Instead, Nalan does not suggest any action against Sikander and even recommends that he should be complimented for keeping an eye on general misconduct.'

'That sounds like the deal,' Lina said. 'I agree with Ashok.'

Bhaskar disagreed. 'That couldn't have been the deal. Mahesh Bansi would have never allowed his son to be expelled. He couldn't have remained the party president after that; his rivals would have ensured it. No, Mahesh Bansi had to demonstrate his clout by protecting his son. Although, on a personal level, I'm sure he must have already disowned every action of Sikander.'

'If that's not the deal,' Munshi asked, 'then why did Sikander ask for Nalan to head the investigation against him?'

No one had an answer to that.

'Mira could have given us an idea about how Sikander thinks,' Dubey observed sadly. Then asked, 'What do you think, Salat? You are a knower too.'

Salat had stood near the wall in silence and observed her with worry. But Dubey's question focused him. 'I only know a few things about Sikander,' he replied, 'especially after meeting him here yesterday. He is highly intelligent, motivated and intimidated neither by strategy nor by force. He knew his plan was perfect, that's why he risked bringing Mira into it. And yet, he made one mistake and that cost him everything.'

Salat paused. 'His targets in the published tapes were all chosen with precision,' he explained. 'This worked on two levels; it exposed the corruption and also helped his political career. And there was nothing anyone could do in retaliation. He himself was in hiding, and his frayed relationship with his father was well known. He doesn't have close friends, and is unmarried and unattached.'

Salat felt his heart slowly fill up. 'But even Sikander, despite his meticulous planning, missed something—that he would fall for Mira.' Salat turned to her again. 'That surprises me, you know. A man who could see into the future of his rivals and manipulate their present was blind to his own heart. That was his only mistake.'

Munshi asked, 'Then that's the deal? That she should be safe?'

'If I know Sikander,' he answered, 'that's why he surrendered to Nalan.'

'So you're saying Nalan was behind the attack on Mira?' Bhaskar asked.

'I don't know that,' Salat said, unsure. 'But perhaps Nalan can keep it from happening again.'

There was a thoughtful silence in the room. It was clear that even though Salat's analysis might be the truth, there was simply no way to prove it.

Dubey cleared his throat. 'I'm sure the news channels would run through the entire report by tonight, and there would be little left for us to write in tomorrow morning's newspaper. However, the channels won't have the time to play the complete recording of Nalan's questioning of Sikander. I think there may be a few stories lurking there that we can work on.'

'All right,' Munshi said. 'Let us listen to the interview.'

Dubey set up the laptop on the table and played the recording. They heard Nalan's cool, comforting voice fill the silence like a drop of blue ink in water, owning it slowly.

'Today is 3 August. This is the formal interview of Sikander Bansi for the People's Party panel investigating allegations of corruption against Parliamentarians. I'm Nalan Malik.'

There was a pause. Then he said, 'Sikander, I have been directed to ask you questions to explain your role in the recordings that have come to be known as the Parliament tapes. Five critical questions have been selected and endorsed by the party leadership, and I request you to answer them as accurately and elaborately as possible. To aid you in this, I have already provided you a copy of the questions. Your answers will be made public and form the basis for any legal action that may be contemplated. Now, I hope that is clear?'

'It is,' Sikander answered.

'Question number one,' Nalan said. 'According to the chronology of your tapes, you made the first recording just a few months after you were elected to the Parliament. You must have had no time to study the working of procedures to know their merit. You couldn't have even attended enough sessions of the House to learn how each issue was discussed. Why, with so little effort at learning first, did you go straight to demolishing a system we have come to cherish?'

Sikander's voice was tranquil as usual. 'In the first place, I was interested in contesting for Parliament because I knew its importance and because I wanted to contribute to its working,' he paused. 'But it took me just a few weeks to realize that I was being a fool. I used to come prepared every day to participate in debates and impact policy with my ideas. There was low attendance, the government side

left a junior minister to take notes of the debates and mostly
ignored the suggestions made by the House. The legislations
were already negotiated and decided. Clearly, that was not
happening inside the House. So, I started to check where the
actual debates took place about the bills,' He added quietly,
'It didn't take me long to discover, as you can see.'

'Yes, I can,' Nalan assured him dryly. 'Question number
two: If you had complaints about the way Parliament was
functioning, you could have taken up the issues with the
office-bearers of the parliamentary board of the party. Or, you
could have placed the complaints before the party leadership
at the headquarters to which, if I may mention here, you have
exclusive access. Why didn't you?'

'I did,' Sikander answered. 'I spoke to the minister in
charge of Parliamentary affairs and also to the party whips.
They felt that as a new member, I would take some time to
learn the ropes. By that, I understood that in time I would
get used to the way business was conducted in Parliament.
But that was exactly the point. I didn't want to get used to
it; I wanted to change it.' Then he added with restraint, 'As
for the party leadership, it never took me seriously because
I was his son.'

'Perhaps for good reason,' Nalan observed sardonically.
'Question number three: As you must be aware, according
to article 157, sub section (a)-2 of the party constitution, a
member is prohibited from speaking to the media about the
internal affairs of the party. Why did you violate this rule
by going to a newspaper to publish your tapes? Please show
cause why disciplinary action shouldn't be taken against you.'

'I collected the evidence of deals being made in the
government over everything, ranging from food to foreign
affairs, and I did it with a view to inform the public,' Sikander

said. 'Voters do not know what happens behind the closed doors of Parliament. The televised sessions and press conferences do not mention what takes place in the shadows beyond the limelight. I wanted people to know who made the millions to support a vote or oppose it. I wanted to name the members of Parliament who converted the hopes of their helpless constituents into a meal ticket for themselves. Yes,' Sikander asserted evenly, 'I know of that rule in the party constitution, but I believe that not to correct this situation would have been detrimental to the party's future. And that's in sub-section (b) of the same article.'

'That's a debatable interpretation,' Nalan dismissed him. 'Now, for question number four. Serious allegations have been leveled at senior politicians, bureaucrats and businesses in the tapes. What is the extent and scope of the evidence you have in the tapes that have been published? Can you provide us access to the evidence?'

'Well, for those who are on the tapes,' Sikander politely added, 'such as yourself, it would be evident that each tape is a key that could open many other deals and many other scams. However, to answer your question, yes, I'm ready to pass on to the courts all the evidence and other recordings to support the allegations in each tape. Besides, only five of the tapes were published. There is more unpublished evidence that awaits investigation.'

'There are more tapes?'

Sikander chuckled. 'Your surprise disappoints me.'

Nalan cleared his throat. 'Last question: Why were you in hiding while the tapes were being published? From the clues you gave the know-journalist, whom I shall not name here, it is clear that you knew her well. Why did you collude with her to stay in hiding while her newspaper published the tapes?'

'My disappearance was the only way to keep the tapes from being attributed to me personally,' Sikander replied. 'Without adulterating them with my justifications, which I would have been forced to give, the tapes told the true story exactly the way it happened in each case. It allowed people to judge for themselves what they could see and hear. Besides, I knew I couldn't have survived the collective pressure of the party leadership, Opposition leaders, senior bureaucrats and business houses. I would have been silenced, and the tapes would have never seen the light of day.'

Sikander continued carefully, 'You will agree that we don't usually talk about the personal lives of our friends. It should have been obvious that I wouldn't have used personal information about the know-journalist in widely publicized clues if we were acquainted in any way or if I was even remotely concerned about her interests. She is a stranger to me, and I researched her only because I couldn't have trusted an unknown woman on such a sensitive case.'

'And yet, she is fighting for her life in a hospital, possibly because of you,' Nalan countered.

'That's her choice. I'm sorry, but I'm not responsible for the risks people want to take,' Sikander answered patiently. 'I do wish her a quick recovery.'

'That concludes your questioning, Sikander.' Nalan was terse and added, 'Thank you for your time.'

The tape ended, and Munshi glanced at Salat accusingly.

'Well?' he demanded. 'You got that wrong, haven't you? Sikander didn't surrender to save Mira's life. He did it to save his own political career.'

Upset and shocked by Sikander's words, Salat couldn't answer Munshi.

'That's the story I want tomorrow morning.' Munshi stood up and glared at everyone. 'Get working on how Sikander is encashing the tapes. This is the end of the amnesty we had extended to him because he gave the tapes to our newspaper due to Mira. Now, let's get back to business!'

Later, when everyone left the room, Salat still stood leaning against the wall and studied Mira. Then, he slowly walked to the bed and listened to the effort it took for her to breath. Salat gently held her hand that was cold and sweaty, as if with fever under control with drugs.

'You heard that Mira. I know you did,' he said apologetically. 'I wish I could confront Sikander about his words and prove him wrong, but I can't. No one can, except you.'

He stood there for a long while, praying fervently for a sign of life from her. Then, disappointed, he turned heavily and left.

TWENTY-ONE

Mira frowned slightly as the pain in her stomach woke her up and increased rapidly as she became aware of it. And so, she slipped back under the great black canopy of sleep and looked for her favourite dream.

Ah yes, I found it. This is the dream I love, but usually can't remember when I'm awake. It is about a place that has things that I want and would like to keep. I have a little suitcase to carry them with me, and I walk around, wondering what to choose. There are others in the same place, looking equally lost. It is so beautiful that it is difficult to decide. I can't see what others gather, I can't look into their suitcases. Many go together, guiding each other, but I walk alone. I decide to pick up what I think I would miss the most. Like the moss in the stream and mountain rain, like the smell of cardamom and the kitchen in the morning, like the fatigue and exhilaration of a long walk, like a cool, white pillow on a summer night.

I take some papers with me as well, like my excellent transcripts from university, my first big story at the newspaper, the journalist of the year plaque, and a few thank you messages from my email. I want to take with me the picture of the Gita, but it won't come off the wall, so I leave it behind. I also can't take along the only photo I have of the orphanage in Rishikesh. It won't stay in my hand.

A bell rings somewhere, and we all gather at a place to leave. It is like a platform, but there is no train. None of us know how we will travel, but we are excited somehow about the journey. As people bring their luggage, I see their suitcases are large and many. Worried, I stare at the little trolley that I have, the kind we generally use for cabin baggage in an aircraft. Even children carried bigger suitcases than mine. I wonder if I had forgotten something, if I should have gathered more. But where was all the good stuff? Perhaps I was stuck on the dull side, where there was nothing special. It didn't matter, I tell myself. I like travelling light, and what I don't have in mementoes, I make up in memories.

It always makes me smile, this dream. I smiled the last time I dreamt it. I was twenty-seven years old.

Mira winced as the pain once again forced her awake and opened her eyes weakly. A nurse immediately pressed the bell for the doctor and took her pulse. Mira forgot her agony for a moment and scrutinized the grey wall in front of her bed and the white curtains on the windows. Confused, Mira touched the heavy bandage on her waist where that stranger had stabbed her and then noticed the blue hospital clothes. A doctor arrived and welcomed her back; Mira asked, back from where? He was speechless for a second, and then explained that she had been unconscious for three days.

Mira turned and saw the closed window and the blocked sunlight. It had been raining when she was killed. It had been prefect. Why did she return? What for? This constant torment of the injuries didn't make sense; this wasn't her doing. In the hours that followed, doctors and nurses from the next shift told her the anxious times they went through when she was close to death.

They misunderstood her tears as she heard them and changed her pain medication instead. By that night, however, everyone realized there was something wrong. It was as if she fell apart, and the doctors consulted each other worriedly about her condition. They talked to her and reasoned with her, but she restlessly contradicted the advice in her mind. They didn't understand, Mira argued; she didn't want to 'pull herself together', she didn't want to 'get well' or 'miraculously' live again. She had tried life; she now wanted something better. Then she remembered the identity of the assailant's employers—those who wanted her dead. Why didn't they ensure it? Or did they want her to suffer, here on the edge of life? A fitting punishment, a difficult death! The nurses held her down to the bed as she wouldn't sleep despite sedation. Mira struggled against the grip on her arms, trying to free herself to escape. People rushed around, and urgent voices called. She begged them to let her die, her whispers were lost in the warning sounds of the machines around. Everything was grinding to a halt, and she struggled against the restraints, the needles and the words. She felt her breath fail suddenly and panicked. Warm blood spread on her skin from her injuries, and her heart began to ache. As she choked, she felt fear of death again, but it was still less powerful than her fear of returning to life. She stopped fighting; it was a simple choice. She could feel her body collapse inside her, detach itself from her, and she let it go. There was chaos at the brink, the pain of her wounds dug into her and unravelled the muscles. Her heart ached acutely, and she completely ceased to breathe, lost in the unfamiliar silence. There were noises around her, hands supported her, and machines beeped, but she fell through it all at a speed that frightened her. There was nothing to stop her, no reference points, no memory and no one. Her eyes filled up for the unwanted life she was forced to live, and she willed it resolutely to its end. Vaguely, as if from across a great river, she felt something return, something she had desired: a touch. Delusion, she thought, must be part of the end, part of the brain's survival tactics. The last deception. Such reference points could work with others, not her. Whose touch could she miss? But she was intrigued as warm hands held her face, and someone asked her to wake up. What for, she thought, falling through the images behind her eyes of the places she had never belonged to.

'Mira don't!'

She gasped for air, as the voice pulled her back through the distance she had already travelled. This wasn't fair, she complained as she strained to breath again. Why was she called back? Someone called her name again, the familiar voice afraid and agitated. Did she forget to finish something? Why was she going back? She opened her eyes, puzzled, and could only see the hazy light at first. There were relieved chuckles around the bed, and she found someone holding her close, pushing the hair away from her forehead. It was the same touch that had stopped her, and she glanced up to ask why. She stared at Nalan, confused. His face was serious and grim with worry. Intrigued, Mira frowned; he thought she objected to him and left her. But as he moved away she felt disoriented and reached out, and he quickly held her cold hand again. Mira closed her eyes, tired, and after some time, fell asleep.

Nalan was still there when she woke up a few hours later. He sat in a chair at a distance and worked on his laptop. She noticed as he intently surveyed the screen that lit up his good-looking face. A nurse asked her if she felt better, and that made Nalan glance up.

He quietly walked to her bed.

'You could have told me, you know,' he protested, 'that you were planning this. I had just dropped by, it had become a habit in the last two days. Good I did, though. Might have missed meeting you forever.'

Mira closed her eyes indifferently.

'Yes, you're right,' he said, contemplating. 'I've got to get out of the habit. You won't be here in this hospital for long. And others have their own Nalans.'

That made her smile weakly.

'Maybe I'll get lucky, I agree with you,' he nodded. 'But my days of searching hospitals for true love are over. Really.'

Mira chuckled and opened her eyes. He studied her, then gratefully touched her face. 'I don't know why I came here every day twice,' he said. 'I couldn't be anywhere else, do anything else ...'

She just heard him speak in his beautiful voice.

'And my irate driver informed me today that the hospital doesn't fall on the way to every destination in the city,' Nalan smiled. 'But it will, as long as you are here. So I request you, for the sake of my itinerary, please recover quickly.'

She realized this was what had brought her back, he had to let her go for her to die.

'I don't want to recover,' she whispered with effort, and he leaned forward to hear her better. 'I have to go now,' she begged him. 'Let me. Please.'

He was silent, his brown eyes pained by her request. He didn't speak at once, but reached and held her hand.

'Go where, Mira?' he asked her finally. 'I can't afford another detour!'

She smiled, apologetic; she knew he understood.

'Wherever next you're planning to go,' he said earnestly, 'make sure it falls on my way.'

Mira was aware that he probably didn't mean them, but the words made her eyes fill up, and noticing that, he kissed her hand.

'All right! That hand tasted of the antiseptic!' he said, disgusted.

Mira chuckled again and managed to weakly pull her hand away.

The first visitors the next morning were Salat and Lina. They brought the newspapers with them and told her about Sikander's interview to Nalan. They were puzzled by his harsh comments about her. The doctors didn't let her sit up yet, and she often fell into long spells of fatigued sleep. But every time she woke up, she found herself thinking only about Sikander. His words enraged her. What did he mean he couldn't trust her with a sensitive case? Perhaps she would ask him when he came to see her, but he never did.

The following day, Nalan was visiting her when Sita Patnaik came to check on her informally. Overlooking the nurse's protests, Nalan and Sita helped Mira sit up on the bed with the support of the pillows. Nalan left his chair for Sita and leaned against the window. They talked of the case and the progress.

Then Sita smiled a little contritely. 'I need a bit of your help, Miraji. We can't seem to place the assailant.'

'Don't bother,' Mira said, her voice was still a low whisper. 'No one can.'

'You were stabbed twice from the front,' Sita noted. 'You must have seen him. What did you make of your assailant?'

'Well, let me remember.' Mira closed her eyes. 'He was about six feet tall, forty-five years old, well built, fair with dark hair, small eyes, no glasses, a watch with a silver dial, no ring and black shoes with rubber soles. He takes the labels off his clothes, he even wears shoes that don't belong to him. He loves being invisible, and it is not just because he doesn't leave footprints or fingerprints. He wouldn't even leave traces of his life behind when he moves from one place to another. He will own nothing that can't fit in his pocket. His assets will be inaccessible but online and so would be his entire work.' Mira opened her eyes. 'He will be impossible to catch in the real world, he will have no physical address.'

Amused, Nalan glanced at Sita's stunned face.

'Right,' Sita recovered. "I should've known.'

Mira just smiled.

'It was a symbolic assault,' Sita said. 'Your hands were tied to make the point. However, the man could have easily killed you. Instead, he left you to die. That's very interesting.'

'Why is that *interesting*?' Nalan was offended.

'It saved her life,' Sita calmly explained to him. 'It made the rescue possible.' She turned to Mira again. 'Can you remember anything more about the two phone calls you said he had made?'

'When he called before the attack, he was instructed to ask me if I wanted to say something or have something, like a last wish.' Mira stopped for breath, then said, 'It was a meaningless formality that wasted time, which was strange because the assailant said he was in a hurry. The employer wanted the attack delayed.'

Sita was troubled. 'This is most confusing. It seems to be someone who cares for you.'

'And also wants to kill you,' Nalan added meditatively. 'Sounds like my divorce.'

They all laughed. Then Mira continued, 'The person in the second phone call ascertained whether prior instructions were followed about the attack, like I should bleed to death and not killed outright. I thought that was also a bit strange, you know.'

'Did he give any names?' Nalan asked.

'No. The assailant referred to them only as his employers,' Mira answered. 'Presumably, they were the people who sent him to kill me.'

Nalan remarked, 'You know who they are, Mira.'

'I do,' Mira accepted, 'but how can I prove that they were the same people who got hurt due to the Parliament tapes?'

'There are other suspects,' Sita countered. 'You had gone to see Sikander Bansi that morning and returned from Sangam Vihar. Is that correct?'

'Yes, but I had not met him.'

'He says he first checked the room you had rented in the area but didn't find you there. He rushed to your home as he anticipated the danger you might face from the people who were allegedly looking for him.'

'That's possible.'

Sita studied her. 'It's also possible that it was Sikander Bansi himself who sent that man to kill you. That's why he knew where and when to rescue you.'

Mira frowned.

'What nonsense!' Nalan objected. 'Another of your police theories, Sitaji, that you cook up sitting behind your desk? Why would Sikander Bansi want to kill Mira when he cares for her so much?'

'As we just discovered, Mr Malik,' Sita pointed out, 'the assailant's employers also cared for her.'

'Yes, but Sikander left his life in her hands, with clues that led directly to him. He would be grateful that Mira didn't betray him till the end, not get her killed!'

Sita considered him. 'Another of your civilian theories that you cook up sitting in your living room?'

That made Nalan chuckle. He raised his hands, giving up.

Mira responded intrigued. 'Why do you suspect Sikander?'

'Two reasons. He might have needed an excuse to come out of hiding.'

'Oh, come on, Sitaji!' Nalan intervened again impatiently, 'Sikander could have done that anytime. There were enough "excuses" for him to choose from. For example, to save his father's reputation, to save his own political career and to just prove wrong all the doubts about his motives.' Nalan paused, his sharp eyes turned keen. 'But none of them would have been the right excuse. None of them would have made him the martyr he is now. And he surrendered to me, one of the tainted men from the Parliament tapes. It was a priceless political move!'

Mira didn't speak. As usual she could detect only some of Nalan's thoughts and, at that moment, even those were incomplete.

Then she asked Sita, 'What's the second reason?'

'Well, didn't one of Sikander's clues mention death?' Sita inquired, 'Your death?'

'Many of his clues did.'

'Yes, but this one talked about a knife.'

Mira didn't speak. She vividly recollected Sikander's first clue.

'I should have a copy of the clues in the file in my vehicle downstairs,' Sita stood up. 'Let me get that, please excuse me.'

When she was gone, Nalan glanced at Mira. 'Are you all right with this? You don't have to solve the case for the police.'

'I'm fine,' she told him, lost in thought. 'That clue Sita was talking about came with the first tape. It had stated:

'Choose the knife carefully, none of the fancy types will do.
It should be double-edged and long, and made of steel for
a warrior.'

Nalan listened to her, getting enraged.

'These were different ways in which I could end my life,' Mira recalled. Then the clue ended with;

'Come die with me any way you want, but not alone.'

'That murderer!' Nalan said, infuriated. 'I shouldn't have let him off so easily.' He angrily paced the room.

'It was just a clue . . .'

'It was not!' Nalan snapped. 'He advertised how he was going to get you killed, Mira! The arrogant little . . .' He stopped with effort, then asked, 'Don't tell me you can't see that?'

Mira shrugged. 'I don't mind, really. I myself have thought of these ways to die.'

'I would like to change that,' Nalan retorted sternly. 'And I know I can. But Sikander didn't want to even try, he wanted you to die instead.'

Mira watched Nalan in silence. She knew he lied.

Nalan walked to the window. 'I want the police to lodge a case against Sikander for that attack on you. I don't need more proof than this, and I don't care if you do.'

She observed him outlined against the rainless bright day, as he stood straight and strong. It was his nature to believe in himself. That's why he was there with her working out her life, despite her. In a way, she loved that about him.

'Sikander didn't plunge that knife into you,' Nalan reasoned, coldly, 'but he chose that death for you. I care too much about you to let him get away with it.'

'All right, Nalan,' she said, and he turned to her in surprise.

She gently accepted, 'You know him better.'

His angry eyes softened. 'I do.'

'But can you wait a little before you lodge that police complaint?'

'What for?' He gestured to the chair, which Sita had just occupied. 'Let Sitaji return, and she can write down the complaint right now.'

Mira whispered, 'I would like to meet Sikander once.'

Nalan was still. 'Why?'

What could she tell him? Mira wondered. Then said, 'To learn from my mistakes.'

'It was his mistake, not yours.'

'I hope so.'

Nalan was unsure, but finally agreed. 'Fine, I'll wait.'

Mira thanked him and mentioned that she would seek time from Sikander's office. Nalan didn't speak immediately. Then he said, 'I find I can't refuse you anything. It's going to cost me something someday, much more than that terrible lunch at your newspaper canteen I shouldn't have had.'

Mira smiled mischievously. 'Then learn from your mistakes.'

He studied her smile and said, 'This isn't a mistake. This is a disaster.'

She laughed, conceding that, and the healing wounds began to hurt a little less.

A couple of days later, Mira managed to walk around in the hospital room and the doctors felt she could soon return home. Salat helped her to the chair and sat on the bed himself.

'Why don't you come and stay at my house?' he suggested. 'As you saw for yourself, there is enough staff to take care of you and enough space for you to rest without disturbance.'

Mira smiled. 'Good try, Salat, but no.'

'Now really, Mira,' he protested. 'You can't go home. Who'll take care of you?'

She declined, and just then, her cell phone rang. It was Nalan, and she told him that the doctors might send her home in a day or two.

'Yes, but you'll be alone at home.' Nalan was concerned. 'You need to be looked after.'

'Salat was just saying that.' Mira glanced at him. 'He has even generously invited me to his house, as if I could be so cruel.'

Salat smiled at her words and tried to guess whom she talked to.

'I extend to you a similar invitation,' Nalan offered, 'and I hope you are cruel enough to accept it.'

'And you guys think I'm suicidal!'

'Fine! Have it your way and go home,' he said. 'I'll send along my staff to take care of the medicines, food and other things you may need.'

'You won't do any such thing,' she exclaimed. 'I don't need your staff. I would rather stay here at the hospital for a few more days.'

'That was easy!' He chuckled. Then he said he would visit her in the evening and ended the call.

Salat surveyed her, amazed. 'This is the first time I've seen you actually happy!'

Mira laughed. 'It's the stab wounds.'

'This is something special,' Salat noted, curious. 'Who was that on the phone? Sikander?'

Mira's smiled faded. 'Why would you think it was Sikander?'

'Perhaps because he rescued you and saved your life,' he pointed out.

'Not the only one,' she said cryptically.

Intrigued, Salat said, 'But I do find it strange that he should have spoken those words against you, and called you a stranger when he knows you so well. And he hasn't even come to visit you.' Salat then added, hurt, 'He could have at least sent a message.'

'Why should he?' Mira frowned. 'His project is done, Salat. The Parliament tapes are published. He doesn't need me or the newspaper anymore. Please don't confuse his efficiency with emotion. The research about my life, the insightful clues and everything else was part of his larger strategy to reinvent himself.'

Salat reluctantly accepted that. 'Yes, I see that in every news report and political analysis. He is considered a rebel despite his background and is seen as someone who is better than the system because he has exposed its corruption.' He paused. 'Even his re-election, which was in doubt, is assured now.'

'That's fine,' Mira said derisively. 'He has moved ahead in his life and, in time, his enemies will relent. I'm sure you have noted that he has not made even a single demand to ask for specific action against anyone mentioned in his tapes.' She was quietly furious. 'But these facts can't dull the blinding glory of his honesty and his morality. No one, not even the PP, can touch him now. Not just because of his soaring popularity, but because he is armed with the evidence in Parliament tapes that our newspaper helped advertise for him. It was routine journalism for us and it was routine blackmail for him.'

Salat heard her seriously, then reflected, 'I wish we were all more than what we do to succeed.'

'We are exactly what we do to succeed,' she insisted.

Salat was puzzled, 'If it was not Sikander, then who were you talking to on the phone?'

'Nalan Malik.'

'*Who!*'

Mira avoided his stunned eyes.

'Are you sure you can even stand him?' he asked incredulously. 'I mean, he is the same man who forced our newspaper to stop publishing the tapes. And the last tape we did publish gave evidence of his role in the division of a state for corporate purposes!'

Mira remained silent.

Salat sounded dazed. 'I mean, I can see straight patterns in his behaviour that reveal his motives. His interest in you might be because he is committed to bringing down Sikander. He was probably even behind the attack on you.' Salat was disturbed. 'Why are you even talking to him?'

'I like him.'

'You *what*?'

'Look, I know what he did, Salat,' she argued. 'His deals, his politics, all that our newspaper tried to expose and all that he did to prevent us from doing so. But you forget that it was not Nalan who decided *not to publish* the last tape on weapons dealers. It was the editor of our newspaper.'

Salat tolerantly pointed out, 'You know Nalan forced that decision. He is a dangerous man, Mira.'

'More than Sikander?' she asked him evenly.

Salat weighed that. 'Probably not.'

'I have recorded the thoughts of both men,' she told him, her voice forlorn. 'I can't hate either of them.'

He noticed her drawn face. 'Well, I guess I was wrong,' he said easily. 'I thought you hated Nalan.'

She chuckled. 'Hate a man who is here morning and evening to meet me looking like this?' Mira gestured to the hospital clothes. 'Even I'm beginning to believe.'

Salat smiled. 'That he is more than what he does to succeed?'

'Or less, in his case,' she replied.

Salat laughed. Then he remembered something.

'What is it?' Mira asked, observing his troubled face.

'There was something I never wanted to tell you about Sikander.' Salat spoke uncertainly. 'I thought you liked him too much and that it might upset you.'

'Are you serious?' Mira chided him. 'When did you not upset me?'

But he was anxious as he said, 'Sikander seemed to know who was behind the attack.'

She was suddenly still. 'Who did he say it was?'

'Bhaskar asked him but he wouldn't say. He just mentioned that it was his score to settle.'

'His score?' Mira repeated, frowning.

'So I accused him of protecting the assailant.'

'Please, Salat,' she protested. 'Wasn't that going too far?'

'Perhaps,' he admitted. 'But he didn't deny it.'

Mira's dark eyes sharpened with interest.

'He said your blood spoke to him,' Salat fell silent, tormented, as he recalled the stains on Sikander's shirt. 'He said he shed your blood, and you won't stop thanking him for it.'

She remained silent, distressed; Sikander referred to his first clue that suggested death by knife, the clue that Sita thought made him a suspect in the case.

'I'm sorry,' Salat said remorsefully, noticing her expression. 'I shouldn't have told you this.'

Mira took a deep breath and managed to smile at him. 'You haven't told me anything I didn't know already. You just confirmed something I wasn't sure of.'

'What's that?'

'That it was probably good I survived the attack,' Mira reflected. 'This is no time to die.'

TWENTY-TWO

The following days saw many agitations across the country that demanded action against people exposed in Sikander's Parliament tapes. There were demonstrations, hunger strikes, boycotts and symbolic arrests. But the movement seemed to have no leaders, no organizers and no spokespersons. In other words, there was no politics. There was also no corporate support and no media support. In other words, there was no money. And yet people gathered in parks, at crossings, outside government buildings and inside school playgrounds. Experts sitting in Delhi analysed this rapid mobilization and mistook it for a revolution against an elected government. There was outrage against the undemocratic uprising, and the government prepared to retaliate. And then, just on the brink of a conflict, Sikander made a statement to clarify that the movement should not be about taking over of power. Instead, it should only be about making power more accountable to people.

That simple explanation, which he had Tweeted one morning over a cup of tea, forced the government to wait and stalled the planned crackdown against the agitators. It also instantly made Sikander a hero. His Tweet was re-Tweeted, made into posters and even T-shirts and caps. Then someone proposed that if his statement crossed over 10,000 re-Tweets, he should be declared leader of the movement. It took just three hours to cross that mark, and the question was settled. However, no one had anticipated Sikander's answer when he turned down the offer. But by refusing power over people, he became the most qualified man to wield it. He was asked about it often; why wasn't he ready to take the credit for the Parliament tapes and lead the movement for better accountability? And he repeated the same answer every time, that he had done the job for which he was elected as a member of Parliament—to serve the best interests of the people. There was no need to give him credit for it, he mentioned, he already drew a salary. Delhi was not used to this, at least not from one of its own.

There was an uproar of support for him from across the country. And yet, he stayed home, allowing himself to be photographed with his books and friends. He was a recluse in the middle of a crowd, a silence that made the chaos around him stand still and make sense. He seemed to have no ambition, no motive, no need for wealth and no desire for power. There is always demand for such people at all times of history, and there is always a short supply.

The PP had no choice but to treat Sikander like a star. He was the only clean face they had in the party. He stood against the corruption of his own party's government and, therefore, neutralized the Opposition parties' campaigns. The PP knew the next election would be about the Parliament tapes, and it was prudent to own them than denounce them.

However, everyone in the PP knew what Sikander had done was treacherous. They needed him politically, but they didn't respect him personally. Their respect was reserved for Nalan, especially for his effortless handling of the investigation against Sikander in a way that no one was hurt. He was also admired for the way he had braved the risk of facing action himself, when he had made his bold recommendation based on the investigation. That had made him a favourite among all the others named in the published tapes or expected to be named in the unpublished ones. He too was constantly petitioned to lead a front within the party against Sikander. It already had the support of the leadership that was tired of Mahesh, and also the cooperation of other political parties angry with Sikander. Such a rebellion could have split the PP and created a new party in which a new leader could have emerged and assumed control. There was possibility of power, and there was certainty of money. And yet, just like Sikander, Nalan didn't make a move. They both seemed to wait for something to happen.

Mira returned home after a week's stay in the hospital, and, just as everyone had warned, found it difficult to manage alone. It helped that Salat's staff brought food and other supplies, and the landlady sent her own housekeeper to do the chores. But it was Nalan who was to be always found in the house, usually talking on his phone, pacing the living room or sitting with his feet up, reading one of her stories from old newspaper clippings. Mira wondered about his way of thinking. He sought nothing of her and gave everything of himself, without her ever asking. So, she wanted to find out what if she asked him for something. For instance, the apples she loved? He would get her a few dozen, she thought, make sure she was never short of apples. Instead, he brought one apple every time he met her and sliced it himself carefully, as if he valued something she liked. It almost changed the taste of apples forever.

Mira had already informed Bhaskar that she would seek time to meet Sikander unofficially and not on behalf of the newspaper. When she had called from the hospital, Sikander's office politely registered her request but never got back. When she called to check, she was told that he was busy. Then, after a few more reminders, his office finally gave her time for the meeting at 4 p.m on that Monday.

Nalan asked her to be careful and not take too long at the meeting, as she was still not fully recovered and too weak. He was on a tour of an eastern state on party work and was expected to be away for three days. But he made up for his absence by calling often, and she kept the cell phone close to her. She felt strangely insufficient without him, as if he was functionally important for her to get through a day. Salat drove her to the Bansi residence and helped her step out of the car. He said he would wait outside and she gave him her cell phone with a request to tell Nalan, who was bound to call, that she would talk to him after the meeting. An aide led her to the separate path on the right side of the main house. It was a sunny day, full of birds and conversations. The garden was green and with rows of empty white chairs, as if a meeting had just ended. Getting breathless with the exertion, she walked slowly and felt the pull of the muscles around the healing wounds. Mira glanced at the tree in the distance, the one that kept secret stories of unseen worlds folded in its foliage. It seemed to have soaked enough rain to start making it the next season. She stopped walking, unable to breathe, and the aide waited anxiously. It had been over ten days since the attack, and there was only a light bandage over the injuries. But the doctors still insisted on rest, and she still couldn't walk without pain and fatigue. Her legs trembled with weakness by the time she reached the door of Sikander's house, and gratefully slumped down in one of the armchairs of the study. She had a glass of water the aide got her and closed her eyes, dealing with the pain. The house had always been silent and settled, as if it had resolved whatever bothered it. But now it felt complete, Mira discovered, and wondered where he was.

Sikander stood at a distance and scrutinized her with a frown. Her face seemed thinner, the khadi shirt she usually wore hung loosely, and the dark trousers were crumpled. The exhaustion of even that short walk had overwhelmed her, the injuries were taking their toll. His worried eyes went to her hand that was pressed to the waist at the wounds. Then his face cleared quickly.

'It couldn't wait?' he said as he walked into the study. 'Good afternoon.'

Startled, Mira opened her eyes and found Sikander stand before her.

She made to get up to move to the sofas, but he gestured her not to and pulled up a chair. The light from the windows fell on him, and Mira was taken aback a little. He was no longer the common-looking man who merged seamlessly into that damp lane in Sangam Vihar, as if he had always belonged to it. He wore a beige cotton jacket and a white shirt, with dark brown trousers and suede shoes. His dark hair was neat and his large eyes were formal. Sikander was once again the man in his picture, the man in his tapes.

'Why haven't you recovered yet?' he asked with precise impatience. 'Never mind, I'll find out from the doctors at the hospital. Let's talk about why you are here.'

Mira sank back in the armchair, her dark eyes still surprised.

'What, you were expecting someone else?' He was amused. 'Nalan Malik, perhaps?'

Mira conceded, weakly. 'I was expecting someone else.'

There was a moment's silence, then Sikander noted, 'That'll be the first thing you have ever said to me.'

She still breathed with effort, and knew it wasn't going to be easy to speak.

'All right,' he said crisply. 'What can I do for you? Why are you here?'

Mira studied him in silence, realizing the futility of her visit. 'I'm sorry,' she whispered. 'I shouldn't have wasted your time. This meeting was not required, and if you could please call your aide, I will leave right now.'

She made to rise from the armchair and realized she may need assistance. Sikander didn't move.

'This may be a waste of time,' he granted, 'but now that the meeting has begun, let's talk. What's on your mind?'

Mira glanced around and searched for the aide who seemed to have left the house.

'You want something?' Sikander inquired. 'You like tea, if I recall. No food, but two shelves full of tea. Your kitchen.'

'Yours as well,' she countered. 'No, I don't want tea, thank you.' She spoke slowly, 'I just want your aide to help me walk out to the gate.'

'I get the distinct feeling that you are trying to escape,' he remarked cordially. 'Naturally, I am concerned that any of my guests should feel so.'

That was a mean trick, Mira thought. He smiled encouragingly.

'I thought I had read you wrong,' she finally told him. 'I came to find out what was the truth: the man I knew or the man you turned out to be.'

Sikander raised his eyebrows. 'And?'

'Now I know that I was not wrong about you,' Mira said, 'and I would like to leave before you convince me otherwise.'

He chuckled. 'May I ask what exactly you were "not wrong" about?'

Mira didn't speak; his thoughts ridiculed her.

'Allow me to guess then,' Sikander offered. 'What has formed the basis of your conclusions about me? The information my father had provided about me, the tapes, the clues, this house, the way I lived in that lane where you found me and now, the result of everything.' He regarded her steadily. 'These are only parts of the picture that is far from complete. You may have concluded that I'm weighed down by my inheritance and don't care too much about it. Such admirable detachment is not my style, although I use the notion often.'

Mira wasn't surprised, that had been her conclusion about his facades.

'As for the tapes,' he glanced at the windows, thinking, his expressive eyes catching the light like water. 'The elected members of our Parliament should no longer function without any sense of accountability to the voters. I wanted to build a case for reforms that would compel MPs to reveal every deal they make, all the negotiations and the understandings they reach during their tenure. As an MP myself, I know that these transactions are mostly settled before the election when businesses start investing in politicians. If the candidate wins the election, he is obliged to pay back the businesses by supporting decisions beneficial to them.' Sikander explained, 'I wanted to raise the question: is it truly a democracy if people don't even know who funds the politician they vote for?'

He turned to her. 'Now, as for my life in the lane that you uncovered brilliantly in just the very third clue . . . I got to know that from the date you rented the room across the lane.' He paused, then continued evenly, 'I'm torn apart daily by the knowledge that I enjoy privileges most of my country cannot afford. I may be used to my destined life, but I don't like to be dependent on it. I have left it often and lived like an ordinary person in different parts of this nation.' He was serious as he added, 'It wasn't something I ever talked about. It wasn't politics. It was just the only way I felt alive, as if my soul was finally happy.'

Mira knew he meant that.

'Therefore, it was easy for me to become someone else for the duration of the publication of the tapes,' Sikander told her. 'I had to disappear to save my father trouble, and allow him to distance himself from my actions. My disguise kept me hidden from the forces that could have pressured me and, at the same time, let me monitor the publication of the tapes from Delhi and their impact.'

Mira forgot to breathe as she detected his next thought.

'As for the clues,' he leaned forward and observed her keenly. 'Trenchant, weren't they? Cut you to the quick, and made you run away from yourself. But you were also drawn by the words, even though they hurt you, because they proved I cared for you. That was worth the pain, wasn't it? I thought so too,' he said, satisfied. 'In the end, I can't say how right you were about me, Mira, but from the first day until today, you have acted exactly as I thought you would and . . .'

He stopped speaking abruptly when he noticed the faint tears in her eyes as they met his. There was silence between them for a long moment.

'That's why you chose me, wasn't it?' she whispered.

Sikander couldn't answer her.

'Your clues, your . . . vicious and loving words?' she accused him. 'You knew I would die before I gave you up. You knew it would be easy.'

He didn't speak at once, but his thoughts made her flinch.

'You call this easy?' he asked her.

'You should have let me go,' she said, helplessly.

'I plan to.'

'Please realize I can discern a lie,' she warned him.

'And please remember I know you,' he responded. 'Down to that photograph, which was not of your parents.'

Mira, disturbed, remained silent.

'Yes, I chose you because you are an orphan,' he said sternly. 'It wasn't to manipulate you but I thought you would understand me. And I was right!' Sikander said to her, upset. 'I chose you also because of the way you read my father's decisions so accurately every time. I knew you could perceive my decisions even if I was in hiding. But you did much more than that,' he said, his voice sincere. 'Your courage forced me to be strong when I had doubts about my own plans. I admire you Mira. I respect you, and you know I'm telling the truth.'

She nodded reluctantly.

He was silent, somehow hurt. Then said, 'And yet you never believed me.'

She uneasily considered him as his dark, deep eyes didn't allow her to look away.

'You found my words in the notebook, but you didn't stay in the lane that morning. I wanted that moment so much, you can't imagine!' He spoke intensely. 'I was sure my life would have changed, but when you left, when I found your room empty . . .' He stopped, then continued softly, 'I would have never hurt you, you know. You were wrong to doubt my affection.'

Mira frowned at the perfection with which he knew her thoughts. Troubled, her hand once again reached the bandage at the wounds that ached dully.

Sikander lowered his eyes. 'Perhaps I'm being selfish to think that you would want me,' he said pensively, 'merely because I need you. I have spent the last six months learning about you, thinking of you and watching you. I can't imagine a future that has nothing to do with you,' he told her simply. 'I don't want to go on without you, it would be like leaving a part of me behind.'

His thoughts were clear like sunlight. Even when he fell silent, she could hear his words in her heart. She answered them.

'That's all right. I didn't mind.'

'But I did!' he said earnestly, not surprised at her perception. 'I should've been there next to you, when you struggled for your life in the hospital. It's far too dangerous for you to be associated with me right now. They are looking for my weakness, the person for whom I can leave everything, do anything. That's why they attacked you, and that's why I had to make that statement in the interview with Nalan Malik.' Then he added, apologetic. 'That's why I didn't agree to meet you at once. Why else would I postpone this meeting?'

His every word was the truth, she noted, his every thought was about her.

'Knowing you made my life worth living, worth waking up for,' he spoke simply, honestly. 'I learnt from you how to live without wanting tomorrow. My life has been all about acquiring the future, but you left every day to itself and expected nothing from the next. I don't care if I never get to live, Mira, only if I get to die with you. I intended the clues, every one of them!' He was vehement as he added, 'For the way you desire death, I have begun desiring it for myself. Freedom; I want it like you do, with my life!'

His thoughts overwhelmed her mind and forced out every other thought.

Sikander leaned forward in his chair again, his speaking eyes were liquid light. 'When I found you dying at your home, I was shaken, Mira, but I was also angry with you. I was upset that you found what you wanted without me. There you were, leaving behind all that pinned you down to this world—the desire to begin and finish, leave and reach, give and take. You were purged of all that, you were purified of your life, your blood.' His voice was passionate as he said, 'You were like God to me that instant, someone I aspired to be but could never be; someone who belonged to a better world.'

Then he fell silent, and it was a silence like she had never heard before. There was nothing else but him, and the longing for his next words. Nothing physical, not even the pain of her wounds mattered.

'I request you to be careful.' He collected himself, his face set with control. 'You must not reach out to me again, or give me any importance, until it's safe for you. Leave me as if I were dead,' he smiled with effort, 'and I shall find you. Every time.'

Mira closed her eyes, memorizing that moment, his lasting words.

Then said, 'You see, Sikander, I have been meaning to tell you.' She said regretfully, 'I know something about masks, I have needed many during my lifetime.'

His concerned eyes sharpened a fraction.

'I have played many different people,' she elaborated. 'Strangely, the most difficult part was to appear happy when I wasn't. Then I got a hang of it; happy child, happy student, happy employee.' She regarded him critically. 'Your masks lack conviction because your life doesn't depend on them as mine had.'

His watched her in silence and noted that her hand stayed at the waist on the bandaged wounds.

Her voice was thin, as she continued, 'Your political life needed to be free of your father's influence, which everyone knows might end with this elections. It was your strategy to become a popular leader by raising a pertinent issue and by demolishing rivals,' she paused for breath. Then said, 'Yes, you wanted the Parliament to be open to scrutiny and correction, but you wanted it for attaining power yourself. So please,' she smiled briefly, 'don't tell me it's not politics.'

Sikander seemed offended but didn't contradict her.

Fatigued, Mira closed her eyes. 'Your masks fooled everyone but not me,' she spoke slowly. 'You loved the life of an ordinary man in that lane, but you also loved the deception of it and the challenge. I saw you when you put up with a difficult boss at work or when you had food with strangers. You loved that they believed your masks,' she whispered weakly, 'your many faces.'

Mira couldn't speak for sometime, and Sikander surveyed her in silence.

'Now, for the clues.' She finally opened her eyes and saw him sit back in his chair, his beautiful eyes deeply wounded. 'Your first clue stumped me, but I was prepared for the second, and I saw through the third. I just hope you don't think I recover my faith from things that I hang on walls.'

'I don't,' he remarked briefly.

Mira acknowledged that. 'Then I thank you for thinking of my safety by deliberately revealing your address to me when the whole world searched for you.'

He politely nodded.

'It was a good alternative that you proposed if I had stayed back in the lane that morning. Such happiness was worth every suffering of my past.' She observed sadly. 'A girl in this country, orphan or otherwise, grows up to believe that the world can easily do without her. Your words made me cry.'

Mira stopped speaking and quickly averted her face as the pain turned suddenly acute. He noticed her frown, and asked if she would rather rest. She didn't answer him.

Then said, 'You didn't consider one thing,' she managed with effort. 'I'm also left stronger by my struggle against my destiny. I'm vulnerable only when I choose to be, lonely when I want to be.' She glanced at him distressed. 'I left the lane that morning because I knew you lied to me.'

Mira paused again as the pain burnt through her; the injuries were beginning to bleed, she could tell, and now she also knew why. She needed to calm down and not get agitated.

'I'm sure you have worked this out, Sikander,' she continued, more collectedly. 'I had the choice not to return home from that lane. I could have escaped and even left the city.'

'I know that,' he said, grateful. 'You did it for me.'

'I knew you needed a reason to end your hiding, a powerful reason that could add to your popularity and also justify your absence. I knew you couldn't resist the opportunity.'

He was now silent, wary.

'You knew there would be an attack on me.' She smiled at his caution. 'You knew because you arranged it.'

Sikander was very still. 'I guess I deserve that.'

'That's quaint!' She mocked and regarded him with contempt. 'The assailant made two calls, one before the attack and one, afterwards. I detected those conversations as I could sense his thoughts as he responded to the callers.' Mira paused, exhausted from the pain. 'I also knew *who* the callers were, as he repeated their identities in his mind.'

Sikander was flustered for the first time.

'You asked him to check if I needed something, like a last wish. And you asked him for my last thoughts,' she told him, quietly outraged. 'I wasn't surprised that you organized that attack and enacted the rescue later. What surprised me was that for someone who knew me so well, you didn't think I would discover the truth.'

Sikander stared at her in realization.

'Remind me,' she said, sarcastic, 'to email you a brief outline of what my special powers can and can't do. It would help you in planning such attacks better!'

He continued to sit in the chair in the same elegant way, but his face was now flushed in anger, and his eyes were darker with hurt.

'Is that all your powers tell you?' he inquired with forced composure. 'And I thought, foolishly in retrospect, that you would give me the credit for thinking of every possible way to keep you safe these past weeks,' he said, as he met her tired eyes. 'Your life was in danger, and to make it worse, you let Nalan Malik get close to you. Did you realize, I wonder, that he visited you regularly to send me the message that he could threaten your life any time he wanted?' He added witheringly, 'Probably not!'

Mira hadn't thought of that.

'The moment I realized you were headed home from the lane,' he was curt, 'I decided to come out of hiding because I knew you were in danger. I didn't have to rescue you if, as you allege, I had lied. I called my aides at once and gave them my location, then contacted everyone who had been hunting for me.' His face turned stormy as he recounted, 'The more I begged them not to harm you, the clearer it became how important you were to me, and you became the target of revenge against me. On way to your home, I finally called Nalan and asked him for help. He too knew of the risk you faced, and was upset that I couldn't prevent you from leaving the lane. Then he called the men waiting for you to negotiate a deal to save your life at whatever cost.' He added gravely. 'And the cost was my life, my career.'

Stunned, Mira heard him in silence and assessed his every word.

'In return,' Sikander continued, 'the concession I got was that I could talk to the assailant and delay him for a while. I accepted it; I had no choice and hoped I would reach your home before the attack took place.' He stopped, disconcerted. 'I was wrong, I reached after.'

Mira waited, as he spoke his mind. And his heart.

'As part of the deal,' he revealed impassively, 'I surrendered to Nalan, and he took charge of the tapes. It didn't really matter.' He stopped, lost in thought. 'I still remember the number of vehicles that waited for me at your gate when I arrived. Everyone knew; the world was convinced of how much I cared for you.' He smiled ironically. 'Everyone except you!'

Mira met his tragic eyes in silence. For just that one moment, she couldn't help wanting to give in, trust him blindly and let go of herself. She wished she could.

'Why play these games, Sikander,' she chided him, hiding her desperation, 'when we both know why you rushed to my rescue? You knew your political career couldn't have survived my murder, but that dramatic rescue to save my life has done wonders to it. You, in fact, rescued yourself.'

He studied her for a while without answering, his dark eyes level with hers. Then he shook his head in disbelief.

'Don't miss much, do you?' he mentioned appreciatively.

There was a long silence between them and even the birds of his garden sounded guilty.

'I did miss one thing though,' she said at length, angry that she felt vulnerable again. 'Why did you have to desecrate my pain? You knew it was all I had in my life that was truly mine.'

Sikander stared at her, speechless. Then made to get up and come to her, but she asked him not to.

'How do I make you believe me?' he demanded, dismayed. 'It's mine too, your pain,' he insisted, anguished. 'You disregard my suffering because I don't matter to you. If I did, you would discover that *I* am *you*, there is no difference.'

She chuckled cynically. 'Those words again! You drove me from that lane with those dangerous words,' she whispered, as her eyes threatened to fill up again. 'You shouldn't have, you know. I was destroyed!'

'And how about me?' he frowned. 'You destroyed me too when you left me in that lane because you feared I might be right!' His voice softened. 'But that's all right, Mira, I fear you too.'

She stared at him, lost. Once again, he was accurate and she looked away hurriedly as her eyes spilled again. He reprimanded himself.

'I'm sorry,' he said, remorseful. 'You're right, no more words from me.'

She couldn't speak. She sat with her head lowered and her palm was now pressed harder to the bandages to control the pain.

'I compliment your strength for coming here today and your strategy,' he said. Then asked her gently, 'What do you want me to do? What is this meeting really about?'

It took time for her to speak. 'I want you to expose the men who planned the attack on me. You must speak about your reasons for hiding, and your motives for making the tapes. You must give an interview, along with Nalan, to the media.'

'I'll speak only to you,' he said. Then pointed out, 'But it would undo the impact of the tapes. Those who are named in the tapes will use the circumstances as an excuse and escape from consequences.'

'Not if you provide evidence you have against them,' she whispered, her voice faint.

'And if I don't?' he asked seriously. 'Will you really expose me, damage me? Don't I mean anything to you?'

She impatiently glanced at him. 'Want to find out?'

He considered her grimly. 'What about Nalan? Or isn't it the same?'

'It's not the same,' she agreed, troubled. 'That is a different mask, a different truth.'

Deciding to leave, she made to stand and held her breath in pain. She moved her hand to hold the chair and discovered the blood on her shirt. Sikander quickly reached out to help, but Mira restrained him again. He glanced at her questioningly, and she waited until he stepped back.

Sikander demanded, 'Why won't you let me help you?'

She weakly apologized. 'It's just that I need to forget your words, thoughts and presence in my life in the past few weeks. It'll be easy, like turning the pages of a book, just a memory,' Mira explained. 'But if I have your touch to forget as well, it'll be tougher; more like burning the pages of a book, a cremation.' She added quietly, 'I don't like to do that.'

He stared at her, stunned.

Mira slowly struggled to her feet, and amid the agony that blinded her, she remembered the words that had made her endure an even more cruel and insidious torment than this. She wanted to leave him with similar injuries, the kind that get deeper with time. He stood at a distance, his hand desperately clutched the back of the chair.

She now answered his message in the notebook, 'Although I packed diligently, there may be things that I leave behind. Put them in a dusty corner somewhere, so you won't stumble upon them everyday. And throw them out of your heart,' she met his devastated eyes with satisfaction, 'when you make space for someone else again.'

There was silence after those words. Even in the garden outside.

TWENTY-THREE

Three days later, on that Thursday afternoon, Mira sat in her living room and read the extensive coverage of the tapes in the previous weekend's magazines. It was a bright day, and the sunlight was extracting memories of rain from the reluctant foliage of trees. She had returned home on Tuesday from the hospital after the second and much briefer stay; Salat had driven her there from the Bansi residence after the meeting with Sikander. The wounds had reopened and bled again, as if she had been attacked again. The doctors didn't believe she had merely talked briefly and only walked a little. They accused her of deliberately sabotaging her recovery, and once again reprimanded her for being suicidal. Mira couldn't explain to them why the wounds were open, why they bled. She had been too weak for that meeting with Sikander. And soon, she would have to confront Nalan Malik. She had known, as the doctor gave her permission to go home the next morning, that she would return to the hospital within a few days.

Nalan had called when she was unconscious, and Salat had briefed him about her condition. She left her stained shirt in the hospital, she didn't want Nalan to find it. But he had sounded deceptively calm on phone when she had talked to him the same evening. He was very understanding about the wounds and did not mention Sikander. Mira smiled to herself now as she turned the pages of a magazine. Like every good politician, Nalan knew the importance of timing.

Mira looked up as the key turned in the lock and the main door opened. People spoke in low voices, and a stranger came in carrying a duffle bag. Alarmed, Mira slowly stood up with the support of the chair. He was equally alarmed and glanced at someone behind him to whisper something.

'What!' she heard Nalan exclaim. 'She is standing in the living room?'

He came into the house and stopped, looking at her in delight. 'And here we were speaking softly, thinking you lay dying in bed.' He dropped the bags he carried and rushed to hug her.

Mira laughed and held him close. 'I'm trying. It takes time to die properly.'

'And practice, by the looks of it!' he said, as his anxious eyes scanned her face. 'You look fatigued.'

Mira didn't know what to say, how to match that affection in his voice.

'No matter. We will set that right soon.'

Then he turned to introduce the men who stood at the main entrance. 'This is my team and our luggage. Hope you don't mind, we'll be here just for a few hours.' He explained that they had come directly from the airport and he had to attend a long meeting in a few hours. So instead of going to his office to work, he had come to see her first. His staff had to prepare the summary of the state tour he had just finished, and he was scheduled to brief the party leadership at that evening's meeting. Mira invited them in and he thanked her, then went to his staff to give some instructions. Two men sat at the desk, and the third settled on the floor near the wall. Nalan pushed the last chair to a corner for her from where she surveyed, impressed, how swiftly her living room was turned into an office. They worked efficiently and fast, finding data, maps and quotes of people interviewed. Nalan paced the room, dictating the report, and his staff completed it with the appropriate references. He seemed weary, his white shirt and dark trousers wrinkled with travel. But when he found her studying him, he smiled and his brilliant eyes sparkled.

After half an hour, Nalan's phone rang, and he walked away to answer it. A break was called by consensus and the men relaxed. By now there was paper everywhere, bottles of water, shoes they had taken off, cell phones, notebooks and other stuff. She nodded as one of them asked if he could make tea. Another went into the balcony to smoke. The third one, who was on the floor, leaned against the wall and closed his eyes. She was wondering if he had gone to sleep so quickly, when his cell phone rang. He answered and introduced it as Nalan's number. He listened for a moment, then explained to someone that the other phone was busy because Nalan presently talked on that line. He promised to give the message to him and ended the call. They heard the main door open again, and Nalan returned. He tolerantly scrutinized his dispersed staff.

'Fine, take a few minutes off!' He smiled helplessly, then pushed one of the empty chairs next to hers and slumped down in it, tired.

The man on the floor said, 'There was a call for you, sir. It was Sikander Bansi. He said he tried calling on the other number, but it was busy. He wanted to know if there was any change in the schedule for tonight.'

Nalan stared at him, speechless.

'He meant the meeting, sir,' the aide mentioned helpfully, 'at your residence.'

Mira glanced at Nalan, waiting.

'I know he meant the meeting,' Nalan answered his aide curtly. 'And yes, tell him it's on.'

Then he turned to her, his brown eyes reflecting the sunlight carefully, as if it could start a fire.

She suggested quietly, 'We should talk.'

He nodded gravely and requested his staff to leave the room. When they were alone, he said, 'Let me explain . . .'

'Please don't.' Mira stood up with effort. 'I don't want to know more than what I believe.'

Nalan watched her anxiously. 'What do you believe?'

'I believe Sikander when he said he gave those instructions to the assailant before he attacked me.'

'Then we should lodge a police complaint against him, shouldn't we?' he asked calmly. 'That's a confession to a crime.'

She stood at the windows. She didn't want to hurt Nalan and it didn't matter what he had done. He was different from Sikander. He didn't show his injuries, he didn't live them like Sikander. He carried his pain like a secret letter in his heart, folded between past and future, hidden in every sliver of time.

'What are you thinking Mira?'

Distracted, she said, 'I don't want you to lodge any police complaint.'

'Why not?'

'As a favour to me.'

'You know the police already suspect Sikander and all they need is evidence.' He pointed out, 'This is evidence.'

'Not if we don't tell the police.'

'Don't tell the police that Sikander plotted to kill you?' Nalan inquired placidly. 'Even after he has brazenly owned it up?'

'That's not the entire truth,' she remarked, her voice subdued.

Nalan didn't speak for a second, then asked cautiously, 'You think he lied?'

'He didn't lie,' she answered, forlorn. 'There is a difference.'

Nalan regarded her for a moment from the chair, then came to stand behind her. He held her shoulders and gently said, 'Tell me, what's the difference?'

She closed her eyes, tensely, as his touch weakened her.

'You want to protect Sikander, isn't it?' his voice was soft with envy. 'You can't hurt him, can you? That's why you believe him and not me.'

She turned to face him, anguished. 'Be kind, Nalan,' she begged him, 'and tell me the truth for once! Don't you think I would be lost if I believed you?'

He was distraught. 'What're you saying, Mira? I would be lost forever if you don't believe me.'

Tired, she leaned against the windows. 'It has been two weeks since the attack and I haven't said a word,' she spoke feebly. 'I thought there may be a better explanation for what I know and I had to meet Sikander to be sure. How I wish I hadn't!' she said, defeated. 'I wanted to believe you, I hoped you would be innocent of my death, not guilty.'

Nalan frowned at her words, and noticed the way her hands trembled as she held the window behind her for support.

'You wanted to find Sikander when he was in hiding,' she whispered. 'You knew the threat to my life would force him to surrender, not just because he cared for me but because he couldn't have survived the controversy. You would have won both ways, even if I had died. There was no downside to this plan, except that you would have lost me. But perhaps,' she paused in thought, 'that's not a downside.'

He didn't speak, although his thoughts told her she was wrong. But she had been fooled by his thoughts before.

'You see,' Mira explained, 'the assailant made two phone calls to his employers. He talked to Sikander on the first call. I discerned Sikander's name in the assailant's thoughts as he received the instructions to find out if I had any last wish. Sikander was on his way to my home, and he was buying time.'

Nalan heard her in watchful silence.

'Then there was a second call,' Mira considered him steadily. 'The assailant made this call just after the attack to give a description of the wounds. He confirmed that he had followed the instructions, and that the injuries were fatal.'

Nalan froze in shock and Mira looked at him resentfully. 'You wanted to know if it was over, if it had been painless. You asked him, "Did she feel it?" He answered, "A little". You even asked if I was bleeding too fast. He said no, but . . .'

'Mira!' Nalan interrupted, shaken.

There was silence for an instant.

She watched him with distrust. 'That first clue from Sikander was the key, wasn't it?'

He didn't answer, still stunned.

Fatigue made her voice faint as she continued, 'Sikander's clue was his confession, and all you needed was a crime to pin it on him. My death could have easily looked like his doing if it was executed the way he suggested. And there had been so many suggestions; the "suicide", the "accident". But you preferred the knife!'

'Why, I wonder?' She struggled to breath. 'Was it because it was to be a punishment, not just a killing? A punishment for being the object of Sikander's interest . . .'

Her legs gave way, and Nalan moved swiftly to keep her from falling. But she weakly pushed him away and leaned against the windows again. Nalan stepped back, his pleading eyes, tormented.

'I got fragments of your thoughts when I mentioned a knife just to distract you when you were here to ask me about Sikander,' she told him. 'I could sense your incomplete thoughts when Sita spoke at the hospital about the knife in Sikander's first clue. You had been waiting for the right moment, round every turn,' she whispered, desperately, 'round every corner, to frame Sikander!'

He folded his hands and heard her in a resigned silence.

'You were with me all these days because you used me as a

hostage,' she accused him. 'You thought that would keep Sikander from bringing out the tapes against you. But he still did.' She smiled weakly. 'You don't know Sikander at all if you thought he would give up the chance to damage a rival for any consideration, even to save my life. He knew you would implicate him if anything happened to me. That's the reason why he wanted me to stay in the lane. And when I didn't, he knew exactly whom to contact to manage the attack and plan the rescue. You!'

Mira faltered and bent forward in pain, holding the bandage at the waist. Nalan observed her in silence, his face set resolutely.

'I had no idea,' he said at length, 'that this was something you wanted to hear. I thought you would be reluctant about the ending this could inevitably bring.' He nodded and then said coldly, 'But I can do this.'

He came up and helped her stand again.

'I realized the moment the first tape was published that there would be more recordings against me. I knew Sikander wouldn't spare me; I wouldn't have, if I had been in his position. So I immediately planned to counter it, and the best way to do that was through you.' He thoughtfully pushed away the hair that fell on her forehead. 'It was easy gaining your confidence, and when the time was right, I commissioned that attack against you. The plan was to kill you, and you are right, I would have ensured the blame fell on Sikander. Well,' he smiled, stiffly, 'things don't always work out the way one plans, do they?'

Astonished, Mira stared at him and made to move but he held her close. 'Why, not the story you expected?' he asked deliberately. 'Let me try again then!'

'The tapes had to be stopped at any cost,' Nalan explained afresh, 'and we all knew that you were the only link to Sikander. I got familiar with you in the hope that you would betray him at some point, but you didn't. So, I planned that attack on you to frame Sikander and forced him to emerge from hiding.' She tried to push him away again, and he held her hands to his chest. 'Now, there is really no need to protest! I thought you did great. We believed you would be the weakest link, but you turned out to be the strongest.' He added furious, 'Stronger than even me!'

Then he left her and walked away to the desk. Picking up the papers, he pondered, 'I should call back the guys and finish this report.'

Mira held her breath and struggled to remain standing. Nalan's admission of guilt was exactly what she had wanted to hear, but it was not the truth. The anguish behind his words now filled her, adding to her pain, and made her wounds ache. She watched him lean against the desk and revise the report.

'Try again,' she whispered, and he glanced at her, questioning.

'The story,' she challenged him, her voice low. 'Try once more.'

Nalan was surprised. 'Somehow I pictured this scene with you crying and begging me not to tell the truth.' He chuckled. 'You would plead that you had never known such happiness and wouldn't throw it all away because of what I had done. I would insist that truth was the most important thing, and you would argue that, no, it was love. I would naturally be convinced.'

'Naturally,' she sympathized. 'Please answer a few questions, Nalan. I can't stand this for long.'

'Good to know that.' He angrily dropped the papers on the desk again. 'Ask your questions.'

'Why did it have to be you? You have a political career to lose. Besides, any one of the watchers would have loved to hurt me.' She paused as her voice shook. Then said, 'Or couldn't you resist it?'

Nalan smiled patiently. 'They were desperate to hurt you, but I forced them to leave it to me.'

'Because you knew I would fall for your caring words?' she charged him. 'Because you discovered I was an orphan?'

His brown eyes were offended. 'Because I knew what they would do to you,' he told her sternly, 'that's why I got involved. They were confident that if you were interrogated long enough, you would reveal where Sikander was. I convinced them that if Sikander found out you were being targeted, he would not contact you again and would vanish.' He seriously regarded her, 'I knew that was a chance they couldn't take. They needed to stop the tapes badly. And so, they listened to me.'

'And they kept listening to you?' Mira marvelled. 'How did you manage that?

'With difficulty,' he retorted. 'They watched us all the time, as I told you once. Every day I failed to find the answers from you, I was a step closer to losing control of the situation. These were not men and women I could displease, I have to survive them daily in Delhi. But they have to survive me as well. That's how I bought more time for you.'

Mira winced in pain and leaned her head back to the window. 'So that attack outside the café was not a warning for me,' she realized. 'It was, in fact, a warning for you.'

He nodded. 'They knew by then that I cared for you and . . .'

Livid, Nalan stopped speaking, as she chuckled, entertained.

'But please don't get me wrong!' he said sarcastically. 'I did want you dead.'

Mira verified with his thoughts that were anything but sarcastic.

'To begin with,' he continued, his voice strained, 'I thought you would appreciate it, having chased death all your life. I wanted to change your mind, wanted you to never think of dying again.' He paused, ruffled. 'So, although I wanted to give you hope, make you love life, I also wanted you dead!'

Mira stared at him, lost.

'Secondly, I did recall the knife in the clue when I came to ask you about Sikander,' he spoke bluntly. 'But somehow, I only remember the henna in your palms and my desperate struggle not to let you know how I felt about you. It wouldn't have been fair to you. The wreckage of my broken marriage was still strewn around.' He added with emphasis, 'So, although I couldn't break your heart with my story, I thought you should be dead instead.'

'Nalan, please . . .!' Mira protested, but he interrupted her.

'Thirdly, the clues of Sikander felt like threats to me,' he told her. 'I studied them closely to know his final intentions. That's how I discovered that you were an orphan. I was deeply concerned that you were all alone,' he said, his voice forlorn. 'Sikander clearly cared for you, but thought of death as the end to your search. That constantly worried me and made me meet you often, even when you didn't want me to.' He added indignantly, 'And although I wanted to protect you, I also wanted you dead!'

She uneasily turned away from him.

'But most of all, I wanted you dead for myself', he confided. 'I can't think of my day without you, without hearing your voice. I love waiting for you, leaving you, finding you. I'm done with everything, I want nothing without you.'

Mira met his angry, confessing eyes, as his unsaid thoughts stifled her mind.

'Next question,' Nalan said punishingly.

It took her time to speak again. 'What did you say to Sikander when he called you that morning of the attack?'

'He mentioned you were on your way home,' Nalan replied, 'and I told him that it was irresponsible of him to have let you leave the lane. The watchers had already informed me that you were missing, and they waited for your return. Sikander knew you would be hurt to teach him a lesson for the tapes, and I knew you would be hurt to teach me a lesson for protecting you. We couldn't stop the attack, but we managed to negotiate a delay.' He spoke somberly. 'I managed to get the assailant report to us. Those were the two calls you heard. Sikander, as he tried to delay the beginning, and I, as I tried to delay the end so that you could be rescued.'

Mira heard him in silence.

He continued absently, 'One of the terms agreed for that negotiation was the manner of Sikander's surrender. He requested for me just like the others wanted, so that we could access all the evidence he had. And he ensured through his father that I headed the internal party investigation, which helped to diffuse the immediate crisis . . .' He saw her wince in pain again. 'You should lie down, Mira. We can talk later.'

Mira nodded and tried to take a few steps. But the pain tore her apart, and she fell to her knees, holding tight to the bandages. Nalan hurried her to the bed in the next room. She buried her face in the pillow, battling to breathe as the wounds hurt and bled.

'You have the fever again,' Nalan said, troubled.

Mira sensed his thoughts were clear, as always, when he focused on her. 'No need to call the doctors,' she whispered. 'They'll only blame me for being suicidal.'

'They would be right,' he informed her harshly. 'You didn't have to interrogate me so soon after Sikander. And I can only imagine how that meeting must have gone!'

'It went well,' she answered unsteadily. 'He was in more pain at the end than I was.'

'As I will be at the end of this talk,' he predicted.

When she finally turned, he demanded, tersely, 'Why did you return home that morning from the lane, Mira? You must have known you were going to your death.'

'That felt a better option than trusting you or Sikander,' she told him. 'Besides, I told you the first time we met, death is the best part of life.'

He shook his head, repentant. 'Please tell me, Mira. What can I do?'

'The same that I asked Sikander to do,' she answered weakly.

'Then I'm sure to do it better than him,' he smiled. 'What is it?'

'Give an interview to the media and speak about the attempts to prevent the publication of the Parliament tapes, the efforts to protect people named in the tapes and how the tapes impacted you. Finally, you can say a few words about who were behind the attempt on my life.' Mira paused, as she discerned his thoughts. 'I sense reluctance.'

'I wonder why,' he said scathingly. 'This could merely be the end of my political career.'

'That's wishful thinking,' she dismissed it. 'Give an interview together with Sikander, so that there is no scope for escapes or excuses.'

'Only if you conduct such an interview.'

'Who else would know if you lied?' she asked wearily.

'It's traditional to go to the police,' he pointed out, 'so that they can blackmail me and Sikander for the rest of our tenures in politics.'

'If you prefer that, sure.' She smiled, exhausted. Then remembered, 'Why are you meeting him tonight?'

'It's nothing, really ...' he fell silent abruptly, then told the truth. 'I called him when I got to know you returned to the hospital after meeting him. I was furious that you were hurt again and said I had several scores to settle with him.' He added quietly, 'He agreed to meet me to sort it out.'

'So even this is leverage for you?'

'And a negotiation for him.'

She remained silent to gather her strength. Then said, 'To answer the question you didn't ask—yes, I can go to the police against you.'

'But how can you, Mira?' he was astonished. 'How can you forget about us? Does love mean nothing to you?'

352 Kota Neelima

'Love is for birds and garden benches,' she whispered. 'You think of it beautifully, with colours I have never known before, like looking through a magical glass at a new world. But it also shatters to pieces when I want it to be true.'

'Then try looking at it through my eyes,' he suggested.

She was too fatigued to answer. Worried, he checked the wounds, and as he moved her hand away from the bandages, he found the blood on her shirt. Shocked, Nalan reached for his cell phone to call the doctors. She could sense the panic in his thoughts, much like the frenzy in Sikander's when he saw her bleed.

'What if you don't get any help?' she wondered, and he glanced at her, startled. 'No one will ever know you let me die here today.'

Nalan couldn't speak; he knew what she meant.

'Just once more, Nalan,' she entreated him. 'Kill me once again.'

He was shattered by her request. Then he managed to smile. 'There may be no need for that, Mira,' he finally said. 'You have an interview to conduct. And I'll probably have to kill myself after that!'

TWENTY-FOUR

Nalan, of course, didn't kill himself, although at the time of the interview it seemed very possible that he might. The interview itself had been the biggest news event of the year. So big that even Munshi didn't know how to handle the publicity it gathered. The rivalry between Nalan and Sikander was well known in politics but not so much among the public. They could just see the man who made the Parliament tapes, and the man who featured on them. For the sheer drama of it, many television channels tried to lure Munshi into a telecast deal, but without success. Everyone also knew, however, that the interview was made possible not because of Munshi, but because of Mira. So, they tried tracking down Mira, and some journalists even managed to get her well-guarded address. But they didn't get to meet her because she was mostly either resting, recovering from the injuries, or at the hospital.

Over a month after the attack on her, Mira interviewed Sikander and Nalan at her office in one of the third floor conference rooms; also present were Salat, Bhaskar and an assistant who handled the recording. There were a few structured questions, but the interview was open ended and guided by what she could detect from their thoughts. Munshi's instructions were to allow only photographers from other newspapers to be present and, that too, only for a few minutes before the interview began.

These were the first photos of the two men together, and have since been used extensively with stories on Parliament tapes or political corruption. Their photographs, however, were not the only things that had become instant legends about the interview. Many of their answers were explosive in their honesty. Like, for example, when Mira asked Sikander about his motives for making the tapes. He was impeccable that day—dressed in a dark suit, blue shirt and brown tie—except when he answered that question, 'You know why, Mira.' He had said grimly, 'I gave people what they wanted. After all, that's politics.' In the months before the elections, the Opposition National Party ran an entire campaign against PP government titled 'That's Politics' and highlighted its double standards.

Many of their answers were also candid about other leaders. For instance, when Mira asked Nalan about who wanted him to bury the Parliament tapes, his answer included names of some of the top brass of political parties in the country. Nalan had added, towards the end of his answer, 'As you know I didn't do everything they asked me to do.' He smiled at her. 'We wouldn't have been here if I had.' Critics decried this as a display of the 'blatant disregard' for ethics in the younger generation of politicians and called Nalan a symptom of the 'malaise that afflicts our society.'

He was far from being a symptom, however, when defending himself on the division of the state. 'Corporate interests had to be addressed. Every politician who wanted to get re-elected with corporate money wanted the division. Don't ask me why, I do not contest elections.'

Sikander as an elected MP had to counter. 'It's good that you don't contest elections. But if you did, you would discover that the affection and respect of the people is enough to win elections. You don't need corporate money.' Then he considered Mira for a moment and retracted, 'All right, that's nonsense!'

There were times that day when the third-floor conference room had appeared too small for the two of them, as neither gave the other an inch. Nalan wore his usual white shirt with dark jacket, along with an unusually patient smile. Sikander was polite as if his life depended on it, until Mira asked them about the attack on her.

'If Sikander had the courage to stay and not disappear during the publication of the tapes,' Nalan reflected calmly, 'you wouldn't have been hurt.'

'And if Mr Malik had the courage to wait until I emerged from hiding,' Sikander remarked politely, 'there would have been no need to hurt you.'

Mira touched her forehead, tired. 'Once again,' she said tolerantly, 'why was I attacked?'

Grateful that her question didn't point fingers at them, they spoke about the various people behind the attack, including the men employed by the Opposition parties, business houses and government agencies that were named in the tapes. They both ended up assuring her that without their intervention, she would have been dead. Mira managed not to analyse that assurance and moved on to the question of reforms.

Sikander's ideas, widely quoted later, were clear and practical. 'We need to make Parliament more accessible to discover the pressures that play on policy and decisions of the government. People must know why members of Parliament vote in favour or against, participate or abstain, debate or protest in the House and why they are bound by party whips. This is not mere procedure; it is the practice of democracy, and people should know how it works.' He asserted, 'We will never cure corruption in our society as long as it thrives behind closed doors in the highest sanctuary of our democracy.'

Nalan's solutions were impractical but revolutionary and now part of the party's reforms resolution. 'We need to take Parliament to the people to expose motives. Every debate in the House should be conducted from the constituencies of MPs and must include selected constituents,' he envisaged. 'This is the best way we can minimize the influence of vested interests on policy and legislation in both Houses.'

Sikander had also noted that the mere telecast of House proceedings wasn't enough. It should be interactive where every MP could answer questions directly from his or her constituents. Nalan, however, had felt that none of the reforms would really work unless the information about funding of political parties was open and accessible to all. To encourage such transparency, he recommended that political donations should be given incentives like tax exemptions. Both felt the gates of Parliament were unfairly shut to common people and sought free access for citizens to reach their lawmakers.

After a few more questions, Mira called for a break to cross-check the answers. Then, registering their thoughts, she glanced inquiringly at Sikander and Nalan. They sat across the conference table with four tape recorders before them. Salat was at her side and Bhaskar was at one end of the table.

'This is no time to go off the record,' she said, in response to their thoughts.

'I just want to say something to you, Mira,' Sikander mentioned in a tightly controlled voice.

'So do I,' Nalan said, his brown eyes infuriated.

Mira nodded to the assistant, and he switched off the tape-recorders.

'I deeply resent, not to mention condemn, the manner in which Mr Malik mislead you about his methods and motives.' Sikander was emphatic, 'I may not be able to say this publicly, but it was behaviour not befitting a gentleman. I wish you remember that and extend Mr Malik no concession for his kindness or his affection for you. He is neither kind nor affectionate to anyone. I want you to promise me you will bear that in mind at all times.'

Mira uneasily glanced around the room and met Bhaskar's amused eyes.

'And I wanted you, Mira,' Nalan insisted, 'to never forget Sikander's cowardice, the way he left you alone to face all the repercussions of what he had done. Unlike him, I don't resent or condemn him, but I find him most devious in his actions. So he may try his best to act different, but whenever you are inclined to think well of him, just recall his past. Promise me you won't forget that.'

Salat checked his notes to hide a smile.

She studied them seriously. 'You neglect to mention that both of you do politics for self-interest but disguise it in the name of the people. You are manipulative and dishonest, and you almost got me killed. Please believe that I wish to have nothing to do with either of you. So stop wasting my time, and continue with the interview.'

Nalan glanced at Sikander, who nodded. They both regarded her, determined. 'Not until you give us an answer.'

'Fine.' She was impatient. 'In view of your warnings, I promise that I won't see either of you again. I suggest you respect my wishes and don't try to contact me or meet me.'

Nalan was decisive. 'That's impossible.'

'And I don't make false promises,' Sikander declared.

'Really?' Nalan marvelled at his words. 'What are you going to do in the January elections then?'

Sikander ignored that but was struck by an idea. 'Let the elections be the deadline,' he suggested to Nalan, who nodded in agreement.

'Don't meet us until the elections,' he then suggested to Mira.

'Yes,' agreed Nalan. 'It'll be easy on us. We will be quite busy.'

'I may need a little more time to forget,' Mira said dryly. 'Let's meet six months after the national elections.'

There was consensus, and the interview resumed.

EPILOGUE

That moment stood still on the bridge over river Yamuna. Dawn was still a few horizons away, and the earth was taking its time. It had just begun to rain, the first rain of the season; it was that honest season again. Mira stood at the metal railings, listening to the darkness of the river below, as the ancient waters mixed half-heartedly with the modern times. It was rain too, the river; only that a river had a name and a destiny. Just like people, made of rain but estranged from it by their search for identity, different forms before everything and everyone was rain again. Like a falling drop, blink and die. It was this that drew her to rain, she realized now. It was the same as death, same as life, and same as waiting for rain. She too was made of raindrops, mixed with a whiff of air, a shovel of earth, few slices of flesh and a pint of blood. She came together because she had wanted to wait on that bridge for this dawn; she had wanted a destiny. She saw the greying waters of the river below the bridge. It would just take one step to end this separation, to let the rain dissolve the skin and reclaim the body. Only one step away. That was close, that was reassuring.

Her deadline had ended yesterday. Mira was reminded by

two text messages, one each from Sikander and Nalan. There was no space in her life for anything but the constant waiting, and everything she did was a preparation. They both knew that, and they knew they couldn't change her. But perhaps, she had changed them, and they didn't want to change back. Mira restlessly glanced up at the lightening skies. She had to decide. She had to answer one of the two messages she had got that morning.

One year, she had believed, would be long enough time to forget, forgive and err again. While she continued to work at the newspaper, both Sikander and Nalan had been busy this year, just as they had predicted. The People's Party had returned to power with a spectacular victory, which had appeared impossible just a few months ago. Under pressure before elections, the PP government had appointed a commission of inquiry to look into the Parliament tapes to show that it was acting tough against the corrupt, even when they were found among its own ranks. But that wasn't the message that went out from the daily news of summons being issued to ministers and MPs, the television footage of senior politicians of the PP walking into the commission office. Everyone appeared guilty in voter perception that didn't wait for verdicts and evidence. To be thus embarrassed by their own government based on evidence provided by one of their own party MP led to deep resentment among the leaders. The PP started bickering like a losing side does before battle. The Opposition NP, it appeared, didn't have to move an inch. Its popularity increased by default, and appeared as a better choice.

In this turmoil, few noticed the growing influence of Nalan Malik who had been deployed by the PP to contain the damage. He was already in charge of the internal party investigation of the tapes, which now began to collaborate closely with the inquiry commission of the government. Steadily, the commission targeted PP rebel leaders and deadwood, which in turn meant they didn't get a candidacy for the election. Then, the commission got after the Opposition leadership with evidence so damning that no one could survive—especially on television news channels. It became apparent, though a little late, what Nalan had done. The commission was hailed as impartial when it targeted powerful PP men, leaders belonging to the ruling party. So, when it targeted the Opposition, there could be no protest citing political motivations.

In November, three months before the election, Nalan was promoted to the post of senior general secretary in charge of election strategy. By then, he had ensured that the party was free of the tainted and the restless. Even though he himself was named twice in the tapes, the manner in which Nalan survived made him a star of the adventure sports of Delhi politics. His promotion also pointed to the unlikely coalition with the party president Mahesh Bansi. Nalan couldn't have been the second most important man in the party unless Mahesh wanted him to be. A similar thaw could be seen in Nalan's relationship with Sikander, although they remained guarded and polite, as if wary of the secrets they shared.

At the end, while it was tradition to attribute the credit for victory in elections to the party president, Sikander was the first one to openly acknowledge that it would have been impossible without Nalan. In his response, Nalan thanked Sikander for turning a defeat into victory by being the new face of the election campaign.

Sikander had also suffered the brunt of the Parliament tapes, more so because of his father's rivals, who deliberately held Mahesh responsible for his son's actions. This was especially vicious in the months before the elections when everyone was nervous, and increasingly supported the idea that only a change in leadership could improve the fortunes of the party. Dissent spread rapidly from Delhi to the ranks and the days of Mahesh Bansi as the party president seemed numbered. To add spice to the situation, the news of the tapes remained alive with the Opposition NP determined not to let it be forgotten. So even the few among the party who supported Mahesh couldn't really speak up in view of the damage being done by Sikander's tapes. The dissent reached new heights after the interview to Mira, and the party faced a serious threat of breaking into two if Mahesh Bansi didn't resign.

That was when, once again without consulting his father, Sikander declared that he would not contest the elections. In a brief statement released directly to the press, Sikander mentioned that he was facing severe criticism within his party for exposing the members of Parliament. It was felt that he had betrayed the PP, but Sikander insisted that he would rather betray the PP than his country, and he would rather have the love of the people than their vote. What happened next did not surprise anyone. The Opposition demanded that he immediately leave a party that didn't value him and offered him the Middle Delhi seat. The PP leadership, realizing how little Mahesh Bansi knew his son, reiterated its support to Sikander's campaign against corruption and organized pro-demonstrations outside their own party headquarters in his favour. The PP dissenters against Mahesh, who had denounced the tapes, found themselves isolated and the only people in favour of protecting the corrupt. So, they were forced to pledge their support to Sikander and organized their own anti-demonstrations against those who targeted Sikander. In the end, Sikander reluctantly agreed to contest the elections but refused to follow the party stand that was against giving candidacy to dissenters as a way of punishment. That was a direct challenge to his father, and the dissenters found it much easier to support Mahesh Bansi's rebel son.

Sikander made history by winning the Middle Delhi seat with the maximum number of votes ever polled for a single candidate. He campaigned for the dissenters as well and won them seats across the country. Then he picked half-a-dozen impossible seats, supervised candidate selection process, campaigned vigorously and won those for the party. Finally, after the elections, he refused a ministerial position in the new government and astounded the nation as usual.

It had been Nalan's conviction and Sikander's courage that won the election for the PP, and their dependence on each other.

Meanwhile, the Parliament tapes dragged through the inquiry commission like a dead whale in fishing net. No one was interested in them anymore. It had always been difficult to keep the focus on issues that mattered, the things that didn't matter were always more interesting. Common people couldn't force politicians to talk about the tapes or force news channels to report about the tapes. And in time, common people were forced, instead, to forget about the Parliament tapes. But it would be wrong to think that this amnesia was easy to achieve or cheap. The tainted politicians were sidelined, the guilty bureaucrats suspended and the investigative agencies were reprimanded, but the tapes had no impact on the one entity that was central to corruption—the money. It funded the national forgetfulness that was necessary for its own survival and multiplication. After a year, end of political corruption sounded vaguely familiar, like an idyllic station at which the express train doesn't stop. The job was done.

Dawn was moments away. Mira's clothes were soaked as she glanced up at the moving sky, the colour of rain. She shivered as a low river breeze passed through her as though she were merely an idea. The rain bleached the colours of the sky and brought the sunrise to the river instead. It was a decision the rain made, a choice, and the waters turned crimson as the dawn mixed slowly with the river. Mira wished she could also leave her decision to the rain. It would know she needed neither the sky nor the river, nor anyone in between. She wanted to meet rain itself, not off ledges or bridges, but in person.

'Do give me an answer before you jump off the bridge,' said someone over the sound of water. 'Have you decided between the two of us?'

Startled, Mira turned and found him standing in the rain, leaning against her blue car.

'So that I know whether to stop you or push you,' he remarked.

She smiled. 'Or jump with me.'

'To be the river?' he asked.

'To be the rain.'

A NOTE ON THE AUTHOR

Kota Neelima has been a journalist for over twenty years, covering politics in New Delhi, India. She is Senior Research Fellow, South Asia Studies at The Paul H. Nitze School of Advanced International Studies, Johns Hopkins University, Washington, DC. Her recent academic research in India on perception seeks to develop a structure based on rural and urban voter choices.

Her previous books include the bestselling *Shoes of the Dead* and *Death of a Moneylender*, among others. Also a well-known painter, Neelima's works are a part of several collections in India and abroad, including the Museum of Sacred Art, Belgium.

www.kotaneelima.com